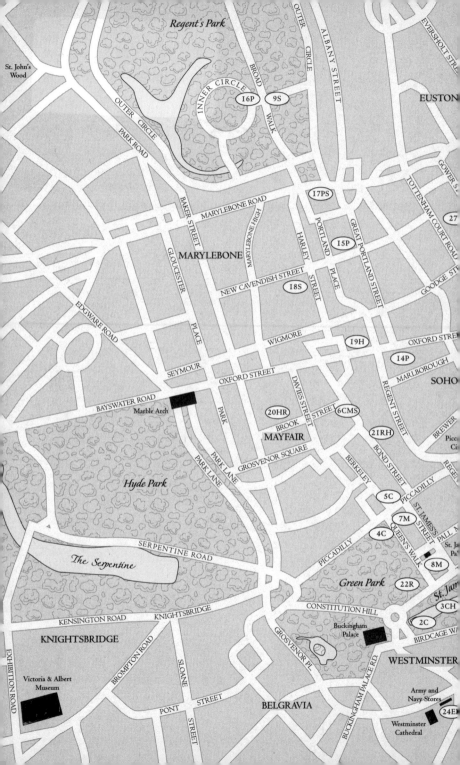

Mrs. Dalloway

Mrs. Dalloway

VIRGINIA
WOOLF

Annotated and with an introduction
by Bonnie Kime Scott

Mark Hussey, General Editor

A Harvest Book • Harcourt, Inc.
Orlando Austin New York San Diego London

For information about permission to
reproduce selections from this book, write to
trade.permissions@hmhco.com or to Permissions,
Houghton Mifflin Harcourt Publishing Company,
3 Park Avenue, 19th Floor, New York, New York 10016.

www.hmhco.com

Library of Congress Cataloging-in-Publication Data
Woolf, Virginia, 1882–1941.
Mrs. Dalloway/Virginia Woolf; annotated and with an introduction
by Bonnie Kime Scott; Mark Hussey, general editor.—1st Harvest ed.
p.   cm.—(A Harvest Book)
Includes bibliographical references.
1. Triangles (Interpersonal relations)—Fiction.   2. Middle aged women—Fiction.
3. London (England)—Fiction.   4. Suicide victims—Fiction.   5. Married women—
Fiction.   6. First loves—Fiction.   7. Parties—Fiction.   8. Regret—Fiction.
I. Scott, Bonnie Kime, 1944–   II. Title.   III. Series.
PR6045.O72M7   2005
823'.912—dc22   2005003378
ISBN 978-0-15-603035-9

Text set in Garamond MT
Designed by Cathy Riggs

Printed in the United States of America

First edition
25 2021
4500841522

Contents

Mrs. Dalloway

VIRGINIA WOOLF

VIRGINIA WOOLF was born into what she once described as "a very communicative, literate, letter writing, visiting, articulate, late nineteenth century world." Her parents, Leslie and Julia Stephen, both previously widowed, began their marriage in 1878 with four young children: Laura (1870–1945), the daughter of Leslie Stephen and his first wife, Harriet Thackeray (1840–1875); and George (1868–1934), Gerald (1870–1937), and Stella Duckworth (1869–1897), the children of Julia Prinsep (1846–1895) and Herbert Duckworth (1833–1870). In the first five years of their marriage, the Stephens had four more children. Their third child, Virginia, was born in 1882, the year her father began work on the monumental *Dictionary of National Biography* that would earn him a knighthood in 1902. Virginia, her sister, Vanessa (1879–1961), and brothers, Thoby (1880–1906) and Adrian (1883–1948), all were born in the tall house at 22 Hyde Park Gate in London where the eight children lived with numerous servants, their eminent and irascible father, and their beautiful mother, who, in Woolf's words, was "in the very centre of that great Cathedral space that was childhood."

Woolf's parents knew many of the intellectual luminaries of the late Victorian era well, counting among their close friends novelists such as George Meredith, Thomas Hardy, and Henry James. Woolf's great-aunt Julia Margaret Cameron was a pioneering photographer who made portraits of the poets Alfred

Tennyson and Robert Browning, of the naturalist Charles Darwin, and of the philosopher and historian Thomas Carlyle, among many others. Beginning in the year Woolf was born, the entire Stephen family moved to Talland House in St. Ives, Cornwall, for the summer. There the younger children would spend their days playing cricket in the garden, frolicking on the beach, or taking walks along the coast, from where they could look out across the bay to the Godrevy lighthouse.

The early years of Woolf's life were marred by traumatic events. When she was thirteen, her mother, exhausted by a punishing schedule of charitable visits among the sick and poor, died from a bout of influenza. Woolf's half sister Stella took over the household responsibilities and bore the brunt of their self-pitying father's sorrow until she escaped into marriage in 1897 with Jack Hills, a young man who had been a favorite of Julia's. Within three months, Stella (who was pregnant) was dead, most likely from peritonitis. In this year, which she called "the first really *lived* year of my life," Woolf began a diary. Over the next twelve years, she would record in its pages her voracious reading, her impressions of people and places, feelings about her siblings, and events in the daily life of the large household.[1]

In addition to the premature deaths of her mother and half sister, there were other miseries in Woolf's childhood. In autobiographical writings and letters, Woolf referred to the sexual abuse she suffered at the hands of her two older half brothers, George and Gerald Duckworth. George, in one instance, explained his behavior to a family doctor as his effort to comfort his half sister for the fatal illness of their father. Sir Leslie died

---

[1]Woolf's early diary is published as *A Passionate Apprentice: The Early Journals, 1897–1909*, edited by Mitchell A. Leaska. A 1909 notebook discovered in 2002 has been published as *Carlyle's House and Other Sketches,* edited by David Bradshaw (London: Hesperus, 2003).

from cancer in 1904, and shortly thereafter the four Stephen children—Vanessa, Virginia, Thoby, and Adrian—moved together to the then-unfashionable London neighborhood of Bloomsbury. When Thoby Stephen began to bring his Cambridge University friends to the house on Thursday evenings, what would later become famous as the "Bloomsbury Group" began to form.

In an article marking the centenary of her father's birth, Woolf recalled his "allowing a girl of fifteen the free run of a large and quite unexpurgated library"—an unusual opportunity for a Victorian young woman, and evidence of the high regard Sir Leslie had for his daughter's intellectual talents. In her diary, she recorded the many different kinds of books her father recommended to her—biographies and memoirs, philosophy, history, and poetry. Although he believed that women should be "as well educated as men," Woolf's mother held that "to serve is the fulfilment of women's highest nature." The young Stephen children were first taught at home by their mother and father, with little success. Woolf herself received no formal education beyond some classes in Greek and Latin in the Ladies' Department of King's College in London, beginning in the fall of 1897. In 1899 she began lessons in Greek with Clara Pater, sister of the renowned Victorian critic Walter Pater, and in 1902 she was tutored in the classics by Janet Case (who also later involved her in work for women's suffrage). Such homeschooling was a source of some bitterness later in her life, as she recognized the advantages that derived from the expensive educations her brothers and half brothers received at private schools and university. Yet she also realized that her father's encouragement of her obviously keen intellect had given her an eclectic foundation. In the early years of Bloomsbury, she reveled in the opportunity to discuss ideas with her brother Thoby and his friends, among whom were Lytton Strachey, Clive Bell, and

E. M. Forster. From them, she heard, too, about an intense young man named Leonard Woolf, whom she had met briefly when visiting Thoby at Cambridge, and also in 1904 when he came to dinner at Gordon Square just before leaving for Ceylon (now called Sri Lanka), where he was to administer a far-flung outpost of the British Empire.

Virginia Woolf's first publications were unsigned reviews and essays in an Anglo-Catholic newspaper called the *Guardian,* beginning in December 1904. In the fall of 1906, she and Vanessa went with a family friend, Violet Dickinson, to meet their brothers in Greece. The trip was spoiled by Vanessa's falling ill, and when she returned to London, Virginia found both her brother Thoby—who had returned earlier—and her sister seriously ill. After a misdiagnosis by his doctors, Thoby died from typhoid fever on November 20, leaving Virginia to maintain a cheerful front while her sister and Violet Dickinson recovered from their own illnesses. Two days after Thoby's death, Vanessa agreed to marry his close friend Clive Bell.

While living in Bloomsbury, Woolf had begun to write a novel that would go through many drafts before it was published in 1915 as *The Voyage Out.* In these early years of independence, her social circle widened. She became close to the art critic Roger Fry, organizer of the First Post-Impressionist Exhibition in London in 1910, and also entered the orbit of the famed literary hostess Lady Ottoline Morrell (cruelly caricatured as Hermione Roddice in D. H. Lawrence's 1920 novel *Women in Love*). Her political consciousness also began to emerge. In 1910 she volunteered for the movement for women's suffrage. She also participated that February in a daring hoax that embarrassed the British Navy and led to questions being asked in the House of Commons: She and her brother Adrian, together with some other Cambridge friends, gained access to a secret warship by dressing up and posing as the Emperor of Abyssinia and his retinue. The "Dreadnought Hoax" was front-page news, complete with photographs of the phony Ethiopians with flowing robes, blackened faces, and false beards.

To the British establishment, one of the most embarrassing aspects of the Dreadnought affair was that a woman had taken part in the hoax. Vanessa Bell was concerned at what might have happened to her sister had she been discovered on the ship. She was also increasingly worried about Virginia's erratic health, and by the early summer 1910 had discussed with Dr. George Savage, one of the family's doctors, the debilitating headaches her sister suffered; Dr. Savage prescribed several weeks in a nursing home. Another element in Vanessa's concern was that Virginia was twenty-eight and still unmarried. Clive Bell and Virginia had, in fact, engaged in a hurtful flirtation soon after the birth of Vanessa's first child in 1908. Although she had been proposed to twice in 1909 and once in 1911, Virginia had not taken these offers very seriously.

Dropping by Vanessa's house on a July evening in 1911, Virginia met Leonard Woolf, recently back on leave from Ceylon. Soon after this, Leonard became a lodger at the house Virginia shared with Adrian, the economist John Maynard Keynes, and the painter Duncan Grant. Leonard decided to resign from the Colonial Service, hoping that Virginia would agree to marry him. After some considerable hesitation, she did, and they married in August 1912.

By the end of that year, Woolf was again suffering from the tremendous headaches that afflicted her throughout her life, and in 1913 she was again sent to a nursing home for what was then called a "rest cure." In September of that year, she took an overdose of a sleeping drug and was under care until the following spring. In early 1915 she suffered a severe breakdown and was ill throughout most of the year in which her first novel was published.

Despite this difficult beginning, Virginia and Leonard Woolf's marriage eventually settled into a pattern of immense productivity and mutual support. Leonard worked for a time for the Women's Cooperative Guild, and became increasingly involved with advising the Labour Party and writing on international politics, as well as editing several periodicals. Virginia began to establish herself as an important novelist and influential critic. In 1917 the Woolfs set up their own publishing house, the Hogarth Press, in their home in Richmond. Their first publication was *Two Stories*—Leonard's "Three Jews" and Virginia's experimental "The Mark on the Wall." They had decided to make their livings by writing, and in 1919, a few months before Woolf's second novel, *Night and Day,* was published, they bought a cottage in the village of Rodmell in Sussex. After moving back into London from Richmond in 1923, Woolf would spend summers at Monk's House, returning to the social whirl of the city in the fall.

"The Mark on the Wall" was one of a number of what Woolf called "sketches" that she began to write around the time she and Leonard bought their printing press. *Night and Day* was the last of her books to be published in England by another press. In 1919 Hogarth published her short story *Kew Gardens,* with two woodcuts by Vanessa Bell, and two years later came *Monday or Tuesday,* the only collection of her short fiction published in Woolf's lifetime. Her next novel was *Jacob's Room* (1922), a slim elegy to the generation of 1914, and to her beloved brother Thoby, whose life of great promise had also been cut short so suddenly. Woolf had written to her friend Margaret Llewelyn Davies in 1916 that the Great War, as it was then called, was a "preposterous masculine fiction" that made her "steadily more feminist," and in her fiction and nonfiction she began to articulate and illuminate the connections between the patriarchal status quo, the relatively subordinate position of

women, and war making. Thinking about a novel she was calling "The Hours," Woolf wrote in her diary in 1923 that she
wanted to criticize "the social system." Her inclusion in the
novel of a shell-shocked war veteran named Septimus Warren
Smith would confuse many of the early reviewers of her fourth
novel, *Mrs. Dalloway* (1925), but others recognized that Woolf
was breaking new ground in the way she rendered consciousness and her understanding of human subjectivity.

By the time she wrote *Mrs. Dalloway,* Woolf was also a sought-
after essayist and reviewer who, like many of her celebrated
contemporaries, was staking out her own particular piece of
modernist territory. The Hogarth Press published radical young
writers like Katherine Mansfield, T. S. Eliot, and Gertrude Stein.
Approached by Harriet Shaw Weaver with part of the manuscript of James Joyce's *Ulysses* in 1918, the Woolfs turned it down.
Their own small press could not cope with the long and com-
plex manuscript, nor could Leonard Woolf find a commercial
printer willing to risk prosecution for obscenity by producing it.
In 1924 the Hogarth Press became the official English publisher
of the works of Sigmund Freud, translated by Lytton Strachey's
brother James. Woolf's own literary criticism was collected in a
volume published in 1925, *The Common Reader*—a title signaling
her distrust of academics and love of broad, eclectic reading.

The staggering range of Woolf's reading is reflected in the
more than five hundred essays and reviews she published during her lifetime. Her critical writing is concerned not only with
the canonical works of English literature from Chaucer to her
contemporaries, but also ranges widely through lives of the obscure, memoirs, diaries, letters, and biographies. Models of the
form, her essays comprise a body of work that has only recently
begun to attract the kind of recognition her fiction has received.

In 1922 Woolf met "the lovely and gifted aristocrat" Vita
Sackville-West, already a well-known poet and novelist. Their

close friendship slowly turned into a love affair, glowing most intensely from about 1925 to 1928, before modulating into friendship once more in the 1930s. The period of their intimacy was extremely creative for both writers, Woolf publishing essays such as "Mr. Bennett and Mrs. Brown" and "Letter to a Young Poet," as well as three very different novels: *To the Lighthouse* (1927), which evoked her own childhood and had at its center the figure of a modernist woman artist, Lily Briscoe; *Orlando* (1928), a fantastic biography inspired by Vita's own remarkable family history; and *The Waves* (1931), a mystical and profoundly meditative work that pushed Woolf's concept of novel form to its limit. Woolf also published a second *Common Reader* in 1932, and the "biography" of *Flush,* Elizabeth Barrett Browning's dog (1933). She went with Sackville-West to Cambridge in the fall of 1928 to deliver the second of the two lectures on which her great feminist essay *A Room of One's Own* (1929) is based.

As the political situation in Europe in the 1930s moved inexorably to its crisis in 1939, Woolf began to collect newspaper clippings about the relations between the sexes in England, France, Germany, and Italy. The scrapbooks she made became the matrix from which developed the perspectives of her penultimate novel, *The Years* (1937), and the arguments of her pacifist-feminist polemic *Three Guineas* (1938). In 1937 Vanessa's eldest son, Julian Bell, was killed serving as an ambulance driver in the Spanish Civil War. Woolf later wrote to Vanessa that she had written *Three Guineas* partly as an argument with Julian. Her work on *The Years* was grindingly slow and difficult. Ironically, given Woolf's reputation as a highbrow, it became a bestseller in the United States, even being published in an Armed Services edition. While she labored over the novel in 1934, the news came of the death of Roger Fry, one of her oldest and closest friends and the former lover of her sister, Vanessa. Reluctantly, given her distaste for the conventions of biography, Woolf agreed to write his life, which was published in 1940.

In 1939, to relieve the strain of writing Fry's biography, Woolf began to write a memoir, "A Sketch of the Past," which remained unpublished until 1976, when the manuscripts were edited by Jeanne Schulkind for a collection of Woolf's autobiographical writings, *Moments of Being*. Withdrawing with Leonard to Monk's House in Sussex, where they could see the German airplanes flying low overhead on their way to bomb London, Woolf continued to write for peace and correspond with anti-war activists in Europe and the United States. She began to write her last novel, *Between the Acts,* in the spring of 1938, but by early 1941 was dissatisfied with it. Before completing her final revisions, Woolf ended her own life, walking into the River Ouse on the morning of March 28, 1941. To her sister, Vanessa, she wrote, "I can hardly think clearly any more. If I could I would tell you what you and the children have meant to me. I think you know." In her last note to Leonard, she told him he had given her "complete happiness," and asked him to destroy all her papers.

BY THE END of the twentieth century, Virginia Woolf had become an iconic figure, a touchstone for the feminism that revived in the 1960s as well as for the conservative backlash of the 1980s. Hailed by many as a radical writer of genius, she has also been dismissed as a narrowly focused snob. Her image adorns T-shirts, postcards, and even a beer advertisement, while phrases from her writings occur in all kinds of contexts, from peace-march slogans to highbrow book reviews. That Woolf is one of those figures upon whom the myriad competing narratives of twentieth- and twenty-first-century Western culture inscribe themselves is testified to by the enormous number of biographical works about her published in the decades since her nephew Quentin Bell broke the ground in 1972 with his two-volume biography of his aunt.

Argument continues about the work and life of Virginia Woolf: about her experience of incest, her madness, her class attitudes, her sexuality, the difficulty of her prose, her politics, her feminism, and her legacy. Perhaps, though, these words from her essay "How Should One Read a Book?" are our best guide: "The only advice, indeed, that one person can give another about reading is to take no advice, to follow your own instincts, to use your own reason, to come to your own conclusions."

—MARK HUSSEY, GENERAL EDITOR

CHRONOLOGY

Information is arranged in this order: 1. Virginia Woolf's family and her works; 2. Cultural and political events; 3. Significant publications and works of art.

1878   Marriage of Woolf's parents, Leslie Stephen (1832–1904) and Julia Prinsep Duckworth (née Jackson) (1846–1895). Leslie Stephen publishes *Samuel Johnson,* first volume in the English Men of Letters series.
England at war in Afghanistan.

1879   Vanessa Stephen (Bell) born (d. 1961). Edward Burne-Jones paints Julia Stephen as the Virgin Mary in *The Annunciation.* Leslie Stephen, *Hours in a Library,* 3rd series.
Somerville and Lady Margaret Hall Colleges for women founded at Oxford University.
Anglo-Zulu war in South Africa.

1880   Thoby Stephen born (d. 1906).
William Gladstone becomes prime minister for second time. First Boer War begins (1880–81). Deaths of Gustave Flaubert (b. 1821) and George Eliot (b. 1819). Lytton Strachey born (d. 1932).
Fyodor Dostoyevsky, *The Brothers Karamazov.*

1881   Leslie Stephen buys lease of Talland House, St. Ives, Cornwall.

Cambridge University Tripos exams opened to women. Henrik Ibsen, *Ghosts;* Henry James, *The Portrait of a Lady, Washington Square;* Christina Rossetti, *A Pageant and Other Poems;* D. G. Rossetti, *Ballads and Sonnets;* Oscar Wilde, *Poems.*

1882   Adeline Virginia Stephen (Virginia Woolf) born January 25. Leslie Stephen begins work as editor of the *Dictionary of National Biography (DNB)*; publishes *The Science of Ethics.* The Stephen family spends its first summer at Talland House.

Married Women's Property Act enables women to buy, sell, and own property and keep their own earnings. Triple Alliance between Germany, Italy, and Austria. Phoenix Park murders of British officials in Dublin, Ireland. James Joyce born (d. 1941). Death of Charles Darwin (b. 1809).

1883   Adrian Leslie Stephen born (d. 1948). Julia Stephen's *Notes from Sick Rooms* published.

Olive Schreiner, *The Story of an African Farm;* Robert Louis Stevenson, *Treasure Island.*

1884   Leslie Stephen delivers the Clark Lectures at Cambridge University.

Third Reform Act extends the franchise in England. Friedrich Engels, *The Origin of the Family, Private Property and the State;* John Ruskin, *The Storm-Cloud of the Nineteenth Century;* Mark Twain, *The Adventures of Huckleberry Finn.*

1885   First volume of Leslie Stephen's *Dictionary of National Biography* published.
Redistribution Act further extends the franchise in England. Ezra Pound born (d. 1972); D. H. Lawrence born (d. 1930).
George Meredith, *Diana of the Crossways;* Émile Zola, *Germinal.*

1887   Queen Victoria's Golden Jubilee.
Arthur Conan Doyle, *A Study in Scarlet;* H. Rider Haggard, *She;* Thomas Hardy, *The Woodlanders.*

1891   Leslie Stephen gives up the *DNB* editorship. Laura Stephen (1870–1945) is placed in an asylum.
William Gladstone elected prime minister of England a fourth time.
Thomas Hardy, *Tess of the D'Urbervilles;* Oscar Wilde, *The Picture of Dorian Gray.*

1895   Death of Julia Stephen.
Armenian Massacres in Turkey. Discovery of X-rays by William Röntgen; Guglielmo Marconi discovers radio; invention of the cinematograph. Trials of Oscar Wilde.
Thomas Hardy, *Jude the Obscure;* H. G. Wells, *The Time Machine;* Oscar Wilde, *The Importance of Being Earnest.*

1896   Vanessa Stephen begins drawing classes three afternoons a week.
Death of William Morris (b. 1834); F. Scott Fitzgerald born (d. 1940).
Anton Chekhov, *The Seagull.*

1897   Woolf attends Greek and history classes at King's College, London, and begins to keep a regular diary. Vanessa, Virginia, and Thoby watch Queen Victoria's Diamond Jubilee procession. Stella Duckworth (b. 1869) marries Jack Hills in April, but dies in July. Gerald Duckworth (1870–1937) establishes a publishing house.
Paul Gauguin, *Where Do We Come From? What Are We? Where Are We Going?*; Bram Stoker, *Dracula*.

1898   Spanish-American War (1898–99). Marie Curie discovers radium. Death of Stéphane Mallarmé (b. 1842).
H. G. Wells, *The War of the Worlds*; Oscar Wilde, *The Ballad of Reading Gaol*.

1899   Woolf begins Latin and Greek lessons with Clara Pater. Thoby Stephen goes up to Trinity College, Cambridge University, entering with Lytton Strachey, Leonard Woolf (1880–1969), and Clive Bell (1881–1964).
The Second Boer War begins (1899–1902) in South Africa. Ernest Hemingway born (d. 1961).

1900   Woolf and Vanessa attend the Trinity College Ball at Cambridge University.
Deaths of Friedrich Nietzsche (b. 1844), John Ruskin (b. 1819), and Oscar Wilde (b. 1854).
Sigmund Freud, *The Interpretation of Dreams*.

1901   Vanessa enters Royal Academy Schools.
Queen Victoria dies January 22. Edward VII becomes king. Marconi sends messages by wireless telegraphy from Cornwall to Newfoundland.

1902   Woolf begins classics lessons with Janet Case. Adrian
        Stephen enters Trinity College, Cambridge University.
        Leslie Stephen is knighted.
        Joseph Conrad, *Heart of Darkness;* Henry James, *The
        Wings of the Dove;* William James, *The Varieties of Religious
        Experience.*

1903   The Wright Brothers fly a biplane 852 feet. Women's
        Social and Political Union founded in England by Em-
        meline Pankhurst.

1904   Sir Leslie Stephen dies. George Duckworth (1868–
        1934) marries Lady Margaret Herbert. The Stephen
        children—Vanessa, Virginia, Thoby, and Adrian—move
        to 46 Gordon Square, in the Bloomsbury district of
        London. Woolf contributes to F. W. Maitland's biogra-
        phy of her father. Leonard Woolf comes to dine before
        sailing for Ceylon. Woolf travels in Italy and France.
        Her first publication is an unsigned review in the
        Guardian, a church weekly.
        "Empire Day" inaugurated in London and in Britain's
        colonies.
        Anton Chekhov, *The Cherry Orchard;* Henry James, *The
        Golden Bowl.*

1905   Woolf begins teaching weekly adult education classes at
        Morley College. Thoby invites Cambridge friends to
        their home for "Thursday Evenings"—the beginnings
        of the Bloomsbury Group. Woolf travels with Adrian to
        Portugal and Spain. The Stephens visit Cornwall for the
        first time since their mother's death.
        Revolution in Russia.

Albert Einstein, *Special Theory of Relativity;* E. M. Forster, *Where Angels Fear to Tread;* Sigmund Freud, *Essays in the Theory of Sexuality;* Edith Wharton, *The House of Mirth;* Oscar Wilde, *De Profundis.*

1906   The Stephens travel to Greece. Vanessa and Thoby fall ill. Thoby dies November 20; on November 22, Vanessa agrees to marry Clive Bell.

Deaths of Paul Cézanne (b. 1839) and Henrik Ibsen (b. 1828). Samuel Beckett born (d. 1989).

1907   Woolf moves with her brother Adrian to Fitzroy Square. Vanessa marries Clive Bell.

First Cubist exhibition in Paris. W. H. Auden born (d. 1973).

Joseph Conrad, *The Secret Agent;* E. M. Forster, *The Longest Journey;* Edmund Gosse, *Father and Son;* Pablo Picasso, *Demoiselles d'Avignon.*

1908   Birth of Vanessa Bell's first child, Julian. Woolf travels to Italy with Vanessa and Clive Bell.

Herbert Asquith becomes prime minister.

E. M. Forster, *A Room with a View;* Gertrude Stein, *Three Lives.*

1909   Woolf receives a legacy of £2,500 on the death of her Quaker aunt, Caroline Emelia Stephen. Lytton Strachey proposes marriage to Woolf, but they both quickly realize this would be a mistake. Woolf meets Lady Ottoline Morrell for the first time. She travels to the Wagner festival in Bayreuth.

Chancellor of the Exchequer David Lloyd George (1863–1945) introduces a "People's Budget," taxing wealth to pay for social reforms. A constitutional crisis ensues when the House of Lords rejects it. Death of George Meredith (b. 1828).

Filippo Marinetti, "The Founding and Manifesto of Futurism"; Henri Matisse, *Dance.*

1910   Woolf participates in the Dreadnought Hoax. She volunteers for the cause of women's suffrage. Birth of Vanessa Bell's second child, Quentin (d. 1996).

First Post-Impressionist Exhibition ("Manet and the Post-Impressionists") organized by Roger Fry (1866–1934) at the Grafton Galleries in London. Edward VII dies May 6. George V becomes king. Death of Leo Tolstoy (b. 1828).

E. M. Forster, *Howards End;* Igor Stravinsky, *The Firebird.*

1911   Woolf rents Little Talland House in Sussex. Leonard Woolf returns from Ceylon; in November, he, Adrian Stephen, John Maynard Keynes (1883–1946), Woolf, and Duncan Grant (1885–1978) share a house together at Brunswick Square in London.

Ernest Rutherford makes first model of atomic structure. Rupert Brooke, *Poems;* Joseph Conrad, *Under Western Eyes;* D. H. Lawrence, *The White Peacock;* Katherine Mansfield, *In a German Pension;* Ezra Pound, *Canzoni;* Edith Wharton, *Ethan Frome.*

1912   Woolf leases Asheham House in Sussex. Marries Leonard on August 10; they move to Clifford's Inn, London.

Captain Robert Scott's expedition reaches the South Pole, but he and his companions die on the return

journey. The *Titanic* sinks. Second Post-Impression-
ist Exhibition, for which Leonard Woolf serves as
secretary.
Marcel Duchamp, *Nude Descending a Staircase;* Wassily
Kandinsky, *Concerning the Spiritual in Art;* Thomas
Mann, *Death in Venice;* George Bernard Shaw, *Pygmalion.*

1913   *The Voyage Out* manuscript delivered to Gerald Duckworth. Woolf enters a nursing home in July; in September, she attempts suicide.
Roger Fry founds the Omega Workshops.
Sigmund Freud, *Totem and Taboo;* D. H. Lawrence, *Sons
and Lovers;* Marcel Proust, *Du côté de chez Swann;* Igor
Stravinsky, *Le Sacre du printemps.*

1914   Leonard Woolf, *The Wise Virgins;* he reviews Freud's
The Psychopathology of Everyday Life.
World War I ("The Great War") begins in August.
Home Rule Bill for Ireland passed.
Clive Bell, *Art;* James Joyce, *Dubliners;* Wyndham Lewis
et al., "Vorticist Manifesto" (in *Blast*); Gertrude Stein,
Tender Buttons.

1915   *The Voyage Out,* Woolf's first novel, published by Duck-
worth. In April the Woolfs move to Hogarth House in
Richmond. Woolf begins again to keep a regular diary.
First Zeppelin attack on London. Death of Rupert
Brooke (b. 1887).
Joseph Conrad, *Victory;* Ford Madox Ford, *The Good Sol-
dier;* D. H. Lawrence, *The Rainbow;* Dorothy Richardson,
Pointed Roofs.

1916   Woolf discovers Charleston, where her sister, Vanessa (no longer living with her husband, Clive), moves in October with her sons, Julian and Quentin, and Duncan Grant (with whom she is in love) and David Garnett (with whom Duncan is in love).

Easter Rising in Dublin. Death of Henry James (b. 1843).

Albert Einstein, *General Theory of Relativity;* James Joyce, *A Portrait of the Artist as a Young Man;* Dorothy Richardson, *Backwater.*

1917   The Hogarth Press established by Leonard and Virginia Woolf in Richmond. Their first publication is their own *Two Stories,* with woodcuts by Dora Carrington (1893–1932).

Russian Bolshevik Revolution destroys the rule of the czar. The United States enters the European war.

T. S. Eliot, *Prufrock and Other Observations;* Sigmund Freud, *Introduction to Psychoanalysis;* Carl Jung, *The Unconscious;* Dorothy Richardson, *Honeycomb;* W. B. Yeats, *The Wild Swans at Coole.*

1918   Woolf meets T. S. Eliot (1888–1965). Harriet Shaw Weaver comes to tea with the manuscript of James Joyce's *Ulysses.* Vanessa Bell and Duncan Grant's daughter, Angelica Garnett, born; her paternity is kept secret from all but a very few intimates.

Armistice signed November 11; Parliamentary Reform Act gives votes in Britain to women of thirty and older and to all men.

G. M. Hopkins, *Poems;* James Joyce, *Exiles;* Katherine Mansfield, *Prelude* (Hogarth Press); Marcel Proust, *À l'ombre des jeunes filles en fleurs;* Lytton Strachey, *Eminent Victorians;* Rebecca West, *The Return of the Soldier.*

1919   The Woolfs buy Monk's House in Sussex. Woolf's second novel, *Night and Day,* is published by Duckworth. Her essay "Modern Novels" (republished in 1925 as "Modern Fiction") appears in the *Times Literary Supplement; Kew Gardens* published by Hogarth Press.
Bauhaus founded by Walter Gropius in Weimar. Sex Disqualification (Removal) Act opens many professions and public offices to women. Election of first woman member of parliament, Nancy Astor. Treaty of Versailles imposes harsh conditions on postwar Germany, opposed by John Maynard Keynes, who writes *The Economic Consequences of the Peace.* League of Nations created. T. S. Eliot, "Tradition and the Individual Talent," *Poems;* Dorothy Richardson, *The Tunnel, Interim;* Robert Wiene, *The Cabinet of Dr. Caligari* (film).

1920   The Memoir Club, comprising thirteen original members of the Bloomsbury Group, meets for the first time. *The Voyage Out* and *Night and Day* are published in the United States by George H. Doran.
Mohandas Gandhi initiates mass passive resistance against British rule in India.
T. S. Eliot, *The Sacred Wood;* Sigmund Freud, *Beyond the Pleasure Principle;* Roger Fry, *Vision and Design;* D. H. Lawrence, *Women in Love;* Katherine Mansfield, *Bliss and Other Stories;* Ezra Pound, *Hugh Selwyn Mauberley;* Marcel Proust, *Le Côté de Guermantes I;* Edith Wharton, *The Age of Innocence.*

1921   Woolf's short story collection *Monday or Tuesday* published by Hogarth Press, which will from this time publish all her books in England. The book is also published in the United States by Harcourt Brace, which from now on is her American publisher.

Aldous Huxley, *Crome Yellow;* Pablo Picasso, *Three Musicians;* Luigi Pirandello, *Six Characters in Search of an Author;* Marcel Proust, *Le Côté de Guermantes II, Sodome et Gomorrhe I;* Dorothy Richardson, *Deadlock;* Lytton Strachey, *Queen Victoria.*

1922   *Jacob's Room* published. Woolf meets Vita Sackville-West (1892–1962) for the first time.

Bonar Law elected prime minister. Mussolini comes to power in Italy. Irish Free State established. British Broadcasting Company (BBC) formed. Discovery of Tutankhamen's tomb in Egypt. Death of Marcel Proust (b. 1871).

T. S. Eliot, *The Waste Land;* James Joyce, *Ulysses;* Katherine Mansfield, *The Garden Party;* Marcel Proust, *Sodome et Gomorrhe II;* Ludwig Wittgenstein, *Tractatus Logico-Philosophicus.*

1923   The Woolfs travel to Spain, stopping in Paris on the way home. Hogarth Press publishes *The Waste Land.*

Stanley Baldwin succeeds Bonar Law as prime minister. Death of Katherine Mansfield (b. 1888).

Mina Loy, *Lunar Baedeker;* Marcel Proust, *La Prisonnière;* Dorothy Richardson, *Revolving Lights;* Rainer Maria Rilke, *Duino Elegies.*

1924   The Woolfs move to Tavistock Square. Woolf lectures on "Character in Fiction" to the Heretics Society at Cambridge University.

The Labour Party takes office for the first time under

the leadership of Ramsay MacDonald but is voted out within the year. Death of Joseph Conrad (b. 1857).

E. M. Forster, *A Passage to India;* Thomas Mann, *The Magic Mountain.*

1925   *Mrs. Dalloway* and *The Common Reader* published. Woolf stays with Vita Sackville-West at her house, Long Barn, for the first time.

Nancy Cunard, *Parallax;* F. Scott Fitzgerald, *The Great Gatsby;* Ernest Hemingway, *In Our Time;* Adolf Hitler, *Mein Kampf;* Franz Kafka, *The Trial;* Alain Locke, ed., *The New Negro;* Marcel Proust, *Albertine disparue;* Dorothy Richardson, *The Trap;* Gertrude Stein, *The Making of Americans.*

1926   Woolf lectures on "How Should One Read a Book?" at Hayes Court School. "Cinema" published in *Arts* (New York), "Impassioned Prose" in *Times Literary Supplement,* and "On Being Ill" in *New Criterion.* Meets Gertrude Stein (1874–1946).

The General Strike in support of mine workers in England lasts nearly two weeks.

Ernest Hemingway, *The Sun Also Rises;* Langston Hughes, *The Weary Blues;* Franz Kafka, *The Castle;* A. A. Milne, *Winnie-the-Pooh.*

1927   *To the Lighthouse,* "The Art of Fiction," "Poetry, Fiction and the Future," and "Street Haunting" published. The Woolfs travel with Vita Sackville-West and her husband, Harold Nicolson, to Yorkshire to see the total eclipse of the sun. They buy their first car.

Charles Lindbergh flies the Atlantic solo.

E. M. Forster, *Aspects of the Novel;* Ernest Hemingway, *Men without Women;* Franz Kafka, *Amerika;* Marcel

Proust, *Le Temps retrouvé;* Gertrude Stein, *Four Saints in Three Acts.*

1928   *Orlando: A Biography* published. In October, Woolf delivers two lectures at Cambridge on which she will base *A Room of One's Own.* Femina-Vie Heureuse prize awarded to *To the Lighthouse.*
The Equal Franchise Act gives the vote to all women over twenty-one. Sound films introduced. Death of Thomas Hardy (b. 1840).
Djuna Barnes, *Ladies Almanack;* Radclyffe Hall, *The Well of Loneliness;* D. H. Lawrence, *Lady Chatterley's Lover;* Evelyn Waugh, *Decline and Fall;* W. B. Yeats, *The Tower.*

1929   *A Room of One's Own* published. "Women and Fiction" in *The Forum* (New York).
Labour Party returned to power under Prime Minister MacDonald. Discovery of penicillin. Museum of Modern Art opens in New York. Wall Street crash.
William Faulkner, *The Sound and the Fury;* Ernest Hemingway, *A Farewell to Arms;* Nella Larsen, *Passing.*

1930   Woolf meets the pioneering composer, writer, and suffragette Ethel Smyth (1858–1944), with whom she forms a close friendship.
Death of D. H. Lawrence (b. 1885).
W. H. Auden, *Poems;* T. S. Eliot, *Ash Wednesday;* William Faulkner, *As I Lay Dying;* Sigmund Freud, *Civilisation and Its Discontents.*

1931   *The Waves* is published. First of six articles by Woolf about London published in *Good Housekeeping;* "Introductory Letter" to *Life As We Have Known It.* Lectures to London branch of National Society for Women's Service on "Professions for Women." Meets John Lehmann (1907–1987), who will become a partner in the Hogarth Press.

Growing financial crisis throughout Europe and beginning of the Great Depression.

1932   *The Common Reader, Second Series* and "Letter to a Young Poet" published. Woolf invited to give the 1933 Clark Lectures at Cambridge, which she declines.

Death of Lytton Strachey (b. 1880).

Aldous Huxley, *Brave New World.*

1933   *Flush: A Biography,* published. The Woolfs travel by car to Italy.

Adolf Hitler becomes chancellor of Germany, establishing the totalitarian dictatorship of his National Socialist (Nazi) Party.

T. S. Eliot, *The Use of Poetry and the Use of Criticism;* George Orwell, *Down and Out in Paris and London;* Gertrude Stein, *The Autobiography of Alice B. Toklas;* Nathanael West, *Miss Lonelyhearts;* W. B. Yeats, *The Collected Poems.*

1934   Woolf meets W. B. Yeats at Ottoline Morrell's house. Writes "Walter Sickert: A Conversation."

George Duckworth dies. Roger Fry dies.

Samuel Beckett, *More Pricks Than Kicks;* Nancy Cunard, ed., *Negro: An Anthology;* F. Scott Fitzgerald, *Tender Is the Night;* Wyndham Lewis, *Men Without Art;* Henry Miller, *Tropic of Cancer;* Ezra Pound, *ABC of Reading;* Evelyn Waugh, *A Handful of Dust.*

1935 The Woolfs travel to Germany, where they accidentally get caught up in a parade for Göring. They return to England via Italy and France.

1936 Woolf reads "Am I a Snob?" to the Memoir Club, and publishes "Why Art Today Follows Politics" in the *Daily Worker*.
Death of George V, who is succeeded by Edward VIII, who then abdicates to marry Wallis Simpson. George VI becomes king. Spanish Civil War (1936–38) begins when General Franco, assisted by Germany and Italy, attacks the Republican government. BBC television begins.
Djuna Barnes, *Nightwood;* Charlie Chaplin, *Modern Times* (film); Aldous Huxley, *Eyeless in Gaza;* J. M. Keynes, *The General Theory of Employment, Interest and Money;* Rose Macaulay, *Personal Pleasures;* Margaret Mitchell, *Gone with the Wind.*

1937 *The Years* published. Woolf's nephew Julian Bell killed in the Spanish Civil War.
Neville Chamberlain becomes prime minister.
Zora Neale Hurston, *Their Eyes Were Watching God;* David Jones, *In Parenthesis;* Pablo Picasso, *Guernica;* John Steinbeck, *Of Mice and Men;* J. R. R. Tolkien, *The Hobbit.*

1938 *Three Guineas* published.
Germany annexes Austria. Chamberlain negotiates the Munich Agreement ("Peace in our time"), ceding Czech territory to Hitler.
Samuel Beckett, *Murphy;* Elizabeth Bowen, *The Death of the Heart;* Jean-Paul Sartre, *La Nausée.*

1939   The Woolfs visit Sigmund Freud, living in exile in London having fled the Nazis. They move to Mecklenburgh Square.

Germany occupies Czechoslovakia; Italy occupies Albania; Russia makes a nonaggression pact with Germany. Germany invades Poland and war is declared by Britain and France on Germany, September 3. Deaths of W. B. Yeats (b. 1865), Sigmund Freud (b. 1856), and Ford Madox Ford (b. 1873).

James Joyce, *Finnegans Wake;* John Steinbeck, *The Grapes of Wrath;* Nathanael West, *The Day of the Locust.*

1940   *Roger Fry: A Biography* published. "Thoughts on Peace in an Air Raid" in the *New Republic.* Woolf lectures on "The Leaning Tower" to the Workers Educational Association in Brighton.

The Battle of Britain leads to German night bombings of English cities. The Woolfs' house at Mecklenburgh Square is severely damaged, as is their former house at Tavistock Square. Hogarth Press is moved out of London.

Ernest Hemingway, *For Whom the Bell Tolls;* Christina Stead, *The Man Who Loved Children.*

1941   Woolf drowns herself, March 28, in the River Ouse in Sussex. *Between the Acts* published in July.

Death of James Joyce (b. 1882).

Rebecca West, *Black Lamb and Grey Falcon.*

INTRODUCTION
BY BONNIE KIME SCOTT

IN HER OWN introduction to *Mrs. Dalloway*,[1] Virginia Woolf took the attitude that "one has too much respect for the reader pure and simple to point out to him what he has missed, or to suggest to him what he should seek" (11). She dealt instead with misconceptions about her work that she felt the critics had encouraged, given their initial preoccupation with fitting the novel into a predefined artistic method. There is much to enjoy in just plunging into *Mrs. Dalloway*, "pure and simple," and no guarantee that the critics will get it right. But as someone who has taught and enjoyed this work for many years, I can't resist pointing out a few things that shouldn't be missed. These include ways that Woolf's method evolved in the course of writing *Mrs. Dalloway*. Woolf helped with this genealogy of the text by leaving behind contemporary notebooks and diary entries commenting on her formal discoveries, as well as early drafts (see Wussow). Woolf also suspects in her introduction that readers will be curious about ways the author is reflected in her work: "Books are the flowers or fruit stuck here and there on a tree which has its roots deep down in the earth of our earliest life, of our first experiences" (11). Along these lines, we will want to consider attitudes as various as Woolf's love of social gatherings enriched by conversation, and her distrust of doctors, based on her own treatments by them. Her remark about the "roots" of her tree betrays her interest in psychology, which plays out in the minds of her characters as they flash back to previous events and early acquaintances.

The novel is set in London on a Wednesday in mid-June 1923.[2] Both the place and the time grow increasingly remote from culture as we know it today. This gulf calls for the identifications and mappings that begin in this introduction and continue in the notes and the map of Mrs. Dalloway's London. With a closer knowledge of place-names, streets, shops, government buildings, and monuments, we can appreciate the rich political contexts and social commentary Woolf has packed into this novel, having said early on, "I want to criticize the social system, & show it at work, at its most intense" (*Diary* 2: 248). Her concerns include the politics of a world war recently ended, of a questionable empire entering decline, and of people in power who have the dangerous options of passing judgment on and even controlling the lives of the outsiders who consistently won Woolf's attention.

Genealogy

WITH *Mrs. Dalloway,* Woolf entered her most productive and confident phase as a writer. At the age of forty, when she was at work on *Mrs. Dalloway,* she had three previous novels to her credit (*The Voyage Out,* 1915; *Night and Day,* 1919; and *Jacob's Room,* 1922), a collection of short fiction (*Monday or Tuesday,* 1921) that included the remarkable experimental works "Kew Gardens" and "The Mark on the Wall" (both written in 1917), and a growing reputation as an essayist and a reviewer of fiction, biography, drama, and art. Her work appeared in such prestigious periodicals as the *Times Literary Supplement, Criterion* (edited by T. S. Eliot), the British *Vogue,* and American publications including the *Dial,* the *New York Herald Tribune,* and the

New Republic. She had entered into critical conversations defining the nature of modern fiction ("Modern Novels," 1919; revised as "Modern Fiction," 1925), and was thinking about the ways that character had changed in the modern world ("Mr. Bennett and Mrs. Brown," 1923). Both of these topics no doubt stimulated the critics' interest in what she might do with her own method. On the political end of the creative spectrum, Woolf was beginning to venture with her essays and speaking engagements into polemics about feminism and imperialism.

Her first novel, *The Voyage Out,* gave Woolf a fine foundation for her future writing. In several ways this work looks ahead to the politics and plot of *Mrs. Dalloway.* Woolf explored a young woman's subjectivity as it developed on her travels out to South America, where she stayed near a hotel populated by English travelers. Rachel Vinrace encounters unfamiliar cultural and geographical terrain, as well as persistent British patriarchal forces, as does Elizabeth Dalloway in *Mrs. Dalloway.* Woolf also plays with the marriage plot in *The Voyage Out,* as Rachel becomes engaged to another vacationer, Terence Hewet, and begins to face up to societal expectations for her future.

Among those Rachel encounters while still aboard her father's ship, the *Euphrosyne,* is a couple named Dalloway. Their behavior, if not their social position, is very different from that of the same-named older pair we encounter in *Mrs. Dalloway.* They impress Rachel—Clarissa, with her exquisite features and air of control; Richard, with his machine-like grasp of politics. This early Clarissa is a delicate, fashionable woman who places a premium upon ladylike behavior as she assesses her shipmates. She is protected from the chill with veils and furs, and unlike the Vinrace women, must lie low from seasickness shortly into her voyage. Clarissa in *The Voyage Out* supports her husband's mission abroad as his photographer and diarist, and acquiesces to his positions, including his denunciation of women's suffrage.

Speaking with Richard in their own cabin, she glories in English identity and his sense of empire—values that Woolf would shift somewhat to other characters in *Mrs. Dalloway,* making her central couple more likable in the later work. The early Clarissa does read *Antigone* (an important text of protest for Woolf), and seems to feel that Rachel will benefit from having her copy of Jane Austen's *Persuasion.* She competes to some extent with Rachel's aunt, Helen Ambrose, in affection for Rachel. One remarkable scene that has invited lesbian analysis finds Helen tumbling Rachel in the pampas grass, anticipating an enduring strain of interest in women loving women in Woolf's texts.

The Richard of *The Voyage Out,* though temporarily voted out of Parliament, is accustomed to being granted special arrangements—like transportation on the Vinraces' ship. He aims at impressing readers of the London *Times* with his ability to gather information about unsettled conditions abroad, and he gains the attention of Rachel with his programs to improve working women's problems at home. When he encounters Rachel alone, Richard exposes his vulnerable listener to his own ungoverned desires, kissing her passionately. Woolf takes us into subsequent nightmares Rachel experiences, and we are left to decide how traumatic this event has been for her. As Rachel dies of a fever, she moves metaphorically and mentally beyond the reach of her intended husband in the final pages of this first novel. Strategic deaths of her protagonists remained a powerful option for Woolf in later novels, including *Mrs. Dalloway.*

Night and Day (1919) was Woolf's most traditionally plotted novel, as author Katherine Mansfield pointed out in a somewhat dismissive review that deeply troubled Woolf. As a representative of the genre of "new woman" fiction, however, it contributes to Woolf's clear feminist trajectory. Woolf is very much concerned with young women's use of their minds. One of the leading characters, Katharine Hilbery, is fascinated with mathematical theory. The second female protagonist, Mary Datchet, labors stoically on behalf of the suffrage movement. As in her former novel, Woolf is concerned with the difficulties of finding a productive partnership between a woman and a man. Katharine's first engagement is to William Rodney, an aspiring writer who aspires also to control her. Katharine has much more to say to the young lawyer Ralph Denham, her eventual partner. Mary Datchet is much admired by both Ralph (whom she loves) and Katharine, suggesting an intricacy of early cross-gendered friendships. Both this sort of multivalent friendship and a woman's choice of a partner to preserve her own autonomy remain important in *Mrs. Dalloway*. Katharine's mother, who is perennially engaged in writing a biography of her poet father and other literary projects unlikely of completion, remains a part of Woolf's fictional universe. Dotty as ever, she attends Mrs. Dalloway's party.

With her third novel, *Jacob's Room* (1922), Woolf launched herself more than ever into experimental form. Her method involved the representation of the young man at its center from the perceptions of the characters who surround him. Politically, Woolf offered a study of the institutions and experiences that shape a young man of her own educated class, often at the expense of the women in their lives. Like so many of his generation, Jacob perishes in World War I. Both the experiment in rendering character, and the interest in the effects of war would persist in *Mrs. Dalloway*. In *Mrs. Dalloway*, we pass the Tomb of the Unknown Warrior, who, like Jacob Flanders, fell in Belgium. Leonard Woolf (who typically read Woolf's novels in manuscript) suggested that she might build upon the discoveries she had made in rendering character for *Jacob's Room* in her subsequent work.

The writer who turned from *Jacob's Room* to new projects late in 1922 was an experienced and determined professional.

She was involved in an impressive variety of tasks, and management of all of them seems to have instilled self-confidence. She had a "quick change theory" that suggested that it was beneficial to switch from fiction to essays (*Diary* 2: 189). In addition to writing two stories that would evolve into the first two segments of *Mrs. Dalloway* ("Mrs. Dalloway in Bond Street" and "The Prime Minister"), Woolf was also writing and revising essays for the collection she would call the *Common Reader* (published in April 1925, less than a month before the publication of *Mrs. Dalloway*). The mixed content of her notebooks attests to this variety of endeavors. Woolf kept up with her diary and letters, did background reading in the classics that contributed to both the fiction and the essays, and spent hours setting type for the Hogarth Press, an enterprise the Woolfs had undertaken in 1917. She muses that without this printing, she would be "an inbreeding rabbit" (*Diary* 2: 323). Anticipating the critics' comments on *Jacob's Room,* she could draw from her variety of projects for an answer: "If they say this is all a clever experiment, I shall produce Mrs Dalloway in Bond Street as the finished product. If they say your fiction is impossible, I shall say what about Miss Ormerod,[3] a fantasy. If they say, You can't make us care a damn for any of your figures—I shall say, read my criticism then" (*Diary* 2: 178–79).

Challenging Personal History

THERE IS another side to this rich array of activities and imagined answers to her critics. As is well known (often to the extent of dominating accounts of her), Woolf was challenged by a pattern of recurrent mental breakdowns, which literary critics have diagnosed after the fact as manic-depressive illness or bipolar disorder (see Caramagno). This condition was complicated by episodes of sexual abuse at the hands of her half brothers, Gerald and George Duckworth, starting in early childhood. Her first obvious episode of mental illness followed the death of her mother in 1895, when Woolf was thirteen. Anxiety over the critical reception of her works may have been a contributing factor to later recurrences of the illness, though something as routine as flu could take her out of action for a week or more. Woolf experienced a particularly severe set of episodes surrounding the publication of *The Voyage Out* (begun by 1907 but not published until 1915). She attempted suicide soon after the manuscript was sent to the publisher, Duckworth (her half brother Gerald's press), in 1913, and had another severe bout of mental illness after its much-delayed publication. Her second novel, *Night and Day*, was begun while she was still confined to bed for a rest cure. A half year of elevated temperature and influenza followed her completion of her third novel, *Jacob's Room*. Thus *Mrs. Dalloway* is the work of a survivor, and indeed takes survival and triumph over illness as a central subject. It also respects a suicide.

Woolf, like her title character in *Mrs. Dalloway*, led a regulated existence in the early 1920s. Readers will note ways that the routine of Mrs. Dalloway is regulated. Her husband, Richard, brings her flowers in the early afternoon, and before departing returns with a pillow and a quilt, admonishing, "An hour's complete rest after luncheon" (117). Clarissa's response is accepting, even appreciative, but also critical. "He would go on saying 'An hour's complete rest after luncheon' to the end of time, because a doctor had ordered it once. It was like him to take what doctors said literally; part of his adorable, divine simplicity" (117). Woolf's husband, Leonard, played a similar role.

Virginia had married Leonard Woolf in 1912, making permanent his visit back to England from a civil service post in the colonial administration of Ceylon. An editor, essayist, and socialist thinker, he was a fine intellectual companion and proved highly supportive of her writing career. Their decision to run their own press would give her the advantage of suiting herself, rather than the whims of publishing houses, for the remainder of her career. It also gave her a special relationship to other writers. She had the pleasure of publishing work by T. S. Eliot and Katherine Mansfield, among others. Woolf would write *Mrs. Dalloway* with Mansfield's criticisms of *Night and Day* very much in mind, and Eliot, through repeated conversations concerning *Ulysses*, would make her conscious of James Joyce as a modernist rival. Leonard Woolf's position as editor of *Nation & Athenaeum*, starting in 1923, would give her a constant outlet for her essays, though she would continue to publish in a variety of journals. These advantages came well into her marriage. Upon discovering the severity of Virginia's illness within their first few months together, Leonard had an immediate impulse to regulate where and when she would work. While some have criticized him for the particular medical advice he pursued—resulting in periods spent in rest homes, restricted social and writing time, and the decision that the couple should not have children—others regard his unflagging support as life preserving.

In 1914 Leonard settled with an ailing Virginia in Richmond. Situated south of the Thames River, this suburban location removed her from the more feverish activities and encounters of London. The Woolfs took walks regularly, sometimes visiting nearby Kew Gardens, often in the company of their current dog. When she was not ill, Woolf had a daily routine that limited her hours of writing, ensured periods of rest, and varied the sorts of work she did at different times of the day. We might find her writing for a few hours in the morning, then turning to reading in the afternoon, and perhaps retyping drafts later in the day. One variation might be the hand setting of type for the press. Woolf occasionally registered her protest against her protected suburban life, as in this diary entry, which also acknowledges the importance of her social self:

> But half the horror is that L. instead of being, as I gathered, sympathetic has the old rigid obstacle — my health. And I cant sacrifice his peace of mind, yet the obstacle is surely now a dead hand, which one should no longer let dominate our short years of life — oh to dwindle them out here, with all these gaps, & abbreviations! Always to catch trains, always to waste time, to sit here & wait for Leonard to come in, to spend hours standing at the box of type with Margery, to wonder what its all for . . . For ever to be suburban. L. I don't think minds any of this as much as I do. But then Lord! . . . what I owe him! What he gives me! Still, I say, surely we could get more from life than we do — isn't he too much of a Puritan, of a disciplinarian, doesn't he through birth & training accept a drastic discipline too tamely, or rather, with too Spartan a self control? There is, I suppose, a very different element in us; my social side, his intellectual side. This social side is very genuine in me. Nor do I think it reprehensible. It is a piece of jewellery I inherit from my mother — a joy in laughter, something that is stimulated, not selfishly wholly or vainly, by contact with my friends. (*Diary* 2: 250)

She wrote this breakaway diary entry on June 28, 1923—very nearly at the time she set *Mrs. Dalloway*.

Although London was a restricted destination for Woolf during the first decade of her marriage, the countryside, and especially the rolling hills near the sea in Sussex, were within reach. Having frequented the area since their early courtship, the Woolfs in 1919 purchased Monk's House in Rodmell as their country retreat. The *Mrs. Dalloway* manuscript traveled back and forth to Sussex, where Woolf wrote in a garden shed (shared with apples in the loft). Though its present action is set in London, *Mrs. Dalloway* goes back in memory to a country setting.

By 1924, when in the finishing stages of *Mrs. Dalloway,* Virginia was doing well enough to convince Leonard that they should again reside in London. She took the initiative to find and negotiate for a residence that would house both themselves and the Hogarth Press at 52 Tavistock Square. She recorded her love of the city, so central to her novel in progress, in her diary as she prepared to settle there again: "London thou art a jewel of jewels, & jasper of jocunditie—music, talk, friendship, city views, books, publishing, something central & inexplicable, all this is now within my reach, as it hasn't been since August 1913, when we left Cliffords Inn, for a series of catastrophes which very nearly ended my life, & would, I'm vain enough to think, have ended Leonard's" (*Diary* 2: 283).

Connections

WOOLF'S long-restricted but much-cherished social life involved members of the Bloomsbury circle, most of whom (including Leonard) were drawn from the group of young men who had surrounded Woolf's older brother, Thoby, when he was a student at Cambridge. Now middle-aged like herself, they might come to Richmond on individual visits. They were also likely to gather at various residences in Bloomsbury, or at Virginia's or Vanessa's country homes in Sussex. Woolf's Bloomsbury friends, moving through the decades, included Vanessa's husband, the art critic Clive Bell; Vanessa's lover, the bisexual artist Duncan Grant; the artist, critic, and founder of the arts and crafts Omega Workshop Roger Fry; the biographer Lytton

Strachey, who had briefly engaged himself to Virginia, despite being a homosexual; the novelist E. M. Forster; and the noted economist John Maynard Keynes, joined by his wife, the Russian ballerina Lydia Lopokova (a recent addition to the group).

Woolf's love of gathering with friends would play a part in the design of *Mrs. Dalloway,* where a party provides the culmination of the day, and the plot. The double dimension of time, which flashes from middle-aged Bloomsbury friendship back to the excitement of youthful acquaintanceship, is also echoed in *Mrs. Dalloway.* Clarissa Dalloway, Richard, Peter Walsh, and Sally Seton move repeatedly in their minds from their middle-aged present, on a single day in London, to intense late-adolescent episodes experienced in the country at Bourton. Both Woolf and numerous critics have noted resources for the characters of *Mrs. Dalloway* in the Bloomsbury set. Lydia Lopokova, for example, helped Woolf imagine the cultural challenges faced by Rezia, the Italian wife of Septimus Smith in *Mrs. Dalloway,* and Rezia bears some of her gestures. In Lytton Strachey, Woolf continued to encounter the man she did not marry, sometimes reflecting on his foibles, as Clarissa does on those of Peter Walsh. Leonard for Virginia, like Richard Dalloway for Clarissa, was the more reliable choice. Such parallels are imperfect, however. Peter's personality was not at all like Strachey's, and for it she might have turned more to Clive Bell. Woolf opportunistically transplanted some of Leonard's experiences as a colonial administrator in Ceylon onto Peter as well, since Peter has just returned to London from his post in India.

Woolf had to look outside Bloomsbury for characters such as Hugh Whitbread, with his allegiance to the society of the royal court, and even for some aspects of Clarissa. Woolf had a model for Hugh in her half brother George Duckworth, who insisted that Virginia accompany him to high-society occasions.

These brought torment to Woolf's teen years, and this is reflected somewhat in the rebellion of Elizabeth Dalloway against her objectification at the Dalloways' party. Another family friend, introduced to the Stephens via their upper-class Duckworth connection, was Kitty Maxse, sometimes seen as a partial model for Clarissa. Woolf recalled Kitty's engagement, which occurred during a visit to the family's vacation house in St. Ives, when Woolf was eight years old. Woolf's diary records Kitty's death from a suspicious fall in October 1922, and expresses regret that she hadn't kept up with this "old friend." She sets down very distinct memories of "her white hair—pink cheeks—how she sat upright—her voice—with its characteristic tones—her green blue floor—which she painted with her own hands: her earrings, her gaiety, yet melancholy; her smartness: her tears, which stayed on her cheek" (*Diary* 2: 206). Woolf worried that Clarissa was a "stiff-glittering & tinsely" character and comforted herself that she could bring other characters to her support (*Diary* 2: 272). Woolf could also study character types and modes of entertainment at a grand country house, Garsington, near Oxford, where Lady Ottoline Morrell entertained her own literary aristocracy. One visit brought out qualities of loathing that suggest the more troubled views of humanity expressed by Septimus Smith in *Mrs. Dalloway*:

> But I cannot describe Garsington. Thirty seven people to tea; a bunch of young men no bigger than asparagus; walking to & fro, round & round; compliments, attentions, & then this slippery mud—which is what interests me at the moment. A loathing overcomes me of human beings—their insincerity, their vanity—A wearisome & rather defiling talk with Ott. last night is the foundation of this complaint—& then the blend in one's own mind of suavity & sweetness with contempt & bitterness. (*Diary* 2: 243)

Also during the period of her writing *Mrs. Dalloway,* Woolf gained fresh insight into aristocrats through her new friend, later her lover and a significant contributor to the Hogarth Press, Vita Sackville-West.

Work in Progress

AT WORK on *Mrs. Dalloway,* Woolf strove "to foresee this book better than the others, & get the utmost out of it. I suppose I could have screwed Jacob up tighter if I had foreseen; but I had to make my path as I went" (*Diary* 2: 209–10). She paced herself by setting goals for scenes to be completed in the next month or two, and planning how fiction should take turns with other tasks. "I am beginning Greek again, & must really make out some plan: today 28th [August 1922]: Mrs Dalloway finished on Sat. 2nd Sept: Sunday 3rd to Friday 8th start Chaucer: Chaucer—that chapter, I mean, should be finished by Sept. 22nd. And then? Shall I write the next chapter of Mrs D.—if she is to have a next chapter; & shall it be The Prime Minister? Which will last till the week we get back—Say Oct. 12th. Then I must be ready to start my Greek chapter" (*Diary* 2: 196).

Woolf's documentation of her progress in diaries, note-books, and letters lets us share in the evolution of the novel, her sense of her own method, and her coping with the problems introduced in specific scenes. She thinks of various possible titles, including "At Home" and "The Party," which eventually become segments of the novel. A third tentative title, "The Hours," furnished a lasting structure recording the passage of a single day in London, and a recurrent motif of clocks rather savagely slicing out "leaden circles" of time. By early October 1922, "MD [had] branched into a book" from the original two stories. Woolf began to have the idea of creating an unusual double for

Mrs. Dalloway in the person of a young clerk, Septimus Smith, who had returned from World War I with a case of shell shock: "I adumbrate here a study of insanity & suicide: the world seen by the sane & the insane side by side" (*Diary* 2: 207). This changed one plan, "that Mrs. Dalloway was originally to kill herself, or perhaps merely to die at the end of the party" (Woolf, Introduction 11). We find Woolf negotiating her writing of the most upsetting passages, where she touched closest to her own mental struggles through the depiction of Smith. She reported to a friend, Gwen Raverat, "It was a subject that I have kept cooling in my mind until I felt I could touch it without bursting into flame all over. You can't think what a raging furnace it is still to me — madness and doctors and being forced" (*Letters* 3: 180). The difficult scenes included the "mad scene in Regent's Park," where Septimus hallucinates the figure of his fallen commanding officer. For this she found she could write but fifty words a day (*Diary* 2: 272). She races through Septimus's suicide scene, as if to protect herself. In February 1923, Woolf reports that she is deriving benefits from the reading she is doing simultaneously: "I wonder if this next lap will be influenced by Proust? I think his French language, tradition, &c, prevents that: yet his command of every resource is so extravagant that one can hardly fail to profit, & must not flinch, through cowardice" (*Diary* 2: 234). She finds in the writing of fiction the "instant nourishment & well being of my entire day."

"I dig out beautiful caves behind my characters: I think that gives exactly what I want; humanity, humour, depth. The idea is that the caves shall connect, and each comes to daylight at the present moment" (*Diary* 2: 213). This famous metaphorical description of Woolf's breakthrough discovery about her method in creating characters, made in the course of writing *Mrs. Dalloway,* holds many conceptual possibilities. It works on both spatial and temporal planes and among a large set of characters.

Taken moment by moment (or scene by scene), it can help us work our way into the experimental nature of this work. Woolf does not mark out chapters for us. She does insert occasional section breaks with a blank line in the text, when there is usually a change of character or scene. Interestingly, two breaks that occur in the British edition of *Mrs. Dalloway* fail to appear in the American edition, upon which this version is based (see notes for their location). As was her usual practice, Woolf marked up separate sets of proofs for the two publications, and may have worked longer, making more changes, on the British set. Whatever the number, the breaks in the text may encourage us readers to start tunneling in a new direction. Transitions between characters often occur via an experience of the present moment that they share—hearing the tone of one of the many chiming clocks, or the alarming backfire on Bond Street, or watching an airplane doing skywriting far above. These are all forms of connecting in the present moment, as called for in the "tunneling process" (*Diary* 2: 272).

Writing character at depth was important for Woolf at this stage of her career because Woolf's *Jacob's Room* had been derided by Arnold Bennett, a prominent novelist and critic of the previous generation. His complaint was that "the characters do not vitally survive in the mind, because the author has been obsessed by details of originality and cleverness" (qtd. *Essays* 3: 388). Woolf mulls over Bennett's comment in her diary, considering her potential weaknesses: "People, like Arnold Bennett, say I cant create, or didn't in J's R, characters that survive. My answer is—but I leave that to the *Nation*: its only the old argument that character is dissipated into shreds now: the old post-Dostoevsky argument." Thus character has changed for modernists—an idea that she would develop further in her essay "Mr. Bennett and Mrs. Brown." She senses that she isn't good at the sort of reality Bennett achieves and praises, and she wonders if she has achieved a different sort of "true reality" that is insubstantial (*Diary* 2: 248). In the same diary entry, she admits, "The design is so queer & so masterful. I'm always having to wrench my substance to fit it. The design certainly original, & interests me hugely" (*Diary* 2: 249). One of the things we might consider is whether it is the approach to character, rather than the characters themselves, that is more memorable in *Mrs. Dalloway*.

Contending with *Ulysses* and Qualifying for Modernism

WOOLF'S SUCCESS, on the verge of *Mrs. Dalloway,* had not come easily, and would not go unchallenged. As she would acknowledge a few years later in *A Room of One's Own,* she did have literary foremothers. Some, such as Mary Wollstonecraft, George Eliot, and Jane Austen, were quite well known. But with the exception of Austen, she finds that they had all struggled with literary forms and critical criteria that strained against their talents and inclinations. There had been many bestselling women novelists in the late nineteenth century whose names were largely forgotten by the twentieth because they had not been taken seriously by those who determined what would be canonized— what qualified as high culture, deserving of further study. In her frequently cited literary essay "Modern Fiction," Woolf gravitated toward defining and practicing what was "modern." She distinguished her method from that of "materialist" Edwardian writers, H. G. Wells, Arnold Bennett, and John Galsworthy. Her own generation placed its accent differently—on random atoms of experience as recorded in the mind (155), or "in the dark places of psychology" (156). Despite advocating a new kind of writing, she was not universally welcomed by key makers of high, avant-garde modernism.

Wyndham Lewis is representative of early gatekeepers of modernism who thought of their project in terms of a masculine reclaiming of culture from decadence and feminization. To him, *Mrs. Dalloway* presented "puerile copies" of the "realistic vigor" offered by James Joyce's 1922 novel *Ulysses* (*Men Without Art* 138–39). Woolf could certainly have been influenced by *Ulysses.* She had read parts of the novel as early as 1918, when they were serialized in the *Little Review* magazine. That same year the Woolfs were offered the manuscript for publication at the Hogarth Press. They turned it down, ostensibly because of its length, but probably also because of their distaste for it. In "Modern Fiction," Woolf takes Joyce as a primary example of her own generation of writers. She credits him with revealing "the flickerings of that innermost flame which flashes its messages through the brain" (155). Her notebooks, "Modern Novels (Joyce)," kept in preparing the earlier version of this essay, have even more positive observations. But in "Modern Fiction," she does criticize *Ulysses,* for being "centered in a self which, in spite of its tremor of susceptibility, never embraces or creates what is outside itself." Woolf also resists "the emphasis laid, perhaps didactically, upon indecency"—a quibble that may register class as well as gender difference between Joyce and Woolf. By the time *Ulysses* was published in full in 1922, Woolf finds it increasingly "unimportant" and doesn't "even trouble conscientiously to make out its meanings" (*Diary* 2: 196). It is a "misfire. Genius it has I think; but of the inferior water. The book is diffuse. It is brackish. It is pretentious. It is underbred." She imagines a schoolboy "full of wits & powers, but so self-conscious & egotistical that he loses his head" (*Diary* 2: 199). As was true with her thoughts about Katherine Mansfield, Woolf sees that envy may explain her reaction to Joyce. She concedes, "I was over stimulated by Tom's [T. S. Eliot's] praises" of *Ulysses* (*Diary* 2: 200).

Eliot's contacts with the Woolfs began in 1918, and the following year they published a group of his poems. By 1922 they were facilitating what proved a fruitless scheme to release him from his job at a bank in order to work full-time on his writing. In a sketchy account of their conversations about *Ulysses,* Woolf is particularly attentive to the few negative concessions Eliot makes regarding Joyce: "I said he was virile — a he-goat; but didn't expect Tom to agree. Tom did tho'; & said he left out many things that were important. . . . Bloom told one nothing. Indeed, he said, this new method of giving the psychology proves to my mind that it doesn't work. It doesn't tell as much as some casual glance from outside often tells" (*Diary* 2: 202–3). Of course, Woolf, like Dorothy Richardson and Marcel Proust, shared the technique of interior monologue with Joyce. Her admiration for his internal flickerings of the mind in "Modern Fiction" seems genuine. Still, in developing this technique, she sought to avoid the "damned egotistical self" she found in both Joyce and Richardson, "narrowing & restricting" their characters (*Diary* 2: 14).

The parallels between these novels by Joyce and Woolf are probably best viewed as representative of formal and political concerns of their age. Both offer urban-centered novels that are confined in their actions to a single day, measuring out the commonplace actions of their characters against the elapsing hours. Both stroll their characters amid the commercial venues and political monuments of their respective cities, leaving the possibility for readers to infer rich cultural readings, particularly with the help of notes. Both enter the consciousness of their characters for extended periods and register variations in their energy levels and moods. Both make an unexpected switch from the character who seems to be central at the start of the novel to an outsider figure, establishing unusual connections that cross ethnicity, class, and age: Joyce's disillusioned young artist, Stephen Dedalus, yielding prominence after three episodes to the middle-

aged Jewish advertising canvasser and scientific amateur, Leopold
Bloom; Woolf turning from her society matron, Mrs. Dalloway,
to follow the intellectually aspiring Septimus Smith, who is of
humble provincial origin and shell-shocked in war service.
While Joyce's characters eventually share actual experiences toward the end of the novel, Woolf's have a final meeting only in
Clarissa Dalloway's mind. The mature characters in both novels
flash back in time to the loves of their youth, testing the marriage plot, and the institution of marriage itself. There are
smaller coincidences. Both books follow the route of an official
vehicle traversing the city: Joyce's showy viceregal procession
surveying colonially administered Dublin; Woolf's enclosed
motorcar conveying a person of consequence—a prince or a
prime minister—on some mission of importance. These dis-
plays demonstrate the appeal of spectacle and power to various
people in the streets and invite the reader's more satirical observations on imperialism and class difference. Shakespeare shad-
ows both stories. *Hamlet* offers an important backdrop for
Stephen Dedalus in *Ulysses.* The plays of Shakespeare both in-
spire Septimus Smith to go to war for England and, later, to suspect human character. The bidding of Shakespeare's *Cymbeline*
to "fear no more" runs through the minds of both of Woolf's
traumatized protagonists. Having shared some of the qualifica-
tions of his admiration for Joyce with Woolf, T. S. Eliot would
eventually focus upon the mythic method of *Ulysses,* with its
classical Homeric underpinnings, in his essay "*Ulysses,* Order
and Myth." Woolf's reading of the *Odyssey* and Greek plays as
she composed *Mrs. Dalloway* resulted in a less formal seepage of
classical literature into her text, but it is a presence that has invited mythical interpretations for her work as well.

Increasingly, as *Ulysses* progresses, Joyce presents a different form for each episode, bringing us in "Oxen of the Sun"
the styles of literature through the centuries, paralleling the

stages of human gestation at the maternity hospital, or the hallucinatory dramas of the "Circe" brothel episode, or what he took to be the eternal feminine in Molly Bloom's culminating "Penelope" monologue in bed. Unlike Joyce, with his well-demarcated episodes keyed to Homer's text, Woolf doesn't offer us chapter breaks but rather "very short intervals, not whole chapters" (Notes, October 6, 1922, in Wussow). In many of these intervals we encounter specialized discourses, some of them serving in her social critique. Going to lunch with Richard Dalloway, we find Hugh Whitbread crafting a persuasive political letter to the *Times* on behalf of Lady Bruton and a racist emigration scheme. Septimus and Rezia Smith hear the repressive voice of Proportion issuing from the mouth of the physician, Dr. Bradshaw. Septimus has hallucinatory episodes symptomatic of what we now call post-traumatic stress disorder, and Peter Walsh has a dream sequence, with a discourse of its own, while snoozing in the park. It remains a rewarding and almost inexhaustible exercise to both compare and contrast *Ulysses* and *Mrs. Dalloway*.

WOOLF WAS brought into the canon of modernism initially for her aesthetic and formal traits that most resembled Joyce, rather than the political departures that later made her appealing to feminist and postmodern critics. Earliest critics did feel challenged by her method, as her 1928 introduction suggests. They sought to achieve a sense of unity or balance between Woolf's very different central characters, Clarissa and Septimus. Through the 1970s, critics focused upon Woolf's experimental craft of fiction, a topic that has endured but also been reconstrued. Critics have continued to note patterns, such as Woolf's strategic use of repetition and richly metaphoric language, applying these increasingly to cultural readings. There was also early interest in the psychology of the work, and Septimus's recourse to suicide. The novel has encouraged spiritual readings that resurrect and negotiate ghosts and mythic figures from the past, to therapeutic effect. By the time deconstruction became a favored theoretical approach in the late 1970s, critics began to set less of a priority on unity, and favored more the various ways that Woolf challenged prevailing systems of order and masculine authority.

The 1980s brought a flourishing of feminist approaches to Woolf, beginning with her critique of patriarchy, and extending this focus into her biography, including her private accounts of her own treatments by physicians. By the 1990s the feminist interest in identities and sexualities found expression in lesbian studies, centering on Clarissa's feelings for Sally Seton, and extending to Miss Kilman's involvement with Elizabeth Dalloway, Septimus's feeling for his lost commanding officer, Evans, and to a queering or skewing of representation. The '90s also brought increased attention to ways that various systems of identification, including sexuality, class, and nation, interact with gender to produce a sense of self. Interest in global politics, and particularly the postcolonial critique of imperialism, emerged by the late '90s. The concept of modernity, with its typical urban setting, its awareness of technology, commodification, and international capitalism, all are relevant to Woolf's novel, which is frequently mentioned in illustrating modernity. *Mrs. Dalloway* has entered a new era of creative appropriation and popularization. It has been adapted for opera and film, and creatively reconceived for Michael Cunningham's novel *The Hours,* which has been further adapted as a film, and for Robin Lippincott's novella *Mr. Dalloway.* Despite its increasing remoteness in time, *Mrs. Dalloway* as well as other Woolf works like *Orlando* have moved with the times, proving applicable to enduring concerns.

Digging into Character and Politics

WE TAKE our first plunge into the caves Woolf described digging behind her characters with Mrs. Dalloway, her name conveniently supplied in the first two words of the novel. This moment occurs toward the start of a day that will culminate for many of its characters in Mrs. Dalloway's party. The slightness of having a party as the culmination of a plot is in keeping with the liberation from traditional form Woolf had claimed for her generation in "Modern Fiction" (154). Woolf's digging into an individual character proceeds with the play of the mind of each person she follows into an ordinary situation, calling up associations and memories—a process akin to psychoanalysis. The squeak of hinges on the door of her London home transports Mrs. Dalloway back to her childhood home at Bourton, where the French doors squeaked as she (when a girl of eighteen) thrust them open to plunge "into the open air" (3). But she also recalls falling into a solemn mood. The caves of characters have come together and surfaced at former moments, like this remembered one. At Bourton, more than twenty years ago, Peter Walsh appears with a critical remark, "Musing among the vegetables" (3), wanting to call attention to himself. He will reappear in the present, later on the same day in London, exposing both familiar and new sides of himself as he calls on Clarissa at her home in Westminster.

By tunneling back to Bourton, we get to the roots of Mrs. Dalloway, set in her home turf, in the company of her father and aunt, but most firmly bonded to her contemporaries. She is at the vulnerable age when marriage was the expectation for young women of her class. The marriage plot, a staple of novels of the eighteenth and nineteenth centuries, is secondary and in need of political excavation in Woolf's modernist feminist novel. This excavation concentrates more on relationships not sanctified and preserved, rather than on the Dalloway marriage, which has survived into the present. At Bourton we mine a rapturous moment for Clarissa in the garden, when she is kissed by Sally Seton, and a disastrous one, when Peter interrupts this scene. Peter has his own catastrophe, when he realizes that it is Richard, and not himself, whom Clarissa will wed. When Clarissa and Richard go off for an evening boating, Peter is left to interact with Clarissa's aunt Helena, and we dig in yet another direction. Miss Parry's botanical ventures, as a single woman of privilege in Burma, make her formidable. As we explore for her connections, we find that she joins with a large cast of characters who have made their way through empire, often uprooting more than orchids in the process. These figures include soldiers whose memorials line Whitehall, the ancestors of Lady Bruton, men sitting around in the Oriental Club, and, eventually, Peter himself.

When we visit Bourton in Peter's memory, more of Clarissa is exposed. We find her prudish and chaste in her reaction to the affair between a neighboring squire and his housemaid that has produced a child—a moment Peter "tickets," or labels, severely, as the "death of her soul" (58). Peter thinks of her father, Justin Parry, in a way that suggests that Peter is still contending with the patriarch who never liked the young men who wanted to marry his daughter. In a moment revelatory of buried trauma, Peter holds Parry responsible for the death of Clarissa's sister, Sylvia, who was killed by a falling tree at Bourton. Peter's meeting with Clarissa in London brings her confirmation of her father's disdain for her suitors, but any trauma over Sylvia seems buried. Sylvia crosses her mind only in matter-of-fact ways. One has to wonder what Woolf must have felt in inventing this lost sister, given her very close connection to her surviving sister, Vanessa, and her loss of two half sisters, Laura Stephen (incarcerated in an institution for mental disability) and Stella

Duckworth (who succumbed to peritonitis, perhaps complicated by early pregnancy). Clarissa also frustrates any curiosity
about her parents. She thinks briefly of standing with her
mother and father by the lake, feeding ducks, and is touched to
tears when the elderly Mrs. Hilbery finds a resemblance between Clarissa and her mother, recollected walking in the garden in a grey hat (171). Woolf's more personal digging at
parental roots would wait for *To the Lighthouse*.

Clarissa is the name that still resonates with Sally, Peter, and
even Richard, but it has largely fallen from usage in her adult
married life, as she deals with servants and merchants, in service
of her domestic sphere, and entertaining colleagues of her husband. This suggested to early feminist critics that in marriage,
Clarissa had relinquished a more feminine world, associated
with the green world of the country (see Abel). This line of association of woman with nature has since been criticized as es-
sentialist. Interestingly, we do not delve back to Bourton in any
significant way through Richard's character, though he has his
own country affiliation with the county of Norfolk.

In London, in middle age, Mrs. Dalloway takes considerable
pleasure in traversing the city. She continues to connect with
others, and indeed makes a project of it with her party. We find
that Miss Pym, the florist she has done business with for years,
likes her and is thankful for some kind of help Clarissa has given
her. There is a "concord" between Mrs. Dalloway and her maid,
Lucy, who treats her umbrella like the "sacred weapon" of a
goddess who has "acquitted herself honourably in the field of
battle" (29). Clarissa is disappointed not to be asked to lunch by
Lady Bruton. Instead we follow Richard to aristocratic Mayfair,
where he serves Lady Bruton's conservative political ends. He
muses, helpfully for character construction: "She should have
been a general of dragoons herself. And Richard would have
served under her, cheerfully; he had the greatest respect for her;

he cherished these romantic views about well-set-up old women of pedigree" (102). Lady Bruton thinks of Clarissa in relation to the analysis of character: "She had never seen the sense of cutting people up, as Clarissa Dalloway did—cutting them up and sticking them together again" (101); she saw little difference between men, at her age. Indeed, we see Clarissa better, thanks to this contrast.

One of the most intriguing connections Clarissa makes, however, is negative and deeply troubling—her reaction to Doris Kilman, the tutor whom she suspects (correctly) of trying to alienate her daughter Elizabeth's affections. As noted above, Clarissa has herself experienced lesbian attraction to Sally Seton. Running naked through the hall at Bourton, bicycling around the parapet, making arrangements of floating flowers, and reading forbidden socialist texts, Sally is a far more attractive figure than Miss Kilman. Although she considers many other factors in analyzing her negative feelings, Clarissa does not address the lesbian potential of her daughter's relationship. Clarissa is able to appreciate other differences with Miss Kilman. We discover the hostile climate faced by people of German nationality on the home front of World War I. Despite her training as a historian, Miss Kilman has been dismissed from her teaching position because of her nationality. She has found solace in religion, and by encouraging Elizabeth to pray, she seems to be working toward the girl's religious conversion. Clarissa is sensitive to difference in class, though the evidence she focuses upon—matters of dress and grooming—suggest snobbery. "Year in year out she wore that coat; she perspired; she was never in the room five minutes without making you feel her superiority, your inferiority; how poor she was; how rich you were" (11).

Clarissa tries to manage her own hatred: "For it was not her one hated but the idea of her, which undoubtedly had gathered in to itself a great deal that was not Miss Kilman; had become one of those spectres with which one battles in the night; one of those spectres who stand astride us and suck up half our life-blood, dominators and tyrants" (12). There is then, in this idea, something that diminishes or even destroys life, touching at a major theme of the novel, and in Woolf's sense of what fiction should be after, "life itself" ("Modern Fiction" 155). Woolf gives us the distinct impression that we have dug into a dark place in Clarissa's psychology: "It rasped her, though, to have stirring about in her this brutal monster! to hear twigs cracking and feel hooves planted down in the depths of that leaf-encumbered forest, the soul" (12). We go with Miss Kilman and Elizabeth Dalloway to the Army and Navy Stores, but leave Miss Kilman there, a deliberate loose end, not neatly channeled into the culminating party.

"The Sane and the Insane Side by Side"

THE TUNNELING process can be pursued in this manner through many people in Clarissa Dalloway's life, and those they touch upon. It functions somewhat differently, it seems, in the case of Septimus Smith. While working on *Mrs. Dalloway,* Woolf makes the perhaps dubious suggestion in her notebook (November 19, 1922, in Wussow) that he "might be left vague—as a mad person is—not so much character as an idea." This presumed difference may have called for a modified method. Contact is limited. A 1999 film version of the novel brings Clarissa Dalloway and Septimus Smith into eye-to-eye contact, whereas Woolf merely places them in Bond Street, where they hear the same backfire from a car. Peter sees the Smiths in Regent's Park, but fails to comprehend their situation. He may hear the siren of the actual ambulance that bears away Septimus's remains, but rather than contemplate the tragedy, Peter goes off on a line of thought that glories in the modernity of the capital city he has just returned to from India. Peter fails to come close to Septimus, unless inadvertently to suggest to readers that he has been sacrificed to supposedly progressive postwar modernity.

The tunneling process may work best where we can compare the variant interpretations of characters who know something about each other. Only Lucrezia Smith knows her husband well enough to present him thoroughly, tunneling to the surface during the war, when they met in Italy, and bringing to light incidents of their marriage, experienced on outings and walks, which bear upon his increasingly alarming symptoms of shell shock. In a limited manner, Septimus can think back to their meeting, and his failure of feeling for Rezia, both then and in the present. He also had a failure of feeling at the death in war of his commander, Evans. With Septimus providing only a few clues, Woolf leaves it to readers to excavate his homoerotic bond to Evans, and a related homophobic panic that led to his marriage. For Septimus, Woolf had to make parallel devices, rather than her tunneled connections, work.

One of the ways that Woolf enables us to see her characters side by side, politically and emotionally, is by allowing them to share images and ideas. Trees offer one of many parallel images. Walking through St. James's Park, Clarissa makes a metaphor for her life as mist in conjunction with the trees: "being part, she was positive, of the trees at home; of the house there, ugly, rambling all to bits and pieces as it was; part of people she had never met; being laid out like a mist between the people she knew best, who lifted her on their branches as she had seen the trees lift the mist, but it spread ever so far, her life, herself" (9). Sitting in Regent's Park, Septimus is excited by "the elm trees rising and falling, rising and falling with all their leaves alight and the colour thinning and thickening from blue to the green of a hollow wave" (21–22). Rezia only briefly brings him back to reality by placing her hand on his knee, or bidding him look at real things. By the time she has strolled briefly apart he is making proclamations, "Men must not cut down trees," and hearing Greek words from birds singing from railings and trees, and sensing that Evans had returned (24).

A threatening or deadly idea that most oppresses Clarissa is Conversion, which she associates with Miss Kilman and religion. Though depressed into thinking of a nunlike existence, she manages her thoughts sufficiently to pull herself out of the most monstrous phase of her thinking. Septimus goes from his hallucinations in the park to an interrogation by Sir William Bradshaw, who is in possession both of the title of knight of the empire and of a prominent address as a Harley Street physician. His car is of the same model that early in the novel transports the mysterious figure of royal or political power. Bradshaw requires almost no contact with Septimus to diagnose him with "complete physical and nervous breakdown" (93). He does not diagnose homosexuality; instead, those around him school Septimus in the manly and patriotic virtues of a British husband. Septimus's sense of having committed a crime resonates with the legal prosecution of homosexuality, most visibly in the case of Oscar Wilde in 1895. Septimus tries to articulate his sense of being pursued, from this point on: "Once you fall . . . human nature is on you" (95). The human nature he laments is suggested by Bradshaw's reasoning, "Health we must have; and health is proportion" (96).

At this point in the novel, Woolf tries on a different discourse that challenges genre description. This is closer to the essay writing that she has been doing by turns with fiction; it partakes of classical figures that could easily have flowed from her concurrent reading of Greek texts; it has some flavor of fantasy but also serves as a parody of masculine oratory: "Proportion, divine proportion, Sir William's goddess, was acquired by Sir William walking hospitals, catching salmon, begetting one son in Harley Street by Lady Bradshaw . . . Worshipping proportion, Sir William not only prospered himself but made England prosper, secluded her lunatics, forbade childbirth, penalised despair, made it impossible for the unfit to propagate their views until they, too, shared his sense of proportion" (97). This strange oration goes on to declare "Proportion has a sister, less smiling, more formidable, a Goddess even now engaged—in the heat and sands of India, the mud and swamp of Africa, the purlieus of London, wherever in short the climate or the devil tempts men to fall from the true belief which is her own . . . Conversion is her name" (97). Woolf's resistance to professional, imperial, and religious authority could not be clearer, even filtered through grandiose, yet witty, phrases. It is interesting to look for the appearance of other goddesses that lead characters in *Mrs. Dalloway* to various causes and dubious destinations: Clarissa is a goddess to her maid, Lucy. Peter has a goddess beckoning him into yet another group of trees. Isabel Pole, through her charisma as a teacher, sends Septimus off to fight for the nation of Shakespeare. With this segment of *Mrs. Dalloway,* Woolf cultivates the political side of herself that will take on Fascism, at home and abroad, thirteen years later in *Three Guineas.*

London, the Party, and Life Itself

THE EARLIEST reviewers of *Mrs. Dalloway* praised the way that Woolf's novel brought London vibrantly to life. We can see this in London's streets and shops and parks, where we receive distinct impressions of individuals from various walks of life, as they cross paths or share public spaces in the course of their day. There is a sort of mechanical vitality as well in London's well-run houses, monumental clocks, marching soldiers, measured and efficient medical consultations, newspaper editions, swift mail service, delivery vehicles, automobiles, and even the airplane that rises above it all, leaving a commercial message in the sky. As its central character, Mrs. Dalloway, having been ill, finds life precious, and fights the deadly effects of hate and fear with thoughts of connection. Her party, which culminates the novel, serves a concept of unity, which was precious to modernists and their interpreters, at least until postmodern concepts gained critical authority.

Woolf was concerned that her central character might be too slight and artificial to stand at the center of her novel. Indeed, Clarissa has had her detractors, starting with Lytton Strachey, who found Woolf alternately laughing at her female protagonist and covering her with aspects of herself (*Diary* 3: 32). Some recent interpreters see Clarissa as representative of a social class that Woolf subjected to satire. It is easy to discover Mrs. Dalloway in unflattering moments, where she may patronize her servants, exhibit snobbery in making up her guest list or ignorance in pondering Richard's dealings with Armenians, or is it Albanians, when in fact the plight of the Armenians was desperate indeed (see notes, page 211).

But Clarissa—or should we say Virginia Woolf?—does not give a trivial party. That parties get trivialized is in itself a political point. Parties are a form of domestic labor, in this case, of woman's work. We find a female collaboration across class where the cook, the maid, and Mrs. Dalloway cooperate in production. Standing up to those who trivialize her efforts, Clarissa functions as the outsider within patriarchy, building a mood and sensing, with the beating back of a curtain, that the party itself finally takes life. The early Mrs. Dalloway of *The Voyage Out* and the present Lady Bradshaw can be seen operating very much in the service of their husbands' careers, and Lady Bradshaw goes

under in the process. Mrs. Dalloway's party is not centrally concerned with advancing her husband. Richard makes it clear that
he could do without Clarissa's parties, particularly if they put a
strain upon her health. While the Prime Minister does make a
much-anticipated appearance, Clarissa focuses elsewhere. Some
sort of discussion between him and Lady Bruton takes place in
a separate room, but we can hardly think this is of great significance, knowing the eugenicist nature of the idea Lady Bruton
was advancing to the *Times*. Clarissa has invited the Bradshaws
as part of their social circle, but she reserves the right to dislike
them. There is a remote chance that by bringing Richard Dalloway and Bradshaw together on the evening of Septimus's suicide, something may be done toward helping victims of shell
shock. But Bradshaw is still an appalling snob as he scrutinizes
the paintings, and so Woolf's satire is sustained. This is not a
group one leaves confidently in charge of the nation.

The party includes some people Clarissa hadn't originally
planned on, and they make a difference. She invites Peter to attend after he shows up at her house in the morning. Sally Seton
comes uninvited, when she finds herself in London on the evening of the party. Clarissa gives a last-minute invitation to her
dull relative Ellie Henderson, providing Woolf with an outsider
to offer her specialized perspective on the party. Clarissa had
feared that her daughter would not attend, but Elizabeth has ex-
tricated herself from Miss Kilman (who never would have
come, even if invited). In a social situation where she is the object of scrutiny and floral metaphor, Elizabeth stages a quiet rebellion. She leaves us to wonder about the future of a young
woman who a few hours earlier had exulted in riding on the top
of a bus through lively areas of the Strand, where her family
rarely ventured.

While we might expect Clarissa to be completed by the re-
assembly of her beloved trio, formed with Sally and Peter at the

party, she postpones their reunion beyond the end of the novel. Her absence lets us sample the kind of conversational intimacy that Woolf liked at parties, as we find Sally and Peter reconstructing Bourton days once again, while they wait for her. This pair could not care less about the society assembled before them. But neither of them is very remarkable as an adult. Our sense of Peter's failures has grown through the day. Sally may not have gone under like Mrs. Bradshaw, but she has lost every radical bone in her body. The party has a ghostly visitor in the form of Septimus Smith, and having heard of his death from the Bradshaws, Clarissa draws apart to accommodate him. She finds an affirmation of life from his throwing it away, her thoughts echoing his own feelings of the event. Even the earliest interpreters of *Mrs. Dalloway* were fascinated by the old woman Clarissa watches in the window opposite, another liminal visitor to the party, another affirmation of life going on in the simple act of going alone to bed. Thus the end of *Mrs. Dalloway* takes life into another register, remote, spiritual, and respectful of the difficulty of surviving even a single day. Survival has its fragmented pleasures, like Mrs. Dalloway's plunging into a perfect London morning in June, or Rezia and Septimus assembling an absurd little hat together, or Peter experiencing ecstasy and terror as the woman he once loved so desperately stands before him as we leave the party.

NOTES

[1]Woolf composed this introduction for a 1928 edition of her novel published by Random House for the Modern Library of the World's Best Books edition. It is the only commentary of its sort that she wrote for any of her works.

[2]Having found that evidence from actual newspaper accounts does not correspond to what is in newspaper accounts of cricket matches read by characters in the novel, David Bradshaw argues that *Mrs. Dalloway* is set on an *imaginary* Wednesday in mid-June 1923 (182–83). Arguments for the actual

dates of June 13 and June 20 have been made by Harvena Richter and Morris Beja, respectively.

[3] Woolf refers here to one of three "Lives of the Obscure," published in the American edition of *The Common Reader.* "Miss Ormerod" is an imaginative rendering of scenes from the life of Eleanor Ormerod, a specialist on destructive insects.

———

For their painstaking reading of drafts of this introduction, and their useful suggestions, I should like to thank Mark Hussey, Suzette Henke, Susan Gubar, and Heidi Cathryn Molly Scott.

WORKS CITED

Abel, Elizabeth. "Narrative Structure(s) and Female Development: The Case of *Mrs. Dalloway.*" In *The Voyage In: Fictions of Female Development,* edited by Elizabeth Abel, Marianne Hirsch, and Elizabeth Langland, 161–85. Hanover, NH: University Press of New England, 1983.

Beja, Morris. Introduction to *Mrs. Dalloway,* by Virginia Woolf, xi–xxxi. Oxford: Shakespeare Head Press, 1996.

Bradshaw, David. "Explanatory Notes." In *Mrs. Dalloway,* by Virginia Woolf, 166–85. Oxford: Oxford University Press, 2000.

Caramagno, Thomas. *The Flight of the Mind: Virginia Woolf's Art and Manic-Depressive Illness.* Berkeley: University of California Press, 1992.

Lewis, Wyndham. *Men Without Art.* Santa Rosa, CA: Black Sparrow Press, 1987. Originally published in 1934.

Richter, Harvena. "The *Ulysses* Connection: Clarissa Dalloway's Bloomsday." *Studies in the Novel* 21.3 (Fall 1989): 305–19.

Virginia Woolf's Mrs. Dalloway. Produced by Lisa Katselas Paré and Stephen Bayly. Directed by Marleen Gorris. Screenplay by Eileen Atkins. First Look Pictures, 1999.

Woolf, Virginia. *The Diary of Virginia Woolf. Volume Two: 1920–1924.* Edited by Anne Olivier Bell, with Andrew McNeillie. New York: Harcourt Brace Jovanovich, 1978.

———. *The Essays of Virginia Woolf. Volume 3: 1919–1924.* Edited by Andrew McNeillie. San Diego: Harcourt Brace Jovanovich, 1988.

———. "An Introduction to *Mrs. Dalloway.*" In *The Mrs. Dalloway Reader.* Edited by Francine Prose, 10–12. Orlando: Harcourt, 2003. Originally published in 1928.

————. *The Letters of Virginia Woolf. Volume Three: 1923–1928.* Edited by Nigel Nicolson and Joanne Trautmann. New York: Harcourt Brace Jovanovich, 1977.

————. "Modern Fiction." *The Common Reader,* 150–58. New York: Harcourt, Brace & World, 1953. Originally published in 1925.

————. "Modern Novels (Joyce)." Edited by Suzette Henke. In *The Gender of Modernism.* Edited by Bonnie Kime Scott, 642–45. Bloomington: Indiana University Press, 1990.

Wussow, Helen M., ed. *Virginia Woolf 'The Hours': The British Museum Manuscript of* Mrs. Dalloway. New York: Pace University Press, 1997.

Mrs. Dalloway

MRS. DALLOWAY SAID she would buy the flowers herself.

For Lucy had her work cut out for her. The doors would be taken off their hinges; Rumpelmayer's men were coming. And then, thought Clarissa Dalloway, what a morning—fresh as if issued to children on a beach.

What a lark! What a plunge! For so it had always seemed to her, when, with a little squeak of the hinges, which she could hear now, she had burst open the French windows and plunged at Bourton into the open air. How fresh, how calm, stiller than this of course, the air was in the early morning; like the flap of a wave; the kiss of a wave; chill and sharp and yet (for a girl of eighteen as she then was) solemn, feeling as she did, standing there at the open window, that something awful was about to happen; looking at the flowers, at the trees with the smoke winding off them and the rooks rising, falling; standing and looking until Peter Walsh said, "Musing among the vegetables?"—was that it?—"I prefer men to cauliflowers"—was that it? He must have said it at breakfast one morning when she had gone out on to the terrace—Peter Walsh. He would be back from India one of these days, June or July, she forgot which, for his letters were awfully dull; it was his sayings one remembered; his eyes, his pocket-knife, his smile, his grumpiness and, when millions of things had utterly vanished—how strange it was!—a few sayings like this about cabbages.

She stiffened a little on the kerb, waiting for Durtnall's van to pass. A charming woman, Scrope Purvis thought her (knowing her as one does know people who live next door to one in Westminster); a touch of the bird about her, of the jay, blue-green, light, vivacious, though she was over fifty, and grown very white since her illness. There she perched, never seeing him, waiting to cross, very upright.

For having lived in Westminster—how many years now? over twenty,—one feels even in the midst of the traffic, or waking at night, Clarissa was positive, a particular hush, or solemnity; an indescribable pause; a suspense (but that might be her heart, affected, they said, by influenza) before Big Ben strikes. There! Out it boomed. First a warning, musical; then the hour, irrevocable. The leaden circles dissolved in the air. Such fools we are, she thought, crossing Victoria Street. For Heaven only knows why one loves it so, how one sees it so, making it up, building it round one, tumbling it, creating it every moment afresh; but the veriest frumps, the most dejected of miseries sitting on doorsteps (drink their downfall) do the same; can't be dealt with, she felt positive, by Acts of Parliament for that very reason: they love life. In people's eyes, in the swing, tramp, and trudge; in the bellow and the uproar; the carriages, motor cars, omnibuses, vans, sandwich men shuffling and swinging; brass bands; barrel organs; in the triumph and the jingle and the strange high singing of some aeroplane overhead was what she loved; life; London; this moment of June.

For it was the middle of June. The War was over, except for some one like Mrs. Foxcroft at the Embassy last night eating her heart out because that nice boy was killed and now the old Manor House must go to a cousin; or Lady Bexborough who opened a bazaar, they said, with the telegram in her hand, John, her favourite, killed; but it was over; thank Heaven—over. It was June. The King and Queen were at the Palace. And everywhere, though it was still so early, there was a beating, a stirring of galloping ponies, tapping of cricket bats; Lords, Ascot, Ranelagh and all the rest of it; wrapped in the soft mesh of the grey-blue morning air, which, as the day wore on, would unwind them, and set down on their lawns and pitches the bouncing ponies whose forefeet just struck the ground and up they sprung, the whirling young men, and laughing girls in their transparent muslins who, even now, after dancing all night, were taking their absurd woolly dogs for a run; and even now, at this hour, discreet old dowagers were shooting out in their motor cars on errands of mystery; and the shopkeepers were fidgeting in their windows with their paste and diamonds, their lovely old sea-green brooches in eighteenth-century settings to tempt Americans (but one must economise, not buy things rashly for Elizabeth), and she, too, loving it as she did with an absurd and faithful passion, being part of it, since her people were courtiers once in the time of the Georges, she, too, was going that very night to kindle and illuminate; to give her party. But how strange, on entering the Park, the silence; the mist; the hum; the slow-swimming happy ducks; the pouched birds waddling; and who should be coming along with his back against the Government buildings, most appropriately, carrying a despatch box stamped with the Royal Arms, who but Hugh Whitbread; her old friend Hugh—the admirable Hugh!

"Good-morning to you, Clarissa!" said Hugh, rather extravagantly, for they had known each other as children. "Where are you off to?"

"I love walking in London," said Mrs. Dalloway. "Really it's better than walking in the country."

They had just come up—unfortunately—to see doctors. Other people came to see pictures; go to the opera; take their daughters out; the Whitbreads came "to see doctors." Times without number Clarissa had visited Evelyn Whitbread in a nursing home. Was Evelyn ill again? Evelyn was a good deal out of sorts, said Hugh, intimating by a kind of pout or swell of his very well-covered, manly, extremely handsome, perfectly uphol-stered body (he was almost too well dressed always, but pre-sumably had to be, with his little job at Court) that his wife had some internal ailment, nothing serious, which, as an old friend, Clarissa Dalloway would quite understand without requiring him to specify. Ah yes, she did of course; what a nuisance; and felt very sisterly and oddly conscious at the same time of her hat. Not the right hat for the early morning, was that it? For Hugh always made her feel, as he bustled on, raising his hat rather extravagantly and assuring her that she might be a girl of eighteen, and of course he was coming to her party to-night, Evelyn absolutely insisted, only a little late he might be after the party at the Palace to which he had to take one of Jim's boys,—she always felt a little skimpy beside Hugh; schoolgirlish; but at-tached to him, partly from having known him always, but she did think him a good sort in his own way, though Richard was nearly driven mad by him, and as for Peter Walsh, he had never to this day forgiven her for liking him.

She could remember scene after scene at Bourton—Peter furious; Hugh not, of course, his match in any way, but still not a positive imbecile as Peter made out; not a mere barber's block. When his old mother wanted him to give up shooting or to take her to Bath he did it, without a word; he was really unselfish, and as for saying, as Peter did, that he had no heart, no brain, nothing but the manners and breeding of an English gentleman, that was only her dear Peter at his worst; and he could be intol-erable; he could be impossible; but adorable to walk with on a morning like this.

(June had drawn out every leaf on the trees. The mothers of Pimlico gave suck to their young. Messages were passing from the Fleet to the Admiralty. Arlington Street and Piccadilly seemed to chafe the very air in the Park and lift its leaves hotly, brilliantly, on waves of that divine vitality which Clarissa loved. To dance, to ride, she had adored all that.)

For they might be parted for hundreds of years, she and Peter; she never wrote a letter and his were dry sticks; but suddenly it would come over her, If he were with me now what would he say?—some days, some sights bringing him back to her calmly, without the old bitterness; which perhaps was the reward of having cared for people; they came back in the middle of St. James's Park on a fine morning—indeed they did. But Peter—however beautiful the day might be, and the trees and the grass, and the little girl in pink—Peter never saw a thing of all that. He would put on his spectacles, if she told him to; he would look. It was the state of the world that interested him; Wagner, Pope's poetry, people's characters eternally, and the defects of her own soul. How he scolded her! How they argued! She would marry a Prime Minister and stand at the top of a staircase; the perfect hostess he called her (she had cried over it in her bedroom), she had the makings of the perfect hostess, he said.

So she would still find herself arguing in St. James's Park, still making out that she had been right—and she had too—not to marry him. For in marriage a little licence, a little independence there must be between people living together day in day out in the same house; which Richard gave her, and she him. (Where was he this morning for instance? Some committee, she never asked what.) But with Peter everything had to be shared; everything gone into. And it was intolerable, and when it came to that scene in the little garden by the fountain, she had to break with him or they would have been destroyed, both of them ruined, she was convinced; though she had borne about with her for years like an arrow sticking in her heart the grief, the anguish; and then the horror of the moment when some one told her at a concert that he had married a woman met on the boat going to India! Never should she forget all that! Cold, heartless, a prude, he called her. Never could she understand how he cared. But those Indian women did presumably—silly, pretty, flimsy nincompoops. And she wasted her pity. For he was quite happy, he assured her—perfectly happy, though he had never done a thing that they talked of; his whole life had been a failure. It made her angry still.

She had reached the Park gates. She stood for a moment, looking at the omnibuses in Piccadilly.

She would not say of any one in the world now that they were this or were that. She felt very young; at the same time unspeakably aged. She sliced like a knife through everything; at the same time was outside, looking on. She had a perpetual sense, as she watched the taxi cabs, of being out, out, far out to sea and alone; she always had the feeling that it was very, very dangerous to live even one day. Not that she thought herself clever, or much out of the ordinary. How she had got through life on the few twigs of knowledge Fräulein Daniels gave them she could not think. She knew nothing; no language, no history; she scarcely read a book now, except memoirs in bed; and yet to her it was absolutely absorbing; all this; the cabs passing; and she would not say of Peter, she would not say of herself, I am this, I am that.

Her only gift was knowing people almost by instinct, she thought, walking on. If you put her in a room with some one, up went her back like a cat's; or she purred. Devonshire House, Bath House, the house with the china cockatoo, she had seen them all lit up once; and remembered Sylvia, Fred, Sally

Seton—such hosts of people; and dancing all night; and the waggons plodding past to market; and driving home across the Park. She remembered once throwing a shilling into the Serpentine. But every one remembered; what she loved was this, here, now, in front of her; the fat lady in the cab. Did it matter then, she asked herself, walking towards Bond Street, did it matter that she must inevitably cease completely; all this must go on without her; did she resent it; or did it not become consoling to believe that death ended absolutely? but that somehow in the streets of London, on the ebb and flow of things, here, there, she survived, Peter survived, lived in each other, she being part, she was positive, of the trees at home; of the house there, ugly, rambling all to bits and pieces as it was; part of people she had never met; being laid out like a mist between the people she knew best, who lifted her on their branches as she had seen the trees lift the mist, but it spread ever so far, her life, herself. But what was she dreaming as she looked into Hatchards' shop window? What was she trying to recover? What image of white dawn in the country, as she read in the book spread open:

> Fear no more the heat o' the sun
> Nor the furious winter's rages.

This late age of the world's experience had bred in them all, all men and women, a well of tears. Tears and sorrows; courage and endurance; a perfectly upright and stoical bearing. Think, for example, of the woman she admired most, Lady Bexborough, opening the bazaar.

There were Jorrocks' *Jaunts and Jollities;* there were *Soapy Sponge* and Mrs. Asquith's *Memoirs* and *Big Game Shooting in Nigeria,* all spread open. Ever so many books there were; but none that seemed exactly right to take to Evelyn Whitbread in her nursing home. Nothing that would serve to amuse her and make that indescribably dried-up little woman look, as Clarissa came in, just for a moment cordial; before they settled down for the usual interminable talk of women's ailments. How much she wanted it—that people should look pleased as she came in, Clarissa thought and turned and walked back towards Bond Street, annoyed, because it was silly to have other reasons for doing things. Much rather would she have been one of those people like Richard who did things for themselves, whereas, she thought, waiting to cross, half the time she did things not simply, not for themselves; but to make people think this or that; perfect idiocy she knew (and now the policeman held up his hand) for no one was ever for a second taken in. Oh if she could have had her life over again! she thought, stepping on to the pavement, could have looked even differently!

She would have been, in the first place, dark like Lady Bexborough, with a skin of crumpled leather and beautiful eyes. She would have been, like Lady Bexborough, slow and stately; rather large; interested in politics like a man; with a country house; very dignified, very sincere. Instead of which she had a narrow pea-stick figure; a ridiculous little face, beaked like a bird's. That she held herself well was true; and had nice hands and feet; and dressed well, considering that she spent little. But often now this body she wore (she stopped to look at a Dutch picture), this body, with all its capacities, seemed nothing— nothing at all. She had the oddest sense of being herself invisible, unseen; unknown; there being no more marrying, no more having of children now, but only this astonishing and rather solemn progress with the rest of them, up Bond Street, this being Mrs. Dalloway; not even Clarissa any more; this being Mrs. Richard Dalloway.

Bond Street fascinated her; Bond Street early in the morning in the season; its flags flying; its shops; no splash; no glitter;

one roll of tweed in the shop where her father had bought his suits for fifty years; a few pearls; salmon on an iceblock.

"That is all," she said, looking at the fishmonger's. "That is all," she repeated, pausing for a moment at the window of a glove shop where, before the War, you could buy almost perfect gloves. And her old Uncle William used to say a lady is known by her shoes and her gloves. He had turned on his bed one morning in the middle of the War. He had said, "I have had enough." Gloves and shoes; she had a passion for gloves; but her own daughter, her Elizabeth, cared not a straw for either of them.

Not a straw, she thought, going on up Bond Street to a shop where they kept flowers for her when she gave a party. Elizabeth really cared for her dog most of all. The whole house this morning smelt of tar. Still, better poor Grizzle than Miss Kilman; better distemper and tar and all the rest of it than sitting mewed in a stuffy bedroom with a prayer book! Better anything, she was inclined to say. But it might be only a phase, as Richard said, such as all girls go through. It might be falling in love. But why with Miss Kilman? who had been badly treated of course; one must make allowances for that, and Richard said she was very able, had a really historical mind. Anyhow they were inseparable, and Elizabeth, her own daughter, went to Communion; and how she dressed, how she treated people who came to lunch she did not care a bit, it being her experience that the religious ecstasy made people callous (so did causes); dulled their feelings, for Miss Kilman would do anything for the Russians, starved herself for the Austrians, but in private inflicted positive torture, so insensitive was she, dressed in a green mackintosh coat. Year in year out she wore that coat; she perspired; she was never in the room five minutes without making you feel her superiority, your inferiority; how poor she was; how rich you were;

how she lived in a slum without a cushion or a bed or a rug or whatever it might be, all her soul rusted with that grievance sticking in it, her dismissal from school during the War—poor embittered unfortunate creature! For it was not her one hated but the idea of her, which undoubtedly had gathered in to itself a great deal that was not Miss Kilman; had become one of those spectres with which one battles in the night; one of those spectres who stand astride us and suck up half our life-blood, dominators and tyrants; for no doubt with another throw of the dice, had the black been uppermost and not the white, she would have loved Miss Kilman! But not in this world. No.

It rasped her, though, to have stirring about in her this brutal monster! to hear twigs cracking and feel hooves planted down in the depths of that leaf-encumbered forest, the soul; never to be content quite, or quite secure, for at any moment the brute would be stirring, this hatred, which, especially since her illness, had power to make her feel scraped, hurt in her spine; gave her physical pain, and made all pleasure in beauty, in friendship, in being well, in being loved and making her home delightful rock, quiver, and bend as if indeed there were a monster grubbing at the roots, as if the whole panoply of content were nothing but self love! this hatred!

Nonsense, nonsense! she cried to herself, pushing through the swing doors of Mulberry's the florists.

She advanced, light, tall, very upright, to be greeted at once by button-faced Miss Pym, whose hands were always bright red, as if they had been stood in cold water with the flowers.

There were flowers: delphiniums, sweet peas, bunches of lilac; and carnations, masses of carnations. There were roses; there were irises. Ah yes—so she breathed in the earthy garden sweet smell as she stood talking to Miss Pym who owed her help, and thought her kind, for kind she had been years ago; very kind, but she looked older, this year, turning her head from side to side among the irises and roses and nodding tufts of lilac with her eyes half closed, snuffing in, after the street uproar, the delicious scent, the exquisite coolness. And then, opening her eyes, how fresh like frilled linen clean from a laundry laid in wicker trays the roses looked; and dark and prim the red carnations, holding their heads up; and all the sweet peas spreading in their bowls, tinged violet, snow white, pale — as if it were the evening and girls in muslin frocks came out to pick sweet peas and roses after the superb summer's day, with its almost blue-black sky, its delphiniums, its carnations, its arum lilies was over; and it was the moment between six and seven when every flower — roses, carnations, irises, lilac — glows; white, violet, red, deep orange; every flower seems to burn by itself, softly, purely in the misty beds; and how she loved the grey-white moths spinning in and out, over the cherry pie, over the evening primroses!

And as she began to go with Miss Pym from jar to jar, choosing, nonsense, nonsense, she said to herself, more and more gently, as if this beauty, this scent, this colour, and Miss Pym liking her, trusting her, were a wave which she let flow over her and surmount that hatred, that monster, surmount it all; and it lifted her up and up when — oh! a pistol shot in the street outside!

"Dear, those motor cars," said Miss Pym, going to the window to look, and coming back and smiling apologetically with her hands full of sweet peas, as if those motor cars, those tyres of motor cars, were all *her* fault.

THE VIOLENT explosion which made Mrs. Dalloway jump and Miss Pym go to the window and apologise came from a motor car which had drawn to the side of the pavement precisely opposite Mulberry's shop window. Passers-by who, of course, stopped and stared, had just time to see a face of the very greatest importance against the dove-grey upholstery, before a male hand drew the blind and there was nothing to be seen except a square of dove grey.

Yet rumours were at once in circulation from the middle of Bond Street to Oxford Street on one side, to Atkinson's scent shop on the other, passing invisibly, inaudibly, like a cloud, swift, veil-like upon hills, falling indeed with something of a cloud's sudden sobriety and stillness upon faces which a second before had been utterly disorderly. But now mystery had brushed them with her wing; they had heard the voice of authority; the spirit of religion was abroad with her eyes bandaged tight and her lips gaping wide. But nobody knew whose face had been seen. Was it the Prince of Wales's, the Queen's, the Prime Minister's? Whose face was it? Nobody knew.

Edgar J. Watkiss, with his roll of lead piping round his arm, said audibly, humorously of course: "The Proime Minister's kyar."

Septimus Warren Smith, who found himself unable to pass, heard him.

Septimus Warren Smith, aged about thirty, pale-faced, beak-nosed, wearing brown shoes and a shabby overcoat, with hazel eyes which had that look of apprehension in them which makes complete strangers apprehensive too. The world has raised its whip; where will it descend?

Everything had come to a standstill. The throb of the motor engines sounded like a pulse irregularly drumming through an entire body. The sun became extraordinarily hot because the motor car had stopped outside Mulberry's shop window; old ladies on the tops of omnibuses spread their black parasols; here a green, here a red parasol opened with a little pop. Mrs. Dalloway, coming to the window with her arms full of sweet peas, looked out with her little pink face pursed in enquiry. Every one looked at the motor car. Septimus looked. Boys on bicycles sprang off. Traffic accumulated. And there the motor car stood, with drawn blinds, and upon them a curious pattern like a tree, Septimus thought, and this gradual drawing together of everything to one centre before his eyes, as if some horror had come almost to the surface and was about to burst into flames, terrified him. The world wavered and quivered and threatened to burst into flames. It is I who am blocking the way, he thought. Was he not being looked at and pointed at; was he not weighted there, rooted to the pavement, for a purpose? But for what purpose?

"Let us go on, Septimus," said his wife, a little woman, with large eyes in a sallow pointed face; an Italian girl.

But Lucrezia herself could not help looking at the motor car and the tree pattern on the blinds. Was it the Queen in there — the Queen going shopping?

The chauffeur, who had been opening something, turning something, shutting something, got on to the box.

"Come on," said Lucrezia.

But her husband, for they had been married four, five years now, jumped, started, and said, "All right!" angrily, as if she had interrupted him.

People must notice; people must see. People, she thought, looking at the crowd staring at the motor car; the English people, with their children and their horses and their clothes, which she admired in a way; but they were "people" now, because Septimus had said, "I will kill myself"; an awful thing to say. Suppose they had heard him? She looked at the crowd. Help, help! she wanted to cry out to butchers' boys and women. Help! Only last autumn she and Septimus had stood on the Embankment wrapped in the same cloak and, Septimus reading a paper instead of talking, she had snatched it from him and laughed in the old man's face who saw them! But failure one conceals. She must take him away into some park.

"Now we will cross," she said.

She had a right to his arm, though it was without feeling. He would give her, who was so simple, so impulsive, only twenty-four, without friends in England, who had left Italy for his sake, a piece of bone.

The motor car with its blinds drawn and an air of inscrutable reserve proceeded towards Piccadilly, still gazed at, still ruffling the faces on both sides of the street with the same dark breath of veneration whether for Queen, Prince, or Prime Minister nobody knew. The face itself had been seen only once by three people for a few seconds. Even the sex was now in dispute. But there could be no doubt that greatness was seated within; greatness was passing, hidden, down Bond Street, removed only by a hand's-breadth from ordinary people who might now, for the first and last time, be within speaking distance of the majesty of England, of the enduring symbol of the state which will be known to curious antiquaries, sifting the ruins of time, when London is a grass-grown path and all those hurrying along the pavement this Wednesday morning are but bones with a few wedding rings mixed up in their dust and the gold stoppings of innumerable decayed teeth. The face in the motor car will then be known.

It is probably the Queen, thought Mrs. Dalloway, coming out of Mulberry's with her flowers; the Queen. And for a second she wore a look of extreme dignity standing by the flower shop in the sunlight while the car passed at a foot's pace, with its blinds drawn. The Queen going to some hospital; the Queen opening some bazaar, thought Clarissa.

The crush was terrific for the time of day. Lords, Ascot, Hurlingham, what was it? she wondered, for the street was blocked. The British middle classes sitting sideways on the tops of omnibuses with parcels and umbrellas, yes, even furs on a day like this, were, she thought, more ridiculous, more unlike anything there has ever been than one could conceive; and the

Queen herself held up; the Queen herself unable to pass. Clarissa was suspended on one side of Brook Street; Sir John Buckhurst, the old Judge on the other, with the car between them (Sir John had laid down the law for years and liked a well-dressed woman) when the chauffeur, leaning ever so slightly, said or showed something to the policeman, who saluted and raised his arm and jerked his head and moved the omnibus to the side and the car passed through. Slowly and very silently it took its way.

Clarissa guessed; Clarissa knew of course; she had seen something white, magical, circular, in the footman's hand, a disc inscribed with a name,—the Queen's, the Prince of Wales's, the Prime Minister's?—which, by force of its own lustre, burnt its way through (Clarissa saw the car diminishing, disappearing), to blaze among candelabras, glittering stars, breasts stiff with oak leaves, Hugh Whitbread and all his colleagues, the gentlemen of England, that night in Buckingham Palace. And Clarissa, too, gave a party. She stiffened a little; so she would stand at the top of her stairs.

The car had gone, but it had left a slight ripple which flowed through glove shops and hat shops and tailors' shops on both sides of Bond Street. For thirty seconds all heads were inclined the same way—to the window. Choosing a pair of gloves—should they be to the elbow or above it, lemon or pale grey?—ladies stopped; when the sentence was finished something had happened. Something so trifling in single instances that no mathematical instrument, though capable of transmitting shocks in China, could register the vibration; yet in its fulness rather formidable and in its common appeal emotional; for in all the hat shops and tailors' shops strangers looked at each other and thought of the dead; of the flag; of Empire. In a public house in a back street a Colonial insulted the House of Windsor which led to words, broken beer glasses, and a general shindy, which echoed strangely across the way in the ears of girls buying white underlinen threaded with pure white ribbon for their weddings. For the surface agitation of the passing car as it sunk grazed something very profound.

Gliding across Piccadilly, the car turned down St. James's Street. Tall men, men of robust physique, well-dressed men with their tail-coats and their white slips and their hair raked back who, for reasons difficult to discriminate, were standing in the bow window of Brooks's with their hands behind the tails of their coats, looking out, perceived instinctively that greatness was passing, and the pale light of the immortal presence fell upon them as it had fallen upon Clarissa Dalloway. At once they stood even straighter, and removed their hands, and seemed ready to attend their Sovereign, if need be, to the cannon's mouth, as their ancestors had done before them. The white busts and the little tables in the background covered with copies of the *Tatler* and syphons of soda water seemed to approve; seemed to indicate the flowing corn and the manor houses of England; and to return the frail hum of the motor wheels as the walls of a whispering gallery return a single voice expanded and made sonorous by the might of a whole cathedral. Shawled Moll Pratt with her flowers on the pavement wished the dear boy well (it was the Prince of Wales for certain) and would have tossed the price of a pot of beer—a bunch of roses—into St. James's Street out of sheer light-heartedness and contempt of poverty had she not seen the constable's eye upon her, discouraging an old Irishwoman's loyalty. The sentries at St. James's saluted; Queen Alexandra's policeman approved.

A small crowd meanwhile had gathered at the gates of Buckingham Palace. Listlessly, yet confidently, poor people all of them, they waited; looked at the Palace itself with the flag flying; at Victoria, billowing on her mound, admired her shelves of running water, her geraniums; singled out from the motor cars in the Mall first this one, then that; bestowed emotion, vainly, upon commoners out for a drive; recalled their tribute to keep it unspent while this car passed and that; and all the time let rumour accumulate in their veins and thrill the nerves in their thighs at the thought of Royalty looking at them; the Queen bowing; the Prince saluting; at the thought of the heavenly life divinely bestowed upon Kings; of the equerries and deep curtsies; of the Queen's old doll's house; of Princess Mary married to an Englishman, and the Prince—ah! the Prince! who took wonderfully, they said, after old King Edward, but was ever so much slimmer. The Prince lived at St. James's; but he might come along in the morning to visit his mother.

So Sarah Bletchley said with her baby in her arms, tipping her foot up and down as though she were by her own fender in Pimlico, but keeping her eyes on the Mall, while Emily Coates ranged over the Palace windows and thought of the housemaids, the innumerable housemaids, the bedrooms, the innumerable bedrooms. Joined by an elderly gentleman with an Aberdeen terrier, by men without occupation, the crowd increased. Little Mr. Bowley, who had rooms in the Albany and was sealed with wax over the deeper sources of life but could be unsealed suddenly, inappropriately, sentimentally, by this sort of thing—poor women waiting to see the Queen go past—poor women, nice little children, orphans, widows, the War—tut-tut—actually had tears in his eyes. A breeze flaunting ever so warmly down the Mall through the thin trees, past the bronze heroes, lifted some flag flying in the British breast of Mr. Bowley and he raised his hat as the car turned into the Mall and held it high as the car approached; and let the poor mothers of Pimlico press close to him, and stood very upright. The car came on.

Suddenly Mrs. Coates looked up into the sky. The sound of an aeroplane bored ominously into the ears of the crowd. There it was coming over the trees, letting out white smoke from behind, which curled and twisted, actually writing something! making letters in the sky! Every one looked up.

Dropping dead down the aeroplane soared straight up, curved in a loop, raced, sank, rose, and whatever it did, wherever it went, out fluttered behind it a thick ruffled bar of white smoke which curled and wreathed upon the sky in letters. But what letters? A C was it? an E, then an L? Only for a moment did they lie still; then they moved and melted and were rubbed out up in the sky, and the aeroplane shot further away and again, in a fresh space of sky, began writing a K, an E, a Y perhaps?

"Glaxo," said Mrs. Coates in a strained, awe-stricken voice, gazing straight up, and her baby, lying stiff and white in her arms, gazed straight up.

"Kreemo," murmured Mrs. Bletchley, like a sleepwalker. With his hat held out perfectly still in his hand, Mr. Bowley gazed straight up. All down the Mall people were standing and looking up into the sky. As they looked the whole world became perfectly silent, and a flight of gulls crossed the sky, first one gull leading, then another, and in this extraordinary silence and peace, in this pallor, in this purity, bells struck eleven times, the sound fading up there among the gulls.

The aeroplane turned and raced and swooped exactly where it liked, swiftly, freely, like a skater—

"That's an E," said Mrs. Bletchley—or a dancer—

"It's toffee," murmured Mr. Bowley—(and the car went in at the gates and nobody looked at it), and shutting off the smoke, away and away it rushed, and the smoke faded and assembled itself round the broad white shapes of the clouds.

It had gone; it was behind the clouds. There was no sound. The clouds to which the letters E, G, or L had attached themselves moved freely, as if destined to cross from West to East on a mission of the greatest importance which would never be revealed, and yet certainly so it was—a mission of the greatest importance. Then suddenly, as a train comes out of a tunnel, the aeroplane rushed out of the clouds again, the sound boring into the ears of all people in the Mall, in the Green Park, in Piccadilly, in Regent Street, in Regent's Park, and the bar of smoke curved behind and it dropped down, and it soared up and wrote one letter after another—but what word was it writing?

Lucrezia Warren Smith, sitting by her husband's side on a seat in Regent's Park in the Broad Walk, looked up.

"Look, look, Septimus!" she cried. For Dr. Holmes had told her to make her husband (who had nothing whatever seriously the matter with him but was a little out of sorts) take an interest in things outside himself.

So, thought Septimus, looking up, they are signalling to me. Not indeed in actual words; that is, he could not read the language yet; but it was plain enough, this beauty, this exquisite beauty, and tears filled his eyes as he looked at the smoke words languishing and melting in the sky and bestowing upon him in their inexhaustible charity and laughing goodness one shape after another of unimaginable beauty and signalling their intention to provide him, for nothing, for ever, for looking merely, with beauty, more beauty! Tears ran down his cheeks.

It was toffee; they were advertising toffee, a nursemaid told Rezia. Together they began to spell t...o...f...

"K...R..." said the nursemaid, and Septimus heard her say "Kay Arr" close to his ear, deeply, softly, like a mellow organ, but with a roughness in her voice like a grasshopper's, which rasped his spine deliciously and sent running up into his brain waves of sound which, concussing, broke. A marvellous discovery indeed—that the human voice in certain atmospheric conditions (for one must be scientific, above all scientific) can quicken trees into life! Happily Rezia put her hand with a tremendous weight on his knee so that he was weighted down, transfixed, or the excitement of the elm trees rising and falling,

rising and falling with all their leaves alight and the colour thinning and thickening from blue to the green of a hollow wave,
like plumes on horses' heads, feathers on ladies', so proudly they
rose and fell, so superbly, would have sent him mad. But he
would not go mad. He would shut his eyes; he would see no
more.

But they beckoned; leaves were alive; trees were alive. And
the leaves being connected by millions of fibres with his own
body, there on the seat, fanned it up and down; when the branch
stretched he, too, made that statement. The sparrows fluttering,
rising, and falling in jagged fountains were part of the pattern;
the white and blue, barred with black branches. Sounds made
harmonies with premeditation; the spaces between them were
as significant as the sounds. A child cried. Rightly far away a
horn sounded. All taken together meant the birth of a new
religion—

"Septimus!" said Rezia. He started violently. People must
notice.

"I am going to walk to the fountain and back," she said.

For she could stand it no longer. Dr. Holmes might say
there was nothing the matter. Far rather would she that he were
dead! She could not sit beside him when he stared so and did
not see her and made everything terrible; sky and tree, children
playing, dragging carts, blowing whistles, falling down; all were
terrible. And he would not kill himself; and she could tell no
one. "Septimus has been working too hard"—that was all she
could say to her own mother. To love makes one solitary, she
thought. She could tell nobody, not even Septimus now, and
looking back, she saw him sitting in his shabby overcoat alone,
on the seat, hunched up, staring. And it was cowardly for a man
to say he would kill himself, but Septimus had fought; he was
brave; he was not Septimus now. She put on her lace collar. She
put on her new hat and he never noticed; and he was happy

without her. Nothing could make her happy without him! Nothing! He was selfish. So men are. For he was not ill. Dr. Holmes said there was nothing the matter with him. She spread her hand before her. Look! Her wedding ring slipped—she had grown so thin. It was she who suffered—but she had nobody to tell.

Far was Italy and the white houses and the room where her sisters sat making hats, and the streets crowded every evening with people walking, laughing out loud, not half alive like people here, huddled up in Bath chairs, looking at a few ugly flowers stuck in pots!

"For you should see the Milan gardens," she said aloud. But to whom?

There was nobody. Her words faded. So a rocket fades. Its sparks, having grazed their way into the night, surrender to it, dark descends, pours over the outlines of houses and towers; bleak hillsides soften and fall in. But though they are gone, the night is full of them; robbed of colour, blank of windows, they exist more ponderously, give out what the frank daylight fails to transmit—the trouble and suspense of things conglomerated there in the darkness; huddled together in the darkness; reft of the relief which dawn brings when, washing the walls white and grey, spotting each windowpane, lifting the mist from the fields, showing the red brown cows peacefully grazing, all is once more decked out to the eye; exists again. I am alone; I am alone! she cried, by the fountain in Regent's Park (staring at the Indian and his cross), as perhaps at midnight, when all boundaries are lost, the country reverts to its ancient shape, as the Romans saw it, lying cloudy, when they landed, and the hills had no names and rivers wound they knew not where—such was her darkness; when suddenly, as if a shelf were shot forth and she stood on it, she said how she was his wife, married years ago in Milan, his wife, and would never, never tell that he was mad! Turning, the shelf fell; down, down she dropped. For he was gone, she thought—gone, as he threatened, to kill himself—to throw himself under a cart! But no; there he was; still sitting alone on the seat, in his shabby overcoat, his legs crossed, staring, talking aloud.

Men must not cut down trees. There is a God. (He noted such revelations on the backs of envelopes.) Change the world. No one kills from hatred. Make it known (he wrote it down). He waited. He listened. A sparrow perched on the railing opposite chirped Septimus, Septimus, four or five times over and went on, drawing its notes out, to sing freshly and piercingly in Greek words how there is no crime and, joined by another sparrow, they sang in voices prolonged and piercing in Greek words, from trees in the meadow of life beyond a river where the dead walk, how there is no death.

There was his hand; there the dead. White things were assembling behind the railings opposite. But he dared not look. Evans was behind the railings!

"What are you saying?" said Rezia suddenly, sitting down by him.

Interrupted again! She was always interrupting.

Away from people—they must get away from people, he said (jumping up), right away over there, where there were chairs beneath a tree and the long slope of the park dipped like a length of green stuff with a ceiling cloth of blue and pink smoke high above, and there was a rampart of far irregular houses hazed in smoke, the traffic hummed in a circle, and on the right, dun-coloured animals stretched long necks over the Zoo palings, barking, howling. There they sat down under a tree.

"Look," she implored him, pointing at a little troop of boys carrying cricket stumps, and one shuffled, spun round on his heel and shuffled, as if he were acting a clown at the music hall.

"Look," she implored him, for Dr. Holmes had told her to make him notice real things, go to a music hall, play cricket— that was the very game, Dr. Holmes said, a nice out-of-door game, the very game for her husband.

"Look," she repeated.

Look the unseen bade him, the voice which now communicated with him who was the greatest of mankind, Septimus, lately taken from life to death, the Lord who had come to renew society, who lay like a coverlet, a snow blanket smitten only by the sun, for ever unwasted, suffering for ever, the scapegoat, the eternal sufferer, but he did not want it, he moaned, putting from him with a wave of his hand that eternal suffering, that eternal loneliness.

"Look," she repeated, for he must not talk aloud to himself out of doors.

"Oh look," she implored him. But what was there to look at? A few sheep. That was all.

The way to Regent's Park Tube station—could they tell her the way to Regent's Park Tube station—Maisie Johnson wanted to know. She was only up from Edinburgh two days ago.

"Not this way—over there!" Rezia exclaimed, waving her aside, lest she should see Septimus.

Both seemed queer, Maisie Johnson thought. Everything seemed very queer. In London for the first time, come to take up a post at her uncle's in Leadenhall Street, and now walking through Regent's Park in the morning, this couple on the chairs gave her quite a turn; the young woman seeming foreign, the man looking queer; so that should she be very old she would still remember and make it jangle again among her memories how she had walked through Regent's Park on a fine summer's morning fifty years ago. For she was only nineteen and had got her way at last, to come to London; and now how queer it was, this couple she had asked the way of, and the girl started and jerked her hand, and the man—he seemed awfully odd; quarrelling, perhaps; parting for ever, perhaps; something was up, she knew; and now all these people (for she returned to the Broad Walk), the stone basins, the prim flowers, the old men and women, invalids most of them in Bath chairs—all seemed, after Edinburgh, so queer. And Maisie Johnson, as she joined that gently trudging, vaguely gazing, breeze-kissed company— squirrels perching and preening, sparrow fountains fluttering for crumbs, dogs busy with the railings, busy with each other, while the soft warm air washed over them and lent to the fixed unsurprised gaze with which they received life something whimsical and mollified—Maisie Johnson positively felt she must cry Oh! (for that young man on the seat had given her quite a turn. Something was up, she knew.)

Horror! horror! she wanted to cry. (She had left her people; they had warned her what would happen.)

Why hadn't she stayed at home? she cried, twisting the knob of the iron railing.

That girl, thought Mrs. Dempster (who saved crusts for the squirrels and often ate her lunch in Regent's Park), don't know a thing yet; and really it seemed to her better to be a little stout, a little slack, a little moderate in one's expectations. Percy drank. Well, better to have a son, thought Mrs. Dempster. She had had a hard time of it, and couldn't help smiling at a girl like that. You'll get married, for you're pretty enough, thought Mrs. Dempster. Get married, she thought, and then you'll know. Oh, the cooks, and so on. Every man has his ways. But whether I'd have chosen quite like that if I could have known, thought Mrs. Dempster, and could not help wishing to whisper a word to Maisie Johnson; to feel on the creased pouch of her worn old face the kiss of pity. For it's been a hard life, thought Mrs.

Dempster. What hadn't she given to it? Roses; figure; her feet too. (She drew the knobbed lumps beneath her skirt.)

Roses, she thought sardonically. All trash, m'dear. For really, what with eating, drinking, and mating, the bad days and good, life had been no mere matter of roses, and what was more, let me tell you, Carrie Dempster had no wish to change her lot with any woman's in Kentish Town! But, she implored, pity. Pity, for the loss of roses. Pity she asked of Maisie Johnson, standing by the hyacinth beds.

Ah, but that aeroplane! Hadn't Mrs. Dempster always longed to see foreign parts? She had a nephew, a missionary. It soared and shot. She always went on the sea at Margate, not out o' sight of land, but she had no patience with women who were afraid of water. It swept and fell. Her stomach was in her mouth. Up again. There's a fine young feller aboard of it, Mrs. Dempster wagered, and away and away it went, fast and fading, away and away the aeroplane shot; soaring over Greenwich and all the masts; over the little island of grey churches, St. Paul's and the rest till, on either side of London, fields spread out and dark brown woods where adventurous thrushes hopping boldly, glancing quickly, snatched the snail and tapped him on a stone, once, twice, thrice.

Away and away the aeroplane shot, till it was nothing but a bright spark; an aspiration; a concentration; a symbol (so it seemed to Mr. Bentley, vigorously rolling his strip of turf at Greenwich) of man's soul; of his determination, thought Mr. Bentley, sweeping round the cedar tree, to get outside his body, beyond his house, by means of thought, Einstein, speculation, mathematics, the Mendelian theory—away the aeroplane shot.

Then, while a seedy-looking nondescript man carrying a leather bag stood on the steps of St. Paul's Cathedral, and hesitated, for within was what balm, how great a welcome, how many tombs with banners waving over them, tokens of victories not over armies, but over, he thought, that plaguy spirit of truth seeking which leaves me at present without a situation, and more than that, the cathedral offers company, he thought, invites you to membership of a society; great men belong to it; martyrs have died for it; why not enter in, he thought, put this leather bag stuffed with pamphlets before an altar, a cross, the symbol of something which has soared beyond seeking and questing and knocking of words together and has become all spirit, disembodied, ghostly—why not enter in? he thought and while he hesitated out flew the aeroplane over Ludgate Circus.

It was strange; it was still. Not a sound was to be heard above the traffic. Unguided it seemed; sped of its own free will. And now, curving up and up, straight up, like something mounting in ecstasy, in pure delight, out from behind poured white smoke looping, writing a T, an O, an F.

"WHAT ARE they looking at?" said Clarissa Dalloway to the maid who opened her door.

The hall of the house was cool as a vault. Mrs. Dalloway raised her hand to her eyes, and, as the maid shut the door to, and she heard the swish of Lucy's skirts, she felt like a nun who has left the world and feels fold round her the familiar veils and the response to old devotions. The cook whistled in the kitchen. She heard the click of the typewriter. It was her life, and, bending her head over the hall table, she bowed beneath the influence, felt blessed and purified, saying to herself, as she took the pad with the telephone message on it, how moments like this are buds on the tree of life, flowers of darkness they are, she thought (as if some lovely rose had blossomed for her eyes only); not for a moment did she believe in God; but all the more, she thought, taking up the pad, must one repay in daily life to servants, yes, to dogs and canaries, above all to Richard her husband, who was the foundation of it—of the gay sounds, of the green lights, of the cook even whistling, for Mrs. Walker was Irish and whistled all day long—one must pay back from this secret deposit of exquisite moments, she thought, lifting the pad, while Lucy stood by her, trying to explain how

"Mr. Dalloway, ma'am"—

Clarissa read on the telephone pad, "Lady Bruton wishes to know if Mr. Dalloway will lunch with her to-day."

"Mr. Dalloway, ma'am, told me to tell you he would be lunching out."

"Dear!" said Clarissa, and Lucy shared as she meant her to her disappointment (but not the pang); felt the concord between them; took the hint; thought how the gentry love; gilded her own future with calm; and, taking Mrs. Dalloway's parasol, handled it like a sacred weapon which a Goddess, having acquitted herself honourably in the field of battle, sheds, and placed it in the umbrella stand.

"Fear no more," said Clarissa. Fear no more the heat o' the sun; for the shock of Lady Bruton asking Richard to lunch without her made the moment in which she had stood shiver, as a plant on the river-bed feels the shock of a passing oar and shivers: so she rocked: so she shivered.

Millicent Bruton, whose lunch parties were said to be extraordinarily amusing, had not asked her. No vulgar jealousy could separate her from Richard. But she feared time itself, and read on Lady Bruton's face, as if it had been a dial cut in impassive stone, the dwindling of life; how year by year her share was sliced; how little the margin that remained was capable any longer of stretching, of absorbing, as in the youthful years, the colours, salts, tones of existence, so that she filled the room she entered, and felt often as she stood hesitating one moment on the threshold of her drawing-room, an exquisite suspense, such as might stay a diver before plunging while the sea darkens and brightens beneath him, and the waves which threaten to break, but only gently split their surface, roll and conceal and encrust as they just turn over the weeds with pearl.

She put the pad on the hall table. She began to go slowly upstairs, with her hand on the bannisters, as if she had left a party, where now this friend now that had flashed back her face, her voice; had shut the door and gone out and stood alone, a single figure against the appalling night, or rather, to be accurate, against the stare of this matter-of-fact June morning; soft with the glow of rose petals for some, she knew, and felt it, as she paused by the open staircase window which let in blinds flapping, dogs barking, let in, she thought, feeling herself suddenly shrivelled, aged, breastless, the grinding, blowing, flowering of the day, out of doors, out of the window, out of her body and brain which now failed, since Lady Bruton, whose lunch parties were said to be extraordinarily amusing, had not asked her.

Like a nun withdrawing, or a child exploring a tower, she went upstairs, paused at the window, came to the bathroom. There was the green linoleum and a tap dripping. There was an emptiness about the heart of life; an attic room. Women must put off their rich apparel. At midday they must disrobe. She pierced the pincushion and laid her feathered yellow hat on the bed. The sheets were clean, tight stretched in a broad white band from side to side. Narrower and narrower would her bed be. The candle was half burnt down and she had read deep in Baron Marbot's *Memoirs*. She had read late at night of the retreat from Moscow. For the House sat so long that Richard insisted, after her illness, that she must sleep undisturbed. And really she preferred to read of the retreat from Moscow. He knew it. So the room was an attic; the bed narrow; and lying there reading, for she slept badly, she could not dispel a virginity preserved through childbirth which clung to her like a sheet. Lovely in girl-

hood, suddenly there came a moment—for example on the
river beneath the woods at Clieveden—when, through some
contraction of this cold spirit, she had failed him. And then at
Constantinople, and again and again. She could see what she
lacked. It was not beauty; it was not mind. It was something
central which permeated; something warm which broke up surfaces and rippled the cold contact of man and woman, or of
women together. For *that* she could dimly perceive. She resented
it, had a scruple picked up Heaven knows where, or, as she felt,
sent by Nature (who is invariably wise); yet she could not resist
sometimes yielding to the charm of a woman, not a girl, of a
woman confessing, as to her they often did, some scrape, some
folly. And whether it was pity, or their beauty, or that she was
older, or some accident—like a faint scent, or a violin next door
(so strange is the power of sounds at certain moments), she did
undoubtedly then feel what men felt. Only for a moment; but
it was enough. It was a sudden revelation, a tinge like a blush
which one tried to check and then, as it spread, one yielded to
its expansion, and rushed to the farthest verge and there quivered and felt the world come closer, swollen with some astonishing significance, some pressure of rapture, which split its thin
skin and gushed and poured with an extraordinary alleviation
over the cracks and sores! Then, for that moment, she had seen
an illumination; a match burning in a crocus; an inner meaning
almost expressed. But the close withdrew; the hard softened. It
was over—the moment. Against such moments (with women
too) there contrasted (as she laid her hat down) the bed and
Baron Marbot and the candle half-burnt. Lying awake, the floor
creaked; the lit house was suddenly darkened, and if she raised
her head she could just hear the click of the handle released as
gently as possible by Richard, who slipped upstairs in his socks
and then, as often as not, dropped his hot-water bottle and
swore! How she laughed!

But this question of love (she thought, putting her coat away), this falling in love with women. Take Sally Seton; her relation in the old days with Sally Seton. Had not that, after all, been love?

She sat on the floor—that was her first impression of Sally—she sat on the floor with her arms round her knees, smoking a cigarette. Where could it have been? The Mannings? The Kinloch-Jones's? At some party (where, she could not be certain), for she had a distinct recollection of saying to the man she was with, "Who is *that*?" And he had told her, and said that Sally's parents did not get on (how that shocked her—that one's parents should quarrel!). But all that evening she could not take her eyes off Sally. It was an extraordinary beauty of the kind she most admired, dark, large-eyed, with that quality which, since she hadn't got it herself, she always envied—a sort of abandonment, as if she could say anything, do anything; a quality much commoner in foreigners than in Englishwomen. Sally always said she had French blood in her veins, an ancestor had been with Marie Antoinette, had his head cut off, left a ruby ring. Perhaps that summer she came to stay at Bourton, walking in quite unexpectedly without a penny in her pocket, one night after dinner, and upsetting poor Aunt Helena to such an extent that she never forgave her. There had been some quarrel at home. She literally hadn't a penny that night when she came to them—had pawned a brooch to come down. She had rushed off in a passion. They sat up till all hours of the night talking. Sally it was who made her feel, for the first time, how sheltered the life at Bourton was. She knew nothing about sex—nothing about social problems. She had once seen an old man who had dropped dead in a field—she had seen cows just after their calves were born. But Aunt Helena never liked discussion of anything (when Sally gave her William Morris, it had to be wrapped in brown paper). There they sat, hour after hour, talking in her bedroom at the top of the house, talking about life, how they were to reform the world. They meant to found a society to abolish private property, and actually had a letter written, though not sent out. The ideas were Sally's, of course — but very soon she was just as excited — read Plato in bed before breakfast; read Morris; read Shelley by the hour.

Sally's power was amazing, her gift, her personality. There was her way with flowers, for instance. At Bourton they always had stiff little vases all the way down the table. Sally went out, picked hollyhocks, dahlias — all sorts of flowers that had never been seen together — cut their heads off, and made them swim on the top of water in bowls. The effect was extraordinary — coming in to dinner in the sunset. (Of course Aunt Helena thought it wicked to treat flowers like that.) Then she forgot her sponge, and ran along the passage naked. That grim old housemaid, Ellen Atkins, went about grumbling — "Suppose any of the gentlemen had seen?" Indeed she did shock people. She was untidy, Papa said.

The strange thing, on looking back, was the purity, the integrity, of her feeling for Sally. It was not like one's feeling for a man. It was completely disinterested, and besides, it had a quality which could only exist between women, between women just grown up. It was protective, on her side; sprang from a sense of being in league together, a presentiment of something that was bound to part them (they spoke of marriage always as a catastrophe), which led to this chivalry, this protective feeling which was much more on her side than Sally's. For in those days she was completely reckless; did the most idiotic things out of bravado; bicycled round the parapet on the terrace; smoked cigars. Absurd, she was — very absurd. But the charm was overpowering, to her at least, so that she could remember standing in her bedroom at the top of the house holding the hot-water can in her hands and saying aloud, "She is beneath this roof. . . . She is beneath this roof!"

No, the words meant absolutely nothing to her now. She could not even get an echo of her old emotion. But she could remember going cold with excitement, and doing her hair in a kind of ecstasy (now the old feeling began to come back to her, as she took out her hairpins, laid them on the dressing-table, began to do her hair), with the rooks flaunting up and down in the pink evening light, and dressing, and going downstairs, and feeling as she crossed the hall "if it were now to die 'twere now to be most happy." That was her feeling—Othello's feeling, and she felt it, she was convinced, as strongly as Shakespeare meant Othello to feel it, all because she was coming down to dinner in a white frock to meet Sally Seton!

She was wearing pink gauze—was that possible? She *seemed*, anyhow, all light, glowing, like some bird or air ball that has flown in, attached itself for a moment to a bramble. But nothing is so strange when one is in love (and what was this except being in love?) as the complete indifference of other people. Aunt Helena just wandered off after dinner; Papa read the paper. Peter Walsh might have been there, and old Miss Cummings; Joseph Breitkopf certainly was, for he came every summer, poor old man, for weeks and weeks, and pretended to read German with her, but really played the piano and sang Brahms without any voice.

All this was only a background for Sally. She stood by the fireplace talking, in that beautiful voice which made everything she said sound like a caress, to Papa, who had begun to be attracted rather against his will (he never got over lending her one of his books and finding it soaked on the terrace), when suddenly she said, "What a shame to sit indoors!" and they all went out on to the terrace and walked up and down. Peter Walsh and

Joseph Breitkopf went on about Wagner. She and Sally fell a little behind. Then came the most exquisite moment of her whole life passing a stone urn with flowers in it. Sally stopped; picked a flower; kissed her on the lips. The whole world might have turned upside down! The others disappeared; there she was alone with Sally. And she felt that she had been given a present, wrapped up, and told just to keep it, not to look at it— a diamond, something infinitely precious, wrapped up, which, as they walked (up and down, up and down), she uncovered, or the radiance burnt through, the revelation, the religious feeling!— when old Joseph and Peter faced them:

"Star-gazing?" said Peter.

It was like running one's face against a granite wall in the darkness! It was shocking; it was horrible!

Not for herself. She felt only how Sally was being mauled already, maltreated; she felt his hostility; his jealousy; his determination to break into their companionship. All this she saw as one sees a landscape in a flash of lightning—and Sally (never had she admired her so much!) gallantly taking her way unvanquished. She laughed. She made old Joseph tell her the names of the stars, which he liked doing very seriously. She stood there: she listened. She heard the names of the stars.

"Oh this horror!" she said to herself, as if she had known all along that something would interrupt, would embitter her moment of happiness.

Yet, after all, how much she owed to him later. Always when she thought of him she thought of their quarrels for some reason—because she wanted his good opinion so much, perhaps. She owed him words: "sentimental," "civilised"; they started up every day of her life as if he guarded her. A book was sentimental; an attitude to life sentimental. "Sentimental," perhaps she was to be thinking of the past. What would he think, she wondered, when he came back?

That she had grown older? Would he say that, or would she see him thinking when he came back, that she had grown older? It was true. Since her illness she had turned almost white.

Laying her brooch on the table, she had a sudden spasm, as if, while she mused, the icy claws had had the chance to fix in her. She was not old yet. She had just broken into her fifty-second year. Months and months of it were still untouched. June, July, August! Each still remained almost whole, and, as if to catch the falling drop, Clarissa (crossing to the dressing-table) plunged into the very heart of the moment, transfixed it, there—the moment of this June morning on which was the pressure of all the other mornings, seeing the glass, the dressing-table, and all the bottles afresh, collecting the whole of her at one point (as she looked into the glass), seeing the delicate pink face of the woman who was that very night to give a party; of Clarissa Dalloway; of herself.

How many million times she had seen her face, and always with the same imperceptible contraction! She pursed her lips when she looked in the glass. It was to give her face point. That was her self—pointed; dartlike; definite. That was her self when some effort, some call on her to be her self, drew the parts together, she alone knew how different, how incompatible and composed so for the world only into one centre, one diamond, one woman who sat in her drawing-room and made a meeting-point, a radiancy no doubt in some dull lives, a refuge for the lonely to come to, perhaps; she had helped young people, who were grateful to her; had tried to be the same always, never showing a sign of all the other sides of her—faults, jealousies, vanities, suspicions, like this of Lady Bruton not asking her to lunch; which, she thought (combing her hair finally), is utterly base! Now, where was her dress?

Her evening dresses hung in the cupboard. Clarissa, plunging her hand into the softness, gently detached the green dress

and carried it to the window. She had torn it. Some one had trod
on the skirt. She had felt it give at the Embassy party at the top
among the folds. By artificial light the green shone, but lost its
colour now in the sun. She would mend it. Her maids had too
much to do. She would wear it to-night. She would take her silks,
her scissors, her—what was it?—her thimble, of course, down
into the drawing-room, for she must also write, and see that
things generally were more or less in order.

Strange, she thought, pausing on the landing, and assembling that diamond shape, that single person, strange how a mistress knows the very moment, the very temper of her house!
Faint sounds rose in spirals up the well of the stairs; the swish
of a mop; tapping; knocking; a loudness when the front door
opened; a voice repeating a message in the basement; the chink
of silver on a tray; clean silver for the party. All was for the party.

(And Lucy, coming into the drawing-room with her tray
held out, put the giant candlesticks on the mantelpiece, the silver casket in the middle, turned the crystal dolphin towards the
clock. They would come; they would stand; they would talk in
the mincing tones which she could imitate, ladies and gentlemen. Of all, her mistress was loveliest—mistress of silver, of
linen, of china, for the sun, the silver, doors off their hinges,
Rumpelmayer's men, gave her a sense, as she laid the paper-
knife on the inlaid table, of something achieved. Behold! Behold! she said, speaking to her old friends in the baker's shop,
where she had first seen service at Caterham, prying into the
glass. She was Lady Angela, attending Princess Mary, when in
came Mrs. Dalloway.)

"Oh Lucy," she said, "the silver does look nice!"

"And how," she said, turning the crystal dolphin to stand
straight, "how did you enjoy the play last night?" "Oh, they had
to go before the end!" she said. "They had to be back at ten!"
she said. "So they don't know what happened," she said. "That

does seem hard luck," she said (for her servants stayed later, if they asked her). "That does seem rather a shame," she said, taking the old bald-looking cushion in the middle of the sofa and putting it in Lucy's arms, and giving her a little push, and crying:

"Take it away! Give it to Mrs. Walker with my compliments! Take it away!" she cried.

And Lucy stopped at the drawing-room door, holding the cushion, and said, very shyly, turning a little pink, Couldn't she help to mend that dress?

But, said Mrs. Dalloway, she had enough on her hands already, quite enough of her own to do without that.

"But, thank you, Lucy, oh, thank you," said Mrs. Dalloway, and thank you, thank you, she went on saying (sitting down on the sofa with her dress over her knees, her scissors, her silks), thank you, thank you, she went on saying in gratitude to her servants generally for helping her to be like this, to be what she wanted, gentle, generous-hearted. Her servants liked her. And then this dress of hers—where was the tear? and now her needle to be threaded. This was a favourite dress, one of Sally Parker's, the last almost she ever made, alas, for Sally had now retired, living at Ealing, and if ever I have a moment, thought Clarissa (but never would she have a moment any more), I shall go and see her at Ealing. For she was a character, thought Clarissa, a real artist. She thought of little out-of-the-way things; yet her dresses were never queer. You could wear them at Hatfield; at Buckingham Palace. She had worn them at Hatfield; at Buckingham Palace.

Quiet descended on her, calm, content, as her needle, drawing the silk smoothly to its gentle pause, collected the green folds together and attached them, very lightly, to the belt. So on a summer's day waves collect, overbalance, and fall; collect and fall; and the whole world seems to be saying "that is all" more and more ponderously, until even the heart in the body which lies in the sun on the beach says too, That is all. Fear no more, says the heart. Fear no more, says the heart, committing its burden to some sea, which sighs collectively for all sorrows, and renews, begins, collects, lets fall. And the body alone listens to the passing bee; the wave breaking; the dog barking, far away barking and barking.

"Heavens, the front-door bell!" exclaimed Clarissa, staying her needle. Roused, she listened.

"Mrs. Dalloway will see me," said the elderly man in the hall. "Oh yes, she will see *me*," he repeated, putting Lucy aside very benevolently, and running upstairs ever so quickly. "Yes, yes, yes," he muttered as he ran upstairs. "She will see me. After five years in India, Clarissa will see me."

"Who can—what can," asked Mrs. Dalloway (thinking it was outrageous to be interrupted at eleven o'clock on the morning of the day she was giving a party), hearing a step on the stairs. She heard a hand upon the door. She made to hide her dress, like a virgin protecting chastity, respecting privacy. Now the brass knob slipped. Now the door opened, and in came— for a single second she could not remember what he was called! so surprised she was to see him, so glad, so shy, so utterly taken aback to have Peter Walsh come to her unexpectedly in the morning! (She had not read his letter.)

"And how are you?" said Peter Walsh, positively trembling; taking both her hands; kissing both her hands. She's grown older, he thought, sitting down. I shan't tell her anything about it, he thought, for she's grown older. She's looking at me, he thought, a sudden embarrassment coming over him, though he had kissed her hands. Putting his hand into his pocket, he took out a large pocket-knife and half opened the blade.

Exactly the same, thought Clarissa; the same queer look; the same check suit; a little out of the straight his face is, a little thinner, dryer, perhaps, but he looks awfully well, and just the same.

"How heavenly it is to see you again!" she exclaimed. He had his knife out. That's so like him, she thought.

He had only reached town last night, he said; would have to go down into the country at once; and how was everything, how was everybody—Richard? Elizabeth?

"And what's all this?" he said, tilting his pen-knife towards her green dress.

He's very well dressed, thought Clarissa; yet he always criticises *me*.

Here she is mending her dress; mending her dress as usual, he thought; here she's been sitting all the time I've been in India; mending her dress; playing about; going to parties; running to the House and back and all that, he thought, growing more and more irritated, more and more agitated, for there's nothing in the world so bad for some women as marriage, he thought; and politics; and having a Conservative husband, like the admirable Richard. So it is, so it is, he thought, shutting his knife with a snap.

"Richard's very well. Richard's at a Committee," said Clarissa.

And she opened her scissors, and said, did he mind her just finishing what she was doing to her dress, for they had a party that night?

"Which I shan't ask you to," she said. "My dear Peter!" she said.

But it was delicious to hear her say that—my dear Peter! Indeed, it was all so delicious—the silver, the chairs; all so delicious!

Why wouldn't she ask him to her party? he asked.

Now of course, thought Clarissa, he's enchanting! perfectly enchanting! Now I remember how impossible it was ever to make up my mind—and why did I make up my mind—not to marry him? she wondered, that awful summer?

"But it's so extraordinary that you should have come this morning!" she cried, putting her hands, one on top of another, down on her dress.

"Do you remember," she said, "how the blinds used to flap at Bourton?"

"They did," he said; and he remembered breakfasting alone, very awkwardly, with her father; who had died; and he had not written to Clarissa. But he had never got on well with old Parry, that querulous, weak-kneed old man, Clarissa's father, Justin Parry.

"I often wish I'd got on better with your father," he said.

"But he never liked any one who—our friends," said Clarissa; and could have bitten her tongue for thus reminding Peter that he had wanted to marry her.

Of course I did, thought Peter; it almost broke my heart too, he thought; and was overcome with his own grief, which rose like a moon looked at from a terrace, ghastly beautiful with light from the sunken day. I was more unhappy than I've ever been since, he thought. And as if in truth he were sitting there on the terrace he edged a little towards Clarissa; put his hand out; raised it; let it fall. There above them it hung, that moon. She too seemed to be sitting with him on the terrace, in the moonlight.

"Herbert has it now," she said. "I never go there now," she said.

Then, just as happens on a terrace in the moonlight, when one person begins to feel ashamed that he is already bored, and yet as the other sits silent, very quiet, sadly looking at the moon, does not like to speak, moves his foot, clears his throat, notices some iron scroll on a table leg, stirs a leaf, but says nothing— so Peter Walsh did now. For why go back like this to the past? he thought. Why make him think of it again? Why make him suffer, when she had tortured him so infernally? Why?

"Do you remember the lake?" she said, in an abrupt voice, under the pressure of an emotion which caught her heart, made the muscles of her throat stiff, and contracted her lips in a spasm as she said "lake." For she was a child, throwing bread to the ducks, between her parents, and at the same time a grown woman coming to her parents who stood by the lake, holding her life in her arms which, as she neared them, grew larger and larger in her arms, until it became a whole life, a complete life, which she put down by them and said, "This is what I have made of it! This!" And what had she made of it? What, indeed? sitting there sewing this morning with Peter.

She looked at Peter Walsh; her look, passing through all that time and that emotion, reached him doubtfully; settled on him tearfully; and rose and fluttered away, as a bird touches a branch and rises and flutters away. Quite simply she wiped her eyes.

"Yes," said Peter. "Yes, yes, yes," he said, as if she drew up to the surface something which positively hurt him as it rose. Stop! Stop! he wanted to cry. For he was not old; his life was not over; not by any means. He was only just past fifty. Shall I tell her, he thought, or not? He would like to make a clean breast of it all. But she is too cold, he thought; sewing, with her scissors; Daisy would look ordinary beside Clarissa. And she would think me a failure, which I am in their sense, he thought; in the Dalloways' sense. Oh yes, he had no doubt about that; he was a failure, compared with all this—the inlaid table, the mounted paper-knife, the dolphin and the candlesticks, the chair-covers and the old valuable English tinted prints—he was a failure! I detest the smugness of the whole affair, he thought; Richard's doing, not Clarissa's; save that she married him. (Here Lucy came into the room, carrying silver, more silver, but charming, slender, graceful she looked, he thought, as she stooped to put it down.) And this has been going on all the time! he thought; week after week; Clarissa's life; while I—he thought; and at once everything seemed to radiate from him; journeys; rides; quarrels; adventures; bridge parties; love affairs; work; work,

work! and he took out his knife quite openly—his old horn-handled knife which Clarissa could swear he had had these thirty years—and clenched his fist upon it.

What an extraordinary habit that was, Clarissa thought; always playing with a knife. Always making one feel, too, frivolous; empty-minded; a mere silly chatterbox, as he used. But I too, she thought, and, taking up her needle, summoned, like a Queen whose guards have fallen asleep and left her unprotected (she had been quite taken aback by this visit—it had upset her) so that any one can stroll in and have a look at her where she lies with the brambles curving over her, summoned to her help the things she did; the things she liked; her husband; Elizabeth; her self, in short, which Peter hardly knew now, all to come about her and beat off the enemy.

"Well, and what's happened to you?" she said. So before a battle begins, the horses paw the ground; toss their heads; the light shines on their flanks; their necks curve. So Peter Walsh and Clarissa, sitting side by side on the blue sofa, challenged each other. His powers chafed and tossed in him. He assembled from different quarters all sorts of things; praise; his career at Oxford; his marriage, which she knew nothing whatever about; how he had loved; and altogether done his job.

"Millions of things!" he exclaimed, and, urged by the assembly of powers which were now charging this way and that and giving him the feeling at once frightening and extremely exhilarating of being rushed through the air on the shoulders of people he could no longer see, he raised his hands to his forehead.

Clarissa sat very upright; drew in her breath.

"I am in love," he said, not to her however, but to some one raised up in the dark so that you could not touch her but must lay your garland down on the grass in the dark.

"In love," he repeated, now speaking rather dryly to Clarissa Dalloway; "in love with a girl in India." He had deposited his garland. Clarissa could make what she would of it.

"In love!" she said. That he at his age should be sucked under in his little bow-tie by that monster! And there's no flesh on his neck; his hands are red; and he's six months older than I am! her eye flashed back to her; but in her heart she felt, all the same, he is in love. He has that, she felt; he is in love.

But the indomitable egotism which for ever rides down the hosts opposed to it, the river which says on, on, on; even though, it admits, there may be no goal for us whatever, still on, on; this indomitable egotism charged her cheeks with colour; made her look very young; very pink; very bright-eyed as she sat with her dress upon her knee, and her needle held to the end of green silk, trembling a little. He was in love! Not with her. With some younger woman, of course.

"And who is she?" she asked.

Now this statue must be brought from its height and set down between them.

"A married woman, unfortunately," he said; "the wife of a Major in the Indian Army."

And with a curious ironical sweetness he smiled as he placed her in this ridiculous way before Clarissa.

(All the same, he is in love, thought Clarissa.)

"She has," he continued, very reasonably, "two small children; a boy and a girl; and I have come over to see my lawyers about the divorce."

There they are! he thought. Do what you like with them, Clarissa! There they are! And second by second it seemed to him that the wife of the Major in the Indian Army (his Daisy) and her two small children became more and more lovely as Clarissa looked at them; as if he had set light to a grey pellet on a plate and there had risen up a lovely tree in the brisk sea-salted air of their intimacy (for in some ways no one understood him, felt with him, as Clarissa did)—their exquisite intimacy.

She flattered him; she fooled him, thought Clarissa; shaping the woman, the wife of the Major in the Indian Army, with three strokes of a knife. What a waste! What a folly! All his life long Peter had been fooled like that; first getting sent down from Oxford; next marrying the girl on the boat going out to India; now the wife of a Major in the Indian Army—thank Heaven she had refused to marry him! Still, he was in love; her old friend, her dear Peter, he was in love.

"But what are you going to do?" she asked him. Oh the lawyers and solicitors, Messrs. Hooper and Grateley of Lincoln's Inn, they were going to do it, he said. And he actually pared his nails with his pocket-knife.

For Heaven's sake, leave your knife alone! she cried to herself in irrepressible irritation; it was his silly unconventionality, his weakness; his lack of the ghost of a notion what any one else was feeling that annoyed her, had always annoyed her; and now at his age, how silly!

I know all that, Peter thought; I know what I'm up against, he thought, running his finger along the blade of his knife, Clarissa and Dalloway and all the rest of them; but I'll show Clarissa—and then to his utter surprise, suddenly thrown by those uncontrollable forces thrown through the air, he burst into tears; wept; wept without the least shame, sitting on the sofa, the tears running down his cheeks.

And Clarissa had leant forward, taken his hand, drawn him to her, kissed him,—actually had felt his face on hers before she could down the brandishing of silver flashing—plumes like pampas grass in a tropic gale in her breast, which, subsiding, left her holding his hand, patting his knee and, feeling as she sat back extraordinarily at her ease with him and light-hearted, all in a clap it came over her, If I had married him, this gaiety would have been mine all day!

It was all over for her. The sheet was stretched and the bed narrow. She had gone up into the tower alone and left them blackberrying in the sun. The door had shut, and there among the dust of fallen plaster and the litter of birds' nests how distant the view had looked, and the sounds came thin and chill (once on Leith Hill, she remembered), and Richard, Richard! she cried, as a sleeper in the night starts and stretches a hand in the dark for help. Lunching with Lady Bruton, it came back to her. He has left me; I am alone for ever, she thought, folding her hands upon her knee.

Peter Walsh had got up and crossed to the window and stood with his back to her, flicking a bandanna handkerchief from side to side. Masterly and dry and desolate he looked, his thin shoulder-blades lifting his coat slightly; blowing his nose violently. Take me with you, Clarissa thought impulsively, as if he were starting directly upon some great voyage; and then, next moment, it was as if the five acts of a play that had been very exciting and moving were now over and she had lived a lifetime in them and had run away, had lived with Peter, and it was now over.

Now it was time to move, and, as a woman gathers her things together, her cloak, her gloves, her opera-glasses, and gets up to go out of the theatre into the street, she rose from the sofa and went to Peter.

And it was awfully strange, he thought, how she still had the power, as she came tinkling, rustling, still had the power as she came across the room, to make the moon, which he detested, rise at Bourton on the terrace in the summer sky.

"Tell me," he said, seizing her by the shoulders. "Are you happy, Clarissa? Does Richard—"

The door opened.

"Here is my Elizabeth," said Clarissa, emotionally, histrion-ically, perhaps.

"How d'y do?" said Elizabeth coming forward.

The sound of Big Ben striking the half-hour struck out between them with extraordinary vigour, as if a young man, strong, indifferent, inconsiderate, were swinging dumb-bells this way and that.

"Hullo, Elizabeth!" cried Peter, stuffing his handkerchief into his pocket, going quickly to her, saying "Good-bye, Clarissa" without looking at her, leaving the room quickly, and running downstairs and opening the hall door.

"Peter! Peter!" cried Clarissa, following him out on to the landing. "My party to-night! Remember my party to-night!" she cried, having to raise her voice against the roar of the open air, and, overwhelmed by the traffic and the sound of all the clocks striking, her voice crying "Remember my party to-night!" sounded frail and thin and very far away as Peter Walsh shut the door.

REMEMBER MY PARTY, remember my party, said Peter Walsh as he stepped down the street, speaking to himself rhythmically, in time with the flow of the sound, the direct downright sound of Big Ben striking the half-hour. (The leaden circles dissolved in the air.) Oh these parties, he thought; Clarissa's parties. Why does she give these parties, he thought. Not that he blamed her or this effigy of a man in a tail-coat with a carnation in his button-hole coming towards him. Only one person in the world could be as he was, in love. And there he was, this fortunate man, himself, reflected in the plate-glass window of a motor-car manufacturer in Victoria Street. All India lay behind him; plains, mountains; epidemics of cholera; a district twice as big as Ire-land; decisions he had come to alone—he, Peter Walsh; who

was now really for the first time in his life, in love. Clarissa had
grown hard, he thought; and a trifle sentimental into the bar-
gain, he suspected, looking at the great motor-cars capable of
doing—how many miles on how many gallons? For he had a
turn for mechanics; had invented a plough in his district, had ordered wheel-barrows from England, but the coolies wouldn't
use them, all of which Clarissa knew nothing whatever about.

The way she said "Here is my Elizabeth!"—that annoyed
him. Why not "Here's Elizabeth" simply? It was insincere. And
Elizabeth didn't like it either. (Still the last tremors of the great
booming voice shook the air round him; the half-hour; still
early; only half-past eleven still.) For he understood young
people; he liked them. There was always something cold in
Clarissa, he thought. She had always, even as a girl, a sort of
timidity, which in middle age becomes conventionality, and then
it's all up, it's all up, he thought, looking rather drearily into the
glassy depths, and wondering whether by calling at that hour he
had annoyed her; overcome with shame suddenly at having
been a fool; wept; been emotional; told her everything, as usual,
as usual.

As a cloud crosses the sun, silence falls on London; and
falls on the mind. Effort ceases. Time flaps on the mast. There
we stop; there we stand. Rigid, the skeleton of habit alone
upholds the human frame. Where there is nothing, Peter Walsh
said to himself; feeling hollowed out, utterly empty within.
Clarissa refused me, he thought. He stood there thinking,
Clarissa refused me.

Ah, said St. Margaret's, like a hostess who comes into her
drawing-room on the very stroke of the hour and finds her
guests there already. I am not late. No, it is precisely half-past
eleven, she says. Yet, though she is perfectly right, her voice,
being the voice of the hostess, is reluctant to inflict its individ-
uality. Some grief for the past holds it back; some concern for

the present. It is half-past eleven, she says, and the sound of St. Margaret's glides into the recesses of the heart and buries itself in ring after ring of sound, like something alive which wants to confide itself, to disperse itself, to be, with a tremor of delight, at rest—like Clarissa herself, thought Peter Walsh, coming down the stairs on the stroke of the hour in white. It is Clarissa herself, he thought, with a deep emotion, and an extraordinarily clear, yet puzzling, recollection of her, as if this bell had come into the room years ago, where they sat at some moment of great intimacy, and had gone from one to the other and had left, like a bee with honey, laden with the moment. But what room? What moment? And why had he been so profoundly happy when the clock was striking? Then, as the sound of St. Margaret's languished, he thought, She has been ill, and the sound expressed languor and suffering. It was her heart, he remembered; and the sudden loudness of the final stroke tolled for death that surprised in the midst of life, Clarissa falling where she stood, in her drawing room. No! No! he cried. She is not dead! I am not old, he cried, and marched up Whitehall, as if there rolled down to him, vigorous, unending, his future.

He was not old, or set, or dried in the least. As for caring what they said of him—the Dalloways, the Whitbreads, and their set, he cared not a straw—not a straw (though it was true he would have, some time or other, to see whether Richard couldn't help him to some job). Striding, staring, he glared at the statue of the Duke of Cambridge. He had been sent down from Oxford—true. He had been a Socialist, in some sense a failure—true. Still the future of civilisation lies, he thought, in the hands of young men like that; of young men such as he was, thirty years ago; with their love of abstract principles; getting books sent out to them all the way from London to a peak in the Himalayas; reading science; reading philosophy. The future lies in the hands of young men like that, he thought.

A patter like the patter of leaves in a wood came from behind, and with it a rustling, regular thudding sound, which as it
overtook him drummed his thoughts, strict in step, up Whitehall, without his doing. Boys in uniform, carrying guns, marched
with their eyes ahead of them, marched, their arms stiff, and on
their faces an expression like the letters of a legend written
round the base of a statue praising duty, gratitude, fidelity, love
of England.

It is, thought Peter Walsh, beginning to keep step with
them, a very fine training. But they did not look robust. They
were weedy for the most part, boys of sixteen, who might, to-
morrow, stand behind bowls of rice, cakes of soap on counters.
Now they wore on them unmixed with sensual pleasure or daily
preoccupations the solemnity of the wreath which they had
fetched from Finsbury Pavement to the empty tomb. They had
taken their vow. The traffic respected it; vans were stopped.

I can't keep up with them, Peter Walsh thought, as they
marched up Whitehall, and sure enough, on they marched, past
him, past every one, in their steady way, as if one will worked
legs and arms uniformly, and life, with its varieties, its irreti-
cences, had been laid under a pavement of monuments and
wreaths and drugged into a stiff yet staring corpse by discipline.
One had to respect it; one might laugh; but one had to respect
it, he thought. There they go, thought Peter Walsh, pausing at
the edge of the pavement; and all the exalted statues, Nelson,
Gordon, Havelock, the black, the spectacular images of great
soldiers stood looking ahead of them, as if they too had made
the same renunciation (Peter Walsh felt he too had made it, the
great renunciation), trampled under the same temptations, and
achieved at length a marble stare. But the stare Peter Walsh did
not want for himself in the least; though he could respect it in
others. He could respect it in boys. They don't know the
troubles of the flesh yet, he thought, as the marching boys dis-

appeared in the direction of the Strand—all that I've been through, he thought, crossing the road, and standing under Gordon's statue, Gordon whom as a boy he had worshipped; Gordon standing lonely with one leg raised and his arms crossed,—poor Gordon, he thought.

And just because nobody yet knew he was in London, except Clarissa, and the earth, after the voyage, still seemed an island to him, the strangeness of standing alone, alive, unknown, at half-past eleven in Trafalgar Square overcame him. What is it? Where am I? And why, after all, does one do it? he thought, the divorce seeming all moonshine. And down his mind went flat as a marsh, and three great emotions bowled over him; understanding; a vast philanthropy; and finally, as if the result of the others, an irrepressible, exquisite delight; as if inside his brain by another hand strings were pulled, shutters moved, and he, having nothing to do with it, yet stood at the opening of endless avenues, down which if he chose he might wander. He had not felt so young for years.

He had escaped! was utterly free—as happens in the downfall of habit when the mind, like an unguarded flame, bows and bends and seems about to blow from its holding. I haven't felt so young for years! thought Peter, escaping (only of course for an hour or so) from being precisely what he was, and feeling like a child who runs out of doors, and sees, as he runs, his old nurse waving at the wrong window. But she's extraordinarily attractive, he thought, as, walking across Trafalgar Square in the direction of the Haymarket, came a young woman who, as she passed Gordon's statue, seemed, Peter Walsh thought (susceptible as he was), to shed veil after veil, until she became the very woman he had always had in mind; young, but stately; merry, but discreet; black, but enchanting.

Straightening himself and stealthily fingering his pocket-knife he started after her to follow this woman, this excitement, which seemed even with its back turned to shed on him a light which connected them, which singled him out, as if the random uproar of the traffic had whispered through hollowed hands his name, not Peter, but his private name which he called himself in his own thoughts. "You," she said, only "you," saying it with her white gloves and her shoulders. Then the thin long cloak which the wind stirred as she walked past Dent's shop in Cockspur Street blew out with an enveloping kindness, a mournful tenderness, as of arms that would open and take the tired——

But she's not married; she's young; quite young, thought Peter, the red carnation he had seen her wear as she came across Trafalgar Square burning again in his eyes and making her lips red. But she waited at the kerbstone. There was a dignity about her. She was not worldly, like Clarissa; not rich, like Clarissa. Was she, he wondered as she moved, respectable? Witty, with a lizard's flickering tongue, he thought (for one must invent, must allow oneself a little diversion), a cool waiting wit, a darting wit; not noisy.

She moved; she crossed; he followed her. To embarrass her was the last thing he wished. Still if she stopped he would say "Come and have an ice," he would say, and she would answer, perfectly simply, "Oh yes."

But other people got between them in the street, obstructing him, blotting her out. He pursued; she changed. There was colour in her cheeks; mockery in her eyes; he was an adventurer, reckless, he thought, swift, daring, indeed (landed as he was last night from India) a romantic buccaneer, careless of all these damned proprieties, yellow dressing-gowns, pipes, fishing-rods, in the shop windows; and respectability and evening parties and spruce old men wearing white slips beneath their waistcoats. He was a buccaneer. On and on she went, across Piccadilly, and up Regent Street, ahead of him, her cloak, her gloves, her shoulders combining with the fringes and the laces and the feather boas in the windows to make the spirit of finery and whimsy which dwindled out of the shops on to the pavement, as the light of a lamp goes wavering at night over hedges in the darkness.

Laughing and delightful, she had crossed Oxford Street and Great Portland Street and turned down one of the little streets, and now, and now, the great moment was approaching, for now she slackened, opened her bag, and with one look in his direction, but not at him, one look that bade farewell, summed up the whole situation and dismissed it triumphantly, for ever, had fitted her key, opened the door, and gone! Clarissa's voice saying, Remember my party, Remember my party, sang in his ears. The house was one of those flat red houses with hanging flower-baskets of vague impropriety. It was over.

Well, I've had my fun; I've had it, he thought, looking up at the swinging baskets of pale geraniums. And it was smashed to atoms—his fun, for it was half made up, as he knew very well; invented, this escapade with the girl; made up, as one makes up the better part of life, he thought—making oneself up; making her up; creating an exquisite amusement, and something more. But odd it was, and quite true; all this one could never share— it smashed to atoms.

He turned; went up the street, thinking to find somewhere to sit, till it was time for Lincoln's Inn—for Messrs. Hooper and Grateley. Where should he go? No matter. Up the street, then, towards Regent's Park. His boots on the pavement struck out "no matter"; for it was early, still very early.

It was a splendid morning too. Like the pulse of a perfect heart, life struck straight through the streets. There was no fumbling—no hesitation. Sweeping and swerving, accurately, punctually, noiselessly, there, precisely at the right instant, the motor-car stopped at the door. The girl, silk-stockinged, feathered, evanescent, but not to him particularly attractive (for he had had his fling), alighted. Admirable butlers, tawny chow dogs, halls laid in black and white lozenges with white blinds blowing, Peter saw through the opened door and approved of. A splendid achievement in its own way, after all, London; the season; civilisation. Coming as he did from a respectable Anglo-Indian family which for at least three generations had administered the affairs of a continent (it's strange, he thought, what a sentiment I have about that, disliking India, and empire, and army as he did), there were moments when civilisation, even of this sort, seemed dear to him as a personal possession; moments of pride in England; in butlers; chow dogs; girls in their security. Ridiculous enough, still there it is, he thought. And the doctors and men of business and capable women all going about their business, punctual, alert, robust, seemed to him wholly admirable, good fellows, to whom one would entrust one's life, companions in the art of living, who would see one through. What with one thing and another, the show was really very tolerable; and he would sit down in the shade and smoke.

There was Regent's Park. Yes. As a child he had walked in Regent's Park—odd, he thought, how the thought of childhood keeps coming back to me—the result of seeing Clarissa, perhaps; for women live much more in the past than we do, he thought. They attach themselves to places; and their fathers— a woman's always proud of her father. Bourton was a nice place, a very nice place, but I could never get on with the old man, he thought. There was quite a scene one night—an argument about something or other, what, he could not remember. Politics presumably.

Yes, he remembered Regent's Park; the long straight walk; the little house where one bought air-balls to the left; an absurd statue with an inscription somewhere or other. He looked for an empty seat. He did not want to be bothered (feeling a little drowsy as he did) by people asking him the time. An elderly grey nurse, with a baby asleep in its perambulator—that was the best he could do for himself; sit down at the far end of the seat by that nurse.

She's a queer-looking girl, he thought, suddenly remembering Elizabeth as she came into the room and stood by her mother. Grown big; quite grown-up, not exactly pretty; handsome rather; and she can't be more than eighteen. Probably she doesn't get on with Clarissa. "There's my Elizabeth"—that sort of thing—why not "Here's Elizabeth" simply?—trying to make out, like most mothers, that things are what they're not. She trusts to her charm too much, he thought. She overdoes it.

The rich benignant cigar smoke eddied coolly down his throat; he puffed it out again in rings which breasted the air bravely for a moment; blue, circular—I shall try and get a word alone with Elizabeth to-night, he thought—then began to wobble into hour-glass shapes and taper away; odd shapes they take, he thought. Suddenly he closed his eyes, raised his hand with an effort, and threw away the heavy end of his cigar. A great brush swept smooth across his mind, sweeping across it moving branches, children's voices, the shuffle of feet, and people passing, and humming traffic, rising and falling traffic. Down, down he sank into the plumes and feathers of sleep, sank, and was muffled over.

THE GREY NURSE resumed her knitting as Peter Walsh, on the hot seat beside her, began snoring. In her grey dress, moving her hands indefatigably yet quietly, she seemed like the champion of the rights of sleepers, like one of those spectral presences which rise in twilight in woods made of sky and branches. The solitary traveller, haunter of lanes, disturber of ferns, and devastator of great hemlock plants, looking up, suddenly sees the giant figure at the end of the ride.

By conviction an atheist perhaps, he is taken by surprise with moments of extraordinary exaltation. Nothing exists outside us except a state of mind, he thinks; a desire for solace, for relief, for something outside these miserable pigmies, these feeble, these ugly, these craven men and women. But if he can conceive of her, then in some sort she exists, he thinks, and advancing down the path with his eyes upon sky and branches he rapidly endows them with womanhood; sees with amazement how grave they become; how majestically, as the breeze stirs them, they dispense with a dark flutter of the leaves charity, comprehension, absolution, and then, flinging themselves suddenly aloft, confound the piety of their aspect with a wild carouse.

Such are the visions which proffer great cornucopias full of fruit to the solitary traveller, or murmur in his ear like sirens lolloping away on the green sea waves, or are dashed in his face like bunches of roses, or rise to the surface like pale faces which fishermen flounder through floods to embrace.

Such are the visions which ceaselessly float up, pace beside, put their faces in front of, the actual thing; often overpowering the solitary traveller and taking away from him the sense of the earth, the wish to return, and giving him for substitute a general peace, as if (so he thinks as he advances down the forest ride) all this fever of living were simplicity itself; and myriads of things merged in one thing; and this figure, made of sky and branches as it is, had risen from the troubled sea (he is elderly, past fifty now) as a shape might be sucked up out of the waves to shower down from her magnificent hands compassion, comprehension, absolution. So, he thinks, may I never go back to the lamplight; to the sitting-room; never finish my book; never knock out my pipe; never ring for Mrs. Turner to clear away; rather let me walk straight on to this great figure, who will, with a toss of her head, mount me on her streamers and let me blow to nothingness with the rest.

Such are the visions. The solitary traveller is soon beyond the wood; and there, coming to the door with shaded eyes, possibly to look for his return, with hands raised, with white apron blowing, is an elderly woman who seems (so powerful is this infirmity) to seek, over a desert, a lost son; to search for a rider destroyed; to be the figure of the mother whose sons have been killed in the battles of the world. So, as the solitary traveller advances down the village street where the women stand knitting and the men dig in the garden, the evening seems ominous; the figures still; as if some august fate, known to them, awaited without fear, were about to sweep them into complete annihilation.

Indoors among ordinary things, the cupboard, the table, the window-sill with its geraniums, suddenly the outline of the landlady, bending to remove the cloth, becomes soft with light, an adorable emblem which only the recollection of cold human contacts forbids us to embrace. She takes the marmalade; she shuts it in the cupboard.

"There is nothing more to-night, sir?"

But to whom does the solitary traveller make reply?

So the elderly nurse knitted over the sleeping baby in Regent's Park. So Peter Walsh snored.

He woke with extreme suddenness, saying to himself, "The death of the soul."

"Lord, Lord!" he said to himself out loud, stretching and opening his eyes. "The death of the soul." The words attached themselves to some scene, to some room, to some past he had been dreaming of. It became clearer; the scene, the room, the past he had been dreaming of.

It was at Bourton that summer, early in the 'nineties, when he was so passionately in love with Clarissa. There were a great many people there, laughing and talking, sitting round a table after tea and the room was bathed in yellow light and full of cigarette smoke. They were talking about a man who had married his housemaid, one of the neighbouring squires, he had forgotten his name. He had married his housemaid, and she had been brought to Bourton to call—an awful visit it had been. She was absurdly over-dressed, "like a cockatoo," Clarissa had said, imitating her, and she never stopped talking. On and on she went, on and on. Clarissa imitated her. Then somebody said—Sally Seton it was—did it make any real difference to one's feelings to know that before they'd married she had had a baby? (In those days, in mixed company, it was a bold thing to say.) He could see Clarissa now, turning bright pink; somehow contracting; and saying, "Oh, I shall never be able to speak to her again!" Whereupon the whole party sitting round the tea-table seemed to wobble. It was very uncomfortable.

He hadn't blamed her for minding the fact, since in those days a girl brought up as she was, knew nothing, but it was her manner that annoyed him; timid; hard; something arrogant; unimaginative; prudish. "The death of the soul." He had said that instinctively, ticketing the moment as he used to do—the death of her soul.

Every one wobbled; every one seemed to bow, as she spoke, and then to stand up different. He could see Sally Seton, like a child who has been in mischief, leaning forward, rather flushed, wanting to talk, but afraid, and Clarissa did frighten people. (She was Clarissa's greatest friend, always about the place, totally unlike her, an attractive creature, handsome, dark, with the reputation in those days of great daring and he used to give her cigars, which she smoked in her bedroom. She had either been engaged to somebody or quarrelled with her family and old Parry disliked them both equally, which was a great bond.) Then Clarissa, still with an air of being offended with them all, got up, made some excuse, and went off, alone. As she opened the door, in came that great shaggy dog which ran after sheep. She flung herself upon him, went into raptures. It was as if she said to Peter—it was all aimed at him, he knew—"I know you thought me absurd about that woman just now; but see how extraordinarily sympathetic I am; see how I love my Rob!"

They had always this queer power of communicating without words. She knew directly he criticised her. Then she would do something quite obvious to defend herself, like this fuss with the dog—but it never took him in, he always saw through Clarissa. Not that he said anything, of course; just sat looking glum. It was the way their quarrels often began.

She shut the door. At once he became extremely depressed. It all seemed useless—going on being in love; going on quarrelling; going on making it up, and he wandered off alone, among outhouses, stables, looking at the horses. (The place was quite a humble one; the Parrys were never very well off; but there were always grooms and stable-boys about—Clarissa loved riding—and an old coachman—what was his name?—an old nurse, old Moody, old Goody, some such name they called her, whom one was taken to visit in a little room with lots of photographs, lots of bird-cages.)

It was an awful evening! He grew more and more gloomy, not about that only; about everything. And he couldn't see her; couldn't explain to her; couldn't have it out. There were always people about—she'd go on as if nothing had happened. That was the devilish part of her—this coldness, this woodenness, something very profound in her, which he had felt again this morning talking to her; an impenetrability. Yet Heaven knows he loved her. She had some queer power of fiddling on one's nerves, turning one's nerves to fiddle-strings, yes.

He had gone in to dinner rather late, from some idiotic idea of making himself felt, and had sat down by old Miss Parry—Aunt Helena—Mr. Parry's sister, who was supposed to preside. There she sat in her white Cashmere shawl, with her head against the window—a formidable old lady, but kind to him, for he had found her some rare flower, and she was a great botanist, marching off in thick boots with a black collecting-box slung between her shoulders. He sat down beside her, and couldn't speak. Everything seemed to race past him; he just sat there, eating. And then half-way through dinner he made himself look across at Clarissa for the first time. She was talking to a young man on her right. He had a sudden revelation. "She will marry that man," he said to himself. He didn't even know his name.

For of course it was that afternoon, that very afternoon, that Dalloway had come over; and Clarissa called him "Wickham"; that was the beginning of it all. Somebody had brought him over; and Clarissa got his name wrong. She introduced him to everybody as Wickham. At last he said "My name is Dalloway!"— that was his first view of Richard — a fair young man, rather awkward, sitting on a deck-chair, and blurting out "My name is Dalloway!" Sally got hold of it; always after that she called him "My name is Dalloway!"

He was a prey to revelations at that time. This one — that she would marry Dalloway — was blinding — overwhelming at the moment. There was a sort of — how could he put it? — a sort of ease in her manner to him; something maternal; something gentle. They were talking about politics. All through dinner he tried to hear what they were saying.

Afterwards he could remember standing by old Miss Parry's chair in the drawing-room. Clarissa came up, with her perfect manners, like a real hostess, and wanted to introduce him to some one — spoke as if they had never met before, which enraged him. Yet even then he admired her for it. He admired her courage; her social instinct; he admired her power of carrying things through. "The perfect hostess," he said to her, whereupon she winced all over. But he meant her to feel it. He would have done anything to hurt her after seeing her with Dalloway. So she left him. And he had a feeling that they were all gathered together in a conspiracy against him—laughing and talking—behind his back. There he stood by Miss Parry's chair as though he had been cut out of wood, he talking about wild flowers. Never, never had he suffered so infernally! He must have forgotten even to pretend to listen; at last he woke up; he saw Miss Parry looking rather disturbed, rather indignant, with her prominent eyes fixed. He almost cried out that he couldn't attend because he was in Hell! People began going out of the room. He heard them talking about fetching cloaks; about its being cold on the water, and so on. They were going boating on the lake by moonlight—one of Sally's mad ideas. He could hear her describing the moon. And they all went out. He was left quite alone.

"Don't you want to go with them?" said Aunt Helena—old Miss Parry!—she had guessed. And he turned round and there was Clarissa again. She had come back to fetch him. He was overcome by her generosity—her goodness.

"Come along," she said. "They're waiting."

He had never felt so happy in the whole of his life! Without a word they made it up. They walked down to the lake. He had twenty minutes of perfect happiness. Her voice, her laugh, her dress (something floating, white, crimson), her spirit, her adventurousness; she made them all disembark and explore the island; she startled a hen; she laughed; she sang. And all the time, he knew perfectly well, Dalloway was falling in love with her; she was falling in love with Dalloway; but it didn't seem to matter. Nothing mattered. They sat on the ground and talked—he and Clarissa. They went in and out of each other's minds without any effort. And then in a second it was over. He said to himself as they were getting into the boat, "She will marry that man," dully, without any resentment; but it was an obvious thing. Dalloway would marry Clarissa.

Dalloway rowed them in. He said nothing. But somehow as they watched him start, jumping on to his bicycle to ride twenty miles through the woods, wobbling off down the drive, waving his hand and disappearing, he obviously did feel, instinctively, tremendously, strongly, all that; the night; the romance; Clarissa. He deserved to have her.

For himself, he was absurd. His demands upon Clarissa (he could see it now) were absurd. He asked impossible things. He made terrible scenes. She would have accepted him still, perhaps, if he had been less absurd. Sally thought so. She wrote him all that summer long letters; how they had talked of him; how she had praised him, how Clarissa burst into tears! It was an extraordinary summer—all letters, scenes, telegrams—arriving at Bourton early in the morning, hanging about till the servants were up; appalling *tête-à-têtes* with old Mr. Parry at breakfast; Aunt Helena formidable but kind; Sally sweeping him off for talks in the vegetable garden; Clarissa in bed with headaches.

The final scene, the terrible scene which he believed had mattered more than anything in the whole of his life (it might be an exaggeration—but still so it did seem now) happened at three o'clock in the afternoon of a very hot day. It was a trifle that led up to it—Sally at lunch saying something about Dalloway, and calling him "My name is Dalloway"; whereupon Clarissa suddenly stiffened, coloured, in a way she had, and rapped out sharply, "We've had enough of that feeble joke." That was all; but for him it was precisely as if she had said, "I'm only amusing myself with you; I've an understanding with Richard Dalloway." So he took it. He had not slept for nights. "It's got to be finished one way or the other," he said to himself. He sent a note to her by Sally asking her to meet him by the fountain at three. "Something very important has happened," he scribbled at the end of it.

The fountain was in the middle of a little shrubbery, far from the house, with shrubs and trees all round it. There she came, even before the time, and they stood with the fountain between them, the spout (it was broken) dribbling water incessantly. How sights fix themselves upon the mind! For example, the vivid green moss.

She did not move. "Tell me the truth, tell me the truth," he kept on saying. He felt as if his forehead would burst. She seemed contracted, petrified. She did not move. "Tell me the truth," he repeated, when suddenly that old man Breitkopf popped his head in carrying the *Times*; stared at them; gaped; and went away. They neither of them moved. "Tell me the truth," he repeated. He felt that he was grinding against something physically hard; she was unyielding. She was like iron, like flint, rigid up the backbone. And when she said, "It's no use. It's no use. This is the end"—after he had spoken for hours, it seemed, with the tears running down his cheeks—it was as if she had hit him in the face. She turned, she left him, went away.

"Clarissa!" he cried. "Clarissa!" But she never came back. It was over. He went away that night. He never saw her again.

It was awful, he cried, awful, awful!

Still, the sun was hot. Still, one got over things. Still, life had a way of adding day to day. Still, he thought, yawning and beginning to take notice—Regent's Park had changed very little since he was a boy, except for the squirrels—still, presumably there were compensations—when little Elise Mitchell, who had been picking up pebbles to add to the pebble collection which she and her brother were making on the nursery mantelpiece, plumped her handful down on the nurse's knee and scudded off again full tilt into a lady's legs. Peter Walsh laughed out.

But Lucrezia Warren Smith was saying to herself, It's wicked; why should I suffer? she was asking, as she walked down the broad path. No; I can't stand it any longer, she was saying, having left Septimus, who wasn't Septimus any longer, to say hard, cruel, wicked things, to talk to himself, to talk to a dead man, on the seat over there; when the child ran full tilt into her, fell flat, and burst out crying.

That was comforting rather. She stood her upright, dusted her frock, kissed her.

But for herself she had done nothing wrong; she had loved Septimus; she had been happy; she had had a beautiful home, and there her sisters lived still, making hats. Why should *she* suffer?

The child ran straight back to its nurse, and Rezia saw her scolded, comforted, taken up by the nurse who put down her knitting, and the kind-looking man gave her his watch to blow open to comfort her—but why should *she* be exposed? Why not left in Milan? Why tortured? Why?

Slightly waved by tears the broad path, the nurse, the man in grey, the perambulator, rose and fell before her eyes. To be rocked by this malignant torturer was her lot. But why? She was like a bird sheltering under the thin hollow of a leaf, who blinks at the sun when the leaf moves; starts at the crack of a dry twig. She was exposed; she was surrounded by the enormous trees, vast clouds of an indifferent world, exposed; tortured; and why should she suffer? Why?

She frowned; she stamped her foot. She must go back again to Septimus since it was almost time for them to be going to Sir William Bradshaw. She must go back and tell him, go back to him sitting there on the green chair under the tree, talking to himself, or to that dead man Evans, whom she had only seen once for a moment in the shop. He had seemed a nice quiet man; a great friend of Septimus's, and he had been killed in the War. But such things happen to every one. Every one has friends who were killed in the War. Every one gives up something when they marry. She had given up her home. She had come to live here, in this awful city. But Septimus let himself think about horrible things, as she could too, if she tried. He had grown stranger and stranger. He said people were talking behind the bedroom walls. Mrs. Filmer thought it odd. He saw things too—he had seen an old woman's head in the middle of a fern. Yet he could be happy when he chose. They went to Hampton Court on top of a bus, and they were perfectly happy. All the little red and yellow flowers were out on the grass, like floating lamps he said, and talked and chattered and laughed, making up stories. Suddenly he said, "Now we will kill ourselves," when they were standing by the river, and he looked at it with a look which she had seen in his eyes when a train went by, or an omnibus—a look as if something fascinated him; and she felt he was going from her and she caught him by the arm. But going home he was perfectly quiet—perfectly reasonable. He would argue with her about killing themselves; and explain how wicked people were; how he could see them making up lies as they passed in the street. He knew all their thoughts, he said; he knew everything. He knew the meaning of the world, he said. Then when they got back he could hardly walk. He lay on the sofa and made her hold his hand to prevent him from falling down, down, he cried, into the flames! and saw faces laughing at him, calling him horrible disgusting names, from the walls, and hands pointing round the screen. Yet they were quite alone. But he began to talk aloud, answering people, arguing, laughing, crying, getting very excited and making her write things down. Perfect nonsense it was; about death; about Miss Isabel Pole. She could stand it no longer. She would go back.

She was close to him now, could see him staring at the sky, muttering, clasping his hands. Yet Dr. Holmes said there was nothing the matter with him. What then had happened—why had he gone, then, why, when she sat by him, did he start, frown at her, move away, and point at her hand, take her hand, look at it terrified?

Was it that she had taken off her wedding ring? "My hand has grown so thin," she said. "I have put it in my purse," she told him.

He dropped her hand. Their marriage was over, he thought, with agony, with relief. The rope was cut; he mounted; he was free, as it was decreed that he, Septimus, the lord of men, should be free; alone (since his wife had thrown away her wedding ring; since she had left him), he, Septimus, was alone, called forth in advance of the mass of men to hear the truth, to learn the meaning, which now at last, after all the toils of civilisation—Greeks, Romans, Shakespeare, Darwin, and now himself—was to be given whole to.... "To whom?" he asked aloud. "To the Prime Minister," the voices which rustled above his head replied. The supreme secret must be told to the Cabinet; first that trees are alive; next there is no crime; next love, universal love, he muttered, gasping, trembling, painfully drawing out these profound truths which needed, so deep were they, so difficult, an immense effort to speak out, but the world was entirely changed by them for ever.

No crime; love; he repeated, fumbling for his card and pencil, when a Skye terrier snuffed his trousers and he started in an agony of fear. It was turning into a man! He could not watch it happen! It was horrible, terrible to see a dog become a man! At once the dog trotted away.

Heaven was divinely merciful, infinitely benignant. It spared him, pardoned his weakness. But what was the scientific explanation (for one must be scientific above all things)? Why could he see through bodies, see into the future, when dogs will become men? It was the heat wave presumably, operating upon a brain made sensitive by eons of evolution. Scientifically speaking, the flesh was melted off the world. His body was macerated until only the nerve fibres were left. It was spread like a veil upon a rock.

He lay back in his chair, exhausted but upheld. He lay resting, waiting, before he again interpreted, with effort, with
agony, to mankind. He lay very high, on the back of the world.
The earth thrilled beneath him. Red flowers grew through his
flesh; their stiff leaves rustled by his head. Music began clang-
ing against the rocks up here. It is a motor horn down in the
street, he muttered; but up here it cannoned from rock to rock,
divided, met in shocks of sound which rose in smooth columns
(that music should be visible was a discovery) and became an
anthem, an anthem twined round now by a shepherd boy's piping (That's an old man playing a penny whistle by the public-
house, he muttered) which, as the boy stood still came bubbling
from his pipe, and then, as he climbed higher, made its exquisite plaint while the traffic passed beneath. This boy's elegy is
played among the traffic, thought Septimus. Now he withdraws
up into the snows, and roses hang about him—the thick red
roses which grow on my bedroom wall, he reminded himself.
The music stopped. He has his penny, he reasoned it out, and
has gone on to the next public-house.

But he himself remained high on his rock, like a drowned
sailor on a rock. I leant over the edge of the boat and fell down,
he thought. I went under the sea. I have been dead, and yet am
now alive, but let me rest still; he begged (he was talking to himself again—it was awful, awful!); and as, before waking, the
voices of birds and the sound of wheels chime and chatter in a
queer harmony, grow louder and louder and the sleeper feels
himself drawing to the shores of life, so he felt himself drawing
towards life, the sun growing hotter, cries sounding louder,
something tremendous about to happen.

He had only to open his eyes; but a weight was on them; a
fear. He strained; he pushed; he looked; he saw Regent's Park
before him. Long streamers of sunlight fawned at his feet. The
trees waved, brandished. We welcome, the world seemed to say;

we accept; we create. Beauty, the world seemed to say. And as if
to prove it (scientifically) wherever he looked at the houses, at
the railings, at the antelopes stretching over the palings, beauty
sprang instantly. To watch a leaf quivering in the rush of air was
an exquisite joy. Up in the sky swallows swooping, swerving,
flinging themselves in and out, round and round, yet always
with perfect control as if elastics held them; and the flies rising
and falling; and the sun spotting now this leaf, now that, in
mockery, dazzling it with soft gold in pure good temper; and
now and again some chime (it might be a motor horn) tinkling
divinely on the grass stalks—all of this, calm and reasonable as
it was, made out of ordinary things as it was, was the truth now;
beauty, that was the truth now. Beauty was everywhere.

"It is time," said Rezia.

The word "time" split its husk; poured its riches over him;
and from his lips fell like shells, like shavings from a plane, without his making them, hard, white, imperishable words, and flew
to attach themselves to their places in an ode to Time; an immortal ode to Time. He sang. Evans answered from behind the
tree. The dead were in Thessaly, Evans sang, among the orchids.
There they waited till the War was over, and now the dead, now
Evans himself—

"For God's sake don't come!" Septimus cried out. For he
could not look upon the dead.

But the branches parted. A man in grey was actually walking towards them. It was Evans! But no mud was on him;
no wounds; he was not changed. I must tell the whole world,
Septimus cried, raising his hand (as the dead man in the grey
suit came nearer), raising his hand like some colossal figure who
has lamented the fate of man for ages in the desert alone with
his hands pressed to his forehead, furrows of despair on his
cheeks, and now sees light on the desert's edge which broadens
and strikes the iron-black figure (and Septimus half rose from

his chair), and with legions of men prostrate behind him he, the giant mourner, receives for one moment on his face the whole—

"But I am so unhappy, Septimus," said Rezia trying to make him sit down.

The millions lamented; for ages they had sorrowed. He would turn round, he would tell them in a few moments, only a few moments more, of this relief, of this joy, of this astonishing revelation—

"The time, Septimus," Rezia repeated. "What is the time?"

He was talking, he was starting, this man must notice him. He was looking at them.

"I will tell you the time," said Septimus, very slowly, very drowsily, smiling mysteriously. As he sat smiling at the dead man in the grey suit the quarter struck—the quarter to twelve.

And that is being young, Peter Walsh thought as he passed them. To be having an awful scene—the poor girl looked absolutely desperate—in the middle of the morning. But what was it about, he wondered, what had the young man in the overcoat been saying to her to make her look like that; what awful fix had they got themselves into, both to look so desperate as that on a fine summer morning? The amusing thing about coming back to England, after five years, was the way it made, anyhow the first days, things stand out as if one had never seen them before; lovers squabbling under a tree; the domestic family life of the parks. Never had he seen London look so enchanting—the softness of the distances; the richness; the greenness; the civilisation, after India, he thought, strolling across the grass.

This susceptibility to impressions had been his undoing no doubt. Still at his age he had, like a boy or a girl even, these alternations of mood; good days, bad days, for no reason whatever, happiness from a pretty face, downright misery at the sight of a frump. After India of course one fell in love with every woman one met. There was a freshness about them; even the poorest dressed better than five years ago surely; and to his eye the fashions had never been so becoming; the long black cloaks; the slimness; the elegance; and then the delicious and apparently universal habit of paint. Every woman, even the most respectable, had roses blooming under glass; lips cut with a knife; curls of Indian ink; there was design, art, everywhere; a change of some sort had undoubtedly taken place. What did the young people think about? Peter Walsh asked himself.

Those five years—1918 to 1923—had been, he suspected, somehow very important. People looked different. Newspapers seemed different. Now for instance there was a man writing quite openly in one of the respectable weeklies about water-closets. That you couldn't have done ten years ago—written quite openly about water-closets in a respectable weekly. And then this taking out a stick of rouge, or a powder-puff and making up in public. On board ship coming home there were lots of young men and girls—Betty and Bertie he remembered in particular—carrying on quite openly; the old mother sitting and watching them with her knitting, cool as a cucumber. The girl would stand still and powder her nose in front of every one. And they weren't engaged; just having a good time; no feelings hurt on either side. As hard as nails she was—Betty What'shername—; but a thorough good sort. She would make a very good wife at thirty—she would marry when it suited her to marry; marry some rich man and live in a large house near Manchester.

Who was it now who had done that? Peter Walsh asked himself, turning into the Broad Walk,—married a rich man and lived in a large house near Manchester? Somebody who had written him a long, gushing letter quite lately about "blue hydrangeas." It was seeing blue hydrangeas that made her think of him and the old days—Sally Seton, of course! It was Sally Seton—the last person in the world one would have expected to marry a rich man and live in a large house near Manchester, the wild, the daring, the romantic Sally!

But of all that ancient lot, Clarissa's friends—Whitbreads, Kinderleys, Cunninghams, Kinloch-Jones's—Sally was probably the best. She tried to get hold of things by the right end anyhow. She saw through Hugh Whitbread anyhow—the admirable Hugh—when Clarissa and the rest were at his feet.

"The Whitbreads?" he could hear her saying. "Who are the Whitbreads? Coal merchants. Respectable tradespeople."

Hugh she detested for some reason. He thought of nothing but his own appearance, she said. He ought to have been a Duke. He would be certain to marry one of the Royal Princesses. And of course Hugh had the most extraordinary, the most natural, the most sublime respect for the British aristocracy of any human being he had ever come across. Even Clarissa had to own that. Oh, but he was such a dear, so unselfish, gave up shooting to please his old mother—remembered his aunts' birthdays, and so on.

Sally, to do her justice, saw through all that. One of the things he remembered best was an argument one Sunday morning at Bourton about women's rights (that antediluvian topic), when Sally suddenly lost her temper, flared up, and told Hugh that he represented all that was most detestable in British middle-class life. She told him that she considered him responsible for the state of "those poor girls in Piccadilly"—Hugh, the perfect gentleman, poor Hugh!—never did a man look more horrified! She did it on purpose she said afterwards (for they used to get together in the vegetable garden and compare notes). "He's read nothing, thought nothing, felt nothing," he could hear her saying in that very emphatic voice which carried so much farther than she knew. The stable-boys had more life in them than Hugh, she said. He was a perfect specimen of the public school type, she said. No country but England could have produced him. She was really spiteful, for some reason; had some grudge against him. Something had happened—he forgot what—in the smoking-room. He had insulted her—kissed her? Incredible! Nobody believed a word against Hugh of course. Who could? Kissing Sally in the smoking-room! If it had been some Honourable Edith or Lady Violet, perhaps; but not that ragamuffin Sally without a penny to her name, and a father or a mother gambling at Monte Carlo. For of all the people he had ever met Hugh was the greatest snob—the most obsequious—no, he didn't cringe exactly. He was too much of a prig for that. A first-rate valet was the obvious comparison—somebody who walked behind carrying suit cases; could be trusted to send telegrams—indispensable to hostesses. And he'd found his job—married his Honourable Evelyn; got some little post at Court, looked after the King's cellars, polished the Imperial shoe-buckles, went about in knee-breeches and lace ruffles. How remorseless life is! A little job at Court!

He had married this lady, the Honourable Evelyn, and they lived hereabouts, so he thought (looking at the pompous houses overlooking the Park), for he had lunched there once in a house which had, like all Hugh's possessions, something that no other house could possibly have—linen cupboards it might have been. You had to go and look at them—you had to spend a great deal of time always admiring whatever it was—linen cupboards, pillow-cases, old oak furniture, pictures, which Hugh had picked up for an old song. But Mrs. Hugh sometimes gave the show away. She was one of those obscure mouse-like little women who admire big men. She was almost negligible. Then suddenly she would say something quite unexpected—something sharp. She had the relics of the grand manner perhaps. The steam coal was a little too strong for her—it made the atmosphere thick. And so there they lived, with their linen cupboards and their old masters and their pillow-cases fringed with real lace at the rate of five or ten thousand a year presumably, while he, who was two years older than Hugh, cadged for a job.

At fifty-three he had to come and ask them to put him into some secretary's office, to find him some usher's job teaching little boys Latin, at the beck and call of some mandarin in an office, something that brought in five hundred a year; for if he married Daisy, even with his pension, they could never do on less. Whitbread could do it presumably; or Dalloway. He didn't mind what he asked Dalloway. He was a thorough good sort; a bit limited; a bit thick in the head; yes; but a thorough good sort. Whatever he took up he did in the same matter-of-fact sensible way; without a touch of imagination, without a spark of brilliancy, but with the inexplicable niceness of his type. He ought to have been a country gentleman—he was wasted on politics. He was at his best out of doors, with horses and dogs—how good he was, for instance, when that great shaggy dog of Clarissa's got caught in a trap and had its paw half torn off, and Clarissa turned faint and Dalloway did the whole thing; bandaged, made splints; told Clarissa not to be a fool. That was what she liked him for perhaps—that was what she needed. "Now, my dear, don't be a fool. Hold this—fetch that," all the time talking to the dog as if it were a human being.

But how could she swallow all that stuff about poetry? How could she let him hold forth about Shakespeare? Seriously and solemnly Richard Dalloway got on his hind legs and said that no decent man ought to read Shakespeare's sonnets because it was like listening at keyholes (besides the relationship was not one that he approved). No decent man ought to let his wife visit a deceased wife's sister. Incredible! The only thing to do was to pelt him with sugared almonds—it was at dinner. But Clarissa sucked it all in; thought it so honest of him; so independent of him; Heaven knows if she didn't think him the most original mind she'd ever met!

That was one of the bonds between Sally and himself. There was a garden where they used to walk, a walled-in place, with rose-bushes and giant cauliflowers—he could remember Sally tearing off a rose, stopping to exclaim at the beauty of the cabbage leaves in the moonlight (it was extraordinary how vividly it all came back to him, things he hadn't thought of for years), while she implored him, half laughing of course, to carry off Clarissa, to save her from the Hughs and the Dalloways and all the other "perfect gentlemen" who would "stifle her soul" (she wrote reams of poetry in those days), make a mere hostess of her, encourage her worldliness. But one must do Clarissa justice. She wasn't going to marry Hugh anyhow. She had a perfectly clear notion of what she wanted. Her emotions were all on the surface. Beneath, she was very shrewd—a far better judge of character than Sally, for instance, and with it all, purely feminine; with that extraordinary gift, that woman's gift, of making a world of her own wherever she happened to be. She came into a room; she stood, as he had often seen her, in a doorway with lots of people round her. But it was Clarissa one remembered. Not that she was striking; not beautiful at all; there was nothing picturesque about her; she never said anything specially clever; there she was, however; there she was.

No, no, no! He was not in love with her any more! He only felt, after seeing her that morning, among her scissors and silks, making ready for the party, unable to get away from the thought of her; she kept coming back and back like a sleeper jolting against him in a railway carriage; which was not being in love, of course; it was thinking of her, criticising her, starting again, after thirty years, trying to explain her. The obvious thing to say of her was that she was worldly; cared too much for rank and society and getting on in the world—which was true in a sense; she had admitted it to him. (You could always get her to own up if you took the trouble; she was honest.) What she would say was that she hated frumps, fogies, failures, like himself presumably; thought people had no right to slouch about with their hands in their pockets; must do something, be something; and these great swells, these Duchesses, these hoary old Countesses one met in her drawing-room, unspeakably remote as he felt them to be from anything that mattered a straw, stood for something real to her. Lady Bexborough, she said once, held herself upright (so did Clarissa herself; she never lounged in any sense of the word; she was straight as a dart, a little rigid in fact). She said they had a kind of courage which the older she grew the more she respected. In all this there was a great deal of Dalloway, of course; a great deal of the public-spirited, British Empire, tariff-reform, governing-class spirit, which had grown on her, as it tends to do. With twice his wits, she had to see things through his eyes—one of the tragedies of married life. With a mind of her own, she must always be quoting Richard—as if one couldn't know to a tittle what Richard thought by reading the *Morning Post* of a morning! These parties for example were all for him, or for her idea of him (to do Richard justice he would have been happier farming in Norfolk). She made her drawing-room a sort of meeting-place; she had a genius for it. Over and over again he had seen her take some raw youth, twist him, turn him, wake him up; set him going. Infinite numbers of dull people conglomerated round her of course. But odd unexpected people turned up; an artist sometimes; sometimes a writer; queer fish in that atmosphere. And behind it all was that network of visiting, leaving cards, being kind to people; running about with bunches of flowers, little presents; So-and-so was going to France—must have an air-cushion; a real drain on her strength; all that interminable traffic that women of her sort keep up; but she did it genuinely, from a natural instinct.

Oddly enough, she was one of the most thorough-going sceptics he had ever met, and possibly (this was a theory he used to make up to account for her, so transparent in some ways, so inscrutable in others), possibly she said to herself, As we are a doomed race, chained to a sinking ship (her favourite reading as a girl was Huxley and Tyndall, and they were fond of these nautical metaphors), as the whole thing is a bad joke, let us, at any rate, do our part; mitigate the sufferings of our fellow-prisoners (Huxley again); decorate the dungeon with flowers and air-cushions; be as decent as we possibly can. Those ruffians, the Gods, shan't have it all their own way,—her notion being that the Gods, who never lost a chance of hurting, thwarting and spoiling human lives were seriously put out if, all the same, you behaved like a lady. That phase came directly after Sylvia's death—that horrible affair. To see your own sister killed by a falling tree (all Justin Parry's fault—all his carelessness) before your very eyes, a girl too on the verge of life, the most gifted of them, Clarissa always said, was enough to turn one bitter. Later she wasn't so positive perhaps; she thought there were no Gods; no one was to blame; and so she evolved this atheist's religion of doing good for the sake of goodness.

And of course she enjoyed life immensely. It was her nature to enjoy (though goodness only knows, she had her reserves; it was a mere sketch, he often felt, that even he, after all these years, could make of Clarissa). Anyhow there was no bitterness in her; none of that sense of moral virtue which is so repulsive in good women. She enjoyed practically everything. If you walked with her in Hyde Park now it was a bed of tulips, now a child in a perambulator, now some absurd little drama she made up on the spur of the moment. (Very likely, she would have talked to those lovers, if she had thought them unhappy.) She had a sense of comedy that was really exquisite, but she needed people, always people, to bring it out, with the inevitable result that she frittered her time away, lunching, dining, giving these incessant parties of hers, talking nonsense, saying things she didn't mean, blunting the edge of her mind, losing her discrimination. There she would sit at the head of the table taking infinite pains with some old buffer who might be useful to Dalloway—they knew the most appalling bores in Europe—or in came Elizabeth and everything must give way to *her*. She was at a High School, at the inarticulate stage last time he was over, a round-eyed, pale-faced girl, with nothing of her mother in her, a silent stolid creature, who took it all as a matter of course, let her mother make a fuss of her, and then said "May I go now?" like a child of four; going off, Clarissa explained, with that mixture of amusement and pride which Dalloway himself seemed to rouse in her, to play hockey. And now Elizabeth was "out," presumably; thought him an old fogy, laughed at her mother's friends. Ah well, so be it. The compensation of growing old, Peter Walsh thought, coming out of Regent's Park, and holding his hat in hand, was simply this; that the passions remain as strong as ever, but one has gained—at last!—the power which adds the supreme flavour to existence,—the power of taking hold of experience, of turning it round, slowly, in the light.

A terrible confession it was (he put his hat on again), but now, at the age of fifty-three one scarcely needed people any more. Life itself, every moment of it, every drop of it, here, this instant, now, in the sun, in Regent's Park, was enough. Too much indeed. A whole lifetime was too short to bring out, now that one had acquired the power, the full flavour; to extract every ounce of pleasure, every shade of meaning; which both were so much more solid than they used to be, so much less personal. It was impossible that he should ever suffer again as Clarissa had made him suffer. For hours at a time (pray God that one might say these things without being overheard!), for hours and days he never thought of Daisy.

Could it be that he was in love with her then, remembering the misery, the torture, the extraordinary passion of those days?

It was a different thing altogether—a much pleasanter thing—
the truth being, of course, that now *she* was in love with *him*.
And that perhaps was the reason why, when the ship actually
sailed, he felt an extraordinary relief, wanted nothing so much
as to be alone; was annoyed to find all her little attentions—
cigars, notes, a rug for the voyage—in his cabin. Every one if
they were honest would say the same; one doesn't want people
after fifty; one doesn't want to go on telling women they are
pretty; that's what most men of fifty would say, Peter Walsh
thought, if they were honest.

But then these astonishing accesses of emotion—bursting
into tears this morning, what was all that about? What could
Clarissa have thought of him? thought him a fool presumably,
not for the first time. It was jealousy that was at the bottom of
it—jealousy which survives every other passion of mankind,
Peter Walsh thought, holding his pocket-knife at arm's length.
She had been meeting Major Orde, Daisy said in her last letter;
said it on purpose he knew; said it to make him jealous; he could
see her wrinkling her forehead as she wrote, wondering what
she could say to hurt him; and yet it made no difference; he was
furious! All this pother of coming to England and seeing
lawyers wasn't to marry her, but to prevent her from marrying
anybody else. That was what tortured him, that was what came
over him when he saw Clarissa so calm, so cold, so intent on
her dress or whatever it was; realising what she might have
spared him, what she had reduced him to—a whimpering,
snivelling old ass. But women, he thought, shutting his pocket-
knife, don't know what passion is. They don't know the meaning of it to men. Clarissa was as cold as an icicle. There she
would sit on the sofa by his side, let him take her hand, give him
one kiss—Here he was at the crossing.

A sound interrupted him; a frail quivering sound, a voice
bubbling up without direction, vigour, beginning or end, run-

ning weakly and shrilly and with an absence of all human meaning into

                    ee um fah um so
                    foo swee too eem oo—

the voice of no age or sex, the voice of an ancient spring spout-
ing from the earth; which issued, just opposite Regent's Park
Tube station from a tall quivering shape, like a funnel, like a
rusty pump, like a wind-beaten tree for ever barren of leaves
which lets the wind run up and down its branches singing

                    ee um fah um so
                    foo swee too eem oo

and rocks and creaks and moans in the eternal breeze.

Through all ages—when the pavement was grass, when it
was swamp, through the age of tusk and mammoth, through the
age of silent sunrise, the battered woman—for she wore a
skirt—with her right hand exposed, her left clutching at her side,
stood singing of love—love which has lasted a million years, she
sang, love which prevails, and millions of years ago, her lover,
who had been dead these centuries, had walked, she crooned,
with her in May; but in the course of ages, long as summer days,
and flaming, she remembered, with nothing but red asters, he
had gone; death's enormous sickle had swept those tremendous
hills, and when at last she laid her hoary and immensely aged
head on the earth, now become a mere cinder of ice, she implored the Gods to lay by her side a bunch of purple heather,
there on her high burial place which the last rays of the last sun
caressed; for then the pageant of the universe would be over.

As the ancient song bubbled up opposite Regent's Park
Tube station still the earth seemed green and flowery; still,

though it issued from so rude a mouth, a mere hole in the earth, muddy too, matted with root fibres and tangled grasses, still the old bubbling burbling song, soaking through the knotted roots of infinite ages, and skeletons and treasure, streamed away in rivulets over the pavement and all along the Marylebone Road, and down towards Euston, fertilising, leaving a damp stain.

Still remembering how once in some primeval May she had walked with her lover, this rusty pump, this battered old woman with one hand exposed for coppers the other clutching her side, would still be there in ten million years, remembering how once she had walked in May, where the sea flows now, with whom it did not matter—he was a man, oh yes, a man who had loved her. But the passage of ages had blurred the clarity of that ancient May day; the bright petalled flowers were hoar and silver frosted; and she no longer saw, when she implored him (as she did now quite clearly) "look in my eyes with thy sweet eyes intently," she no longer saw brown eyes, black whiskers or sunburnt face but only a looming shape, a shadow shape, to which, with the bird-like freshness of the very aged she still twittered "give me your hand and let me press it gently" (Peter Walsh couldn't help giving the poor creature a coin as he stepped into his taxi), "and if some one should see, what matter they?" she demanded; and her fist clutched at her side, and she smiled, pocketing her shilling, and all peering inquisitive eyes seemed blotted out, and the passing generations—the pavement was crowded with bustling middle-class people—vanished, like leaves, to be trodden under, to be soaked and steeped and made mould of by that eternal spring—

ee um fah um so
foo swee too eem oo

"POOR OLD WOMAN," said Rezia Warren Smith, waiting to cross.

Oh poor old wretch!

Suppose it was a wet night? Suppose one's father, or somebody who had known one in better days had happened to pass, and saw one standing there in the gutter? And where did she sleep at night?

Cheerfully, almost gaily, the invincible thread of sound wound up into the air like the smoke from a cottage chimney, winding up clean beech trees and issuing in a tuft of blue smoke among the topmost leaves. "And if some one should see, what matter they?"

Since she was so unhappy, for weeks and weeks now, Rezia had given meanings to things that happened, almost felt sometimes that she must stop people in the street, if they looked good, kind people, just to say to them "I am unhappy"; and this old woman singing in the street "if some one should see, what matter they?" made her suddenly quite sure that everything was going to be right. They were going to Sir William Bradshaw; she thought his name sounded nice; he would cure Septimus at once. And then there was a brewer's cart, and the grey horses had upright bristles of straw in their tails; there were newspaper placards. It was a silly, silly dream, being unhappy.

So they crossed, Mr. and Mrs. Septimus Warren Smith, and was there, after all, anything to draw attention to them, anything to make a passer-by suspect here is a young man who carries in him the greatest message in the world, and is, moreover, the happiest man in the world, and the most miserable? Perhaps they walked more slowly than other people, and there was something hesitating, trailing, in the man's walk, but what more natural for a clerk, who has not been in the West End on a weekday at this hour for years, than to keep looking at the sky, looking at this, that and the other, as if Portland Place were a room he had come into when the family are away, the chandeliers being hung in holland bags, and the caretaker, as she lets in

long shafts of dusty light upon deserted, queer-looking arm-
chairs, lifting one corner of the long blinds, explains to the visitors what a wonderful place it is; how wonderful, but at the
same time, he thinks, as he looks at chairs and tables, how
strange.

To look at, he might have been a clerk, but of the better sort;
for he wore brown boots; his hands were educated; so, too, his
profile — his angular, big-nosed, intelligent, sensitive profile; but
not his lips altogether, for they were loose; and his eyes (as eyes
tend to be), eyes merely; hazel, large; so that he was, on the
whole, a border case, neither one thing nor the other, might end
with a house at Purley and a motor car, or continue renting
apartments in back streets all his life; one of those half-educated,
self-educated men whose education is all learnt from books bor-
rowed from public libraries, read in the evening after the day's
work, on the advice of well-known authors consulted by letter.

As for the other experiences, the solitary ones, which
people go through alone, in their bedrooms, in their offices,
walking the fields and the streets of London, he had them; had
left home, a mere boy, because of his mother; she lied; because
he came down to tea for the fiftieth time with his hands un-
washed; because he could see no future for a poet in Stroud;
and so, making a confidant of his little sister, had gone to London leaving an absurd note behind him, such as great men have
written, and the world has read later when the story of their
struggles has become famous.

London has swallowed up many millions of young men
called Smith; thought nothing of fantastic Christian names like
Septimus with which their parents have thought to distinguish
them. Lodging off the Euston Road, there were experiences,
again experiences, such as change a face in two years from a
pink innocent oval to a face lean, contracted, hostile. But of all
this what could the most observant of friends have said except

what a gardener says when he opens the conservatory door in the morning and finds a new blossom on his plant:—It has flowered; flowered from vanity, ambition, idealism, passion, loneliness, courage, laziness, the usual seeds, which all muddled up (in a room off the Euston Road), made him shy, and stammering, made him anxious to improve himself, made him fall in love with Miss Isabel Pole, lecturing in the Waterloo Road upon Shakespeare.

Was he not like Keats? she asked; and reflected how she might give him a taste of *Antony and Cleopatra* and the rest; lent him books; wrote him scraps of letters; and lit in him such a fire as burns only once in a lifetime, without heat, flickering a red gold flame infinitely ethereal and insubstantial over Miss Pole; *Antony and Cleopatra;* and the Waterloo Road. He thought her beautiful, believed her impeccably wise; dreamed of her, wrote poems to her, which, ignoring the subject, she corrected in red ink; he saw her, one summer evening, walking in a green dress in a square. "It has flowered," the gardener might have said, had he opened the door; had he come in, that is to say, any night about this time, and found him writing; found him tearing up his writing; found him finishing a masterpiece at three o'clock in the morning and running out to pace the streets, and visiting churches, and fasting one day, drinking another, devouring Shakespeare, Darwin, *The History of Civilisation,* and Bernard Shaw.

Something was up, Mr. Brewer knew; Mr. Brewer, managing clerk at Sibleys and Arrowsmiths, auctioneers, valuers, land and estate agents; something was up, he thought, and, being paternal with his young men, and thinking very highly of Smith's abilities, and prophesying that he would, in ten or fifteen years, succeed to the leather arm-chair in the inner room under the skylight with the deed-boxes round him, "if he keeps his health," said Mr. Brewer, and that was the danger—he looked weakly; advised football, invited him to supper and was seeing his way to consider recommending a rise of salary, when something happened which threw out many of Mr. Brewer's calculations, took away his ablest young fellows, and eventually, so prying and insidious were the fingers of the European War, smashed a plaster cast of Ceres, ploughed a hole in the geranium beds, and utterly ruined the cook's nerves at Mr. Brewer's establishment at Muswell Hill.

Septimus was one of the first to volunteer. He went to France to save an England which consisted almost entirely of Shakespeare's plays and Miss Isabel Pole in a green dress walking in a square. There in the trenches the change which Mr. Brewer desired when he advised football was produced instantly; he developed manliness; he was promoted; he drew the attention, indeed the affection of his officer, Evans by name. It was a case of two dogs playing on a hearth-rug; one worrying a paper screw, snarling, snapping, giving a pinch, now and then, at the old dog's ear; the other lying somnolent, blinking at the fire, raising a paw, turning and growling good-temperedly. They had to be together, share with each other, fight with each other, quarrel with each other. But when Evans (Rezia who had only seen him once called him "a quiet man," a sturdy red-haired man, undemonstrative in the company of women), when Evans was killed, just before the Armistice, in Italy, Septimus, far from showing any emotion or recognising that here was the end of a friendship, congratulated himself upon feeling very little and very reasonably. The War had taught him. It was sublime. He had gone through the whole show, friendship, European War, death, had won promotion, was still under thirty and was bound to survive. He was right there. The last shells missed him. He watched them explode with indifference. When peace came he was in Milan, billeted in the house of an innkeeper with a courtyard, flowers in tubs, little tables in the open, daughters making hats, and to Lucrezia, the younger daughter, he became engaged one evening when the panic was on him—that he could not feel.

For now that it was all over, truce signed, and the dead buried, he had, especially in the evening, these sudden thunderclaps of fear. He could not feel. As he opened the door of the room where the Italian girls sat making hats, he could see them; could hear them; they were rubbing wires among coloured beads in saucers; they were turning buckram shapes this way and that; the table was all strewn with feathers, spangles, silks, ribbons; scissors were rapping on the table; but something failed him; he could not feel. Still, scissors rapping, girls laughing, hats being made protected him; he was assured of safety; he had a refuge. But he could not sit there all night. There were moments of waking in the early morning. The bed was falling; he was falling. Oh for the scissors and the lamplight and the buckram shapes! He asked Lucrezia to marry him, the younger of the two, the gay, the frivolous, with those little artist's fingers that she would hold up and say "It is all in them." Silk, feathers, what not were alive to them.

"It is the hat that matters most," she would say, when they walked out together. Every hat that passed, she would examine; and the cloak and the dress and the way the woman held herself. Ill-dressing, over-dressing she stigmatised, not savagely, rather with impatient movements of the hands, like those of a painter who puts from him some obvious well-meant glaring imposture; and then, generously, but always critically, she would welcome a shopgirl who had turned her little bit of stuff gallantly, or praise, wholly, with enthusiastic and professional understanding, a French lady descending from her carriage, in chinchilla, robes, pearls.

"Beautiful!" she would murmur, nudging Septimus, that he might see. But beauty was behind a pane of glass. Even taste

(Rezia liked ices, chocolates, sweet things) had no relish to him. He put down his cup on the little marble table. He looked at people outside; happy they seemed, collecting in the middle of the street, shouting, laughing, squabbling over nothing. But he could not taste, he could not feel. In the teashop among the tables and the chattering waiters the appalling fear came over him—he could not feel. He could reason; he could read, Dante for example, quite easily ("Septimus, do put down your book," said Rezia, gently shutting the *Inferno*), he could add up his bill; his brain was perfect; it must be the fault of the world then—that he could not feel.

"The English are so silent," Rezia said. She liked it, she said. She respected these Englishmen, and wanted to see London, and the English horses, and the tailor-made suits, and could remember hearing how wonderful the shops were, from an Aunt who had married and lived in Soho.

It might be possible, Septimus thought, looking at England from the train window, as they left Newhaven; it might be possible that the world itself is without meaning.

At the office they advanced him to a post of considerable responsibility. They were proud of him; he had won crosses. "You have done your duty; it is up to us—" began Mr. Brewer; and could not finish, so pleasurable was his emotion. They took admirable lodgings off the Tottenham Court Road.

Here he opened Shakespeare once more. That boy's business of the intoxication of language—*Antony and Cleopatra*—had shrivelled utterly. How Shakespeare loathed humanity—the putting on of clothes, the getting of children, the sordidity of the mouth and the belly! This was now revealed to Septimus; the message hidden in the beauty of words. The secret signal which one generation passes, under disguise, to the next is loathing, hatred, despair. Dante the same. Aeschylus (translated) the same. There Rezia sat at the table trimming hats. She trimmed hats for Mrs. Filmer's friends; she trimmed hats by the hour. She looked pale, mysterious, like a lily, drowned, under water, he thought.

"The English are so serious," she would say, putting her arms round Septimus, her cheek against his.

Love between man and woman was repulsive to Shakespeare. The business of copulation was filth to him before the end. But, Rezia said, she must have children. They had been married five years.

They went to the Tower together; to the Victoria and Albert Museum; stood in the crowd to see the King open Parliament. And there were the shops—hat shops, dress shops, shops with leather bags in the window, where she would stand staring. But she must have a boy.

She must have a son like Septimus, she said. But nobody could be like Septimus; so gentle; so serious; so clever. Could she not read Shakespeare too? Was Shakespeare a difficult author? she asked.

One cannot bring children into a world like this. One cannot perpetuate suffering, or increase the breed of these lustful animals, who have no lasting emotions, but only whims and vanities, eddying them now this way, now that.

He watched her snip, shape, as one watches a bird hop, flit in the grass, without daring to move a finger. For the truth is (let her ignore it) that human beings have neither kindness, nor faith, nor charity beyond what serves to increase the pleasure of the moment. They hunt in packs. Their packs scour the desert and vanish screaming into the wilderness. They desert the fallen. They are plastered over with grimaces. There was Brewer at the office, with his waxed moustache, coral tie-pin, white slip, and pleasurable emotions—all coldness and clamminess within,—his geraniums ruined in the War—his cook's nerves destroyed; or Amelia What'shername, handing round cups of tea punctually

at five—a leering, sneering obscene little harpy; and the Toms
and Berties in their starched shirt fronts oozing thick drops of
vice. They never saw him drawing pictures of them naked at their
antics in his notebook. In the street, vans roared past him; brutality blared out on placards; men were trapped in mines; women
burnt alive; and once a maimed file of lunatics being exercised or
displayed for the diversion of the populace (who laughed aloud),
ambled and nodded and grinned past him, in the Tottenham
Court Road, each half apologetically, yet triumphantly, inflicting
his hopeless woe. And would *he* go mad?

At tea Rezia told him that Mrs. Filmer's daughter was ex-
pecting a baby. *She* could not grow old and have no children! She
was very lonely, she was very unhappy! She cried for the first
time since they were married. Far away he heard her sobbing;
he heard it accurately, he noticed it distinctly; he compared it to
a piston thumping. But he felt nothing.

His wife was crying, and he felt nothing; only each time she
sobbed in this profound, this silent, this hopeless way, he descended another step into the pit.

At last, with a melodramatic gesture which he assumed me-
chanically and with complete consciousness of its insincerity,
he dropped his head on his hands. Now he had surrendered;
now other people must help him. People must be sent for. He
gave in.

Nothing could rouse him. Rezia put him to bed. She sent
for a doctor—Mrs. Filmer's Dr. Holmes. Dr. Holmes examined
him. There was nothing whatever the matter, said Dr. Holmes.
Oh, what a relief! What a kind man, what a good man! thought
Rezia. When he felt like that he went to the Music Hall, said Dr.
Holmes. He took a day off with his wife and played golf. Why
not try two tabloids of bromide dissolved in a glass of water at
bedtime? These old Bloomsbury houses, said Dr. Holmes, tapping the wall, are often full of very fine panelling, which the

landlords have the folly to paper over. Only the other day, visiting a patient, Sir Somebody Something in Bedford Square—

So there was no excuse; nothing whatever the matter, except the sin for which human nature had condemned him to death; that he did not feel. He had not cared when Evans was killed; that was worst; but all the other crimes raised their heads and shook their fingers and jeered and sneered over the rail of the bed in the early hours of the morning at the prostrate body which lay realising its degradation; how he had married his wife without loving her; had lied to her; seduced her; outraged Miss Isabel Pole, and was so pocked and marked with vice that women shuddered when they saw him in the street. The verdict of human nature on such a wretch was death.

Dr. Holmes came again. Large, fresh coloured, handsome, flicking his boots, looking in the glass, he brushed it all aside—headaches, sleeplessness, fears, dreams—nerve symptoms and nothing more, he said. If Dr. Holmes found himself even half a pound below eleven stone six, he asked his wife for another plate of porridge at breakfast. (Rezia would learn to cook porridge.) But, he continued, health is largely a matter in our own control. Throw yourself into outside interests; take up some hobby. He opened Shakespeare—*Antony and Cleopatra*; pushed Shakespeare aside. Some hobby, said Dr. Holmes, for did he not owe his own excellent health (and he worked as hard as any man in London) to the fact that he could always switch off from his patients on to old furniture? And what a very pretty comb, if he might say so, Mrs. Warren Smith was wearing!

When the damned fool came again, Septimus refused to see him. Did he indeed? said Dr. Holmes, smiling agreeably. Really he had to give that charming little lady, Mrs. Smith, a friendly push before he could get past her into her husband's bedroom.

"So you're in a funk," he said agreeably, sitting down by his patient's side. He had actually talked of killing himself to his wife, quite a girl, a foreigner, wasn't she? Didn't that give her a very odd idea of English husbands? Didn't one owe perhaps a duty to one's wife? Wouldn't it be better to do something instead of lying in bed? For he had had forty years' experience behind him; and Septimus could take Dr. Holmes's word for it—there was nothing whatever the matter with him. And next time Dr. Holmes came he hoped to find Smith out of bed and not making that charming little lady his wife anxious about him.

Human nature, in short, was on him—the repulsive brute, with the blood-red nostrils. Holmes was on him. Dr. Holmes came quite regularly every day. Once you stumble, Septimus wrote on the back of a postcard, human nature is on you. Holmes is on you. Their only chance was to escape, without letting Holmes know; to Italy—anywhere, anywhere, away from Dr. Holmes.

But Rezia could not understand him. Dr. Holmes was such a kind man. He was so interested in Septimus. He only wanted to help them, he said. He had four little children and he had asked her to tea, she told Septimus.

So he was deserted. The whole world was clamouring: Kill yourself, kill yourself, for our sakes. But why should he kill himself for their sakes? Food was pleasant; the sun hot; and this killing oneself, how does one set about it, with a table knife, uglily, with floods of blood,—by sucking a gaspipe? He was too weak; he could scarcely raise his hand. Besides, now that he was quite alone, condemned, deserted, as those who are about to die are alone, there was a luxury in it, an isolation full of sublimity; a freedom which the attached can never know. Holmes had won of course; the brute with the red nostrils had won. But even Holmes himself could not touch this last relic straying on the edge of the world, this outcast, who gazed back at the inhabited regions, who lay, like a drowned sailor, on the shore of the world.

It was at that moment (Rezia gone shopping) that the great revelation took place. A voice spoke from behind the screen. Evans was speaking. The dead were with him.

"Evans, Evans!" he cried.

Mr. Smith was talking aloud to himself, Agnes the servant girl cried to Mrs. Filmer in the kitchen. "Evans, Evans," he had said as she brought in the tray. She jumped, she did. She scuttled downstairs.

And Rezia came in, with her flowers, and walked across the room, and put the roses in a vase, upon which the sun struck directly, and it went laughing, leaping round the room.

She had had to buy the roses, Rezia said, from a poor man in the street. But they were almost dead already, she said, arranging the roses.

So there was a man outside; Evans presumably; and the roses, which Rezia said were half dead, had been picked by him in the fields of Greece. "Communication is health; communication is happiness, communication—" he muttered.

"What are you saying, Septimus?" Rezia asked, wild with terror, for he was talking to himself.

She sent Agnes running for Dr. Holmes. Her husband, she said, was mad. He scarcely knew her.

"You brute! You brute!" cried Septimus, seeing human nature, that is Dr. Holmes, enter the room.

"Now what's all this about?" said Dr. Holmes in the most amiable way in the world. "Talking nonsense to frighten your wife?" But he would give him something to make him sleep. And if they were rich people, said Dr. Holmes, looking ironically round the room, by all means let them go to Harley Street; if they had no confidence in him, said Dr. Holmes, looking not quite so kind.

It was precisely twelve o'clock; twelve by Big Ben; whose stroke was wafted over the northern part of London; blent with

that of other clocks, mixed in a thin ethereal way with the clouds
and wisps of smoke, and died up there among the seagulls—
twelve o'clock struck as Clarissa Dalloway laid her green dress
on her bed, and the Warren Smiths walked down Harley Street.
Twelve was the hour of their appointment. Probably, Rezia
thought, that was Sir William Bradshaw's house with the grey
motor car in front of it. The leaden circles dissolved in the air.

Indeed it was—Sir William Bradshaw's motor car; low,
powerful, grey with plain initials interlocked on the panel, as if
the pomps of heraldry were incongruous, this man being the
ghostly helper, the priest of science; and, as the motor car was
grey, so to match its sober suavity, grey furs, silver grey rugs
were heaped in it, to keep her ladyship warm while she waited.
For often Sir William would travel sixty miles or more down
into the country to visit the rich, the afflicted, who could afford
the very large fee which Sir William very properly charged for
his advice. Her ladyship waited with the rugs about her knees
an hour or more, leaning back, thinking sometimes of the
patient, sometimes, excusably, of the wall of gold, mounting
minute by minute while she waited; the wall of gold that was
mounting between them and all shifts and anxieties (she had
borne them bravely; they had had their struggles) until she felt
wedged on a calm ocean, where only spice winds blow; respected, admired, envied, with scarcely anything left to wish for,
though she regretted her stoutness; large dinner-parties every
Thursday night to the profession; an occasional bazaar to be
opened; Royalty greeted; too little time, alas, with her husband,
whose work grew and grew; a boy doing well at Eton; she would
have liked a daughter too; interests she had, however, in plenty;
child welfare; the after-care of the epileptic, and photography,
so that if there was a church building, or a church decaying, she
bribed the sexton, got the key and took photographs, which

were scarcely to be distinguished from the work of professionals, while she waited.

Sir William himself was no longer young. He had worked very hard; he had won his position by sheer ability (being the son of a shopkeeper); loved his profession; made a fine figurehead at ceremonies and spoke well—all of which had by the time he was knighted given him a heavy look, a weary look (the stream of patients being so incessant, the responsibilities and privileges of his profession so onerous), which weariness, together with his grey hairs, increased the extraordinary distinction of his presence and gave him the reputation (of the utmost importance in dealing with nerve cases) not merely of lightning skill, and almost infallible accuracy in diagnosis but of sympathy; tact; understanding of the human soul. He could see the first moment they came into the room (the Warren Smiths they were called); he was certain directly he saw the man; it was a case of extreme gravity. It was a case of complete breakdown—complete physical and nervous breakdown, with every symptom in an advanced stage, he ascertained in two or three minutes (writing answers to questions, murmured discreetly, on a pink card).

How long had Dr. Holmes been attending him?

Six weeks.

Prescribed a little bromide? Said there was nothing the matter? Ah yes (those general practitioners! thought Sir William. It took half his time to undo their blunders. Some were irreparable).

"You served with great distinction in the War?"

The patient repeated the word "war" interrogatively.

He was attaching meanings to words of a symbolical kind. A serious symptom, to be noted on the card.

"The War?" the patient asked. The European War—that

little shindy of schoolboys with gunpowder? Had he served with distinction? He really forgot. In the War itself he had failed.

"Yes, he served with the greatest distinction," Rezia assured the doctor; "he was promoted."

"And they have the very highest opinion of you at your office?" Sir William murmured, glancing at Mr. Brewer's very generously worded letter. "So that you have nothing to worry you, no financial anxiety, nothing?"

He had committed an appalling crime and been condemned to death by human nature.

"I have—I have," he began, "committed a crime—"

"He has done nothing wrong whatever," Rezia assured the doctor. If Mr. Smith would wait, said Sir William, he would speak to Mrs. Smith in the next room. Her husband was very seriously ill, Sir William said. Did he threaten to kill himself?

Oh, he did, she cried. But he did not mean it, she said. Of course not. It was merely a question of rest, said Sir William; of rest, rest, rest; a long rest in bed. There was a delightful home down in the country where her husband would be perfectly looked after. Away from her? she asked. Unfortunately, yes; the people we care for most are not good for us when we are ill. But he was not mad, was he? Sir William said he never spoke of "madness"; he called it not having a sense of proportion. But her husband did not like doctors. He would refuse to go there. Shortly and kindly Sir William explained to her the state of the case. He had threatened to kill himself. There was no alternative. It was a question of law. He would lie in bed in a beautiful house in the country. The nurses were admirable. Sir William would visit him once a week. If Mrs. Warren Smith was quite sure she had no more questions to ask—he never hurried his patients—they would return to her husband. She had nothing more to ask—not of Sir William.

So they returned to the most exalted of mankind; the crim-

inal who faced his judges; the victim exposed on the heights; the
fugitive; the drowned sailor; the poet of the immortal ode; the
Lord who had gone from life to death; to Septimus Warren
Smith, who sat in the arm-chair under the skylight staring at a
photograph of Lady Bradshaw in Court dress, muttering messages about beauty.

"We have had our little talk," said Sir William.

"He says you are very, very ill," Rezia cried.

"We have been arranging that you should go into a home,"
said Sir William.

"One of Holmes's homes?" sneered Septimus.

The fellow made a distasteful impression. For there was in
Sir William, whose father had been a tradesman, a natural respect for breeding and clothing, which shabbiness nettled;
again, more profoundly, there was in Sir William, who had never
had time for reading, a grudge, deeply buried, against cultivated
people who came into his room and intimated that doctors,
whose profession is a constant strain upon all the highest facul-
ties, are not educated men.

"One of *my* homes, Mr. Warren Smith," he said, "where we
will teach you to rest."

And there was just one thing more.

He was quite certain that when Mr. Warren Smith was well
he was the last man in the world to frighten his wife. But he had
talked of killing himself.

"We all have our moments of depression," said Sir William.

Once you fall, Septimus repeated to himself, human nature
is on you. Holmes and Bradshaw are on you. They scour the
desert. They fly screaming into the wilderness. The rack and the
thumbscrew are applied. Human nature is remorseless.

"Impulses came upon him sometimes?" Sir William asked,
with his pencil on a pink card.

That was his own affair, said Septimus.

"Nobody lives for himself alone," said Sir William, glancing at the photograph of his wife in Court dress.

"And you have a brilliant career before you," said Sir William. There was Mr. Brewer's letter on the table. "An exceptionally brilliant career."

But if he confessed? If he communicated? Would they let him off then, his torturers?

"I—I—" he stammered.

But what was his crime? He could not remember it.

"Yes?" Sir William encouraged him. (But it was growing late.)

Love, trees, there is no crime—what was his message?

He could not remember it.

"I—I—" Septimus stammered.

"Try to think as little about yourself as possible," said Sir William kindly. Really, he was not fit to be about.

Was there anything else they wished to ask him? Sir William would make all arrangements (he murmured to Rezia) and he would let her know between five and six that evening he murmured.

"Trust everything to me," he said, and dismissed them.

Never, never had Rezia felt such agony in her life! She had asked for help and been deserted! He had failed them! Sir William Bradshaw was not a nice man.

The upkeep of that motor car alone must cost him quite a lot, said Septimus, when they got out into the street.

She clung to his arm. They had been deserted.

But what more did she want?

To his patients he gave three-quarters of an hour; and if in this exacting science which has to do with what, after all, we know nothing about—the nervous system, the human brain—a doctor loses his sense of proportion, as a doctor he fails. Health we must have; and health is proportion; so that when a man comes into your room and says he is Christ (a common delusion), and has a message, as they mostly have, and threatens, as they often do, to kill himself, you invoke proportion; order rest in bed; rest in solitude; silence and rest; rest without friends, without books, without messages; six months' rest; until a man who went in weighing seven stone six comes out weighing twelve.

Proportion, divine proportion, Sir William's goddess, was acquired by Sir William walking hospitals, catching salmon, begetting one son in Harley Street by Lady Bradshaw, who caught salmon herself and took photographs scarcely to be distinguished from the work of professionals. Worshipping proportion, Sir William not only prospered himself but made England prosper, secluded her lunatics, forbade childbirth, penalised despair, made it impossible for the unfit to propagate their views until they, too, shared his sense of proportion—his, if they were men, Lady Bradshaw's if they were women (she embroidered, knitted, spent four nights out of seven at home with her son), so that not only did his colleagues respect him, his subordinates fear him, but the friends and relations of his patients felt for him the keenest gratitude for insisting that these prophetic Christs and Christesses, who prophesied the end of the world, or the advent of God, should drink milk in bed, as Sir William ordered; Sir William with his thirty years' experience of these kinds of cases, and his infallible instinct, this is madness, this sense; in fact, his sense of proportion.

But Proportion has a sister, less smiling, more formidable, a Goddess even now engaged—in the heat and sands of India, the mud and swamp of Africa, the purlieus of London, wherever in short the climate or the devil tempts men to fall from the true belief which is her own—is even now engaged in dashing down shrines, smashing idols, and setting up in their place her own stern countenance. Conversion is her name and she feasts on the wills of the weakly, loving to impress, to impose, adoring her own features stamped on the face of the populace. At Hyde Park Corner on a tub she stands preaching; shrouds herself in white and walks penitentially disguised as brotherly love through factories and parliaments; offers help, but desires power; smites out of her way roughly the dissentient, or dissatisfied; bestows her blessing on those who, looking upward, catch submissively from her eyes the light of their own. This lady too (Rezia Warren Smith divined it) had her dwelling in Sir William's heart, though concealed, as she mostly is, under some plausible disguise; some venerable name; love, duty, self sacrifice. How he would work — how toil to raise funds, propagate reforms, initiate institutions! But conversion, fastidious Goddess, loves blood better than brick, and feasts most subtly on the human will. For example, Lady Bradshaw. Fifteen years ago she had gone under. It was nothing you could put your finger on; there had been no scene, no snap; only the slow sinking, water-logged, of her will into his. Sweet was her smile, swift her submission; dinner in Harley Street, numbering eight or nine courses, feeding ten or fifteen guests of the professional classes, was smooth and urbane. Only as the evening wore on a very slight dulness, or uneasiness perhaps, a nervous twitch, fumble, stumble and confusion indicated, what it was really painful to believe — that the poor lady lied. Once, long ago, she had caught salmon freely: now, quick to minister to the craving which lit her husband's eye so oilily for dominion, for power, she cramped, squeezed, pared, pruned, drew back, peeped through; so that without knowing precisely what made the evening disagreeable, and caused this pressure on the top of the head (which might well be imputed to the professional conversation, or the fatigue of a great doctor whose life, Lady Bradshaw said, "is not his own but his patients'") disagreeable it was: so that guests, when the clock struck ten, breathed in the air of

Harley Street even with rapture; which relief, however, was de-
nied to his patients.

There in the grey room, with the pictures on the wall, and
the valuable furniture, under the ground glass skylight, they
learnt the extent of their transgressions; huddled up in arm-
chairs, they watched him go through, for their benefit, a curious
exercise with the arms, which he shot out, brought sharply back
to his hip, to prove (if the patient was obstinate) that Sir William
was master of his own actions, which the patient was not. There
some weakly broke down; sobbed, submitted; others, inspired
by Heaven knows what intemperate madness, called Sir William
to his face a damnable humbug; questioned, even more impi-
ously, life itself. Why live? they demanded. Sir William replied
that life was good. Certainly Lady Bradshaw in ostrich feathers
hung over the mantelpiece, and as for his income it was quite
twelve thousand a year. But to us, they protested, life has given
no such bounty. He acquiesced. They lacked a sense of proportion. And perhaps, after all, there is no God? He shrugged his
shoulders. In short, this living or not living is an affair of our
own? But there they were mistaken. Sir William had a friend in
Surrey where they taught, what Sir William frankly admitted was
a difficult art—a sense of proportion. There were, moreover,
family affection; honour; courage; and a brilliant career. All of
these had in Sir William a resolute champion. If they failed him,
he had to support police and the good of society, which, he re-
marked very quietly, would take care, down in Surrey, that these
unsocial impulses, bred more than anything by the lack of good
blood, were held in control. And then stole out from her hiding-
place and mounted her throne that Goddess whose lust is to
override opposition, to stamp indelibly in the sanctuaries of others the image of herself. Naked, defenceless, the exhausted, the
friendless received the impress of Sir William's will. He swooped;
he devoured. He shut people up. It was this combination of

decision and humanity that endeared Sir William so greatly to the relations of his victims.

But Rezia Warren Smith cried, walking down Harley Street, that she did not like that man.

Shredding and slicing, dividing and subdividing, the clocks of Harley Street nibbled at the June day, counselled submission, upheld authority, and pointed out in chorus the supreme advantages of a sense of proportion, until the mound of time was so far diminished that a commercial clock, suspended above a shop in Oxford Street, announced, genially and fraternally, as if it were a pleasure to Messrs. Rigby and Lowndes to give the information gratis, that it was half-past one.

Looking up, it appeared that each letter of their names stood for one of the hours; subconsciously one was grateful to Rigby and Lowndes for giving one time ratified by Greenwich; and this gratitude (so Hugh Whitbread ruminated, dallying there in front of the shop window), naturally took the form later of buying off Rigby and Lowndes socks or shoes. So he ruminated. It was his habit. He did not go deeply. He brushed surfaces; the dead languages, the living, life in Constantinople, Paris, Rome; riding, shooting, tennis, it had been once. The malicious asserted that he now kept guard at Buckingham Palace, dressed in silk stockings and knee-breeches, over what nobody knew. But he did it extremely efficiently. He had been afloat on the cream of English society for fifty-five years. He had known Prime Ministers. His affections were understood to be deep. And if it were true that he had not taken part in any of the great movements of the time or held important office, one or two humble reforms stood to his credit; an improvement in public shelters was one; the protection of owls in Norfolk another; servant girls had reason to be grateful to him; and his name at the end of letters to the *Times,* asking for funds, appealing to the public to protect, to preserve, to clear up litter, to abate smoke, and stamp out immorality in parks, commanded respect.

A magnificent figure he cut too, pausing for a moment (as the sound of the half hour died away) to look critically, magisterially, at socks and shoes; impeccable, substantial, as if he beheld the world from a certain eminence, and dressed to match; but realised the obligations which size, wealth, health, entail, and observed punctiliously even when not absolutely necessary, little courtesies, old-fashioned ceremonies which gave a quality to his manner, something to imitate, something to remember him by, for he would never lunch, for example, with Lady Bruton, whom he had known these twenty years, without bringing her in his outstretched hand a bunch of carnations and asking Miss Brush, Lady Bruton's secretary, after her brother in South Africa, which, for some reason, Miss Brush, deficient though she was in every attribute of female charm, so much resented that she said "Thank you, he's doing very well in South Africa," when, for half a dozen years, he had been doing badly in Portsmouth.

Lady Bruton herself preferred Richard Dalloway, who arrived at the next moment. Indeed they met on the doorstep.

Lady Bruton preferred Richard Dalloway of course. He was made of much finer material. But she wouldn't let them run down her poor dear Hugh. She could never forget his kindness—he had been really remarkably kind—she forgot precisely upon what occasion. But he had been—remarkably kind. Anyhow, the difference between one man and another does not amount to much. She had never seen the sense of cutting people up, as Clarissa Dalloway did—cutting them up and sticking them together again; not at any rate when one was sixty-two. She took Hugh's carnations with her angular grim smile. There was nobody else coming, she said. She had got them there on false pretences, to help her out of a difficulty—

"But let us eat first," she said.

And so there began a soundless and exquisite passing to and fro through swing doors of aproned white-capped maids, hand-maidens not of necessity, but adepts in a mystery or grand deception practised by hostesses in Mayfair from one-thirty to two, when, with a wave of the hand, the traffic ceases, and there rises instead this profound illusion in the first place about the food—how it is not paid for; and then that the table spreads itself voluntarily with glass and silver, little mats, saucers of red fruit; films of brown cream mask turbot; in casseroles severed chickens swim; coloured, undomestic, the fire burns; and with the wine and the coffee (not paid for) rise jocund visions before musing eyes; gently speculative eyes; eyes to whom life appears musical, mysterious; eyes now kindled to observe genially the beauty of the red carnations which Lady Bruton (whose movements were always angular) had laid beside her plate, so that Hugh Whitbread, feeling at peace with the entire universe and at the same time completely sure of his standing, said, resting his fork,

"Wouldn't they look charming against your lace?"

Miss Brush resented this familiarity intensely. She thought him an underbred fellow. She made Lady Bruton laugh.

Lady Bruton raised the carnations, holding them rather stiffly with much the same attitude with which the General held the scroll in the picture behind her; she remained fixed, tranced. Which was she now, the General's great-grand-daughter? great-great-grand-daughter? Richard Dalloway asked himself. Sir Roderick, Sir Miles, Sir Talbot—that was it. It was remarkable how in that family the likeness persisted in the women. She should have been a general of dragoons herself. And Richard would have served under her, cheerfully; he had the greatest respect for her; he cherished these romantic views about well-set-up old women of pedigree, and would have liked, in his good-humoured way, to bring some young hot-heads of his acquaintance to lunch with her; as if a type like hers could be bred of amiable tea-drinking enthusiasts! He knew her country. He knew her people. There was a vine, still bearing, which either Lovelace or Herrick—she never read a word of poetry herself, but so the story ran—had sat under. Better wait to put before them the question that bothered her (about making an appeal to the public; if so, in what terms and so on), better wait until they have had their coffee, Lady Bruton thought; and so laid the carnations down beside her plate.

"How's Clarissa?" she asked abruptly.

Clarissa always said that Lady Bruton did not like her. Indeed, Lady Bruton had the reputation of being more interested in politics than people; of talking like a man; of having had a finger in some notorious intrigue of the eighties, which was now beginning to be mentioned in memoirs. Certainly there was an alcove in her drawing-room, and a table in that alcove, and a photograph upon that table of General Sir Talbot Moore, now deceased, who had written there (one evening in the eighties) in Lady Bruton's presence, with her cognisance, perhaps advice, a telegram ordering the British troops to advance upon an historical occasion. (She kept the pen and told the story.) Thus, when she said in her offhand way "How's Clarissa?" husbands had difficulty in persuading their wives and indeed, however devoted, were secretly doubtful themselves, of her interest in women who often got in their husbands' way, prevented them from accepting posts abroad, and had to be taken to the seaside in the middle of the session to recover from influenza. Nevertheless her inquiry, "How's Clarissa?" was known by women infallibly, to be a signal from a well-wisher, from an almost silent companion, whose utterances (half a dozen perhaps in the course of a lifetime) signified recognition of some feminine comradeship which went beneath masculine lunch parties and united Lady Bruton and Mrs. Dalloway, who seldom met, and appeared when they did meet indifferent and even hostile, in a singular bond.

"I met Clarissa in the Park this morning," said Hugh Whitbread, diving into the casserole, anxious to pay himself this little tribute, for he had only to come to London and he met everybody at once; but greedy, one of the greediest men she had ever known, Milly Brush thought, who observed men with unflinching rectitude, and was capable of everlasting devotion, to her own sex in particular, being knobbed, scraped, angular, and entirely without feminine charm.

"D'you know who's in town?" said Lady Bruton suddenly bethinking her. "Our old friend, Peter Walsh."

They all smiled. Peter Walsh! And Mr. Dalloway was genuinely glad, Milly Brush thought; and Mr. Whitbread thought only of his chicken.

Peter Walsh! All three, Lady Bruton, Hugh Whitbread, and Richard Dalloway, remembered the same thing—how passionately Peter had been in love; been rejected; gone to India; come a cropper; made a mess of things; and Richard Dalloway had a very great liking for the dear old fellow too. Milly Brush saw that; saw a depth in the brown of his eyes; saw him hesitate; consider; which interested her, as Mr. Dalloway always interested her, for what was he thinking, she wondered, about Peter Walsh?

That Peter Walsh had been in love with Clarissa; that he would go back directly after lunch and find Clarissa; that he would tell her, in so many words, that he loved her. Yes, he would say that.

Milly Brush once might almost have fallen in love with these silences; and Mr. Dalloway was always so dependable; such a gentleman too. Now, being forty, Lady Bruton had only to nod, or turn her head a little abruptly, and Milly Brush took the signal, however deeply she might be sunk in these reflections of a detached spirit, of an uncorrupted soul whom life could not bamboozle, because life had not offered her a trinket of the slightest value; not a curl, smile, lip, cheek, nose; nothing whatever; Lady Bruton had only to nod, and Perkins was instructed to quicken the coffee.

"Yes; Peter Walsh has come back," said Lady Bruton. It was vaguely flattering to them all. He had come back, battered, unsuccessful, to their secure shores. But to help him, they reflected, was impossible; there was some flaw in his character. Hugh Whitbread said one might of course mention his name to So-and-so. He wrinkled lugubriously, consequentially, at the thought of the letters he would write to the heads of Government offices about "my old friend, Peter Walsh," and so on. But it wouldn't lead to anything—not to anything permanent, because of his character.

"In trouble with some woman," said Lady Bruton. They had all guessed that *that* was at the bottom of it.

"However," said Lady Bruton, anxious to leave the subject, "we shall hear the whole story from Peter himself."

(The coffee was very slow in coming.)

"The address?" murmured Hugh Whitbread; and there was at once a ripple in the grey tide of service which washed round Lady Bruton day in, day out, collecting, intercepting, enveloping her in a fine tissue which broke concussions, mitigated interruptions, and spread round the house in Brook Street a fine net where things lodged and were picked out accurately, instantly, by grey-haired Perkins, who had been with Lady Bruton these thirty years and now wrote down the address; handed it to Mr. Whitbread, who took out his pocketbook, raised his eyebrows, and slipping it in among documents of the highest importance, said that he would get Evelyn to ask him to lunch.

(They were waiting to bring the coffee until Mr. Whitbread had finished.)

Hugh was very slow, Lady Bruton thought. He was getting fat, she noticed. Richard always kept himself in the pink of condition. She was getting impatient; the whole of her being was setting positively, undeniably, domineeringly brushing aside all this unnecessary trifling (Peter Walsh and his affairs) upon that subject which engaged her attention, and not merely her attention, but that fibre which was the ramrod of her soul, that essential part of her without which Millicent Bruton would not have been Millicent Bruton; that project for emigrating young people of both sexes born of respectable parents and setting them up with a fair prospect of doing well in Canada. She exaggerated. She had perhaps lost her sense of proportion. Emigration was not to others the obvious remedy, the sublime conception. It was not to them (not to Hugh, or Richard, or even to devoted Miss Brush) the liberator of the pent egotism, which a strong martial woman, well nourished, well descended, of direct impulses, downright feelings, and little introspective power (broad and simple—why could not every one be broad and simple? she asked) feels rise within her, once youth is past, and must eject upon some object—it may be Emigration, it may be Emancipation; but whatever it be, this object round which the essence of her soul is daily secreted, becomes inevitably prismatic, lustrous, half looking-glass, half precious stone; now carefully hidden in case people should sneer at it; now proudly displayed. Emigration had become, in short, largely Lady Bruton.

But she had to write. And one letter to the *Times*, she used to say to Miss Brush, cost her more than to organise an expedition to South Africa (which she had done in the war). After a morning's battle beginning, tearing up, beginning again, she used to feel the futility of her own womanhood as she felt it on no other occasion, and would turn gratefully to the thought of Hugh Whitbread who possessed—no one could doubt it—the art of writing letters to the *Times*.

A being so differently constituted from herself, with such a command of language; able to put things as editors like them put; had passions which one could not call simply greed. Lady Bruton often suspended judgement upon men in deference to the mysterious accord in which they, but no woman, stood to the laws of the universe; knew how to put things; knew what was said; so that if Richard advised her, and Hugh wrote for her, she was sure of being somehow right. So she let Hugh eat his soufflé; asked after poor Evelyn; waited until they were smoking, and then said,

"Milly, would you fetch the papers?"

And Miss Brush went out, came back; laid papers on the table; and Hugh produced his fountain pen; his silver fountain pen, which had done twenty years' service, he said, unscrewing the cap. It was still in perfect order; he had shown it to the makers; there was no reason, they said, why it should ever wear out; which was somehow to Hugh's credit, and to the credit of the sentiments which his pen expressed (so Richard Dalloway felt) as Hugh began carefully writing capital letters with rings round them in the margin, and thus marvellously reduced Lady Bruton's tangles to sense, to grammar such as the editor of the *Times,* Lady Bruton felt, watching the marvellous transformation, must respect. Hugh was slow. Hugh was pertinacious. Richard said one must take risks. Hugh proposed modifications in deference to people's feelings, which, he said rather tartly when Richard laughed, "had to be considered," and read out "how, therefore, we are of opinion that the times are ripe . . . the superfluous youth of our ever-increasing population . . . what we owe to the dead . . ." which Richard thought all stuffing and bunkum, but no harm in it, of course, and Hugh went on drafting sentiments in alphabetical order of the highest nobility, brushing the cigar ash from his waistcoat, and summing up now and then the progress they had made until, finally, he read out the draft of a letter which Lady Bruton felt certain was a masterpiece. Could her own meaning sound like that?

Hugh could not guarantee that the editor would put it in; but he would be meeting somebody at luncheon.

Whereupon Lady Bruton, who seldom did a graceful thing, stuffed all Hugh's carnations into the front of her dress, and flinging her hands out called him "My Prime Minister!" What she would have done without them both she did not know. They rose. And Richard Dalloway strolled off as usual to have a look at the General's portrait, because he meant, whenever he had a moment of leisure, to write a history of Lady Bruton's family.

And Millicent Bruton was very proud of her family. But they could wait, they could wait, she said, looking at the picture; meaning that her family, of military men, administrators, admirals, had been men of action, who had done their duty; and Richard's first duty was to his country, but it was a fine face, she said; and all the papers were ready for Richard down at Aldmixton whenever the time came; the Labour Government she meant. "Ah, the news from India!" she cried.

And then, as they stood in the hall taking yellow gloves from the bowl on the malachite table and Hugh was offering Miss Brush with quite unnecessary courtesy some discarded ticket or other compliment, which she loathed from the depths of her heart and blushed brick red, Richard turned to Lady Bruton, with his hat in his hand, and said,

"We shall see you at our party to-night?" whereupon Lady Bruton resumed the magnificence which letter-writing had shattered. She might come; or she might not come. Clarissa had wonderful energy. Parties terrified Lady Bruton. But then, she was getting old. So she intimated, standing at her doorway; handsome; very erect; while her chow stretched behind her, and

Miss Brush disappeared into the background with her hands full of papers.

And Lady Bruton went ponderously, majestically, up to her room, lay, one arm extended, on the sofa. She sighed, she snored, not that she was asleep, only drowsy and heavy, drowsy and heavy, like a field of clover in the sunshine this hot June day, with the bees going round and about and the yellow butterflies. Always she went back to those fields down in Devonshire, where she had jumped the brooks on Patty, her pony, with Mortimer and Tom, her brothers. And there were the dogs; there were the rats; there were her father and mother on the lawn under the trees, with the tea-things out, and the beds of dahlias, the hollyhocks, the pampas grass; and they, little wretches, always up to some mischief! stealing back through the shrubbery, so as not to be seen, all bedraggled from some roguery. What old nurse used to say about her frocks!

Ah dear, she remembered—it was Wednesday in Brook Street. Those kind good fellows, Richard Dalloway, Hugh Whitbread, had gone this hot day through the streets whose growl came up to her lying on the sofa. Power was hers, position, income. She had lived in the forefront of her time. She had had good friends; known the ablest men of her day. Murmuring London flowed up to her, and her hand, lying on the sofa back, curled upon some imaginary baton such as her grandfathers might have held, holding which she seemed, drowsy and heavy, to be commanding battalions marching to Canada, and those good fellows walking across London, that territory of theirs, that little bit of carpet, Mayfair.

And they went further and further from her, being attached to her by a thin thread (since they had lunched with her) which would stretch and stretch, get thinner and thinner as they walked across London; as if one's friends were attached to one's body, after lunching with them, by a thin thread, which (as she dozed there) became hazy with the sound of bells, striking the hour or ringing to service, as a single spider's thread is blotted with rain-drops, and, burdened, sags down. So she slept.

And Richard Dalloway and Hugh Whitbread hesitated at the corner of Conduit Street at the very moment that Millicent Bruton, lying on the sofa, let the thread snap; snored. Contrary winds buffeted at the street corner. They looked in at a shop window; they did not wish to buy or to talk but to part, only with contrary winds buffeting the street corner, with some sort of lapse in the tides of the body, two forces meeting in a swirl, morning and afternoon, they paused. Some newspaper placard went up in the air, gallantly, like a kite at first, then paused, swooped, fluttered; and a lady's veil hung. Yellow awnings trembled. The speed of the morning traffic slackened, and single carts rattled carelessly down half-empty streets. In Norfolk, of which Richard Dalloway was half thinking, a soft warm wind blew back the petals; confused the waters; ruffled the flowering grasses. Haymakers, who had pitched beneath hedges to sleep away the morning toil, parted curtains of green blades; moved trembling globes of cow parsley to see the sky; the blue, the steadfast, the blazing summer sky.

Aware that he was looking at a silver two-handled Jacobean mug, and that Hugh Whitbread admired condescendingly with airs of connoisseurship a Spanish necklace which he thought of asking the price of in case Evelyn might like it—still Richard was torpid; could not think or move. Life had thrown up this wreckage; shop windows full of coloured paste, and one stood stark with the lethargy of the old, stiff with the rigidity of the old, looking in. Evelyn Whitbread might like to buy this Spanish necklace—so she might. Yawn he must. Hugh was going into the shop.

"Right you are!" said Richard, following.

Goodness knows he didn't want to go buying necklaces with Hugh. But there are tides in the body. Morning meets afternoon. Borne like a frail shallop on deep, deep floods, Lady Bruton's great-grandfather and his memoir and his campaigns in North America were whelmed and sunk. And Millicent Bruton too. She went under. Richard didn't care a straw what became of Emigration; about that letter, whether the editor put it in or not. The necklace hung stretched between Hugh's admirable fingers. Let him give it to a girl, if he must buy jewels — any girl, any girl in the street. For the worthlessness of this life did strike Richard pretty forcibly — buying necklaces for Evelyn. If he'd had a boy he'd have said, Work, work. But he had his Elizabeth; he adored his Elizabeth.

"I should like to see Mr. Dubonnet," said Hugh in his curt worldly way. It appeared that this Dubonnet had the measurements of Mrs. Whitbread's neck, or, more strangely still, knew her views upon Spanish jewellery and the extent of her possessions in that line (which Hugh could not remember). All of which seemed to Richard Dalloway awfully odd. For he never gave Clarissa presents, except a bracelet two or three years ago, which had not been a success. She never wore it. It pained him to remember that she never wore it. And as a single spider's thread after wavering here and there attaches itself to the point of a leaf, so Richard's mind, recovering from its lethargy, set now on his wife, Clarissa, whom Peter Walsh had loved so passionately; and Richard had had a sudden vision of her there at luncheon; of himself and Clarissa; of their life together; and he drew the tray of old jewels towards him, and taking up first this brooch then that ring, "How much is that?" he asked, but doubted his own taste. He wanted to open the drawing-room door and come in holding out something; a present for Clarissa. Only what? But Hugh was on his legs again. He was unspeakably pompous. Really, after dealing here for thirty-five years he was not going to be put off by a mere boy who did not know his business. For Dubonnet, it seemed, was out, and Hugh would not buy anything until Mr. Dubonnet chose to be in; at which the youth flushed and bowed his correct little bow. It was all perfectly correct. And yet Richard couldn't have said that to save his life! Why these people stood that damned insolence he could not conceive. Hugh was becoming an intolerable ass. Richard Dalloway could not stand more than an hour of his society. And, flicking his bowler hat by way of farewell, Richard turned at the corner of Conduit Street eager, yes, very eager, to travel that spider's thread of attachment between himself and Clarissa; he would go straight to her, in Westminster.

But he wanted to come in holding something. Flowers? Yes, flowers, since he did not trust his taste in gold; any number of flowers, roses, orchids, to celebrate what was, reckoning things as you will, an event; this feeling about her when they spoke of Peter Walsh at luncheon; and they never spoke of it; not for years had they spoken of it; which, he thought, grasping his red and white roses together (a vast bunch in tissue paper), is the greatest mistake in the world. The time comes when it can't be said; one's too shy to say it, he thought, pocketing his sixpence or two of change, setting off with his great bunch held against his body to Westminster to say straight out in so many words (whatever she might think of him), holding out his flowers, "I love you." Why not? Really it was a miracle thinking of the war, and thousands of poor chaps, with all their lives before them, shovelled together, already half forgotten; it was a miracle. Here he was walking across London to say to Clarissa in so many words that he loved her. Which one never does say, he thought. Partly one's lazy; partly one's shy. And Clarissa—it was difficult to think of her; except in starts, as at luncheon, when he saw her quite distinctly; their whole life. He stopped at the crossing; and repeated—being simple by nature, and undebauched, because he had tramped, and shot; being pertinacious and dogged, having championed the downtrodden and followed his instincts in the House of Commons; being preserved in his simplicity yet at the same time grown rather speechless, rather stiff—he repeated that it was a miracle that he should have married Clarissa; a miracle—his life had been a miracle, he thought; hesitating to cross. But it did make his blood boil to see little creatures of five or six crossing Piccadilly alone. The police ought to have stopped the traffic at once. He had no illusions about the London police. Indeed, he was collecting evidence of their malpractices; and those costermongers, not allowed to stand their barrows in the streets; and prostitutes, good Lord, the fault wasn't in them, nor in young men either, but in our detestable social system and so forth; all of which he considered, could be seen considering, grey, dogged, dapper, clean, as he walked across the Park to tell his wife that he loved her.

For he would say it in so many words, when he came into the room. Because it is a thousand pities never to say what one feels, he thought, crossing the Green Park and observing with pleasure how in the shade of the trees whole families, poor families, were sprawling; children kicking up their legs; sucking milk; paper bags thrown about, which could easily be picked up (if people objected) by one of those fat gentlemen in livery; for he was of opinion that every park, and every square, during the summer months should be open to children (the grass of the park flushed and faded, lighting up the poor mothers of Westminster and their crawling babies, as if a yellow lamp were moved beneath). But what could be done for female vagrants like that poor creature, stretched on her elbow (as if she had flung herself on the earth, rid of all ties, to observe curiously, to speculate boldly, to consider the whys and the wherefores, impudent, loose-lipped, humorous), he did not know. Bearing his flowers like a weapon, Richard Dalloway approached her; intent

he passed her; still there was time for a spark between them—
she laughed at the sight of him, he smiled good-humouredly,
considering the problem of the female vagrant; not that they
would ever speak. But he would tell Clarissa that he loved her,
in so many words. He had, once upon a time, been jealous of
Peter Walsh; jealous of him and Clarissa. But she had often said
to him that she had been right not to marry Peter Walsh; which,
knowing Clarissa, was obviously true; she wanted support. Not
that she was weak; but she wanted support.

As for Buckingham Palace (like an old prima donna facing
the audience all in white) you can't deny it a certain dignity, he
considered, nor despise what does, after all, stand to millions of
people (a little crowd was waiting at the gate to see the King
drive out) for a symbol, absurd though it is; a child with a box
of bricks could have done better, he thought; looking at the memorial to Queen Victoria (whom he could remember in her
horn spectacles driving through Kensington), its white mound,
its billowing motherliness; but he liked being ruled by the descendant of Horsa; he liked continuity; and the sense of handing on the traditions of the past. It was a great age in which to
have lived. Indeed, his own life was a miracle; let him make no
mistake about it; here he was, in the prime of life, walking to his
house in Westminster to tell Clarissa that he loved her. Happiness is this, he thought.

It is this, he said, as he entered Dean's Yard. Big Ben was
beginning to strike, first the warning, musical; then the hour, irrevocable. Lunch parties waste the entire afternoon, he thought,
approaching his door.

The sound of Big Ben flooded Clarissa's drawing-room,
where she sat, ever so annoyed, at her writing-table; worried; annoyed. It was perfectly true that she had not asked Ellie Henderson to her party; but she had done it on purpose. Now Mrs.

Marsham wrote "she had told Ellie Henderson she would ask Clarissa—Ellie so much wanted to come."

But why should she invite all the dull women in London to her parties? Why should Mrs. Marsham interfere? And there was Elizabeth closeted all this time with Doris Kilman. Anything more nauseating she could not conceive. Prayer at this hour with that woman. And the sound of the bell flooded the room with its melancholy wave; which receded, and gathered itself together to fall once more, when she heard, distractingly, something fumbling, something scratching at the door. Who at this hour? Three, good Heavens! Three already! For with overpowering directness and dignity the clock struck three; and she heard nothing else; but the door handle slipped round and in came Richard! What a surprise! In came Richard, holding out flowers. She had failed him, once at Constantinople; and Lady Bruton, whose lunch parties were said to be extraordinarily amusing, had not asked her. He was holding out flowers— roses, red and white roses. (But he could not bring himself to say he loved her; not in so many words.)

But how lovely, she said, taking his flowers. She understood; she understood without his speaking; his Clarissa. She put them in vases on the mantelpiece. How lovely they looked! she said. And was it amusing, she asked? Had Lady Bruton asked after her? Peter Walsh was back. Mrs. Marsham had written. Must she ask Ellie Henderson? That woman Kilman was upstairs.

"But let us sit down for five minutes," said Richard.

It all looked so empty. All the chairs were against the wall. What had they been doing? Oh, it was for the party; no, he had not forgotten, the party. Peter Walsh was back. Oh yes; she had had him. And he was going to get a divorce; and he was in love with some woman out there. And he hadn't changed in the slightest. There she was, mending her dress. . . .

"Thinking of Bourton," she said.

"Hugh was at lunch," said Richard. She had met him too! Well, he was getting absolutely intolerable. Buying Evelyn necklaces; fatter than ever; an intolerable ass.

"And it came over me 'I might have married you,'" she said, thinking of Peter sitting there in his little bow-tie; with that knife, opening it, shutting it. "Just as he always was, you know."

They were talking about him at lunch, said Richard. (But he could not tell her he loved her. He held her hand. Happiness is this, he thought.) They had been writing a letter to the *Times* for Millicent Bruton. That was about all Hugh was fit for.

"And our dear Miss Kilman?" he asked. Clarissa thought the roses absolutely lovely; first bunched together; now of their own accord starting apart.

"Kilman arrives just as we've done lunch," she said. "Elizabeth turns pink. They shut themselves up. I suppose they're praying."

Lord! He didn't like it; but these things pass over if you let them.

"In a mackintosh with an umbrella," said Clarissa.

He had not said "I love you"; but he held her hand. Happiness is this, is this, he thought.

"But why should I ask all the dull women in London to my parties?" said Clarissa. And if Mrs. Marsham gave a party, did *she* invite her guests?

"Poor Ellie Henderson," said Richard—it was a very odd thing how much Clarissa minded about her parties, he thought.

But Richard had no notion of the look of a room. However—what was he going to say?

If she worried about these parties he would not let her give them. Did she wish she had married Peter? But he must go.

He must be off, he said, getting up. But he stood for a moment as if he were about to say something; and she wondered what? Why? There were the roses.

"Some Committee?" she asked, as he opened the door.

"Armenians," he said; or perhaps it was "Albanians."

And there is a dignity in people; a solitude; even between husband and wife a gulf; and that one must respect, thought Clarissa, watching him open the door; for one would not part with it oneself, or take it, against his will, from one's husband, without losing one's independence, one's self-respect—something, after all, priceless.

He returned with a pillow and a quilt.

"An hour's complete rest after luncheon," he said. And he went.

How like him! He would go on saying "An hour's complete rest after luncheon" to the end of time, because a doctor had ordered it once. It was like him to take what doctors said literally; part of his adorable, divine simplicity, which no one had to the same extent; which made him go and do the thing while she and Peter frittered their time away bickering. He was already halfway to the House of Commons, to his Armenians, his Albanians, having settled her on the sofa, looking at his roses. And people would say, "Clarissa Dalloway is spoilt." She cared much more for her roses than for the Armenians. Hunted out of existence, maimed, frozen, the victims of cruelty and injustice (she had heard Richard say so over and over again)—no, she could feel nothing for the Albanians, or was it the Armenians? but she loved her roses (didn't that help the Armenians?)—the only flowers she could bear to see cut. But Richard was already at the House of Commons; at his Committee, having settled all her difficulties. But no; alas, that was not true. He did not see the reasons against asking Ellie Henderson. She would do it, of course, as he wished it. Since he had brought the pillows, she would lie down. . . . But—but—why did she suddenly feel, for no reason that she could discover, desperately unhappy? As a person who has dropped some grain of pearl or diamond into the grass and parts the tall blades very carefully, this way and that, and searches here and there vainly, and at last spies it there at the roots, so she went through one thing and another; no, it was not Sally Seton saying that Richard would never be in the Cabinet because he had a second-class brain (it came back to her); no, she did not mind that; nor was it to do with Elizabeth either and Doris Kilman; those were facts. It was a feeling, some unpleasant feeling, earlier in the day perhaps; something that Peter had said, combined with some depression of her own, in her bedroom, taking off her hat; and what Richard had said had added to it, but what had he said? There were his roses. Her parties! That was it! Her parties! Both of them criticised her very unfairly, laughed at her very unjustly, for her parties. That was it! That was it!

Well, how was she going to defend herself? Now that she knew what it was, she felt perfectly happy. They thought, or Peter at any rate thought, that she enjoyed imposing herself; liked to have famous people about her; great names; was simply a snob in short. Well, Peter might think so. Richard merely thought it foolish of her to like excitement when she knew it was bad for her heart. It was childish, he thought. And both were quite wrong. What she liked was simply life.

"That's what I do it for," she said, speaking aloud, to life.

Since she was lying on the sofa, cloistered, exempt, the presence of this thing which she felt to be so obvious became physically existent; with robes of sound from the street, sunny, with hot breath, whispering, blowing out the blinds. But suppose Peter said to her, "Yes, yes, but your parties—what's the sense of your parties?" all she could say was (and nobody could be expected to understand): They're an offering; which sounded horribly vague. But who was Peter to make out that life was all plain

sailing?—Peter always in love, always in love with the wrong
woman? What's your love? she might say to him. And she knew
his answer; how it is the most important thing in the world and
no woman possibly understood it. Very well. But could any man
understand what she meant either? about life? She could not
imagine Peter or Richard taking the trouble to give a party for
no reason whatever.

But to go deeper, beneath what people said (and these
judgements, how superficial, how fragmentary they are!) in her
own mind now, what did it mean to her, this thing she called
life? Oh, it was very queer. Here was So-and-so in South Kensington; some one up in Bayswater; and somebody else, say, in
Mayfair. And she felt quite continuously a sense of their existence; and she felt what a waste; and she felt what a pity; and
she felt if only they could be brought together; so she did it.
And it was an offering; to combine, to create; but to whom?

An offering for the sake of offering, perhaps. Anyhow, it
was her gift. Nothing else had she of the slightest importance;
could not think, write, even play the piano. She muddled Armenians and Turks; loved success; hated discomfort; must be liked;
talked oceans of nonsense: and to this day, ask her what the
Equator was, and she did not know.

All the same, that one day should follow another; Wednesday, Thursday, Friday, Saturday; that one should wake up in the
morning; see the sky; walk in the park; meet Hugh Whitbread;
then suddenly in came Peter; then these roses; it was enough.
After that, how unbelievable death was!—that it must end; and
no one in the whole world would know how she had loved it all;
how, every instant . . .

The door opened. Elizabeth knew that her mother was resting. She came in very quietly. She stood perfectly still. Was it that
some Mongol had been wrecked on the coast of Norfolk (as
Mrs. Hilbery said), had mixed with the Dalloway ladies, perhaps,

a hundred years ago? For the Dalloways, in general, were fair-haired; blue-eyed; Elizabeth, on the contrary, was dark; had Chinese eyes in a pale face; an Oriental mystery; was gentle, considerate, still. As a child, she had had a perfect sense of humour; but now at seventeen, why, Clarissa could not in the least understand, she had become very serious; like a hyacinth, sheathed in glossy green, with buds just tinted, a hyacinth which has had no sun.

She stood quite still and looked at her mother; but the door was ajar, and outside the door was Miss Kilman, as Clarissa knew; Miss Kilman in her mackintosh, listening to whatever they said.

Yes, Miss Kilman stood on the landing, and wore a mackintosh; but had her reasons. First, it was cheap; second, she was over forty; and did not, after all, dress to please. She was poor, moreover; degradingly poor. Otherwise she would not be taking jobs from people like the Dalloways; from rich people, who liked to be kind. Mr. Dalloway, to do him justice, had been kind. But Mrs. Dalloway had not. She had been merely condescending. She came from the most worthless of all classes—the rich, with a smattering of culture. They had expensive things everywhere; pictures, carpets, lots of servants. She considered that she had a perfect right to anything that the Dalloways did for her.

She had been cheated. Yes, the word was no exaggeration, for surely a girl has a right to some kind of happiness? And she had never been happy, what with being so clumsy and so poor. And then, just as she might have had a chance at Miss Dolby's school, the war came; and she had never been able to tell lies. Miss Dolby thought she would be happier with people who shared her views about the Germans. She had had to go. It was true that the family was of German origin; spelt the name Kiehlman in the eighteenth century; but her brother had been killed. They turned her out because she would not pretend that the Germans were all villains—when she had German friends, when the only happy days of her life had been spent in Germany! And after all, she could read history. She had had to take whatever she could get. Mr. Dalloway had come across her working for the Friends. He had allowed her (and that was really generous of him) to teach his daughter history. Also she did a little Extension lecturing and so on. Then Our Lord had come to her (and here she always bowed her head). She had seen the light two years and three months ago. Now she did not envy women like Clarissa Dalloway; she pitied them.

She pitied and despised them from the bottom of her heart, as she stood on the soft carpet, looking at the old engraving of a little girl with a muff. With all this luxury going on, what hope was there for a better state of things? Instead of lying on a sofa—"My mother is resting," Elizabeth had said—she should have been in a factory; behind a counter; Mrs. Dalloway and all the other fine ladies!

Bitter and burning, Miss Kilman had turned in to a church two years three months ago. She had heard the Rev. Edward Whittaker preach; the boys sing; had seen the solemn lights descend, and whether it was the music, or the voices (she herself when alone in the evening found comfort in a violin; but the sound was excruciating; she had no ear), the hot and turbulent feelings which boiled and surged in her had been assuaged as she sat there, and she had wept copiously, and gone to call on Mr. Whittaker at his private house in Kensington. It was the hand of God, he said. The Lord had shown her the way. So now, whenever the hot and painful feelings boiled within her, this hatred of Mrs. Dalloway, this grudge against the world, she thought of God. She thought of Mr. Whittaker. Rage was succeeded by calm. A sweet savour filled her veins, her lips parted, and, standing formidable upon the landing in her mackintosh, she looked with steady and sinister serenity at Mrs. Dalloway, who came out with her daughter.

Elizabeth said she had forgotten her gloves. That was because Miss Kilman and her mother hated each other. She could not bear to see them together. She ran upstairs to find her gloves.

But Miss Kilman did not hate Mrs. Dalloway. Turning her large gooseberry-coloured eyes upon Clarissa, observing her small pink face, her delicate body, her air of freshness and fashion, Miss Kilman felt, Fool! Simpleton! You who have known neither sorrow nor pleasure; who have trifled your life away! And there rose in her an overmastering desire to overcome her; to unmask her. If she could have felled her it would have eased her. But it was not the body; it was the soul and its mockery that she wished to subdue; make feel her mastery. If only she could make her weep; could ruin her; humiliate her; bring her to her knees crying, You are right! But this was God's will, not Miss Kilman's. It was to be a religious victory. So she glared; so she glowered.

Clarissa was really shocked. This a Christian—this woman! This woman had taken her daughter from her! She in touch with invisible presences! Heavy, ugly, commonplace, without kindness or grace, she know the meaning of life!

"You are taking Elizabeth to the Stores?" Mrs. Dalloway said.

Miss Kilman said she was. They stood there. Miss Kilman was not going to make herself agreeable. She had always earned her living. Her knowledge of modern history was thorough in the extreme. She did out of her meagre income set aside so much for causes she believed in; whereas this woman did nothing, believed nothing; brought up her daughter—but here was Elizabeth, rather out of breath, the beautiful girl.

So they were going to the Stores. Odd it was, as Miss Kilman stood there (and stand she did, with the power and taciturnity of some prehistoric monster armoured for primeval warfare), how, second by second, the idea of her diminished, how hatred (which was for ideas, not people) crumbled, how she lost her malignity, her size, became second by second merely Miss Kilman, in a mackintosh, whom Heaven knows Clarissa would have liked to help.

At this dwindling of the monster, Clarissa laughed. Saying good-bye, she laughed.

Off they went together, Miss Kilman and Elizabeth, downstairs.

With a sudden impulse, with a violent anguish, for this woman was taking her daughter from her, Clarissa leant over the bannisters and cried out, "Remember the party! Remember our party to-night!"

But Elizabeth had already opened the front door; there was a van passing; she did not answer.

Love and religion! thought Clarissa, going back into the drawing-room, tingling all over. How detestable, how detestable they are! For now that the body of Miss Kilman was not before her, it overwhelmed her—the idea. The cruelest things in the world, she thought, seeing them clumsy, hot, domineering, hypocritical, eavesdropping, jealous, infinitely cruel and unscrupulous, dressed in a mackintosh coat, on the landing; love and religion. Had she ever tried to convert any one herself? Did she not wish everybody merely to be themselves? And she watched out of the window the old lady opposite climbing upstairs. Let her climb upstairs if she wanted to; let her stop; then let her, as Clarissa had often seen her, gain her bedroom, part her curtains, and disappear again into the background. Somehow one respected that—that old woman looking out of the window, quite unconscious that she was being watched. There was something solemn in it—but love and religion would destroy that, whatever it was, the privacy of the soul. The odious Kilman would destroy it. Yet it was a sight that made her want to cry.

Love destroyed too. Everything that was fine, everything that was true went. Take Peter Walsh now. There was a man, charming, clever, with ideas about everything. If you wanted to know about Pope, say, or Addison, or just to talk nonsense, what people were like, what things meant, Peter knew better than any one. It was Peter who had helped her; Peter who had lent her books. But look at the women he loved—vulgar, trivial, commonplace. Think of Peter in love—he came to see her after all these years, and what did he talk about? Himself. Horrible passion! she thought. Degrading passion! she thought, thinking of Kilman and her Elizabeth walking to the Army and Navy Stores.

Big Ben struck the half-hour.

How extraordinary it was, strange, yes, touching, to see the old lady (they had been neighbours ever so many years) move away from the window, as if she were attached to that sound, that string. Gigantic as it was, it had something to do with her. Down, down, into the midst of ordinary things the finger fell making the moment solemn. She was forced, so Clarissa imagined, by that sound, to move, to go—but where? Clarissa tried to follow her as she turned and disappeared, and could still just see her white cap moving at the back of the bedroom. She was still there moving about at the other end of the room. Why creeds and prayers and mackintoshes? when, thought Clarissa, that's the miracle, that's the mystery; that old lady, she meant, whom she could see going from chest of drawers to dressing-table. She could still see her. And the supreme mystery which Kilman might say she had solved, or Peter might say he had solved, but Clarissa didn't believe either of them had the ghost of an idea of solving, was simply this: here was one room; there another. Did religion solve that, or love?

Love—but here the other clock, the clock which always struck two minutes after Big Ben, came shuffling in with its lap full of odds and ends, which it dumped down as if Big Ben were all very well with his majesty laying down the law, so solemn, so just, but she must remember all sorts of little things besides— Mrs. Marsham, Ellie Henderson, glasses for ices—all sorts of little things came flooding and lapping and dancing in on the wake of that solemn stroke which lay flat like a bar of gold on the sea. Mrs. Marsham, Ellie Henderson, glasses for ices. She must telephone now at once.

Volubly, troublously, the late clock sounded, coming in on the wake of Big Ben, with its lap full of trifles. Beaten up, broken up by the assault of carriages, the brutality of vans, the eager advance of myriads of angular men, of flaunting women, the domes and spires of offices and hospitals, the last relics of this lap full of odds and ends seemed to break, like the spray of an exhausted wave, upon the body of Miss Kilman standing still in the street for a moment to mutter "It is the flesh."

It was the flesh that she must control. Clarissa Dalloway had insulted her. That she expected. But she had not triumphed; she had not mastered the flesh. Ugly, clumsy, Clarissa Dalloway had laughed at her for being that; and had revived the fleshly desires, for she minded looking as she did beside Clarissa. Nor could she talk as she did. But why wish to resemble her? Why? She despised Mrs. Dalloway from the bottom of her heart. She was not serious. She was not good. Her life was a tissue of vanity and deceit. Yet Doris Kilman had been overcome. She had, as a matter of fact, very nearly burst into tears when Clarissa Dalloway laughed at her. "It is the flesh, it is the flesh," she muttered (it being her habit to talk aloud) trying to subdue this turbulent and painful feeling as she walked down Victoria Street. She prayed to God. She could not help being ugly; she could not afford to buy pretty clothes. Clarissa Dalloway had laughed—but she would concentrate her mind upon something else until she had reached the pillar-box. At any rate she had got Elizabeth. But she would think of something else; she would think of Russia; until she reached the pillar-box.

How nice it must be, she said, in the country, struggling, as Mr. Whittaker had told her, with that violent grudge against the world which had scorned her, sneered at her, cast her off, beginning with this indignity—the infliction of her unlovable body which people could not bear to see. Do her hair as she might, her forehead remained like an egg, bald, white. No clothes suited her. She might buy anything. And for a woman, of course, that meant never meeting the opposite sex. Never would she come first with any one. Sometimes lately it had seemed to her that, except for Elizabeth, her food was all that she lived for; her comforts; her dinner, her tea; her hot-water bottle at night. But one must fight; vanquish; have faith in God. Mr. Whittaker had said she was there for a purpose. But no one knew the agony! He said, pointing to the crucifix, that God knew. But why should she have to suffer when other women, like Clarissa Dalloway, escaped? Knowledge comes through suffering, said Mr. Whittaker.

She had passed the pillar-box, and Elizabeth had turned into the cool brown tobacco department of the Army and Navy Stores while she was still muttering to herself what Mr. Whittaker had said about knowledge coming through suffering and the flesh. "The flesh," she muttered.

What department did she want? Elizabeth interrupted her.

"Petticoats," she said abruptly, and stalked straight on to the lift.

Up they went. Elizabeth guided her this way and that; guided her in her abstraction as if she had been a great child, an unwieldy battleship. There were the petticoats, brown, decorous, striped, frivolous, solid, flimsy; and she chose, in her abstraction, portentously, and the girl serving thought her mad.

Elizabeth rather wondered, as they did up the parcel, what Miss Kilman was thinking. They must have their tea, said Miss Kilman, rousing, collecting herself. They had their tea.

Elizabeth rather wondered whether Miss Kilman could be hungry. It was her way of eating, eating with intensity, then looking, again and again, at a plate of sugared cakes on the table next them; then, when a lady and a child sat down and the child took the cake, could Miss Kilman really mind it? Yes, Miss Kilman did mind it. She had wanted that cake — the pink one. The pleasure of eating was almost the only pure pleasure left her, and then to be baffled even in that!

When people are happy, they have a reserve, she had told Elizabeth, upon which to draw, whereas she was like a wheel without a tyre (she was fond of such metaphors), jolted by every pebble, so she would say staying on after the lesson standing by the fire-place with her bag of books, her "satchel," she called it, on a Tuesday morning, after the lesson was over. And she talked too about the war. After all, there were people who did not think the English invariably right. There were books. There were meetings. There were other points of view. Would Elizabeth like to come with her to listen to So-and-so (a most extraordinary looking old man)? Then Miss Kilman took her to some church in Kensington and they had tea with a clergyman. She had lent her books. Law, medicine, politics, all professions are open to women of your generation, said Miss Kilman. But for herself, her career was absolutely ruined and was it her fault? Good gracious, said Elizabeth, no.

And her mother would come calling to say that a hamper had come from Bourton and would Miss Kilman like some flowers? To Miss Kilman she was always very, very nice, but

Miss Kilman squashed the flowers all in a bunch, and hadn't any small talk, and what interested Miss Kilman bored her mother, and Miss Kilman and she were terrible together; and Miss Kilman swelled and looked very plain. But then Miss Kilman was frightfully clever. Elizabeth had never thought about the poor. They lived with everything they wanted,— her mother had breakfast in bed every day; Lucy carried it up; and she liked old women because they were Duchesses, and being descended from some Lord. But Miss Kilman said (one of those Tuesday mornings when the lesson was over), "My grandfather kept an oil and colour shop in Kensington." Miss Kilman made one feel so small.

Miss Kilman took another cup of tea. Elizabeth, with her oriental bearing, her inscrutable mystery, sat perfectly upright; no, she did not want anything more. She looked for her gloves— her white gloves. They were under the table. Ah, but she must not go! Miss Kilman could not let her go! this youth, that was so beautiful, this girl, whom she genuinely loved! Her large hand opened and shut on the table.

But perhaps it was a little flat somehow, Elizabeth felt. And really she would like to go.

But said Miss Kilman, "I've not quite finished yet."

Of course, then, Elizabeth would wait. But it was rather stuffy in here.

"Are you going to the party to-night?" Miss Kilman said. Elizabeth supposed she was going; her mother wanted her to go. She must not let parties absorb her, Miss Kilman said, fingering the last two inches of a chocolate éclair.

She did not much like parties, Elizabeth said. Miss Kilman opened her mouth, slightly projected her chin, and swallowed down the last inches of the chocolate éclair, then wiped her fingers, and washed the tea round in her cup.

She was about to split asunder, she felt. The agony was so

terrific. If she could grasp her, if she could clasp her, if she could make her hers absolutely and forever and then die; that was all she wanted. But to sit here, unable to think of anything to say; to see Elizabeth turning against her; to be felt repulsive even by her—it was too much; she could not stand it. The thick fingers curled inwards.

"I never go to parties," said Miss Kilman, just to keep Elizabeth from going. "People don't ask me to parties"—and she knew as she said it that it was this egotism that was her undoing; Mr. Whittaker had warned her; but she could not help it. She had suffered so horribly. "Why should they ask me?" she said. "I'm plain, I'm unhappy." She knew it was idiotic. But it was all those people passing—people with parcels who despised her, who made her say it. However, she was Doris Kilman. She had her degree. She was a woman who had made her way in the world. Her knowledge of modern history was more than respectable.

"I don't pity myself," she said. "I pity"—she meant to say "your mother" but no, she could not, not to Elizabeth. "I pity other people," she said, "more."

Like some dumb creature who has been brought up to a gate for an unknown purpose, and stands there longing to gallop away, Elizabeth Dalloway sat silent. Was Miss Kilman going to say anything more?

"Don't quite forget me," said Doris Kilman; her voice quivered. Right away to the end of the field the dumb creature galloped in terror.

The great hand opened and shut.

Elizabeth turned her head. The waitress came. One had to pay at the desk, Elizabeth said, and went off, drawing out, so Miss Kilman felt, the very entrails in her body, stretching them as she crossed the room, and then, with a final twist, bowing her head very politely, she went.

She had gone. Miss Kilman sat at the marble table among the éclairs, stricken once, twice, thrice by shocks of suffering. She had gone. Mrs. Dalloway had triumphed. Elizabeth had gone. Beauty had gone, youth had gone.

So she sat. She got up, blundered off among the little tables, rocking slightly from side to side, and somebody came after her with her petticoat, and she lost her way, and was hemmed in by trunks specially prepared for taking to India; next got among the accouchement sets, and baby linen; through all the commodities of the world, perishable and permanent, hams, drugs, flowers, stationery, variously smelling, now sweet, now sour she lurched; saw herself thus lurching with her hat askew, very red in the face, full length in a looking-glass; and at last came out into the street.

The tower of Westminster Cathedral rose in front of her, the habitation of God. In the midst of the traffic, there was the habitation of God. Doggedly she set off with her parcel to that other sanctuary, the Abbey, where, raising her hands in a tent before her face, she sat beside those driven into shelter too; the variously assorted worshippers, now divested of social rank, almost of sex, as they raised their hands before their faces; but once they removed them, instantly reverent, middle class, English men and women, some of them desirous of seeing the wax works.

But Miss Kilman held her tent before her face. Now she was deserted; now rejoined. New worshippers came in from the street to replace the strollers, and still, as people gazed round and shuffled past the tomb of the Unknown Warrior, still she barred her eyes with her fingers and tried in this double darkness, for the light in the Abbey was bodiless, to aspire above the vanities, the desires, the commodities, to rid herself both of hatred and of love. Her hands twitched. She seemed to struggle. Yet to others God was accessible and the path to Him smooth. Mr. Fletcher,

retired, of the Treasury, Mrs. Gorham, widow of the famous
K.C., approached Him simply, and having done their praying,
leant back, enjoyed the music (the organ pealed sweetly), and saw
Miss Kilman at the end of the row, praying, praying, and, being
still on the threshold of their underworld, thought of her sympathetically as a soul haunting the same territory; a soul cut out
of immaterial substance; not a woman, a soul.

But Mr. Fletcher had to go. He had to pass her, and being
himself neat as a new pin, could not help being a little distressed
by the poor lady's disorder; her hair down; her parcel on the
floor. She did not at once let him pass. But, as he stood gazing
about him, at the white marbles, grey window panes, and accumulated treasures (for he was extremely proud of the Abbey),
her largeness, robustness, and power as she sat there shifting her
knees from time to time (it was so rough the approach to her
God—so tough her desires) impressed him, as they had impressed Mrs. Dalloway (she could not get the thought of her out
of her mind that afternoon), the Rev. Edward Whittaker, and
Elizabeth too.

And Elizabeth waited in Victoria Street for an omnibus. It
was so nice to be out of doors. She thought perhaps she need
not go home just yet. It was so nice to be out in the air. So she
would get on to an omnibus. And already, even as she stood
there, in her very well cut clothes, it was beginning. . . . People
were beginning to compare her to poplar trees, early dawn, hy-
acinths, fawns, running water, and garden lilies, and it made her
life a burden to her, for she so much preferred being left alone
to do what she liked in the country, but they would compare her
to lilies, and she had to go to parties, and London was so dreary
compared with being alone in the country with her father and
the dogs.

Buses swooped, settled, were off—garish caravans, glisten-
ing with red and yellow varnish. But which should she get on

to? She had no preferences. Of course, she would not push her way. She inclined to be passive. It was expression she needed, but her eyes were fine, Chinese, oriental, and, as her mother said, with such nice shoulders and holding herself so straight, she was always charming to look at; and lately, in the evening especially, when she was interested, for she never seemed excited, she looked almost beautiful, very stately, very serene. What could she be thinking? Every man fell in love with her, and she was really awfully bored. For it was beginning. Her mother could see that—the compliments were beginning. That she did not care more about it—for instance for her clothes—sometimes worried Clarissa, but perhaps it was as well with all those puppies and guinea pigs about having distemper, and it gave her a charm. And now there was this odd friendship with Miss Kilman. Well, thought Clarissa about three o'clock in the morning, reading Baron Marbot for she could not sleep, it proves she has a heart.

Suddenly Elizabeth stepped forward and most competently boarded the omnibus, in front of everybody. She took a seat on top. The impetuous creature—a pirate—started forward, sprang away; she had to hold the rail to steady herself, for a pirate it was, reckless, unscrupulous, bearing down ruthlessly, circumventing dangerously, boldly snatching a passenger, or ignoring a passenger, squeezing eel-like and arrogant in between, and then rushing insolently all sails spread up Whitehall. And did Elizabeth give one thought to poor Miss Kilman who loved her without jealousy, to whom she had been a fawn in the open, a moon in a glade? She was delighted to be free. The fresh air was so delicious. It had been so stuffy in the Army and Navy Stores. And now it was like riding, to be rushing up Whitehall; and to each movement of the omnibus the beautiful body in the fawn-coloured coat responded freely like a rider, like the figurehead of a ship, for the breeze slightly disarrayed her; the heat gave her cheeks the pallor of white painted wood; and her fine eyes, having no eyes to meet, gazed ahead, blank, bright, with the staring incredible innocence of sculpture.

It was always talking about her own sufferings that made Miss Kilman so difficult. And was she right? If it was being on committees and giving up hours and hours every day (she hardly ever saw him in London) that helped the poor, her father did that, goodness knows,—if that was what Miss Kilman meant about being a Christian; but it was so difficult to say. Oh, she would like to go a little further. Another penny was it to the Strand? Here was another penny then. She would go up the Strand.

She liked people who were ill. And every profession is open to the women of your generation, said Miss Kilman. So she might be a doctor. She might be a farmer. Animals are often ill. She might own a thousand acres and have people under her. She would go and see them in their cottages. This was Somerset House. One might be a very good farmer—and that, strangely enough though Miss Kilman had her share in it, was almost entirely due to Somerset House. It looked so splendid, so serious, that great grey building. And she liked the feeling of people working. She liked those churches, like shapes of grey paper, breasting the stream of the Strand. It was quite different here from Westminster, she thought, getting off at Chancery Lane. It was so serious; it was so busy. In short, she would like to have a profession. She would become a doctor, a farmer, possibly go into Parliament, if she found it necessary, all because of the Strand.

The feet of those people busy about their activities, hands putting stone to stone, minds eternally occupied not with trivial chatterings (comparing women to poplars—which was rather exciting, of course, but very silly), but with thoughts of ships, of business, of law, of administration, and with it all so

stately (she was in the Temple), gay (there was the river), pious
(there was the Church), made her quite determined, whatever
her mother might say, to become either a farmer or a doctor.
But she was, of course, rather lazy.

And it was much better to say nothing about it. It seemed
so silly. It was the sort of thing that did sometimes happen,
when one was alone—buildings without architects' names,
crowds of people coming back from the city having more power
than single clergymen in Kensington, than any of the books
Miss Kilman had lent her, to stimulate what lay slumbrous,
clumsy, and shy on the mind's sandy floor to break surface, as a
child suddenly stretches its arms; it was just that, perhaps, a sigh,
a stretch of the arms, an impulse, a revelation, which has its effects for ever, and then down again it went to the sandy floor.
She must go home. She must dress for dinner. But what was the
time?—where was a clock?

She looked up Fleet Street. She walked just a little way towards St. Paul's, shyly, like some one penetrating on tiptoe, exploring a strange house by night with a candle, on edge lest the
owner should suddenly fling wide his bedroom door and ask
her business, nor did she dare wander off into queer alleys,
tempting bye-streets, any more than in a strange house open
doors which might be bedroom doors, or sitting-room doors, or
lead straight to the larder. For no Dalloways came down the
Strand daily; she was a pioneer, a stray, venturing, trusting.

In many ways, her mother felt, she was extremely immature,
like a child still, attached to dolls, to old slippers; a perfect baby;
and that was charming. But then, of course, there was in the Dalloway family the tradition of public service. Abbesses, principals,
head mistresses, dignitaries, in the republic of women—without
being brilliant, any of them, they were that. She penetrated a little
further in the direction of St. Paul's. She liked the geniality, sis-
terhood, motherhood, brotherhood of this uproar. It seemed to

her good. The noise was tremendous; and suddenly there were trumpets (the unemployed) blaring, rattling about in the uproar; military music; as if people were marching; yet had they been dying—had some woman breathed her last and whoever was watching, opening the window of the room where she had just brought off that act of supreme dignity, looked down on Fleet Street, that uproar, that military music would have come triumphing up to him, consolatory, indifferent.

It was not conscious. There was no recognition in it of one's fortune, or fate, and for that very reason even to those dazed with watching for the last shivers of consciousness on the faces of the dying, consoling. Forgetfulness in people might wound, their ingratitude corrode, but this voice, pouring endlessly, year in year out, would take whatever it might be; this vow; this van; this life; this procession, would wrap them all about and carry them on, as in the rough stream of a glacier the ice holds a splinter of bone, a blue petal, some oak trees, and rolls them on.

But it was later than she thought. Her mother would not like her to be wandering off alone like this. She turned back down the Strand.

A puff of wind (in spite of the heat, there was quite a wind) blew a thin black veil over the sun and over the Strand. The faces faded; the omnibuses suddenly lost their glow. For although the clouds were of mountainous white so that one could fancy hacking hard chips off with a hatchet, with broad golden slopes, lawns of celestial pleasure gardens, on their flanks, and had all the appearance of settled habitations assembled for the conference of gods above the world, there was a perpetual movement among them. Signs were interchanged, when, as if to fulfil some scheme arranged already, now a summit dwindled, now a whole block of pyramidal size which had kept its station inalterably advanced into the midst or gravely led the procession to fresh anchorage. Fixed though they seemed at their posts, at rest in perfect unanimity, nothing could be fresher, freer, more sensitive superficially than the snow-white or gold-kindled surface; to change, to go, to dismantle the solemn assemblage was immediately possible; and in spite of the grave fixity, the accumulated robustness and solidity, now they struck light to the earth, now darkness.

Calmly and competently, Elizabeth Dalloway mounted the Westminster omnibus.

Going and coming, beckoning, signalling, so the light and shadow which now made the wall grey, now the bananas bright yellow, now made the Strand grey, now made the omnibuses bright yellow, seemed to Septimus Warren Smith lying on the sofa in the sitting-room; watching the watery gold glow and fade with the astonishing sensibility of some live creature on the roses, on the wall-paper. Outside the trees dragged their leaves like nets through the depths of the air; the sound of water was in the room and through the waves came the voices of birds singing. Every power poured its treasures on his head, and his hand lay there on the back of the sofa, as he had seen his hand lie when he was bathing, floating, on the top of the waves, while far away on shore he heard dogs barking and barking far away. Fear no more, says the heart in the body; fear no more.

He was not afraid. At every moment Nature signified by some laughing hint like that gold spot which went round the wall—there, there, there—her determination to show, by brandishing her plumes, shaking her tresses, flinging her mantle this way and that, beautifully, always beautifully, and standing close up to breathe through her hollowed hands Shakespeare's words, her meaning.

Rezia, sitting at the table twisting a hat in her hands, watched him; saw him smiling. He was happy then. But she could not bear to see him smiling. It was not marriage; it was not being one's husband to look strange like that, always to be starting, laughing, sitting hour after hour silent, or clutching her and telling her to write. The table drawer was full of those writings; about war; about Shakespeare; about great discoveries; how there is no death. Lately he had become excited suddenly for no reason (and both Dr. Holmes and Sir William Bradshaw said excitement was the worst thing for him), and waved his hands and cried out that he knew the truth! He knew everything! That man, his friend who was killed, Evans, had come, he said. He was singing behind the screen. She wrote it down just as he spoke it. Some things were very beautiful; others sheer nonsense. And he was always stopping in the middle, changing his mind; wanting to add something; hearing something new; listening with his hand up.

But she heard nothing.

And once they found the girl who did the room reading one of these papers in fits of laughter. It was a dreadful pity. For that made Septimus cry out about human cruelty—how they tear each other to pieces. The fallen, he said, they tear to pieces. "Holmes is on us," he would say, and he would invent stories about Holmes; Holmes eating porridge; Holmes reading Shakespeare—making himself roar with laughter or rage, for Dr. Holmes seemed to stand for something horrible to him. "Human nature," he called him. Then there were the visions. He was drowned, he used to say, and lying on a cliff with the gulls screaming over him. He would look over the edge of the sofa down into the sea. Or he was hearing music. Really it was only a barrel organ or some man crying in the street. But "Lovely!" he used to cry, and the tears would run down his cheeks, which was to her the most dreadful thing of all, to see a man like Septimus, who had fought, who was brave, crying. And he would lie listening until suddenly he would cry that he was falling down, down into the flames! Actually she would look for flames, it was so vivid. But there was nothing. They were alone in the room. It was a dream, she would tell him and so quiet him at last, but sometimes she was frightened too. She sighed as she sat sewing.

Her sigh was tender and enchanting, like the wind outside a wood in the evening. Now she put down her scissors; now she turned to take something from the table. A little stir, a little crinkling, a little tapping built up something on the table there, where she sat sewing. Through his eyelashes he could see her blurred outline; her little black body; her face and hands; her turning movements at the table, as she took up a reel, or looked (she was apt to lose things) for her silk. She was making a hat for Mrs. Filmer's married daughter, whose name was—he had forgotten her name.

"What is the name of Mrs. Filmer's married daughter?" he asked.

"Mrs. Peters," said Rezia. She was afraid it was too small, she said, holding it before her. Mrs. Peters was a big woman; but she did not like her. It was only because Mrs. Filmer had been so good to them. "She gave me grapes this morning," she said—that Rezia wanted to do something to show that they were grateful. She had come into the room the other evening and found Mrs. Peters, who thought they were out, playing the gramophone.

"Was it true?" he asked. She was playing the gramophone? Yes; she had told him about it at the time; she had found Mrs. Peters playing the gramophone.

He began, very cautiously, to open his eyes, to see whether a gramophone was really there. But real things—real things were too exciting. He must be cautious. He would not go mad. First he looked at the fashion papers on the lower shelf, then, gradually at the gramophone with the green trumpet. Nothing could be more exact. And so, gathering courage, he looked at the sideboard; the plate of bananas; the engraving of Queen Victoria and the Prince Consort; at the mantelpiece, with the jar of roses. None of these things moved. All were still; all were real.

"She is a woman with a spiteful tongue," said Rezia.

"What does Mr. Peters do?" Septimus asked.

"Ah," said Rezia, trying to remember. She thought Mrs. Filmer had said that he travelled for some company. "Just now he is in Hull," she said.

"Just now!" She said that with her Italian accent. She said that herself. He shaded his eyes so that he might see only a little of her face at a time, first the chin, then the nose, then the forehead, in case it were deformed, or had some terrible mark on it. But no, there she was, perfectly natural, sewing, with the pursed lips that women have, the set, the melancholy expression, when sewing. But there was nothing terrible about it, he assured himself, looking a second time, a third time at her face, her hands, for what was frightening or disgusting in her as she sat there in broad daylight, sewing? Mrs. Peters had a spiteful tongue. Mr. Peters was in Hull. Why then rage and prophesy? Why fly scourged and outcast? Why be made to tremble and sob by the clouds? Why seek truths and deliver messages when Rezia sat sticking pins into the front of her dress, and Mr. Peters was in Hull? Miracles, revelations, agonies, loneliness, falling through the sea, down, down into the flames, all were burnt out, for he had a sense, as he watched Rezia trimming the straw hat for Mrs. Peters, of a coverlet of flowers.

"It's too small for Mrs. Peters," said Septimus.

For the first time for days he was speaking as he used to do! Of course it was—absurdly small, she said. But Mrs. Peters had chosen it.

He took it out of her hands. He said it was an organ grinder's monkey's hat.

How it rejoiced her that! Not for weeks had they laughed like this together, poking fun privately like married people. What she meant was that if Mrs. Filmer had come in, or Mrs. Peters or anybody they would not have understood what she and Septimus were laughing at.

"There," she said, pinning a rose to one side of the hat. Never had she felt so happy! Never in her life!

But that was still more ridiculous, Septimus said. Now the poor woman looked like a pig at a fair. (Nobody ever made her laugh as Septimus did.)

What had she got in her work-box? She had ribbons and beads, tassels, artificial flowers. She tumbled them out on the table. He began putting odd colours together—for though he had no fingers, could not even do up a parcel, he had a wonderful eye, and often he was right, sometimes absurd, of course, but sometimes wonderfully right.

"She shall have a beautiful hat!" he murmured, taking up this and that, Rezia kneeling by his side, looking over his shoulder. Now it was finished—that is to say the design; she must stitch it together. But she must be very, very careful, he said, to keep it just as he had made it.

So she sewed. When she sewed, he thought, she made a sound like a kettle on the hob; bubbling, murmuring, always busy, her strong little pointed fingers pinching and poking; her needle flashing straight. The sun might go in and out, on the tassels, on the wallpaper, but he would wait, he thought, stretching out his feet, looking at his ringed sock at the end of the sofa; he would wait in this warm place, this pocket of still air, which one comes on at the edge of a wood sometimes in the evening, when, because of a fall in the ground, or some arrangement of the trees (one must be scientific above all, scientific), warmth lingers, and the air buffets the cheek like the wing of a bird.

"There it is," said Rezia, twirling Mrs. Peters' hat on the tips of her fingers. "That'll do for the moment. Later . . ." her sentence bubbled away drip, drip, drip, like a contented tap left running.

It was wonderful. Never had he done anything which made him feel so proud. It was so real, it was so substantial, Mrs. Peters' hat.

"Just look at it," he said.

Yes, it would always make her happy to see that hat. He had become himself then, he had laughed then. They had been alone together. Always she would like that hat.

He told her to try it on.

"But I must look so queer!" she cried, running over to the glass and looking first this side then that. Then she snatched it off again, for there was a tap at the door. Could it be Sir William Bradshaw? Had he sent already?

No! it was only the small girl with the evening paper.

What always happened, then happened—what happened every night of their lives. The small girl sucked her thumb at the door; Rezia went down on her knees; Rezia cooed and kissed; Rezia got a bag of sweets out of the table drawer. For so it always happened. First one thing, then another. So she built it up, first one thing and then another. Dancing, skipping, round and round the room they went. He took the paper. Surrey was all out, he read. There was a heat wave. Rezia repeated: Surrey was all out. There was a heat wave, making it part of the game she was playing with Mrs. Filmer's grandchild, both of them laughing, chattering at the same time, at their game. He was very tired. He was very happy. He would sleep. He shut his eyes. But directly he saw nothing the sounds of the game became fainter and stranger and sounded like the cries of people seeking and not finding, and passing further and further away. They had lost him!

He started up in terror. What did he see? The plate of bananas on the sideboard. Nobody was there (Rezia had taken the

child to its mother. It was bedtime). That was it: to be alone forever. That was the doom pronounced in Milan when he came
into the room and saw them cutting out buckram shapes with
their scissors; to be alone forever.

He was alone with the sideboard and the bananas. He was
alone, exposed on this bleak eminence, stretched out—but not
on a hill-top; not on a crag; on Mrs. Filmer's sitting-room sofa.
As for the visions, the faces, the voices of the dead, where were
they? There was a screen in front of him, with black bulrushes
and blue swallows. Where he had once seen mountains, where
he had seen faces, where he had seen beauty, there was a screen.

"Evans!" he cried. There was no answer. A mouse had
squeaked, or a curtain rustled. Those were the voices of the
dead. The screen, the coal-scuttle, the sideboard remained to
him. Let him then face the screen, the coal-scuttle and the sideboard . . . but Rezia burst into the room chattering.

Some letter had come. Everybody's plans were changed.
Mrs. Filmer would not be able to go to Brighton after all. There
was no time to let Mrs. Williams know, and really Rezia thought
it very, very annoying, when she caught sight of the hat and
thought . . . perhaps . . . she . . . might just make a little. . . . Her
voice died out in contented melody.

"Ah, damn!" she cried (it was a joke of theirs, her swearing),
the needle had broken. Hat, child, Brighton, needle. She built it
up; first one thing, then another, she built it up, sewing.

She wanted him to say whether by moving the rose she had
improved the hat. She sat on the end of the sofa.

They were perfectly happy now, she said, suddenly, putting
the hat down. For she could say anything to him now. She could
say whatever came into her head. That was almost the first thing
she had felt about him, that night in the café when he had come
in with his English friends. He had come in, rather shyly, looking round him, and his hat had fallen when he hung it up. That

she could remember. She knew he was English, though not one of the large Englishmen her sister admired, for he was always thin; but he had a beautiful fresh colour; and with his big nose, his bright eyes, his way of sitting a little hunched made her think, she had often told him, of a young hawk, that first evening she saw him, when they were playing dominoes, and he had come in—of a young hawk; but with her he was always very gentle. She had never seen him wild or drunk, only suffering sometimes through this terrible war, but even so, when she came in, he would put it all away. Anything, anything in the whole world, any little bother with her work, anything that struck her to say she would tell him, and he understood at once. Her own family even were not the same. Being older than she was and being so clever—how serious he was, wanting her to read Shakespeare before she could even read a child's story in English!—being so much more experienced, he could help her. And she too could help him.

But this hat now. And then (it was getting late) Sir William Bradshaw.

She held her hands to her head, waiting for him to say did he like the hat or not, and as she sat there, waiting, looking down, he could feel her mind, like a bird, falling from branch to branch, and always alighting, quite rightly; he could follow her mind, as she sat there in one of those loose lax poses that came to her naturally and, if he should say anything, at once she smiled, like a bird alighting with all its claws firm upon the bough.

But he remembered Bradshaw said, "The people we are most fond of are not good for us when we are ill." Bradshaw said, he must be taught to rest. Bradshaw said they must be separated.

"Must," "must," why "must"? What power had Bradshaw over him? "What right has Bradshaw to say 'must' to me?" he demanded.

"It is because you talked of killing yourself," said Rezia. (Mercifully, she could now say anything to Septimus.)

So he was in their power! Holmes and Bradshaw were on him! The brute with the red nostrils was snuffing into every secret place! "Must" it could say! Where were his papers? the things he had written?

She brought him his papers, the things he had written, things she had written for him. She tumbled them out on to the sofa. They looked at them together. Diagrams, designs, little men and women brandishing sticks for arms, with wings—were they?—on their backs; circles traced round shillings and sixpences—the suns and stars; zigzagging precipices with mountaineers ascending roped together, exactly like knives and forks; sea pieces with little faces laughing out of what might perhaps be waves: the map of the world. Burn them! he cried. Now for his writings; how the dead sing behind rhododendron bushes; odes to Time; conversations with Shakespeare; Evans, Evans, Evans—his messages from the dead; do not cut down trees; tell the Prime Minister. Universal love: the meaning of the world. Burn them! he cried.

But Rezia laid her hands on them. Some were very beautiful, she thought. She would tie them up (for she had no envelope) with a piece of silk.

Even if they took him, she said, she would go with him. They could not separate them against their wills, she said.

Shuffling the edges straight, she did up the papers, and tied the parcel almost without looking, sitting beside him, he thought, as if all her petals were about her. She was a flowering tree; and through her branches looked out the face of a lawgiver, who had reached a sanctuary where she feared no one; not Holmes; not Bradshaw; a miracle, a triumph, the last and greatest. Staggering he saw her mount the appalling staircase, laden with Holmes and Bradshaw, men who never weighed less than eleven stone six, who sent their wives to Court, men who made ten thousand a year and talked of proportion; who different in their verdicts (for Holmes said one thing, Bradshaw another), yet judges they were; who mixed the vision and the sideboard; saw nothing clear, yet ruled, yet inflicted. "Must" they said. Over them she triumphed.

"There!" she said. The papers were tied up. No one should get at them. She would put them away.

And, she said, nothing should separate them. She sat down beside him and called him by the name of that hawk or crow which being malicious and a great destroyer of crops was precisely like him. No one could separate them, she said.

Then she got up to go into the bedroom to pack their things, but hearing voices downstairs and thinking that Dr. Holmes had perhaps called, ran down to prevent him coming up.

Septimus could hear her talking to Holmes on the staircase.

"My dear lady, I have come as a friend," Holmes was saying.

"No. I will not allow you to see my husband," she said.

He could see her, like a little hen, with her wings spread barring his passage. But Holmes persevered.

"My dear lady, allow me . . ." Holmes said, putting her aside (Holmes was a powerfully built man).

Holmes was coming upstairs. Holmes would burst open the door. Holmes would say "In a funk, eh?" Holmes would get him. But no; not Holmes; not Bradshaw. Getting up rather unsteadily, hopping indeed from foot to foot, he considered Mrs. Filmer's nice clean bread knife with "Bread" carved on the handle. Ah, but one mustn't spoil that. The gas fire? But it was too late now. Holmes was coming. Razors he might have got, but Rezia, who always did that sort of thing, had packed them. There remained only the window, the large Bloomsbury-lodging house window, the tiresome, the troublesome, and rather melodramatic business of opening the window and throwing himself out. It was their idea of tragedy, not his or Rezia's (for she was with him). Holmes and Bradshaw like that sort of thing. (He sat on the sill.) But he would wait till the very last moment. He did not want to die. Life was good. The sun hot. Only human beings—what did *they* want? Coming down the staircase opposite an old man stopped and stared at him. Holmes was at the door. "I'll give it you!" he cried, and flung himself vigorously, violently down on to Mrs. Filmer's area railings.

"The coward!" cried Dr. Holmes, bursting the door open. Rezia ran to the window, she saw; she understood. Dr. Holmes and Mrs. Filmer collided with each other. Mrs. Filmer flapped her apron and made her hide her eyes in the bedroom. There was a great deal of running up and down stairs. Dr. Holmes came in—white as a sheet, shaking all over, with a glass in his hand. She must be brave and drink something, he said (What was it? Something sweet), for her husband was horribly mangled, would not recover consciousness, she must not see him, must be spared as much as possible, would have the inquest to go through, poor young woman. Who could have foretold it? A sudden impulse, no one was in the least to blame (he told Mrs. Filmer). And why the devil he did it, Dr. Holmes could not conceive.

It seemed to her as she drank the sweet stuff that she was opening long windows, stepping out into some garden. But where? The clock was striking—one, two, three: how sensible the sound was; compared with all this thumping and whispering; like Septimus himself. She was falling asleep. But the clock went on striking, four, five, six and Mrs. Filmer waving her apron (they wouldn't bring the body in here, would they?) seemed part of that garden; or a flag. She had once seen a flag slowly rippling out from a mast when she stayed with her aunt at Venice. Men killed in battle were thus saluted, and Septimus had been through the War. Of her memories, most were happy.

She put on her hat, and ran through cornfields—where could it have been?—on to some hill, somewhere near the sea, for there were ships, gulls, butterflies, they sat on a cliff. In London too, there they sat, and, half dreaming, came to her through the bedroom door, rain falling, whisperings, stirrings among dry corn, the caress of the sea, as it seemed to her, hollowing them in its arched shell and murmuring to her laid on shore, strewn she felt, like flying flowers over some tomb.

"He is dead," she said, smiling at the poor old woman who guarded her with her honest light-blue eyes fixed on the door. (They wouldn't bring him in here, would they?) But Mrs. Filmer pooh-poohed. Oh no, oh no! They were carrying him away now. Ought she not to be told? Married people ought to be together, Mrs. Filmer thought. But they must do as the doctor said.

"Let her sleep," said Dr. Holmes, feeling her pulse. She saw the large outline of his body standing dark against the window. So that was Dr. Holmes.

ONE OF the triumphs of civilisation, Peter Walsh thought. It is one of the triumphs of civilisation, as the light high bell of the ambulance sounded. Swiftly, cleanly the ambulance sped to the hospital, having picked up instantly, humanely, some poor devil; some one hit on the head, struck down by disease, knocked over perhaps a minute or so ago at one of these crossings, as might happen to oneself. That was civilisation. It struck him coming back from the East—the efficiency, the organisation, the communal spirit of London. Every cart or carriage of its own accord drew aside to let the ambulance pass. Perhaps it was morbid; or was it not touching rather, the respect which they showed this ambulance with its victim inside—busy men hurrying home yet instantly bethinking them as it passed of some wife; or presumably how easily it might have been them there, stretched on a shelf with a doctor and a nurse. . . . Ah, but thinking became morbid, sentimental, directly one began conjuring up doctors, dead bodies; a little glow of pleasure, a sort of lust too over the visual impression warned one not to go on with that sort of thing any more—fatal to art, fatal to friendship. True. And yet, thought Peter Walsh, as the ambulance turned the corner though the light high bell could be heard down the next street and still farther as it crossed the Tottenham Court Road, chiming constantly, it is the privilege of loneliness; in privacy one may do as one chooses. One might weep if no one saw. It had been his undoing—this susceptibility—in Anglo-Indian society; not weeping at the right time, or laughing either. I have that in me, he thought standing by the pillar-box, which could now dissolve in tears. Why, Heaven knows. Beauty of some sort probably, and the weight of the day, which beginning with that visit to Clarissa had exhausted him with its heat, its intensity, and the drip, drip, of one impression after another down into that cellar where they stood, deep, dark, and no one would ever know. Partly for that reason, its secrecy, complete and inviolable, he had found life like an unknown garden, full of turns and corners, surprising, yes; really it took one's breath away, these moments; there coming to him by the pillar-box opposite the British Museum one of them, a moment, in which things came together; this ambulance; and life and death. It was as if he were sucked up to some very high roof by that rush of emotion and the rest of him, like a white shell-sprinkled beach, left bare. It had been his undoing in Anglo-Indian society—this susceptibility.

Clarissa once, going on top of an omnibus with him somewhere, Clarissa superficially at least, so easily moved, now in despair, now in the best of spirits, all aquiver in those days and such good company, spotting queer little scenes, names, people from the top of a bus, for they used to explore London and bring back bags full of treasures from the Caledonian market— Clarissa had a theory in those days—they had heaps of theo-

ries, always theories, as young people have. It was to explain the
feeling they had of dissatisfaction; not knowing people; not
being known. For how could they know each other? You met
every day; then not for six months, or years. It was unsatisfac-
tory, they agreed, how little one knew people. But she said, sitting on the bus going up Shaftesbury Avenue, she felt herself
everywhere; not "here, here, here"; and she tapped the back of
the seat; but everywhere. She waved her hand, going up Shaftesbury Avenue. She was all that. So that to know her, or any one,
one must seek out the people who completed them; even the
places. Odd affinities she had with people she had never spoken
to, some woman in the street, some man behind a counter—
even trees, or barns. It ended in a transcendental theory which,
with her horror of death, allowed her to believe, or say that she
believed (for all her scepticism), that since our apparitions, the
part of us which appears, are so momentary compared with the
other, the unseen part of us, which spreads wide, the unseen
might survive, be recovered somehow attached to this person or
that, or even haunting certain places after death . . . perhaps—
perhaps.

Looking back over that long friendship of almost thirty
years her theory worked to this extent. Brief, broken, often
painful as their actual meetings had been what with his absences
and interruptions (this morning, for instance, in came Elizabeth, like a long-legged colt, handsome, dumb, just as he was
beginning to talk to Clarissa) the effect of them on his life was
immeasurable. There was a mystery about it. You were given
a sharp, acute, uncomfortable grain—the actual meeting; horribly painful as often as not; yet in absence, in the most unlikely
places, it would flower out, open, shed its scent, let you touch,
taste, look about you, get the whole feel of it and understanding, after years of lying lost. Thus she had come to him; on
board ship; in the Himalayas; suggested by the oddest things (so

Sally Seton, generous, enthusiastic goose! thought of *him* when
she saw blue hydrangeas). She had influenced him more than
any person he had ever known. And always in this way coming
before him without his wishing it, cool, lady-like, critical; or ravishing, romantic, recalling some field or English harvest. He saw
her most often in the country, not in London. One scene after
another at Bourton. . . .

He had reached his hotel. He crossed the hall, with its
mounds of reddish chairs and sofas, its spike-leaved, withered-
looking plants. He got his key off the hook. The young lady
handed him some letters. He went upstairs—he saw her most
often at Bourton, in the late summer, when he stayed there for
a week, or fortnight even, as people did in those days. First on
top of some hill there she would stand, hands clapped to her
hair, her cloak blowing out, pointing, crying to them—she saw
the Severn beneath. Or in a wood, making the kettle boil—very
ineffective with her fingers; the smoke curtseying, blowing in
their faces; her little pink face showing through; begging water
from an old woman in a cottage, who came to the door to watch
them go. They walked always; the others drove. She was bored
driving, disliked all animals, except that dog. They tramped
miles along roads. She would break off to get her bearings, pilot
him back across country; and all the time they argued, discussed
poetry, discussed people, discussed politics (she was a Radical
then); never noticing a thing except when she stopped, cried out
at a view or a tree, and made him look with her; and so on again,
through stubble fields, she walking ahead, with a flower for her
aunt, never tired of walking for all her delicacy; to drop down
on Bourton in the dusk. Then, after dinner, old Breitkopf would
open the piano and sing without any voice, and they would lie
sunk in arm-chairs, trying not to laugh, but always breaking
down and laughing, laughing—laughing at nothing. Breitkopf

was supposed not to see. And then in the morning, flirting up and down like a wagtail in front of the house. . . .

Oh it was a letter from her! This blue envelope; that was her hand. And he would have to read it. Here was another of those meetings, bound to be painful! To read her letter needed the devil of an effort. "How heavenly it was to see him. She must tell him that." That was all.

But it upset him. It annoyed him. He wished she hadn't written it. Coming on top of his thoughts, it was like a nudge in the ribs. Why couldn't she let him be? After all, she had married Dalloway, and lived with him in perfect happiness all these years.

These hotels are not consoling places. Far from it. Any number of people had hung up their hats on those pegs. Even the flies, if you thought of it, had settled on other people's noses. As for the cleanliness which hit him in the face, it wasn't cleanliness, so much as bareness, frigidity; a thing that had to be. Some arid matron made her rounds at dawn sniffing, peering, causing blue-nosed maids to scour, for all the world as if the next visitor were a joint of meat to be served on a perfectly clean platter. For sleep, one bed; for sitting in, one arm-chair; for cleaning one's teeth and shaving one's chin, one tumbler, one looking-glass. Books, letters, dressing-gown, slipped about on the impersonality of the horsehair like incongruous impertinences. And it was Clarissa's letter that made him see all this. "Heavenly to see you. She must say so!" He folded the paper; pushed it away; nothing would induce him to read it again!

To get that letter to him by six o'clock she must have sat down and written it directly he left her; stamped it; sent somebody to the post. It was, as people say, very like her. She was upset by his visit. She had felt a great deal; had for a moment, when she kissed his hand, regretted, envied him even, remembered possibly (for he saw her look it) something he had said—how they would change the world if she married him perhaps; whereas, it was this; it was middle age; it was mediocrity; then forced herself with her indomitable vitality to put all that aside, there being in her a thread of life which for toughness, endurance, power to overcome obstacles, and carry her triumphantly through he had never known the like of. Yes; but there would come a reaction directly he left the room. She would be frightfully sorry for him; she would think what in the world she could do to give him pleasure (short always of the one thing) and he could see her with the tears running down her cheeks going to her writing-table and dashing off that one line which he was to find greeting him. . . . "Heavenly to see you!" And she meant it.

Peter Walsh had now unlaced his boots.

But it would not have been a success, their marriage. The other thing, after all, came so much more naturally.

It was odd; it was true; lots of people felt it. Peter Walsh, who had done just respectably, filled the usual posts adequately, was liked, but thought a little cranky, gave himself airs—it was odd that *he* should have had, especially now that his hair was grey, a contented look; a look of having reserves. It was this that made him attractive to women who liked the sense that he was not altogether manly. There was something unusual about him, or something behind him. It might be that he was bookish—never came to see you without taking up the book on the table (he was now reading, with his bootlaces trailing on the floor); or that he was a gentleman, which showed itself in the way he knocked the ashes out of his pipe, and in his manners of course to women. For it was very charming and quite ridiculous how easily some girl without a grain of sense could twist him round her finger. But at her own risk. That is to say, though he might be ever so easy, and indeed with his gaiety and good-breeding fascinating to be with, it was only up to a point. She said some-thing—no, no; he saw through that. He wouldn't stand that—no, no. Then he could shout and rock and hold his sides to-gether over some joke with men. He was the best judge of cook-ing in India. He was a man. But not the sort of man one had to respect—which was a mercy; not like Major Simmons, for in-stance; not in the least like that, Daisy thought, when, in spite of her two small children, she used to compare them.

He pulled off his boots. He emptied his pockets. Out came with his pocket-knife a snapshot of Daisy on the verandah; Daisy all in white, with a fox-terrier on her knee; very charm-ing, very dark; the best he had ever seen of her. It did come, after all so naturally; so much more naturally than Clarissa. No fuss. No bother. No finicking and fidgeting. All plain sailing. And the dark, adorably pretty girl on the verandah exclaimed (he could hear her). Of course, of course she would give him everything! she cried (she had no sense of discretion) everything he wanted! she cried, running to meet him, whoever might be looking. And she was only twenty-four. And she had two chil-dren. Well, well!

Well indeed he had got himself into a mess at his age. And it came over him when he woke in the night pretty forcibly. Sup-pose they did marry? For him it would be all very well, but what about her? Mrs. Burgess, a good sort and no chatterbox, in whom he had confided, thought this absence of his in England, ostensibly to see lawyers might serve to make Daisy reconsider, think what it meant. It was a question of her position, Mrs. Burgess said; the social barrier; giving up her children. She'd be a widow with a past one of these days, draggling about in the suburbs, or more likely, indiscriminate (you know, she said, what such women get like, with too much paint). But Peter Walsh pooh-poohed all that. He didn't mean to die yet. Anyhow she must settle for herself; judge for herself, he thought, padding

about the room in his socks, smoothing out his dress-shirt, for
he might go to Clarissa's party, or he might go to one of the
Halls, or he might settle in and read an absorbing book written
by a man he used to know at Oxford. And if he did retire, that's
what he'd do — write books. He would go to Oxford and poke
about in the Bodleian. Vainly the dark, adorably pretty girl ran
to the end of the terrace; vainly waved her hand; vainly cried she
didn't care a straw what people said. There he was, the man she
thought the world of, the perfect gentleman, the fascinating,
the distinguished (and his age made not the least difference to
her), padding about a room in an hotel in Bloomsbury, shaving,
washing, continuing, as he took up cans, put down razors, to
poke about in the Bodleian, and get at the truth about one or
two little matters that interested him. And he would have a chat
with whoever it might be, and so come to disregard more and
more precise hours for lunch, and miss engagements, and when
Daisy asked him, as she would, for a kiss, a scene, fail to come
up to the scratch (though he was genuinely devoted to her)—
in short it might be happier, as Mrs. Burgess said, that she
should forget him, or merely remember him as he was in August 1922, like a figure standing at the cross roads at dusk, which
grows more and more remote as the dog-cart spins away, carrying her securely fastened to the back seat, though her arms are
outstretched, and as she sees the figure dwindle and disappear
still she cries out how she would do anything in the world, anything, anything, anything. . . .

He never knew what people thought. It became more and
more difficult for him to concentrate. He become absorbed;
he became busied with his own concerns; now surly, now gay;
dependent on women, absent-minded, moody, less and less
able (so he thought as he shaved) to understand why Clarissa
couldn't simply find them a lodging and be nice to Daisy; introduce her. And then he could just — just do what? just haunt and

hover (he was at the moment actually engaged in sorting out various keys, papers), swoop and taste, be alone, in short, sufficient to himself; and yet nobody of course was more dependent upon others (he buttoned his waistcoat); it had been his undoing. He could not keep out of smoking-rooms, liked colonels, liked golf, liked bridge, and above all women's society, and the fineness of their companionship, and their faithfulness and audacity and greatness in loving which though it had its drawbacks seemed to him (and the dark, adorably pretty face was on top of the envelopes) so wholly admirable, so splendid a flower to grow on the crest of human life, and yet he could not come up to the scratch, being always apt to see round things (Clarissa had sapped something in him permanently), and to tire very easily of mute devotion and to want variety in love, though it would make him furious if Daisy loved anybody else, furious! for he was jealous, uncontrollably jealous by temperament. He suffered tortures! But where was his knife; his watch; his seals, his notecase, and Clarissa's letter which he would not read again but liked to think of, and Daisy's photograph? And now for dinner.

They were eating.

Sitting at little tables round vases, dressed or not dressed, with their shawls and bags laid beside them, with their air of false composure, for they were not used to so many courses at dinner, and confidence, for they were able to pay for it, and strain, for they had been running about London all day shopping, sightseeing; and their natural curiosity, for they looked round and up as the nice-looking gentleman in horn-rimmed spectacles came in, and their good nature, for they would have been glad to do any little service, such as lend a time-table or impart useful information, and their desire, pulsing in them, tugging at them subterraneously, somehow to establish connections if it were only a birthplace (Liverpool, for example) in common or friends of the same name; with their furtive glances, odd silences, and sudden withdrawals into family jocularity and isolation; there they sat eating dinner when Mr. Walsh came in and took his seat at a little table by the curtain.

It was not that he said anything, for being solitary he could only address himself to the waiter; it was his way of looking at the menu, of pointing his forefinger to a particular wine, of hitching himself up to the table, of addressing himself seriously, not gluttonously to dinner, that won him their respect; which, having to remain unexpressed for the greater part of the meal, flared up at the table where the Morrises sat when Mr. Walsh was heard to say at the end of the meal, "Bartlett pears." Why he should have spoken so moderately yet firmly, with the air of a disciplinarian well within his rights which are founded upon justice, neither young Charles Morris, nor old Charles, neither Miss Elaine nor Mrs. Morris knew. But when he said, "Bartlett pears," sitting alone at his table, they felt that he counted on their support in some lawful demand; was champion of a cause which immediately became their own, so that their eyes met his eyes sympathetically, and when they all reached the smoking-room simultaneously, a little talk between them became inevitable.

It was not very profound—only to the effect that London was crowded; had changed in thirty years; that Mr. Morris preferred Liverpool; that Mrs. Morris had been to the Westminster flower-show, and that they had all seen the Prince of Wales. Yet, thought Peter Walsh, no family in the world can compare with the Morrises; none whatever; and their relations to each other are perfect, and they don't care a hang for the upper classes, and they like what they like, and Elaine is training for the family business, and the boy has won a scholarship at Leeds, and the old lady (who is about his own age) has three more children at home; and they have two motor cars, but Mr. Morris still mends the boots on Sunday: it is superb, it is absolutely superb, thought Peter Walsh, swaying a little backwards and forwards with his liqueur glass in his hand among the hairy red chairs and ash-trays, feeling very well pleased with himself, for the Morrises liked him. Yes, they liked a man who said, "Bartlett pears." They liked him, he felt.

He would go to Clarissa's party. (The Morrises moved off; but they would meet again.) He would go to Clarissa's party, because he wanted to ask Richard what they were doing in India—the conservative duffers. And what's being acted? And music. . . . Oh yes, and mere gossip.

For this is the truth about our soul, he thought, our self, who fish-like inhabits deep seas and plies among obscurities threading her way between the boles of giant weeds, over sun-flickered spaces and on and on into gloom, cold, deep, in-scrutable; suddenly she shoots to the surface and sports on the wind-wrinkled waves; that is, has a positive need to brush, scrape, kindle herself, gossiping. What did the Government mean—Richard Dalloway would know—to do about India?

Since it was a very hot night and the paper boys went by with placards proclaiming in huge red letters that there was a heat-wave, wicker chairs were placed on the hotel steps and there, sipping, smoking, detached gentlemen sat. Peter Walsh sat there. One might fancy that day, the London day, was just beginning. Like a woman who had slipped off her print dress and white apron to array herself in blue and pearls, the day changed, put off stuff, took gauze, changed to evening, and with the same sigh of exhilaration that a woman breathes, tumbling petticoats on the floor, it too shed dust, heat, colour; the traffic thinned; motor cars, tinkling, darting, succeeded the lumber of vans; and here and there among the thick foliage of the squares an intense light hung. I resign, the evening seemed to say, as it paled and faded above the battlements and prominences, moulded, pointed, of hotel, flat, and block of shops, I fade, she was beginning, I disappear, but London would have none of it, and rushed her bayonets into the sky, pinioned her, constrained her to partnership in her revelry.

For the great revolution of Mr. Willett's summer time had taken place since Peter Walsh's last visit to England. The prolonged evening was new to him. It was inspiriting, rather. For as the young people went by with their despatch-boxes, awfully glad to be free, proud too, dumbly, of stepping this famous pavement, joy of a kind, cheap, tinselly, if you like, but all the same rapture, flushed their faces. They dressed well too; pink stockings; pretty shoes. They would now have two hours at the pictures. It sharpened, it refined them, the yellow-blue evening light; and on the leaves in the square shone lurid, livid—they looked as if dipped in sea water—the foliage of a submerged city. He was astonished by the beauty; it was encouraging too, for where the returned Anglo-Indian sat by rights (he knew crowds of them) in the Oriental Club biliously summing up the ruin of the world, here was he, as young as ever; envying young people their summer time and the rest of it, and more than suspecting from the words of a girl, from a housemaid's laughter—intangible things you couldn't lay your hands on—that shift in the whole pyramidal accumulation which in his youth had seemed immovable. On top of them it had pressed; weighed them down, the women especially, like those flowers Clarissa's Aunt Helena used to press between sheets of grey blotting-paper with Littré's dictionary on top, sitting under the lamp after dinner. She was dead now. He had heard of her, from Clarissa, losing the sight of one eye. It seemed so fitting—one of nature's masterpieces—that old Miss Parry should turn to glass. She would die like some bird in a frost gripping her perch. She belonged to a different age, but being so entire, so complete, would always stand up on the horizon, stone-white, eminent, like a lighthouse marking some past stage on this adventurous, long, long voyage, this interminable (he felt for a copper to buy a paper and read about Surrey and Yorkshire — he had held out that copper millions of times. Surrey was all out once more)— this interminable life. But cricket was no mere game. Cricket was important. He could never help reading about cricket. He read the scores in the stop press first, then how it was a hot day; then about a murder case. Having done things millions of times enriched them, though it might be said to take the surface off. The past enriched, and experience, and having cared for one or two people, and so having acquired the power which the young lack, of cutting short, doing what one likes, not caring a rap what people say and coming and going without any very great expectations (he left his paper on the table and moved off), which however (and he looked for his hat and coat) was not altogether true of him, not to-night, for here he was starting to go to a party, at his age, with the belief upon him that he was about to have an experience. But what?

Beauty anyhow. Not the crude beauty of the eye. It was not beauty pure and simple — Bedford Place leading into Russell Square. It was straightness and emptiness of course; the symmetry of a corridor; but it was also windows lit up, a piano, a gramophone sounding; a sense of pleasure-making hidden, but now and again emerging when, through the uncurtained window, the window left open, one saw parties sitting over tables, young people slowly circling, conversations between men and women, maids idly looking out (a strange comment theirs, when work was done), stockings drying on top ledges, a parrot, a few plants. Absorbing, mysterious, of infinite richness, this life. And in the large square where the cabs shot and swerved so quick, there were loitering couples, dallying, embracing, shrunk up under the shower of a tree; that was moving; so silent, so absorbed, that one passed, discreetly, timidly, as if in the presence of some sacred ceremony to interrupt which would have been impious. That was interesting. And so on into the flare and glare.

His light overcoat blew open, he stepped with indescribable idiosyncrasy, leant a little forward, tripped, with his hands behind his back and his eyes still a little hawklike; he tripped through London, towards Westminster, observing.

Was everybody dining out, then? Doors were being opened here by a footman to let issue a high-stepping old dame, in buckled shoes, with three purple ostrich feathers in her hair. Doors were being opened for ladies wrapped like mummies in shawls with bright flowers on them, ladies with bare heads. And in respectable quarters with stucco pillars through small front gardens lightly swathed with combs in their hair (having run up to see the children), women came; men waited for them, with their coats blowing open, and the motor started. Everybody was going out. What with these doors being opened, and the descent and the start, it seemed as if the whole of London were embarking in little boats moored to the bank, tossing on the waters, as if the whole place were floating off in carnival. And Whitehall was skated over, silver beaten as it was, skated over by spiders, and there was a sense of midges round the arc lamps; it was so hot that people stood about talking. And here in Westminster was a retired Judge, presumably, sitting four square at his house door dressed all in white. An Anglo-Indian presumably.

And here a shindy of brawling women, drunken women; here only a policeman and looming houses, high houses, domed houses, churches, parliaments, and the hoot of a steamer on the river, a hollow misty cry. But it was her street, this, Clarissa's; cabs were rushing round the corner, like water round the piers of a bridge, drawn together, it seemed to him because they bore people going to her party, Clarissa's party.

The cold stream of visual impressions failed him now as if the eye were a cup that overflowed and let the rest run down its china walls unrecorded. The brain must wake now. The body must contract now, entering the house, the lighted house, where the door stood open, where the motor cars were standing, and bright women descending: the soul must brave itself to endure. He opened the big blade of his pocket-knife.

Lucy came running full tilt downstairs, having just nipped in to the drawing-room to smooth a cover, to straighten a chair, to pause a moment and feel whoever came in must think how clean, how bright, how beautifully cared for, when they saw the beautiful silver, the brass fire-irons, the new chair-covers, and the curtains of yellow chintz: she appraised each; heard a roar of voices; people already coming up from dinner; she must fly!

The Prime Minister was coming, Agnes said: so she had heard them say in the dining-room, she said, coming in with a tray of glasses. Did it matter, did it matter in the least, one Prime Minister more or less? It made no difference at this hour of the night to Mrs. Walker among the plates, saucepans, cullenders, frying-pans, chicken in aspic, ice-cream freezers, pared crusts of bread, lemons, soup tureens, and pudding basins which, however hard they washed up in the scullery seemed to be all on top of her, on the kitchen table, on chairs, while the fire blared and roared, the electric lights glared, and still supper had to be laid. All she felt was, one Prime Minister more or less made not a scrap of difference to Mrs. Walker.

The ladies were going upstairs already, said Lucy; the ladies were going up, one by one, Mrs. Dalloway walking last and almost always sending back some message to the kitchen, "My love to Mrs. Walker," that was it one night. Next morning they would go over the dishes—the soup, the salmon; the salmon, Mrs. Walker knew, as usual underdone, for she always got nervous about the pudding and left it to Jenny; so it happened, the salmon was always underdone. But some lady with fair hair and silver ornaments had said, Lucy said, about the entrée, was it really made at home? But it was the salmon that bothered Mrs. Walker, as she spun the plates round and round, and pulled in dampers and pulled out dampers; and there came a burst of laughter from the dining-room; a voice speaking; then another burst of laughter— the gentlemen enjoying themselves when the ladies had gone. The tokay, said Lucy running in. Mr. Dalloway had sent for the tokay, from the Emperor's cellars, the Imperial Tokay.

It was borne through the kitchen. Over her shoulder Lucy reported how Miss Elizabeth looked quite lovely; she couldn't take her eyes off her; in her pink dress, wearing the necklace Mr. Dalloway had given her. Jenny must remember the dog, Miss Elizabeth's fox-terrier, which, since it bit, had to be shut up and might, Elizabeth thought, want something. Jenny must remember the dog. But Jenny was not going upstairs with all those people about. There was a motor at the door already! There was a ring at the bell—and the gentlemen still in the dining-room, drinking tokay!

There, they were going upstairs; that was the first to come, and now they would come faster and faster, so that Mrs. Parkinson (hired for parties) would leave the hall door ajar, and the hall would be full of gentlemen waiting (they stood waiting, sleeking down their hair) while the ladies took their cloaks off in the room along the passage; where Mrs. Barnet helped them, old Ellen Barnet, who had been with the family for forty years, and came every summer to help the ladies, and remembered mothers when they were girls, and though very unassuming did shake hands; said "milady" very respectfully, yet had a humorous way with her, looking at the young ladies, and ever so tactfully helping Lady Lovejoy, who had some trouble with her underbodice. And they could not help feeling, Lady Lovejoy and Miss Alice, that some little privilege in the matter of brush and comb, was awarded them having known Mrs. Barnet— "thirty years, milady," Mrs. Barnet supplied her. Young ladies did not use to rouge, said Lady Lovejoy, when they stayed at Bourton in the old days. And Miss Alice didn't need rouge, said Mrs. Barnet, looking at her fondly. There Mrs. Barnet would sit, in the cloakroom, patting down the furs, smoothing out the Spanish shawls, tidying the dressing-table, and knowing perfectly well, in spite of the furs and the embroideries, which were nice ladies, which were not. The dear old body, said Lady Lovejoy, mounting the stairs, Clarissa's old nurse.

And then Lady Lovejoy stiffened. "Lady and Miss Lovejoy," she said to Mr. Wilkins (hired for parties). He had an admirable manner, as he bent and straightened himself, bent and straightened himself and announced with perfect impartiality "Lady and Miss Lovejoy . . . Sir John and Lady Needham . . . Miss Weld . . . Mr. Walsh." His manner was admirable; his family life must be irreproachable, except that it seemed impossible that a being with greenish lips and shaven cheeks could ever have blundered into the nuisance of children.

"How delightful to see you!" said Clarissa. She said it to every one. How delightful to see you! She was at her worst— effusive, insincere. It was a great mistake to have come. He should have stayed at home and read his book, thought Peter Walsh; should have gone to a music hall; he should have stayed at home, for he knew no one.

Oh dear, it was going to be a failure; a complete failure, Clarissa felt it in her bones as dear old Lord Lexham stood there apologising for his wife who had caught cold at the Buckingham Palace garden party. She could see Peter out of the tail of her eye, criticising her, there, in that corner. Why, after all, did she do these things? Why seek pinnacles and stand drenched in fire? Might it consume her anyhow! Burn her to cinders! Better anything, better brandish one's torch and hurl it to earth than taper and dwindle away like some Ellie Henderson! It was extraordinary how Peter put her into these states just by coming and standing in a corner. He made her see herself; exaggerate. It was idiotic. But why did he come, then, merely to criticise? Why always take, never give? Why not risk one's one little point of view? There he was wandering off, and she must speak to him. But she would not get the chance. Life was that—humiliation, renunciation. What Lord Lexham was saying was that his wife would not wear her furs at the garden party because "my dear, you ladies are all alike"—Lady Lexham being seventy-five at least! It was delicious, how they petted each other, that old couple. She did like old Lord Lexham. She did think it mattered, her party, and it made her feel quite sick to know that it was all going wrong, all falling flat. Anything, any explosion, any horror was better than people wandering aimlessly, standing in a bunch at a corner like Ellie Henderson, not even caring to hold themselves upright.

Gently the yellow curtain with all the birds of Paradise blew out and it seemed as if there were a flight of wings into the room, right out, then sucked back. (For the windows were open.) Was it draughty, Ellie Henderson wondered? She was subject to chills. But it did not matter that she should come down sneezing tomorrow; it was the girls with their naked shoulders she thought of, being trained to think of others by an old father, an invalid, late vicar of Bourton, but he was dead now; and her chills never went to her chest, never. It was the girls she thought of, the young girls with their bare shoulders, she herself having always been a wisp of a creature, with her thin hair and meagre profile; though now, past fifty, there was beginning to shine through some mild beam, something purified into distinction by years of self-abnegation but obscured again, perpetually, by her distressing gentility, her panic fear, which arose from three hundred pounds' income, and her weaponless state (she could not earn a penny) and it made her timid, and more and more disqualified year by year to meet well-dressed people who did this sort of thing every night of the season, merely telling their maids "I'll wear so and so," whereas Ellie Henderson ran out nervously and bought cheap pink flowers, half a dozen, and then threw a shawl over her old black dress. For her invitation to Clarissa's party had come at the last moment. She was not quite happy about it. She had a sort of feeling that Clarissa had not meant to ask her this year.

Why should she? There was no reason really, except that they had always known each other. Indeed, they were cousins. But naturally they had rather drifted apart, Clarissa being so sought after. It was an event to her, going to a party. It was quite a treat just to see the lovely clothes. Wasn't that Elizabeth, grown up, with her hair done in the fashionable way, in the pink dress? Yet she could not be more than seventeen. She was very, very handsome. But girls when they first came out didn't seem to wear white as they used. (She must remember everything to tell Edith.) Girls wore straight frocks, perfectly tight, with skirts well above the ankles. It was not becoming, she thought.

So, with her weak eyesight, Ellie Henderson craned rather forward, and it wasn't so much she who minded not having any one to talk to (she hardly knew anybody there), for she felt that they were all such interesting people to watch; politicians presumably; Richard Dalloway's friends; but it was Richard himself who felt that he could not let the poor creature go on standing there all the evening by herself.

"Well, Ellie, and how's the world treating *you?*" he said in his genial way, and Ellie Henderson, getting nervous and flushing and feeling that it was extraordinarily nice of him to come and talk to her, said that many people really felt the heat more than the cold.

"Yes, they do," said Richard Dalloway. "Yes."

But what more did one say?

"Hullo, Richard," said somebody, taking him by the elbow, and, good Lord, there was old Peter, old Peter Walsh. He was delighted to see him—ever so pleased to see him! He hadn't changed a bit. And off they went together walking right across the room, giving each other little pats, as if they hadn't met for a long time, Ellie Henderson thought, watching them go, certain she knew that man's face. A tall man, middle aged, rather fine eyes, dark, wearing spectacles, with a look of John Burrows. Edith would be sure to know.

The curtain with its flight of birds of Paradise blew out again. And Clarissa saw—she saw Ralph Lyon beat it back, and go on talking. So it wasn't a failure after all! it was going to be all right now—her party. It had begun. It had started. But it was still touch and go. She must stand there for the present. People seemed to come in a rush.

Colonel and Mrs. Garrod . . . Mr. Hugh Whitbread . . . Mr. Bowley . . . Mrs. Hilbery . . . Lady Mary Maddox . . . Mr. Quin . . . intoned Wilkin. She had six or seven words with each, and they went on, they went into the rooms; into something now, not nothing, since Ralph Lyon had beat back the curtain.

And yet for her own part, it was too much of an effort. She was not enjoying it. It was too much like being—just anybody, standing there; anybody could do it, yet this anybody she did a little admire, couldn't help feeling that she had, anyhow, made this happen, that it marked a stage, this post that she felt herself to have become, for oddly enough she had quite forgotten what she looked like, but felt herself a stake driven in at the top of her stairs. Every time she gave a party she had this feeling of being something not herself, and that every one was unreal in one way; much more real in another. It was, she thought, partly their clothes, partly being taken out of their ordinary ways, partly the background, it was possible to say things you couldn't say anyhow else, things that needed an effort; possible to go much deeper. But not for her; not yet anyhow.

"How delightful to see you!" she said. Dear old Sir Harry! He would know every one.

And what was so odd about it was the sense one had as they came up the stairs one after another, Mrs. Mount and Celia, Herbert Ainsty, Mrs. Dakers—oh and Lady Bruton!

"How awfully good of you to come!" she said, and she meant it—it was odd how standing there one felt them going on, going on, some quite old, some . . .

What name? Lady Rosseter? But who on earth was Lady Rosseter?

"Clarissa!" That voice! It was Sally Seton! Sally Seton! after all these years! She loomed through a mist. For she hadn't looked like *that,* Sally Seton, when Clarissa grasped the hot water can, to think of her under this roof, under this roof! Not like that!

All on top of each other, embarrassed, laughing, words tumbled out—passing through London; heard from Clara Haydon; what a chance of seeing you! So I thrust myself in—without an invitation. . . .

One might put down the hot water can quite composedly. The lustre had gone out of her. Yet it was extraordinary to see her again, older, happier, less lovely. They kissed each other, first this cheek then that, by the drawing-room door, and Clarissa turned, with Sally's hand in hers, and saw her rooms full, heard the roar of voices, saw the candlesticks, the blowing curtains, and the roses which Richard had given her.

"I have five enormous boys," said Sally.

She had the simplest egotism, the most open desire to be thought first always, and Clarissa loved her for being still like that. "I can't believe it!" she cried, kindling all over with pleasure at the thought of the past.

But alas, Wilkins; Wilkins wanted her; Wilkins was emitting in a voice of commanding authority as if the whole company must be admonished and the hostess reclaimed from frivolity, one name:

"The Prime Minister," said Peter Walsh.

The Prime Minister? Was it really? Ellie Henderson marvelled. What a thing to tell Edith!

One couldn't laugh at him. He looked so ordinary. You might have stood him behind a counter and bought biscuits — poor chap, all rigged up in gold lace. And to be fair, as he went his rounds, first with Clarissa then with Richard escorting him, he did it very well. He tried to look somebody. It was amusing to watch. Nobody looked at him. They just went on talking, yet it was perfectly plain that they all knew, felt to the marrow of their bones, this majesty passing; this symbol of what they all stood for, English society. Old Lady Bruton, and she looked very fine too, very stalwart in her lace, swam up, and they withdrew into a little room which at once became spied upon, guarded, and a sort of stir and rustle rippled through every one, openly: the Prime Minister!

Lord, lord, the snobbery of the English! thought Peter Walsh, standing in the corner. How they loved dressing up in gold lace and doing homage! There! That must be, by Jove it was, Hugh Whitbread, snuffing round the precincts of the great, grown rather fatter, rather whiter, the admirable Hugh!

He looked always as if he were on duty, thought Peter, a privileged, but secretive being, hoarding secrets which he would die to defend, though it was only some little piece of tittle-tattle dropped by a court footman, which would be in all the papers to-morrow. Such were his rattles, his baubles, in playing with which he had grown white, come to the verge of old age, enjoying the respect and affection of all who had the privilege of knowing this type of the English public school man. Inevitably one made up things like that about Hugh; that was his style; the style of those admirable letters which Peter had read thousands of miles across the sea in the *Times,* and had thanked God he was out of that pernicious hubble-bubble if it were only to hear baboons chatter and coolies beat their wives. An olive-skinned youth from one of the Universities stood obsequiously by. Him he would patronise, initiate, teach how to get on. For he liked nothing better than doing kindnessses, making the hearts of old ladies palpitate with the joy of being thought of in their age, their affliction, thinking themselves quite forgotten, yet here was dear Hugh driving up and spending an hour talk-ing of the past, remembering trifles, praising the homemade cake, though Hugh might eat cake with a Duchess any day of his life, and, to look at him, probably did spend a good deal of time in that agreeable occupation. The All-judging, the All-merciful, might excuse. Peter Walsh had no mercy. Villains there must be, and God knows the rascals who get hanged for batter-ing the brains of a girl out in a train do less harm on the whole than Hugh Whitbread and his kindness. Look at him now, on tiptoe, dancing forward, bowing and scraping, as the Prime Minister and Lady Bruton emerged, intimating for all the world to see that he was privileged to say something, something pri-vate, to Lady Bruton as she passed. She stopped. She wagged her fine old head. She was thanking him presumably for some piece of servility. She had her toadies, minor officials in Gov-ernment offices who ran about putting through little jobs on her behalf, in return for which she gave them luncheon. But she derived from the eighteenth century. She was all right.

And now Clarissa escorted her Prime Minister down the room, prancing, sparkling, with the stateliness of her grey hair. She wore ear-rings, and a silver-green mermaid's dress. Lollop-ing on the waves and braiding her tresses she seemed, having that gift still; to be; to exist; to sum it all up in the moment as she passed; turned, caught her scarf in some other woman's dress, unhitched it, laughed, all with the most perfect ease and air of a creature floating in its element. But age had brushed her; even as a mermaid might behold in her glass the setting sun on some very clear evening over the waves. There was a breath of tenderness; her severity, her prudery, her woodenness were all warmed through now, and she had about her as she said good-bye to the thick gold-laced man who was doing his best, and good luck to him, to look important, an inexpressible dignity; an exquisite cordiality; as if she wished the whole world well, and must now, being on the very verge and rim of things, take her leave. So she made him think. (But he was not in love.)

Indeed, Clarissa felt, the Prime Minister had been good to come. And, walking down the room with him, with Sally there and Peter there and Richard very pleased, with all those people rather inclined, perhaps, to envy, she had felt that intoxication of the moment, that dilatation of the nerves of the heart itself till it seemed to quiver, steeped, upright;—yes, but after all it was what other people felt, that; for, though she loved it and felt it tingle and sting, still these semblances, these triumphs (dear old Peter, for example, thinking her so brilliant), had a hollow-ness; at arm's length they were, not in the heart; and it might be that she was growing old but they satisfied her no longer as they used; and suddenly, as she saw the Prime Minister go down the stairs, the gilt rim of the Sir Joshua picture of the little girl with a muff brought back Kilman with a rush; Kilman her enemy. That was satisfying; that was real. Ah, how she hated her—hot, hypocritical, corrupt; with all that power; Elizabeth's seducer; the woman who had crept in to steal and defile (Richard would say, What nonsense!). She hated her: she loved her. It was ene-mies one wanted, not friends—not Mrs. Durrant and Clara, Sir William and Lady Bradshaw, Miss Truelock and Eleanor Gibson (whom she saw coming upstairs). They must find her if they wanted her. She was for the party!

There was her old friend Sir Harry.

"Dear Sir Harry!" she said, going up to the fine old fellow who had produced more bad pictures than any other two Academicians in the whole of St. John's Wood (they were always of cattle, standing in sunset pools absorbing moisture, or signifying, for he had a certain range of gesture, by the raising of one foreleg and the toss of the antlers, "the Approach of the Stranger"—all his activities, dining out, racing, were founded on cattle standing absorbing moisture in sunset pools).

"What are you laughing at?" she asked him. For Willie Titcomb and Sir Harry and Herbert Ainsty were all laughing. But no. Sir Harry could not tell Clarissa Dalloway (much though he liked her; of her type he thought her perfect, and threatened to paint her) his stories of the music hall stage. He chaffed her about her party. He missed his brandy. These circles, he said, were above him. But he liked her; respected her, in spite of her damnable, difficult upper-class refinement, which made it impossible to ask Clarissa Dalloway to sit on his knee. And up came that wandering will-o'-the-wisp, that vagulous phosphorescence, old Mrs. Hilbery, stretching her hands to the blaze of his laughter (about the Duke and the Lady), which, as she heard it across the room, seemed to reassure her on a point which sometimes bothered her if she woke early in the morning and did not like to call her maid for a cup of tea; how it is certain we must die.

"They won't tell us their stories," said Clarissa.

"Dear Clarissa!" exclaimed Mrs. Hilbery. She looked tonight, she said, so like her mother as she first saw her walking in a garden in a grey hat.

And really Clarissa's eyes filled with tears. Her mother, walking in a garden! But alas, she must go.

For there was Professor Brierly, who lectured on Milton, talking to little Jim Hutton (who was unable even for a party like this to compass both tie and waistcoat or make his hair lie flat), and even at this distance they were quarrelling, she could see. For Professor Brierly was a very queer fish. With all those degrees, honours, lectureships between him and the scribblers he suspected instantly an atmosphere not favourable to his queer compound; his prodigious learning and timidity; his wintry charm without cordiality; his innocence blent with snobbery; he quivered if made conscious by a lady's unkempt hair, a youth's boots, of an underworld, very creditable doubtless, of rebels, of ardent young people; of would-be geniuses, and intimated with a little toss of the head, with a sniff—Humph!—the value of moderation; of some slight training in the classics in order to appreciate Milton. Professor Brierly (Clarissa could see) wasn't hitting it off with little Jim Hutton (who wore red socks, his black being at the laundry) about Milton. She interrupted.

She said she loved Bach. So did Hutton. That was the bond between them, and Hutton (a very bad poet) always felt that Mrs. Dalloway was far the best of the great ladies who took an interest in art. It was odd how strict she was. About music she was purely impersonal. She was rather a prig. But how charming to look at! She made her house so nice if it weren't for her Professors. Clarissa had half a mind to snatch him off and set him down at the piano in the back room. For he played divinely.

"But the noise!" she said. "The noise!"

"The sign of a successful party." Nodding urbanely, the Professor stepped delicately off.

"He knows everything in the whole world about Milton," said Clarissa.

"Does he indeed?" said Hutton, who would imitate the Professor throughout Hampstead; the Professor on Milton; the Professor on moderation; the Professor stepping delicately off.

But she must speak to that couple, said Clarissa, Lord Gayton and Nancy Blow.

Not that *they* added perceptibly to the noise of the party. They were not talking (perceptibly) as they stood side by side by the yellow curtains. They would soon be off elsewhere, together; and never had very much to say in any circumstances. They looked; that was all. That was enough. They looked so clean, so sound, she with an apricot bloom of powder and paint, but he scrubbed, rinsed, with the eyes of a bird, so that no ball could pass him or stroke surprise him. He struck, he leapt, accurately, on the spot. Ponies' mouths quivered at the end of his reins. He had his honours, ancestral monuments, banners hanging in the church at home. He had his duties; his tenants; a mother and sisters; had been all day at Lords, and that was what they were talking about—cricket, cousins, the movies—when Mrs. Dalloway came up. Lord Gayton liked her most awfully. So did Miss Blow. She had such charming manners.

"It is angelic—it is delicious of you to have come!" she said. She loved Lords; she loved youth, and Nancy, dressed at enormous expense by the greatest artists in Paris, stood there looking as if her body had merely put forth, of its own accord, a green frill.

"I had meant to have dancing," said Clarissa.

For the young people could not talk. And why should they? Shout, embrace, swing, be up at dawn; carry sugar to ponies; kiss and caress the snouts of adorable chows; and then all tingling and streaming, plunge and swim. But the enormous resources of the English language, the power it bestows, after all, of communicating feelings (at their age, she and Peter would have been arguing all the evening), was not for them. They would solidify young. They would be good beyond measure to the people on the estate, but alone, perhaps, rather dull.

"What a pity!" she said. "I had hoped to have dancing."

It was so extraordinarily nice of them to have come! But talk of dancing! The rooms were packed.

There was old Aunt Helena in her shawl. Alas, she must leave them—Lord Gayton and Nancy Blow. There was old Miss Parry, her aunt.

For Miss Helena Parry was not dead: Miss Parry was alive. She was past eighty. She ascended staircases slowly with a stick. She was placed in a chair (Richard had seen to it). People who had known Burma in the 'seventies were always led up to her. Where had Peter got to? They used to be such friends. For at the mention of India, or even Ceylon, her eyes (only one was glass) slowly deepened, became blue, beheld, not human beings—she had no tender memories, no proud illusions about Viceroys, Generals, Mutinies—it was orchids she saw, and mountain passes and herself carried on the backs of coolies in the 'sixties over solitary peaks; or descending to uproot orchids (startling blossoms, never beheld before) which she painted in water-colour; an indomitable Englishwoman, fretful if disturbed by the War, say, which dropped a bomb at her very door, from her deep meditation over orchids and her own figure journeying in the 'sixties in India—but here was Peter.

"Come and talk to Aunt Helena about Burma," said Clarissa.

And yet he had not had a word with her all the evening!

"We will talk later," said Clarissa, leading him up to Aunt Helena, in her white shawl, with her stick.

"Peter Walsh," said Clarissa.

That meant nothing.

Clarissa had asked her. It was tiring; it was noisy; but Clarissa had asked her. So she had come. It was a pity that they lived in London—Richard and Clarissa. If only for Clarissa's health it would have been better to live in the country. But Clarissa had always been fond of society.

"He has been in Burma," said Clarissa.

Ah. She could not resist recalling what Charles Darwin had said about her little book on the orchids of Burma.

(Clarissa must speak to Lady Bruton.)

No doubt it was forgotten now, her book on the orchids of Burma, but it went into three editions before 1870, she told Peter. She remembered him now. He had been at Bourton (and he had left her, Peter Walsh remembered, without a word in the drawing-room that night when Clarissa had asked him to come boating).

"Richard so much enjoyed his lunch party," said Clarissa to Lady Bruton.

"Richard was the greatest possible help," Lady Bruton replied. "He helped me to write a letter. And how are you?"

"Oh, perfectly well!" said Clarissa. (Lady Bruton detested illness in the wives of politicians.)

"And there's Peter Walsh!" said Lady Bruton (for she could never think of anything to say to Clarissa; though she liked her. She had lots of fine qualities; but they had nothing in common—she and Clarissa. It might have been better if Richard had married a woman with less charm, who would have helped him more in his work. He had lost his chance of the Cabinet). "There's Peter Walsh!" she said, shaking hands with that agreeable sinner, that very able fellow who should have made a name for himself but hadn't (always in difficulties with women), and, of course, old Miss Parry. Wonderful old lady!

Lady Bruton stood by Miss Parry's chair, a spectral grenadier, draped in black, inviting Peter Walsh to lunch; cordial; but without small talk, remembering nothing whatever about the flora or fauna of India. She had been there, of course; had stayed with three Viceroys; thought some of the Indian civilians uncommonly fine fellows; but what a tragedy it was—the state of India! The Prime Minister had just been telling her (old Miss Parry huddled up in her shawl, did not care what the Prime

Minister had just been telling her), and Lady Bruton would like to have Peter Walsh's opinion, he being fresh from the centre, and she would get Sir Sampson to meet him, for really it prevented her from sleeping at night, the folly of it, the wickedness she might say, being a soldier's daughter. She was an old woman now, not good for much. But her house, her servants, her good friend Milly Brush—did he remember her?—were all there only asking to be used if—if they could be of help, in short. For she never spoke of England, but this isle of men, this dear, dear land, was in her blood (without reading Shakespeare), and if ever a woman could have worn the helmet and shot the arrow, could have led troops to attack, ruled with indomitable justice barbarian hordes and lain under a shield noseless in a church, or made a green grass mound on some primeval hillside, that woman was Millicent Bruton. Debarred by her sex and some truancy, too, of the logical faculty (she found it impossible to write a letter to the *Times*), she had the thought of Empire always at hand, and had acquired from her association with that armoured goddess her ramrod bearing, her robustness of demeanour, so that one could not figure her even in death parted from the earth or roaming territories over which, in some spiritual shape, the Union Jack had ceased to fly. To be not English even among the dead—no, no! Impossible!

But was it Lady Bruton (whom she used to know)? Was it Peter Walsh grown grey? Lady Rosseter asked herself (who had been Sally Seton). It was old Miss Parry certainly—the old aunt who used to be so cross when she stayed at Bourton. Never should she forget running along the passage naked, and being sent for by Miss Parry! And Clarissa! oh Clarissa! Sally caught her by the arm.

Clarissa stopped beside them.

"But I can't stay," she said. "I shall come later. Wait," she said, looking at Peter and Sally. They must wait, she meant, until all these people had gone.

"I shall come back," she said, looking at her old friends, Sally and Peter, who were shaking hands, and Sally, remembering the past no doubt, was laughing.

But her voice was wrung of its old ravishing richness; her eyes not aglow as they used to be, when she smoked cigars, when she ran down the passage to fetch her sponge bag, without a stitch of clothing on her, and Ellen Atkins asked, What if the gentlemen had met her? But everybody forgave her. She stole a chicken from the larder because she was hungry in the night; she smoked cigars in her bedroom; she left a priceless book in the punt. But everybody adored her (except perhaps Papa). It was her warmth; her vitality—she would paint, she would write. Old women in the village never to this day forgot to ask after "your friend in the red cloak who seemed so bright." She accused Hugh Whitbread, of all people (and there he was, her old friend Hugh, talking to the Portuguese Ambassador), of kissing her in the smoking-room to punish her for saying that women should have votes. Vulgar men did, she said. And Clarissa remembered having to persuade her not to denounce him at family prayers—which she was capable of doing with her daring, her recklessness, her melodramatic love of being the centre of everything and creating scenes, and it was bound, Clarissa used to think, to end in some awful tragedy; her death; her martyrdom; instead of which she had married, quite unexpectedly, a bald man with a large buttonhole who owned, it was said, cotton mills at Manchester. And she had five boys!

She and Peter had settled down together. They were talking: it seemed so familiar—that they should be talking. They would discuss the past. With the two of them (more even than with Richard) she shared her past; the garden; the trees; old Joseph

Breitkopf singing Brahms without any voice; the drawing-room wallpaper; the smell of the mats. A part of this Sally must always be; Peter must always be. But she must leave them. There were the Bradshaws, whom she disliked. She must go up to Lady Bradshaw (in grey and silver, balancing like a sea-lion at the edge of its tank, barking for invitations, Duchesses, the typical successful man's wife), she must go up to Lady Bradshaw and say . . .

But Lady Bradshaw anticipated her.

"We are shockingly late, dear Mrs. Dalloway, we hardly dared to come in," she said.

And Sir William, who looked very distinguished, with his grey hair and blue eyes, said yes; they had not been able to re-sist the temptation. He was talking to Richard about that Bill probably, which they wanted to get through the Commons. Why did the sight of him, talking to Richard, curl her up? He looked what he was, a great doctor. A man absolutely at the head of his profession, very powerful, rather worn. For think what cases came before him—people in the uttermost depths of misery; people on the verge of insanity; husbands and wives. He had to decide questions of appalling difficulty. Yet—what she felt was, one wouldn't like Sir William to see one unhappy. No; not that man.

"How is your son at Eton?" she asked Lady Bradshaw.

He had just missed his eleven, said Lady Bradshaw, because of the mumps. His father minded even more than he did, she thought "being," she said, "nothing but a great boy himself."

Clarissa looked at Sir William, talking to Richard. He did not look like a boy—not in the least like a boy. She had once gone with some one to ask his advice. He had been perfectly right; extremely sensible. But Heavens—what a relief to get out to the street again! There was some poor wretch sobbing, she remembered, in the waiting-room. But she did not know what it was—about Sir William; what exactly she disliked. Only Richard agreed with her, "didn't like his taste, didn't like his smell." But he was extraordinarily able. They were talking about this Bill. Some case, Sir William was mentioning, lowering his voice. It had its bearing upon what he was saying about the deferred effects of shell shock. There must be some provision in the Bill.

Sinking her voice, drawing Mrs. Dalloway into the shelter of a common femininity, a common pride in the illustrious qualities of husbands and their sad tendency to overwork, Lady Bradshaw (poor goose—one didn't dislike her) murmured how, "just as we were starting, my husband was called up on the telephone, a very sad case. A young man (that is what Sir William is telling Mr. Dalloway) had killed himself. He had been in the army." Oh! thought Clarissa, in the middle of my party, here's death, she thought.

She went on, into the little room where the Prime Minister had gone with Lady Bruton. Perhaps there was somebody there. But there was nobody. The chairs still kept the impress of the Prime Minister and Lady Bruton, she turned deferentially, he sitting four-square, authoritatively. They had been talking about India. There was nobody. The party's splendour fell to the floor, so strange it was to come in alone in her finery.

What business had the Bradshaws to talk of death at her party? A young man had killed himself. And they talked of it at her party—the Bradshaws, talked of death. He had killed himself—but how? Always her body went through it first, when she was told, suddenly, of an accident; her dress flamed, her body burnt. He had thrown himself from a window. Up had flashed the ground; through him, blundering, bruising, went the rusty spikes. There he lay with a thud, thud, thud in his brain, and then a suffocation of blackness. So she saw it. But why had he done it? And the Bradshaws talked of it at her party!

She had once thrown a shilling into the Serpentine, never anything more. But he had flung it away. They went on living (she would have to go back; the rooms were still crowded; people kept on coming). They (all day she had been thinking of Bourton, of Peter, of Sally), they would grow old. A thing there was that mattered; a thing, wreathed about with chatter, defaced, obscured in her own life, let drop every day in corruption, lies, chatter. This he had preserved. Death was defiance. Death was an attempt to communicate; people feeling the impossibility of reaching the centre which, mystically, evaded them; closeness drew apart; rapture faded, one was alone. There was an embrace in death.

But this young man who had killed himself—had he plunged holding his treasure? "If it were now to die, 'twere now to be most happy," she had said to herself once, coming down in white.

Or there were the poets and thinkers. Suppose he had had that passion, and had gone to Sir William Bradshaw, a great doctor yet to her obscurely evil, without sex or lust, extremely polite to women, but capable of some indescribable outrage—forcing your soul, that was it—if this young man had gone to him, and Sir William had impressed him, like that, with his power, might he not then have said (indeed she felt it now), Life is made intolerable; they make life intolerable, men like that?

Then (she had felt it only this morning) there was the terror; the overwhelming incapacity, one's parents giving it into one's hands, this life, to be lived to the end, to be walked with serenely; there was in the depths of her heart an awful fear. Even now, quite often if Richard had not been there reading the *Times,* so that she could crouch like a bird and gradually revive, send roaring up that immeasurable delight, rubbing stick to stick, one thing with another, she must have perished. But that young man had killed himself.

Somehow it was her disaster—her disgrace. It was her punishment to see sink and disappear here a man, there a woman, in this profound darkness, and she forced to stand here in her evening dress. She had schemed; she had pilfered. She was never wholly admirable. She had wanted success. Lady Bexborough and the rest of it. And once she had walked on the terrace at Bourton.

It was due to Richard; she had never been so happy. Nothing could be slow enough; nothing last too long. No pleasure could equal, she thought, straightening the chairs, pushing in one book on the shelf, this having done with the triumphs of youth, lost herself in the process of living, to find it, with a shock of delight, as the sun rose, as the day sank. Many a time had she gone, at Bourton when they were all talking, to look at the sky; or seen it between people's shoulders at dinner; seen it in London when she could not sleep. She walked to the window.

It held, foolish as the idea was, something of her own in it, this country sky, this sky above Westminster. She parted the curtains; she looked. Oh, but how surprising!—in the room opposite the old lady stared straight at her! She was going to bed. And the sky. It will be a solemn sky, she had thought, it will be a dusky sky, turning away its cheek in beauty. But there it was— ashen pale, raced over quickly by tapering vast clouds. It was new to her. The wind must have risen. She was going to bed, in the room opposite. It was fascinating to watch her, moving about, that old lady, crossing the room, coming to the window. Could she see her? It was fascinating, with people still laughing and shouting in the drawing-room, to watch that old woman, quite quietly, going to bed. She pulled the blind now. The clock began striking. The young man had killed himself; but she did not pity him; with the clock striking the hour, one, two, three, she did not pity him, with all this going on. There! the old lady had put out her light! the whole house was dark now with this

going on, she repeated, and the words came to her, Fear no
more the heat of the sun. She must go back to them. But what
an extraordinary night! She felt somehow very like him—the
young man who had killed himself. She felt glad that he had
done it; thrown it away. The clock was striking. The leaden
circles dissolved in the air. He made her feel the beauty; made
her feel the fun. But she must go back. She must assemble. She
must find Sally and Peter. And she came in from the little room.

"But where is Clarissa?" said Peter. He was sitting on the
sofa with Sally. (After all these years he really could not call her
"Lady Rosseter.") "Where's the woman gone to?" he asked.
"Where's Clarissa?"

Sally supposed, and so did Peter for the matter of that, that
there were people of importance, politicians, whom neither of
them knew unless by sight in the picture papers, whom Clarissa
had to be nice to, had to talk to. She was with them. Yet there
was Richard Dalloway not in the Cabinet. He hadn't been a success, Sally supposed? For herself, she scarcely ever read the papers. She sometimes saw his name mentioned. But then—well,
she lived a very solitary life, in the wilds, Clarissa would say,
among great merchants, great manufacturers, men, after all,
who did things. She had done things too!

"I have five sons!" she told him.

Lord, Lord, what a change had come over her! the softness
of motherhood; its egotism too. Last time they met, Peter remembered, had been among the cauliflowers in the moonlight,
the leaves "like rough bronze" she had said, with her literary
turn; and she had picked a rose. She had marched him up and
down that awful night, after the scene by the fountain; he was
to catch the midnight train. Heavens, he had wept!

That was his old trick, opening a pocket-knife, thought
Sally, always opening and shutting a knife when he got excited.
They had been very, very intimate, she and Peter Walsh, when

he was in love with Clarissa, and there was that dreadful, ridiculous scene over Richard Dalloway at lunch. She had called Richard "Wickham." Why not call Richard "Wickham"? Clarissa had flared up! and indeed they had never seen each other since, she and Clarissa, not more than half a dozen times perhaps in the last ten years. And Peter Walsh had gone off to India, and she had heard vaguely that he had made an unhappy marriage, and she didn't know whether he had any children, and she couldn't ask him, for he had changed. He was rather shrivelled-looking, but kinder, she felt, and she had a real affection for him, for he was connected with her youth, and she still had a little Emily Brontë he had given her, and he was to write, surely? In those days he was to write.

"Have you written?" she asked him, spreading her hand, her firm and shapely hand, on her knee in a way he recalled.

"Not a word!" said Peter Walsh, and she laughed.

She was still attractive, still a personage, Sally Seton. But who was this Rosseter? He wore two camelias on his wedding day—that was all Peter knew of him. "They have myriads of servants, miles of conservatories," Clarissa wrote; something like that. Sally owned it with a shout of laughter.

"Yes, I have ten thousand a year"—whether before the tax was paid or after, she couldn't remember, for her husband, "whom you must meet," she said, "whom you would like," she said, did all that for her.

And Sally used to be in rags and tatters. She had pawned her grandmother's ring which Marie Antoinette had given her great-grandfather to come to Bourton.

Oh yes, Sally remembered; she had it still, a ruby ring which Marie Antoinette had given her great-grandfather. She never had a penny to her name in those days, and going to Bourton always meant some frightful pinch. But going to Bourton had meant so much to her—had kept her sane, she believed, so unhappy had she been at home. But that was all a thing of the past—all over now, she said. And Mr. Parry was dead; and Miss Parry was still alive. Never had he had such a shock in his life! said Peter. He had been quite certain she was dead. And the marriage had been, Sally supposed, a success? And that very handsome, very self-possessed young woman was Elizabeth, over there, by the curtains, in red.

(She was like a poplar, she was like a river, she was like a hyacinth, Willie Titcomb was thinking. Oh how much nicer to be in the country and do what she liked! She could hear her poor dog howling, Elizabeth was certain.) She was not a bit like Clarissa, Peter Walsh said.

"Oh, Clarissa!" said Sally.

What Sally felt was simply this. She had owed Clarissa an enormous amount. They had been friends, not acquaintances, friends, and she still saw Clarissa all in white going about the house with her hands full of flowers—to this day tobacco plants made her think of Bourton. But—did Peter understand?—she lacked something. Lacked what was it? She had charm; she had extraordinary charm. But to be frank (and she felt that Peter was an old friend, a real friend—did absence matter? did distance matter? She had often wanted to write to him, but torn it up, yet felt he understood, for people understand without things being said, as one realises growing old, and old she was, had been that afternoon to see her sons at Eton, where they had the mumps), to be quite frank then, how could Clarissa have done it?—married Richard Dalloway? a sportsman, a man who cared only for dogs. Literally, when he came into the room he smelt of the stables. And then all this? She waved her hand.

Hugh Whitbread it was, strolling past in his white waistcoat, dim, fat, blind, past everything he looked, except self-esteem and comfort.

"He's not going to recognise *us*," said Sally, and really she hadn't the courage—so that was Hugh! the admirable Hugh!

"And what does he do?" she asked Peter.

He blacked the King's boots or counted bottles at Windsor, Peter told her. Peter kept his sharp tongue still! But Sally must be frank, Peter said. That kiss now, Hugh's.

On the lips, she assured him, in the smoking-room one evening. She went straight to Clarissa in a rage. Hugh didn't do such things! Clarissa said, the admirable Hugh! Hugh's socks were without exception the most beautiful she had ever seen—and now his evening dress. Perfect! And had he children?

"Everybody in the room has six sons at Eton," Peter told her, except himself. He, thank God, had none. No sons, no daughters, no wife. Well, he didn't seem to mind, said Sally. He looked younger, she thought, than any of them.

But it had been a silly thing to do, in many ways, Peter said, to marry like that; "a perfect goose she was," he said, but, he said, "we had a splendid time of it," but how could that be? Sally wondered; what did he mean? and how odd it was to know him and yet not know a single thing that had happened to him. And did he say it out of pride? Very likely, for after all it must be galling for him (though he was an oddity, a sort of sprite, not at all an ordinary man), it must be lonely at his age to have no home, nowhere to go to. But he must stay with them for weeks and weeks. Of course he would; he would love to stay with them, and that was how it came out. All these years the Dalloways had never been once. Time after time they had asked them. Clarissa (for it was Clarissa of course) would not come. For, said Sally, Clarissa was at heart a snob—one had to admit it, a snob. And it was that that was between them, she was convinced. Clarissa thought she had married beneath her, her husband being—she was proud of it—a miner's son. Every penny they had he had earned. As a little boy (her voice trembled) he had carried great sacks.

(And so she would go on, Peter felt, hour after hour; the miner's son; people thought she had married beneath her; her five sons; and what was the other thing—plants, hydrangeas, syringas, very, very rare hibiscus lilies that never grow north of the Suez Canal, but she, with one gardener in a suburb near Manchester, had beds of them, positively beds! Now all that Clarissa had escaped, unmaternal as she was.)

A snob was she? Yes, in many ways. Where was she, all this time? It was getting late.

"Yet," said Sally, "when I heard Clarissa was giving a party, I felt I couldn't *not* come—must see her again (and I'm staying in Victoria Street, practically next door). So I just came without an invitation. But," she whispered, "tell me, do. Who is this?"

It was Mrs. Hilbery, looking for the door. For how late it was getting! And, she murmured, as the night grew later, as people went, one found old friends; quiet nooks and corners; and the loveliest views. Did they know, she asked, that they were surrounded by an enchanted garden? Lights and trees and wonderful gleaming lakes and the sky. Just a few fairy lamps, Clarissa Dalloway had said, in the back garden! But she was a magician! It was a park. . . . And she didn't know their names, but friends she knew they were, friends without names, songs without words, always the best. But there were so many doors, such unexpected places, she could not find her way.

"Old Mrs. Hilbery," said Peter; but who was that? that lady standing by the curtain all the evening, without speaking? He knew her face; connected her with Bourton. Surely she used to cut up underclothes at the large table in the window? Davidson, was that her name?

"Oh, that is Ellie Henderson," said Sally. Clarissa was really very hard on her. She was a cousin, very poor. Clarissa *was* hard on people.

She was rather, said Peter. Yet, said Sally, in her emotional way, with a rush of that enthusiasm which Peter used to love her for, yet dreaded a little now, so effusive she might become — how generous to her friends Clarissa was! and what a rare quality one found it, and how sometimes at night or on Christmas Day, when she counted up her blessings, she put that friendship first. They were young; that was it. Clarissa was pure-hearted; that was it. Peter would think her sentimental. So she was. For she had come to feel that it was the only thing worth saying — what one felt. Cleverness was silly. One must say simply what one felt.

"But I do not know," said Peter Walsh, "what I feel."

Poor Peter, thought Sally. Why did not Clarissa come and talk to them? That was what he was longing for. She knew it. All the time he was thinking only of Clarissa, and was fidgeting with his knife.

He had not found life simple, Peter said. His relations with Clarissa had not been simple. It had spoilt his life, he said. (They had been so intimate — he and Sally Seton, it was absurd not to say it.) One could not be in love twice, he said. And what could she say? Still, it is better to have loved (but he would think her sentimental — he used to be so sharp). He must come and stay with them in Manchester. That is all very true, he said. All very true. He would love to come and stay with them, directly he had done what he had to do in London.

And Clarissa had cared for him more than she had ever cared for Richard. Sally was positive of that.

"No, no, no!" said Peter (Sally should not have said that — she went too far). That good fellow — there he was at the end of the room, holding forth, the same as ever, dear old Richard.

Who was he talking to? Sally asked, that very distinguished-looking man? Living in the wilds as she did, she had an insatiable curiosity to know who people were. But Peter did not know. He did not like his looks, he said, probably a Cabinet Minister. Of them all, Richard seemed to him the best, he said—the most disinterested.

"But what has he done?" Sally asked. Public work, she supposed. And were they happy together? Sally asked (she herself was extremely happy); for, she admitted, she knew nothing about them, only jumped to conclusions, as one does, for what can one know even of the people one lives with every day? she asked. Are we not all prisoners? She had read a wonderful play about a man who scratched on the wall of his cell, and she had felt that was true of life—one scratched on the wall. Despairing of human relationships (people were so difficult), she often went into her garden and got from her flowers a peace which men and women never gave her. But no; he did not like cabbages; he preferred human beings, Peter said. Indeed, the young are beautiful, Sally said, watching Elizabeth cross the room. How unlike Clarissa at her age! Could he make anything of her? She would not open her lips. Not much, not yet, Peter admitted. She was like a lily, Sally said, a lily by the side of a pool. But Peter did not agree that we know nothing. We know everything, he said; at least he did.

But these two, Sally whispered, these two coming now (and really she must go, if Clarissa did not come soon), this distinguished-looking man and his rather common-looking wife who had been talking to Richard—what could one know about people like that?

"That they're damnable humbugs," said Peter, looking at them casually. He made Sally laugh.

But Sir William Bradshaw stopped at the door to look at a picture. He looked in the corner for the engraver's name. His wife looked too. Sir William Bradshaw was so interested in art.

When one was young, said Peter, one was too much excited to know people. Now that one was old, fifty-two to be precise (Sally was fifty-five, in body, she said, but her heart was like a girl's of twenty); now that one was mature then, said Peter, one could watch, one could understand, and one did not lose the power of feeling, he said. No, that is true, said Sally. She felt more deeply, more passionately, every year. It increased, he said, alas, perhaps, but one should be glad of it—it went on increasing in his experience. There was some one in India. He would like to tell Sally about her. He would like Sally to know her. She was married, he said. She had two small children. They must all come to Manchester, said Sally—he must promise before they left.

There's Elizabeth, he said, she feels not half what we feel, not yet. But, said Sally, watching Elizabeth go to her father, one can see they are devoted to each other. She could feel it by the way Elizabeth went to her father.

For her father had been looking at her, as he stood talking to the Bradshaws, and he had thought to himself, Who is that lovely girl? And suddenly he realised that it was his Elizabeth, and he had not recognised her, she looked so lovely in her pink frock! Elizabeth had felt him looking at her as she talked to Willie Titcomb. So she went to him and they stood together, now that the party was almost over, looking at the people going, and the rooms getting emptier and emptier, with things scattered on the floor. Even Ellie Henderson was going, nearly last of all, though no one had spoken to her, but she had wanted to see everything, to tell Edith. And Richard and Elizabeth were rather glad it was over, but Richard was proud of his daughter. And he had not meant to tell her, but he could not help telling her. He had looked at her, he said, and he had wondered, Who is that lovely girl? and it was his daughter! That did make her happy. But her poor dog was howling.

"Richard has improved. You are right," said Sally. "I shall go and talk to him. I shall say good-night. What does the brain matter," said Lady Rosseter, getting up, "compared with the heart?"

"I will come," said Peter, but he sat on for a moment. What is this terror? what is this ecstasy? he thought to himself. What is it that fills me with extraordinary excitement?

It is Clarissa, he said.

For there she was.

Notes to *Mrs. Dalloway*

The walks and rides taken through London by various characters may be followed on the map that appears at the beginning of the book, through references in the notes. Locations are numbered chronologically followed by an initial (C=Clarissa; E=Elizabeth; H=Hugh; K=Miss Kilman; M=motorcar; P=Peter; R=Richard; S=Septimus). (DB) indicates a note that is indebted to David Bradshaw, "Explanatory Notes," in *Mrs. Dalloway,* by Virginia Woolf (Oxford: Oxford University Press, 2000), 166–85. Bradshaw makes extensive use of *The London Encyclopaedia* (London and Basingstoke: Macmillan, 1993), which he recommends.

Rumpelmayer's men [3]   Caterers for Clarissa's party. There was an actual local firm by this name in 1923.

Clarissa [3]   Noteworthy examples of literary predecessors with this name are the heroine of Samuel Richardson's *Clarissa Harlowe* (1747–48), and the Clarissa who provides the scissors to cut the heroine's hair in Alexander Pope's *The Rape of the Lock* (1712).

Bourton [3]   The imaginary home of Clarissa's family, the Parrys, where she grew up. There are two villages with Bourton in their name in the Cotswold Hills of Gloucestershire. This scenic limestone range drains from one side into the Severn River, which is visible from Woolf's fictional Bourton (see 150).

Durtnall's van [4]   Vehicle belonging to an actual transport and warehouse firm.

Westminster [4]   Borough of London, on the north bank of the Thames River, housing many of Britain's principal government buildings, palaces, and the famous Anglican church Westminster Abbey.

influenza [4]   A worldwide pandemic of influenza killed more than 20 million people in 1918 and 1919. Woolf's recurrent bouts with more standard forms of flu interrupted her writing.

Big Ben [4]   Mrs. Dalloway refers first to the "warning, musical" of the famous Westminster Chimes, rung on four bells at the quarter hour. This is followed on the hour by the tolling of the central, thirteen-ton bell, first sounded in 1859. It may have taken its name from the rotund first commissioner of works, Benjamin Hall. The clock tower rises above Westminster Palace, which contains the British Houses of Parliament. At midnight on December 31, 1923, Woolf could have heard Big Ben over the radio for the first time. Big Ben and the bells of other clocks are heard by various characters, interrupting their actions and marking the passage of time, "the leaden circles dissolv[ing] in the air" throughout the novel (e.g., see Peter, 47; the Smiths, the clocks of Harley Street, 100).

Victoria Street [4]   Street connecting Belgravia with Westminster. Residential apartment buildings dating to the 1880s have gradually yielded to modern concrete and glass office buildings and commercial establishments [map 1C].

The King and Queen were at the Palace [5]   Buckingham Palace, the royal residence since Victoria's ascent to the throne [map 2C]. The current occupants were King George V (1865–1936, his reign began in 1910) and Queen Mary (1867–1953).

Lords, Ascot, Ranelagh [5]   Important locations for British sports and the social events that surround them: Lord's, or the Marylebone Cricket Club, in North London (founded by Thomas Lord); the racetrack at Ascot, near Windsor Castle in Berkshire; and the Hurlingham Club in Ranelagh Gardens, where polo was played, in the Southwest London district of Fulham.

in the time of the Georges [5]   Era encompassing the British Kings George I–IV (1714–1830).

the Park [5]   St. James's Park [map 3CH]. The oldest of eight Royal Parks, dating to Henry VIII's deer park (circa 1530). It is dominated by a long central lake featuring varieties of waterfowl. A favorite strolling place for politicians. Hugh Whitbread, who prides himself on government connections, turns up here.

despatch box stamped with the Royal Arms [5]   Boxes marked with heraldic emblems used to carry papers to and from the royal family.

Bath [6]   Celebrated spa town in southwest England, known for the eighteenth-century architecture of public buildings and town house crescents. The Romans enjoyed its hot mineral waters, and left archaeological remains of baths.

Pimlico [7]   Borough of London southwest of Westminster, on the north bank of the Thames. Home to persons of more modest income than the Dalloways.

Messages were passing from the Fleet to the Admiralty [7]   The Admiralty Building, situated in Whitehall, was equipped with an antenna and wireless telegraphy by the Marconi Company (1909). This permitted an exchange of messages with ships at sea (DB).

Wagner [7]   Richard Wilhelm Wagner (1813–1883), German composer noted for his operas.

Pope's poetry [7]   Alexander Pope (1688–1744), English poet and satirist. He makes an appearance in Woolf's novel *Orlando*.

those Indian women [8]   Women, presumably of British descent, sent to India as part of the imperial enterprise.

Park gates . . . Piccadilly [8]   Clarissa has walked north through Green Park and reached the Ritz gate to the park on Piccadilly Lane [map 4C], which borders the stylish borough of Mayfair, to the north. Woolf's proper young women first encounter prostitutes in Piccadilly, farther east, nearer Piccadilly Circus (see 71). Green is another Royal Park, created in 1668.

Fräulein Daniels [8]   Clarissa's governess, who, along with occasional visiting instructors, provided what education she and her sister, Sylvia, received. "Fräulein" suggests she was German.

Devonshire House, Bath House, the house with the china cockatoo [8]   Grand private houses, the settings for high-society parties (DB). All on or near Clarissa's route east on Piccadilly.

the Park . . . the Serpentine [9]   Hyde Park, another of the major Royal Parks, appropriated by Henry VIII (1536), and site for carriage drives by the wealthy. It has as its lake the Serpentine. Hyde Park lies to the west of Clarissa's route.

Bond Street [9]   Major shopping street in Mayfair, which Clarissa accesses via Piccadilly Lane [map 5C].

Hatchards' [9]   In 1923 the actual Hatchard's (preferred spelling) bookshop was at 187 Piccadilly Lane (DB), past where Clarissa turns onto Bond Street.

Fear no more the heat o' the sun / . . . winter's rages [9]   Beginning of the song sung by Shakespeare's characters Arviragus and Guiderius in his *Cymbeline*, Act IV, Scene ii. They presume that the heroine, Imogen, has died. A new edition of *Cymbeline* edited by

Harley Granville Barker came out in August 1923, and this could have been in the window at Hatchard's (DB). Clarissa later repeats the lines several times (29, 182) and Septimus Smith thinks of them as well (136).

Jorrocks' Jaunts and Jollities . . . Soapy Sponge *and Mrs. Asquith's* Memoirs *and* Big Game Shooting in Nigeria [9] Of these books on display, three are factual. Jorrock was a comic Cockney grocer, the creation of Robert Smith Surtees (1803–1864). Soapy Sponge is a character in another Surtees work, *Mr. Sponge's Sporting Tour* (1853). Margot Asquith was the wife of the former prime minister; her two-volume autobiography appeared in 1920. Woolf invented the *Shooting* book, which is representative of a popular genre (DB). Though several male members of her family were hunters, Woolf's objections to the sport appear in several of her essays, including "The Plumage Bill" (1920).

glove shop [11]   In Woolf's story "Mrs. Dalloway in Bond Street" (1923), which in many ways resembles this morning walk, Clarissa's goal is to purchase a pair of gloves. There would have been shops to correspond to those mentioned in this section.

Grizzle [11]   The actual name of the Woolfs' dog at this time. In "The Hours," an earlier draft of *Mrs. Dalloway* (see Wussow transcription), the dog is named Shag, after the Irish terrier the Stephen family acquired in 1892.

Miss Kilman . . . Russians . . . Austrians [11]   Both countries were experiencing economic hardship following, respectively, the Russian Revolution of 1917 and the breakup of the Austro-Hungarian Empire after the defeat of Germany in World War I. Mrs. Dalloway's daughter, Elizabeth, has as a tutor Miss Kilman, whose German ancestry contributed to her being "badly treated" while Britain was at war with Germany.

Mulberry's the florists [12]   Imaginary shop on Bond Street near its intersection with Brook Street [map 6C].

cherry pie [13]   Popular name for the herb valerian, which has white or pink flowers and roots used medicinally. Woolf "botanized" early with her father, but in her diary usually cited flowers she encountered by their common names.

Prince of Wales [14]   One of the many possibilities for who might be in the car that has backfired on Bond Street [map 6M]. The future Edward VIII (1894–1972), whose coronation took place in 1936. That same year he abdicated to marry Wallis Simpson, an American whose two divorces made her unacceptable as queen to the Church of England, of which the king was head.

Septimus [14]   Our first sighting of the second major character of the novel, Septimus Smith, out on a walk of his own with his wife, Rezia [map 6S].

the Embankment [15]   Reclaimed north bank of the Thames between Westminster Bridge and Blackfriars Bridge.

Brook Street [17]   Street intersecting Bond Street, the last position on Clarissa's walk [map 6C].

breasts stiff with oak leaves [17]   A token dating back to the restoration of King Charles II in 1660. On his birthday (May 29), people wore sprigs of oak in thanks for the return of royalty after the Civil War.

a Colonial [17]   A person from one of the colonies or former colonies of the British Empire, for example, Australia.

House of Windsor [17]   British-affiliated name of the royal family assumed in 1917 by King George V, whose lineage was German. This was a diplomatic decision, as Britain was battling Germany in World War I.

St. James's Street [18]   Location of many gentlemen's clubs. Among these is Brooks's [map 7M].

Brooks's [18]   Men's club at 60 St. James's Street. In the second English edition (actually a new impression of the first edition printed by Hogarth Press in September 1925), this was changed to White's, another club at 37–38 St. James's Street, which was preferable because it had the requisite bow window.

the Tatler [18]   Journal founded by Richard Steele, first published in 1709 and revived as a society paper, reporting on clubs and gaming, in 1901.

whispering gallery [18]   An acoustical effect, usually achieved with a curved wall that collects and magnifies a sound carried to another site. The cathedral Woolf had in mind was probably St. Paul's, which has a remarkable whispering gallery. Much of this section is resonant of Englishness—a nostalgic affection for landscapes and customs associated with the nation.

old Irishwoman's loyalty [18]   This was a restive period in Anglo-Irish relations, following the bloody Easter Rising against British rule (1916) and a bitter Civil War (1919–21). Through a Treaty negotiated by Sinn Fein leader Michael Collins (1921), the Irish Free State (founded January 1922) had dominion status in the British Commonwealth, while Northern Ireland remained part of Britain. This compromise outraged many Irish revolutionaries, and led to Collins's assassination (also 1922). The constable who discourages Moll Pratt's floral tribute to British royalty could be an Irishman with more radical politics than Moll's. The incident reminds us of conflicted national loyalties.

sentries at St. James's [18]   Guards at one of the principal royal palaces, constructed by King Henry VIII, located on St. James's Street.

Queen Alexandra [18]   (1844–1925), widow of King Edward VII, lived in Marlborough House, where her own police would have been on duty.

Victoria, billowing [18]   Memorial to the queen, whose matronly sculpture sits surrounded by allegorical figures and basins of cascading water. Designed by Sir Thomas Brock, it was dedicated in 1911. It is positioned outside the main entrance to Buckingham Palace. Richard Dalloway also makes note of it (114).

the Mall [19]   Wide tree-lined avenue on northern side of St. James's Park, suitable for ceremonial processions from Buckingham Palace to the Admiralty Arch. The name comes from the game, pail-mail, played there with ball and mallet (hence "mall"), in the reign of Charles II.

Queen's old doll's house [19]   Queen Mary was given a grand doll house, meticulously furnished with British goods (one inch to the foot), designed by Sir Edwin Lutyens in 1923. It was thus new at the time of the novel. Still on display at Windsor Palace.

Princess Mary . . . the Prince [19]   Princess Mary (1897–1965) was the only daughter of the royal family. Her marriage to Viscount Lascelles occurred in 1922. Prince Edward is compared to Edward VII (1841–1910).

Mr. Bowley [19]   Character recycled from *Jacob's Room,* where he is also out for a walk. His residence, the Albany, housed prominent politicians and writers. He sights the mysterious motorcar turning onto the Mall, moving toward Buckingham Palace [map 8M]. At this point an airplane distracts viewers of the motorcar, and is visible simultaneously from this and other points.

bronze heroes [19]   Sculpture associated with the Royal Artillery Monument (1910), in memory of soldiers fallen in South African and Chinese wars (1889–1902).

letting out white smoke from behind [19–20]   Michael North gives a detailed account of the first ever demonstration of skywriting, which occurred over London in 1922, and notes Woolf's use of the occasion in her novel (*Reading 1922: A Return to the Scene of the Modern* [New York: Oxford University Press, 1999], 81–84).

Glaxo [20]   Brand name for a babies' formula milk product (DB). Its ads must have succeeded, because the firm grew into a large international pharmaceutical company that still exists.

Regent's Park . . . Broad Walk [21]   Large circular park, part of a garden suburb of town houses designed by John Nash (1812), and named for the prince regent (later George IV). In the Marylebone district, north of the areas of London explored to this point. Its widest pedestrian walkway runs north–south through the eastern part of the park [map 9S]. The airplane is visible from here as well.

her sisters [23]   While this suggests that Rezia had multiple sisters, Septimus later recalls marrying the younger daughter, implying she had only one sister (85).

the Indian and his cross [23]   The Victorian Gothic drinking fountain resembles a cross. To one side is a sacred cow under a palm tree. Its fulsome inscription, dating from 1869, expresses the gratitude of its donor, Sir Cowasjee Jehangir, for the protection British rule gave to himself and other Parsees in India. By 1923, Indians were strongly urging self-government. The Amritsar Massacre (April 1919), in which British troops slaughtered unarmed protesters in that Punjabi city (now in Pakistan), created intense anti-British attitudes. The Government of India Act (December 23, 1919) created a dyarchy. Mohandas Gandhi founded the first Non-cooperation Movement (1920–22) in protest to British rule.

Romans saw it . . . darkness [23]   Romans occupied various parts of Britain during the years A.D. 43 to 410. There is an echo of Joseph Conrad's *Heart of Darkness,* which also looks back to the Roman era. Woolf admired Conrad's work and wrote relevant essays and reviews, most notably, "Mr. Conrad: A Conversation" (1923).

sparrow . . . to sing . . . in Greek words [24]   Septimus's perceptions of a sparrow singing in Greek resembles Woolf's own experience of birds singing Greek choruses to her during her 1904 mental breakdown.

Zoo [24]   Collection of the Zoological Society of London, opened in Regent's Park in 1828. Woolf visited the zoo from childhood onward and wrote about its aquarium in "The Sun and the Fish" (1928).

cricket stumps [24]   Three posts, driven into the ground, which together with two horizontal pieces (bails) form the wicket defended by the batsman, who stands before it in the game of cricket.

Tube station [25]   Subway station.

up from Edinburgh [25]   Although the Scottish capital is far north of London, it is customary in England to say one is traveling "up" to London, wherever one is coming from.

Bath chairs [26]   Wheeled and hooded chairs used by invalids.

Kentish Town [27]   District in north London, inhabited by the working class in the 1920s.

Margate [27]   Seaside resort in Kent, seventy-six miles east of London.

Greenwich [27]   Borough of southeast London, south of the Thames, where the Royal Observatory (source of Greenwich Mean Time) and Royal Naval College are located.

St. Paul's and the rest [27]   Of the many churches visible to the rising airplane, the most prominent would be St. Paul's, the
Renaissance-style domed Cathedral of the Bishop of London,
designed by Sir Christopher Wren and completed in 1710.

Mendelian theory [27]   Concerns inherited biological traits. The
Moravian monk Gregor Johann Mendel (1822–1884) conducted
his experiments by cross-pollinating peas.

Ludgate Circus [28]   Traffic circle where Ludgate Hill meets Fleet
Street, west of St. Paul's.

Baron Marbot's Memoirs [30]   Jean-Baptiste-Antoine de Marbot
(1782–1854), French general who accompanied Napoléon on his
retreat from Moscow in 1812. Clarissa would probably have read
from a one-volume translation of the original three-volume
work, published in French (1891).

woods at Clieveden [31]   Woods at Cliveden (note spelling), scenic
forest on one of the most beautiful and popular stretches of the
Thames, north of London beyond Maidenhead. The country
home of the Astor family, Cliveden, is set nearby. Nancy Astor
(first woman member of Parliament, 1919–45) and others of
the "Cliveden set" urged appeasement of the Fascists in the
1930s.

Constantinople [31]   Ancient Byzantine city, with the Hagia Sophia
(church and mosque in various eras) its architectural wonder,
now capital of Turkey. Called Constantinople from A.D. 330,
after Roman Emperor Constantine. Resumed Byzantine name,
Istanbul (1926). Visited by Woolf (1906). Clarissa thinks of this
failure again (115).

The Mannings [32]   In Woolf's 1927 novel, *To the Lighthouse,* Mrs.
Ramsay recalls going on the river at the Mannings' house twenty
years earlier (89–90).

Marie Antoinette [32]   Austrian-born Queen of France (1755–1793), wife of King Louis XVI, known for her extravagance, guillotined during the French Revolution.

William Morris [32]   Poet, leader of and designer for the Arts and Crafts Movement, socialist activist (1834–1896). Sally might have favored his socialist utopian works, *A Dream of John Ball* (1888) and *News from Nowhere* (1891).

Plato [33]   Greek philosopher (c. 429–347 B.C.). His ideal state is described in the *Republic*.

Shelley [33]   Percy Bysshe Shelley (1792–1822), English Romantic poet. Some of his writings, such as *Prometheus Unbound* (1820), inspired political radicals.

cut their heads off [33]   Woolf noted that her sister, Vanessa Bell, engaged in this same unorthodox form of flower arrangement (*Diary* 2: 260).

"if it were now to die … most happy" [34]   Clarissa's quote from Shakespeare's *Othello*, Act II, Scene i, comes as Othello is reunited with Desdemona. She thinks of it again on learning of Septimus's death (see 180).

air ball [34]   Toy balloon.

Brahms [34]   Johannes Brahms (1833–1897), German Romantic composer.

Caterham [37]   Town in county of Surrey, south of London.

Ealing [38]   District in west London.

Hatfield [38]   Jacobean mansion in Hertfordshire built for Sir Robert Cecil in 1608.

Indian Army [44]   British Army stationed in India.

sent down from Oxford [45]   Expelled from the university.

Lincoln's Inn [45]   One of the four Inns of Court, established in the thirteenth century, which provide the legal center of London. Located in central London, south of High Holborn Street and north of the Thames.

Leith Hill [46]   The highest place in southeast England, in Surrey, south of London, famous for its view and paths through woods full of rhododendrons and bluebells.

coolies [48]   Native unskilled laborers—the term applied to workers from India as well as from China.

St. Margaret's [48]   The bells of the parish church of Westminster, on Parliament Square, which dates back to 1485 [map 10P].

Whitehall [49]   Originally the setting of the royal palace of Whitehall, this half mile between Westminster and Charing Cross has since the seventeenth century been the center of government.

Duke of Cambridge [49]   Equestrian statue by Adrian Jones (1907) commemorating George, second Duke of Cambridge (1819–1904), a cousin of Queen Victoria and commander in chief of the British Army (1856–95).

Finsbury Pavement to the empty tomb [50]   The soldiers will return to an area in the district of Moorfields after placing their wreath at the Cenotaph, a memorial to the fallen warriors of World War I. Designed by Lutyens and completed in 1920, it sits in Whitehall [map 11P].

Nelson, Gordon, Havelock, the black [50]   Military heroes whose statues are in Trafalgar Square. Horatio Nelson (1758–1805), the victor at the Battle of Trafalgar, has the tallest memorial. His statue by E. H. Baily (1843) stands atop a 145-foot column. The bronze statue of Charles George Gordon (1833–1885), who died in the Siege of Khartoum, has since been removed. The service of Henry Havelock (1795–1857) as a general in wars in Burma, Afghanistan, and India is commemorated in a bronze statue on the east side of Nelson's column. He perished of dysentery after capturing Lucknow during the Indian Mutiny. The statues appear black, in silhouette [map 12P].

the Strand [51]   Street running east from Trafalgar Square toward the City of London. Its formerly lively character was hailed in the music-hall song "Let's All Go Down the Strand." Elizabeth Dalloway visits this part of London later in the day.

the Haymarket [51]   Site of a sixteenth-century haymarket, this street runs from Coventry Street to Pall Mall. Notable theaters and the Royal Opera arcade are located here.

Cockspur Street [52]   Part of Peter's route in pursuit of an attractive young woman. Woolf may mischievously have chosen a street with a "cock" in it [map 13P]. The young woman takes Peter up Regent Street (52–53) and into Great Portland Street (53), in the direction of Regent's Park [map 14–15P].

an absurd statue [54]   Perhaps the Matilda fountain, with its bronze figure of a milkmaid perched on rocks, shielding her eyes as if to look into the distance. Peter settles on a bench near the Smiths [map 16P].

Wickham [60]   Clarissa may be thinking of Jane Austen's *Pride and Prejudice* and the officer who runs off with Lydia Bennett but is reluctant to marry her until persuaded to do so by Mr. Darcy— not a promising name for a suitor.

his watch to blow open [64]   Possibly a pocket watch with a cover. One could release the catch to the cover as a child blew upon it, as a game.

Hampton Court [65]   Palace whose most famous resident was Henry VIII. He confiscated the site from Cardinal Wolsey, who had started building there in 1514. Architecture includes Tudor gatehouse and east and south wings designed by Christopher Wren. Favorite destination for day trips, open to the public since Victoria's time.

Thessaly [68]   Area in northern Greece.

water-closets [70]   Flush toilets.

Manchester [70]   Large industrial city in Lancashire, in the north of England, where cotton mills flourished.

women's rights (that antediluvian topic) [71]   The British suffrage movement obtained the vote for women thirty and older in 1918. But the topic was hardly antediluvian, as women twenty-one to twenty-nine had to wait until 1928 for the vote.

"those poor girls in Piccadilly" [71]   Prostitutes.

British Empire, tariff-reform, governing-class spirit [75]   Evidence of Richard's conservatism. Tariff reform would have been protective of British goods.

Morning Post [75]   Peter assumes Richard would read this extremely conservative newspaper, though he actually reads the *Times* (DB).

Huxley and Tyndall [76]   Thomas Henry Huxley (1825–1895), biologist and great communicator on Darwin's theory of evolution. He was a friend of Woolf's father and both were agnostics. John

Tyndall (1820–1893), physicist, adept at communicating scientific discoveries, including his own, concerning radiant heat.

Elizabeth was "out" [77]   Peter presumes that in her elite social set, Elizabeth would by now have been presented at Court, and would be participating in an active social season, as would a debutante.

the battered woman [79]   Woolf describes seeing a blind beggar woman, clasping her dog and singing, on June 8, 1920 (*Diary* 2: 47): "It was gay, & yet terrible & fearfully vivid." Her song's evocation of a dead lover returning as on All Souls' Day has been likened by J. Hillis Miller to the Richard Strauss song "Allerseelen." She is located near the Regent's Park tube station [map 17P]. Septimus and Rezia Smith also pass the beggar (80) [map 17S].

"Poor old woman" [80]   Woolf marked her American proofs "leave 2 lines white" above this. The intended break was hitherto masked by the inset quotation, above.

holland bags [81]   Bags made of a cotton treated with an opaque finish, and thus impermeable to dust that might accumulate on chandeliers.

Purley [82]   Unremarkable town in Surrey, south of London.

Stroud [82]   Market town and a center for the cloth industry in Gloucestershire. Woolf vacationed as a girl in Painswick (1897)—a much more scenic Cotswold setting three miles beyond Stroud. Her family's train journey terminated in Stroud, where they returned repeatedly for bicycle repairs and to bring additional visitors from the train by pony cart.

Euston Road [82]   Busy road bordering Bloomsbury, close to a major train station.

Waterloo Road [83]   Runs south from the Thames through what was a working-class district in the 1920s. Miss Pole, like Virginia Woolf (1905–07), taught at Morley College, which held evening classes in the Old Vic Theatre on this road.

Keats [83]   John Keats (1795–1821), English late Romantic poet. In *The Voyage Out,* the early Clarissa Dalloway recites lines from "Adonais," Shelley's elegy for Keats (58).

The History of Civilisation, *and Bernard Shaw* [83]   Thomas Henry Buckle's two-volume work (1857–61) drew attention to the effect of the environment on civilization. George Bernard Shaw was known for his Fabian socialism expressed in essays as well as plays.

Ceres [84]   Ancient Roman goddess of agriculture, the Roman counterpart to the Greek goddess Demeter.

Muswell Hill [84]   Residential area in northern London.

Dante [86]   Dante Alighieri (1265–1321), Italian poet best known for *The Divine Comedy* (1321). The *Inferno,* representing Hell, is the first of its three parts. The journey progresses to Purgatory and, finally, Paradise.

Soho [86]   Central London district north of Shaftesbury Avenue, known since the flight there of French refugees in 1685 for its cosmopolitan atmosphere. Sex shops and film companies have now joined bakeries, delicatessens, and continental restaurants.

Newhaven [86]   Port at mouth of River Ouse, Sussex, near the Woolfs' house at Rodmell. The Smiths may have arrived in England at this port as newlyweds.

Tottenham Court Road [86]   Road running north from Charing Cross Station into Bloomsbury. Furniture stores are prevalent among the commercial businesses it houses.

Aeschylus [86]   Poet (515–456 B.C.) who developed enduring traditions of Greek theater. Major plays: *Agamemnon* from the *Oresteia* trio, *Prometheus Bound,* and *Seven Against Thebes.*

the Tower [87]   Tower of London. Famous fortress and royal residence built into the city wall on the north bank of the Thames. Begun around 1076 for William the Conqueror. Setting for famous imprisonments and executions.

Victoria and Albert Museum [87]   Outstanding museum of applied arts of numerous cultures and eras, designed by Aston Webb, opened 1909. Located on Cromwell Road in South Kensington among numerous other museums.

bromide [88]   Salt of hydrobromic acid. Some varieties were commonly used as a sedative.

Bedford Square [89]   Stylish Georgian residential neighborhood in Bloomsbury.

Harley Street [91]   Favored address of London's most prestigious doctors, a short walk south of Regent's Park [map 18S]. The Smiths are en route via Portland Place.

It was precisely twelve [91]   The first English edition had a section break before this, though the corrected American proofs do not, and the break may not have been intended by Woolf.

Eton [92]   Eton College. One of England's most exclusive private schools for boys, founded 1440. Set in Berkshire near Windsor Castle.

shindy [94]   A rumpus.

question of rest [94]   Septimus is recommended a rest cure comparable to Woolf's own therapy at Burley Park, Twickenham, 1910 and 1912, as recommended by Dr. George Savage.

It was a question of law [94]   Suicide remained illegal in England until 1961. Until a law was passed against the practice in 1823, suicides were routinely buried at crossroads.

sense of proportion [96]   Woolf's consultation with a Harley Street physician, Dr. Sainsbury, in August 1922 brought the advice, "practise equanimity, Mrs. Woolf," recorded sarcastically in her diary (*Diary* 2: 189), and revised slightly as this.

seven stone six . . . twelve [97]   A stone is fourteen pounds, hence a rise from 104 to 168 pounds. Excessive feeding of mental patients was another cure favored by Dr. Savage.

Hyde Park Corner [98]   Woolf probably means Speaker's Corner (DB), at the northeast corner, where, since 1872, common people have been speaking their minds to passersby. Hyde Park Corner is on the southeast corner of the park.

Oxford Street . . . Messrs. Rigby and Lowndes [100]   Imaginary department store. In the days when not everyone had a wristwatch, stores did provide a real service in offering public clocks. This places Hugh Whitbread on Oxford Street, en route to Brook Street, and lunch with Lady Bruton [map 19H].

Norfolk [100]   County of England northeast of London in East Anglia. Celebrated for its agriculture, scenic landscapes, and outdoor sports, including bird-watching. Richard has nostalgia for nature in Norfolk, his place of origin (110, 119).

Portsmouth [101]   City with an important naval harbor. On the south coast of England, southwest of London.

Mayfair [102]   One of the most exclusive parts of London, bounded by Bond Street to the east and Park Lane to the west. Named for a fair held there in May in the seventeenth to mid-eighteenth centuries.

Lovelace or Herrick [103]   So-called Cavalier poets, supporters of Charles I in the English Civil War. Richard Lovelace (1618–1657) and Robert Herrick (1591–1674) both composed light, graceful, gallant lyrics, typically on the subject of love.

come a cropper [104]   To fall headlong, as from a horse. To fail.

Brook Street [105]   The street in Mayfair where Lady Bruton resides [map 20HR]. It runs west from Hanover Square to Grosvenor Square. Clarissa stood on the corner of Brook and Bond Streets earlier, on her early morning walk.

prospect of doing well in Canada [106]   Woolf is representing satirically arguments that actually appeared in the *Times* in 1923, calling for eugenically sound immigrants who would help rather than harm Canada. The British felt indebted to the Canadians for their losses in World War I (DB).

the Labour Government [108]   She anticipated what did happen on January 22, 1924, when the first Labour government came to power. As a Conservative, Richard could be voted out, and thus have time on his hands to write her family history.

Devonshire [109]   Large scenic county in southwest England that has both a north and a south coast, moors, hills, and forests.

Conduit Street [110]   In the company of Hugh, Richard has headed southeast, back toward Parliament and his home. They seem to have walked east on Brook Street, then south on Bond Street to its intersection at Conduit Street. In a lethargic moment, Richard accompanies Hugh into a nearby shop [map 21RH]. Interestingly, Bruton Street runs into Conduit from the west.

costermongers [113]   Sellers of fruit, vegetables, fish, etc., from carts or wheelbarrows set on the sidewalk or in the street.

Green Park [113]   Its greenery is set amid Piccadilly, Constitution Hill, and the Mall. Clarissa passed through earlier (8) and from here Richard largely follows her path in reverse [map 22R].

descendant of Horsa [114]   Of Saxon lineage. The brothers Horsa and Hengist are said in legend to have led the Saxons into England in the fifth century.

Dean's Yard [114]   Once part of the gardens of Westminster Abbey, and hence the yard of its dean. Now a residential area [map 23R].

Armenians . . . Albanians [117]   Armenians in northeast Turkey, a Christian minority, suffered repeated massacres at the hands of the Turks. Some 1.75 million Armenians were forced to emigrate to Syria, Mesopotamia, and what became Soviet Armenia (1915—21). The press and Parliament continued the discussion of the plight they shared with other ethnic minorities.

Bayswater [119]   London borough north of Hyde Park. White stucco apartments are typical architecture.

Mongol [119]   Person from the Asian region of Mongolia. The eyes of Mongols typically have a fold extending from the eyelid over the inner angle of the eye.

Chinese eyes [120]   Eyes of this shape may suggest independence or inscrutability, a quality often attributed to "orientals" by the British. Lily Briscoe of Woolf's *To the Lighthouse* also has Chinese eyes.

hyacinth [120]   Plant grown from a bulb. Its fragrant blooms are composed of bell-shaped flowers massed on a stalk. In myth, the flower sprung from the blood of Hyacinthus, a beautiful boy loved and accidentally killed by Apollo.

the Friends [121]   Religious Society of Friends, the Quakers. Pacifist sect founded by George Fox around 1650. Their headquarters is on the Euston Road in London.

Extension lecturing [121]   Instruction of students who are not matriculated for a complete course of study, often done in the evening.

the Stores [122]   The Army and Navy Stores. Originally a cooperative run by military officers to supply inexpensive goods to military families. The Victoria Street location opened to the general public in 1918. Elizabeth and Miss Kilman arrive here a few minutes later (126) [map 24EK].

Addison [124]   Joseph Addison (1672–1719), essayist who made regular contributions to periodicals (*Tatler, Spectator*), often in association with Richard Steele. He also wrote poetry and plays.

Kensington [127]   Borough of London where many museums and educational institutions are housed.

Westminster Cathedral [130]   Byzantine-style Catholic church designed by J. F. Bentley and erected 1895–1903. Its bell tower rises 284 feet.

the Abbey [130]   Westminster Abbey. Anglican church where monarchs are crowned and buried. Architecture in its present form begun in 1245 by King Henry III [map 25K].

wax works [130]   Wax effigies of monarchs buried in the Abbey, including Elizabeth I and Charles II, housed in the Treasure Museum. Woolf's essay "Waxworks at the Abbey" was later published in the *New Republic* (1928).

tomb of the Unknown Warrior [130]   Memorial at the west end of the nave, where the remains of an unknown World War I soldier lie in earth brought from the battlefields of Flanders. He was interred November 11, 1920.

K.C. [131]   King's Counsel, or lawyer.

Somerset House [133]   Large Palladian building erected 1776–86 on the site of a building begun by the Lord Protector Somerset. Situated between the Strand and the Thames, it houses government offices including the Inland Revenue (tax bureau) and the General Registrar of Births, Marriages and Deaths (useful for genealogy).

Chancery Lane [133]   Narrow street running from Fleet Street north to High Holborn, in the heart of the legal establishment of London. It is named for the Inns of Chancery, which were always subordinate in the legal profession and gradually yielded to the Inns of Court. Lincoln's Inn, one of the Inns of Court, and the offices of the Law Society are on its west side. The Public Record Office stands on its east side.

the Temple [134]   The Middle Temple and the Inner Temple, established by James I (1609), two of the four Inns of Court, at the foot of Chancery Lane between Fleet Street and the Thames. Another of the Inns of Court, Lincoln's Inn, is mentioned by Peter Walsh, who goes there after Regent's Park (45).

the Church [134]   Temple Church, shared by the Middle and Inner Temple. It has a round part in transitional Norman style consecrated in 1185, where lawyers once awaited their clients.

Fleet Street [134]   Center of the British newspaper industry, named for a submerged river. It continues east from the Strand [map 26E].

Fear no more [136]   Septimus here echoes a line from *Cymbeline* recited twice by Clarissa (9, 182). He is back at home off Tottenham Court Road [map 27S].

Prince Consort [139]   Prince Albert of Saxe-Coburg-Gotha (1819–1861), husband of Queen Victoria.

Hull [139]   City in Yorkshire, northeast England, situated on the north bank of the Humber River, where it intersects with the Hull River, and twenty miles from its entry to the North Sea. Major seaport.

Surrey was all out [141]   Newspaper headline indicating Surrey cricket team had ended their first innings in a match against Yorkshire. Peter reads a later edition that reports "Surrey was all out once more," in a final at bat. This does not match anything that appears in the *Cricketers' Almanac* for the year (DB).

Brighton [142]   Resort city on south coast of England in Sussex. Woolf vacationed there with her family after her mother's death.

British Museum [148]   Neoclassical building designed by Robert Smirke (begun 1823), which occupies a city block, fronting on Great Russell Street in Bloomsbury. It houses art and artifacts from ancient and living cultures around the world, including the Elgin Marbles, the Rosetta Stone, and the magnificent reading room featured in Woolf's *A Room of One's Own* and *Jacob's Room*. Peter is a block away from Tottenham Court Road, so he could hear an ambulance carrying Septimus Smith [map 28P]. He has come a bit out of his way in walking from Lincoln's Inn to his hotel.

Caledonian market [148]   Street market held on Fridays at the site of a cattle market in the borough of Islington, north London. Clarissa's treasures were probably bargains.

Shaftesbury Avenue [149]   Route through the theater district in the West End of London in Soho.

Severn [150]   River, 210 miles in length, that rises in central Wales and flows through western England, entering the Bristol Channel.

wagtail [151]   Small European bird that habitually wags its long narrow tail up and down.

To get that letter to him [151]   In London in the 1920s, there were several mail deliveries a day, making it possible to write a letter and have it be received the same day.

Bodleian [154]   Oxford University's main library, which began with Duke Humphrey's library (1409). Scholar Thomas Bodley restored and enlarged it (1602).

to come up to the scratch [154]   To measure up to expectations. Literally, to approach the starting line for a race.

Liverpool [155]   Major port city in northwest England, where the wide Mersey River flows into the Irish Sea.

Bartlett pears [156]   Large yellow juicy variety of pear first distributed in the nineteenth century by Enoch Bartlett of Dorchester, Massachusetts.

Mr. Willett's summer time [158]   Daylight Saving Time, proposed by William Willett and put into force through spring and summer in 1916 to save power during World War I.

Oriental Club [158]   Founded in 1824 to serve members of the East India Company, it was located in Hanover Square in 1923.

Littré's dictionary [158]   Four-volume French-language dictionary compiled by philosopher and lexicographer Maximilien-Paul-Émile Littré, published 1863–73.

a copper [159]   A penny coin.

Bedford Place [159]   Peter is setting out from his hotel near Russell Square for the party [map 29P], passing south through Whitehall, into Westminster. We do not know the name of "her street, this, Clarissa's" (160). But there the mapping ends where it began.

The Prime Minister [161]   Stanley Baldwin (1867–1947), Conservative Party statesman, held this office 1923–24, 1924–29, and 1935–37.

dampers [162]   Movable part that permits regulation of the draft, and hence the heat, of a stove. They might actually be pushed, rather than pulled in.

Imperial Tokay [162]   Aromatic dessert wine produced near city of that name in northeast Hungary; this brand has presumably been stocked in the cellars of royalty.

birds of Paradise [164]   Birds native to New Guinea. Males have colorful, ornamental plumage. The flight of the curtains is mentioned again (166).

public school man [168]   In England, what Americans would consider a private school is called a public school, and hence it is a place of privilege.

Sir Joshua [170]   Sir Joshua Reynolds (1723–1792), eighteenth-century English portrait painter in the "grand style."

Mrs. Durrant and Clara [170]   Mother and daughter who appear in Woolf's *Jacob's Room*. Clara is the sister of Jacob's friend Timothy Durrant, and one of several love interests.

St. John's Wood [171]   Residential area northwest of Regent's Park in London, where artists (including Academicians—members of the Royal Academy) and writers resided. Woolf mentions George Eliot's living there in *A Room of One's Own*. Sir Edwin Landseer, who developed the style attributed to Sir Harry, was also a resident.

will-o'-the-wisp [171]   Flitting phosphorescent light seen at night, attributable to marsh gas, and thus something deluding or misleading.

old Mrs. Hilbery [171]   Character who appears in Woolf's second novel, *Night and Day*.

Hampstead [172]   Village in North London dating from the eighteenth century, where artists and freethinkers have resided. Adjacent is the preserved open space of Hampstead Heath.

Lords [173]   The cricket ground mentioned early in the novel (5).

a green frill [173]   Woolf imagines a similar putting out of a frill by her character Jinny in *The Waves*.

Burma [174]   Now known as Myanmar, a country in southeast Asia on the Bay of Bengal. It was gradually annexed by the British colonial government of India during the three Burma Wars (1824–86).

this isle of men, this dear, dear land [176]   Reminiscent of speech praising England by John of Gaunt in Shakespeare's *Richard II*, Act II, Scene i: "This land of such dear souls, this dear dear land."

armoured goddess [176]   Though this could be the Greek goddess Athena, whose various charges include warfare, the female symbol of the empire is Britannia, represented with trident and helmet, in a seated position.

Union Jack [176]   Great Britain's national flag, which combines Saint George's red cross, representing England; Saint Andrew's white cross on a blue field, representing Scotland; and Saint Patrick's diagonal red on white cross, representing Ireland. Originally flown from the jack staff of a ship.

punt [177]   Small shallow boat with two square ends, propelled by a long pole, often used for outings on rivers in Britain. Boating at Bourton seems to have been a regular activity (see 61).

that Bill [178] . . . *deferred effects of shell shock* [179]   An official inquiry into shell shock had been initiated by the British government's

War Office in 1920. Woolf could have read extensive details of its report, issued in 1922, in the *Times*.

his eleven [178]   His cricket team (composed of eleven players).

"If it were now to die, 'twere now to be most happy" [180]   Repeat of quotation from *Othello* (34).

Fear no more the heat of the sun [182]   Repeat of quotation from *Cymbeline* (9).

"But where is Clarissa?" [182]   The English edition has a section break before this. Woolf called for the break on a set of corrected proofs that she sent to her friend the painter Jacques Raverat, who was dying from multiple sclerosis. (This set is now in the Department of Special Collections, University Research Library, University of California, Los Angeles.) She did not call for the break on the proofs she corrected for her American publisher (now in the Lilly Library at Indiana University).

Emily Brontë [183]   English poet and author of the novel *Wuthering Heights* (1847).

in red [184]   Elizabeth's dress is described by Lucy, Ellie, and Richard as pink (162, 165, 189).

Suez Canal [186]   Canal in Egypt connecting the Mediterranean and Red Seas, constructed 1859–69. It was largely controlled by the British, giving them economic and strategic power in the region (1875–1956). From her own travels and her interest in plants, Vita Sackville-West could have informed Woolf of rare lilies native to the area.

fifty-two to be precise [189]   Peter may have been more "precise" when he registered his age at fifty-three, earlier in the novel (77).

Suggestions for Further Reading:
Virginia Woolf

Editions

The Complete Shorter Fiction. Edited by Susan Dick. 2nd ed. San Diego: Harcourt, 1989.

The Diary of Virginia Woolf. Edited by Anne Olivier Bell. 5 vols. New York: Harcourt, 1977–84.

The Essays of Virginia Woolf. Edited by Andrew McNeillie. 6 vols. [in progress]. San Diego: Harcourt Brace Jovanovich, 1986–.

The Letters of Virginia Woolf. Edited by Nigel Nicolson and Joanne Trautmann. 6 vols. New York: Harcourt Brace Jovanovich, 1975–80.

Moments of Being. Edited by Jeanne Schulkind. San Diego: Harcourt, 1985.

A Passionate Apprentice: The Early Journals, 1897–1909. Edited by Mitchell A. Leaska. San Diego: Harcourt, 1990.

Biographies and Reference Works

Briggs, Julia. *Virginia Woolf: An Inner Life.* San Diego: Harcourt, 2005.

Hussey, Mark. *Virginia Woolf A to Z: A Comprehensive Reference for Students, Teachers, and Common Readers to Her Life, Works, and Critical Reception.* New York: Facts on File, 1995.

Kirkpatrick, B. J., and Stuart N. Clarke. *A Bibliography of Virginia Woolf.* 4th ed. Oxford: Clarendon, 1997.

Lee, Hermione. *Virginia Woolf.* New York: Knopf, 1996.

Marder, Herbert. *The Measure of Life: Virginia Woolf's Last Years.* Ithaca, NY: Cornell University Press, 2000.

Poole, Roger. *The Unknown Virginia Woolf.* 4th ed. Cambridge: Cambridge University Press, 1995.

Reid, Panthea. *Art and Affection: A Life of Virginia Woolf.* New York: Oxford University Press, 1996.

General Criticism

Abel, Elizabeth. *Virginia Woolf and the Fictions of Psychoanalysis.* Chicago: University of Chicago Press, 1989.

Bazin, Nancy Topping. *Virginia Woolf and the Androgynous Vision.* New Brunswick, NJ: Rutgers University Press, 1973.

Beer, Gillian. *Virginia Woolf: The Common Ground.* Ann Arbor: University of Michigan Press, 1996.

Cuddy-Keane, Melba. *Virginia Woolf, the Intellectual, and the Public Sphere.* Cambridge: Cambridge University Press, 2003.

DiBattista, Maria. *Virginia Woolf's Major Novels: The Fables of Anon.* New Haven, CT: Yale University Press, 1980.

Fleishman, Avrom. *Virginia Woolf: A Critical Reading.* Baltimore: Johns Hopkins University Press, 1975.

Froula, Christine. *Virginia Woolf and the Bloomsbury Avant-Garde: War, Civilization, Modernity.* New York: Columbia University Press, 2005.

Guiguet, Jean. *Virginia Woolf and Her Works.* New York: Harcourt Brace Jovanovich, 1965.

Harper, Howard. *Between Language and Silence: The Novels of Virginia Woolf.* Baton Rouge: Louisiana State University Press, 1982.

Hussey, Mark. *The Singing of the Real World: The Philosophy of Virginia Woolf's Fiction.* Columbus: Ohio State University Press, 1986.

———, ed. *Virginia Woolf and War: Fiction, Reality and Myth.* Syracuse, NY: Syracuse University Press, 1991.

Majumdar, Robin, and Allen McLaurin, eds. *Virginia Woolf: The Critical Heritage.* Boston: Routledge, 1975.

Marcus, Jane. *Art and Anger: Reading Like a Woman.* Columbus: Ohio State University Press, 1988.

———, ed. *New Feminist Essays on Virginia Woolf.* Lincoln: University of Nebraska Press, 1981.

———, ed. *Virginia Woolf: A Feminist Slant.* Lincoln: University of Nebraska Press, 1983.

———, ed. *Virginia Woolf and Bloomsbury: A Centenary Celebration.* Bloomington: Indiana University Press, 1987.

———. *Virginia Woolf and the Languages of Patriarchy.* Bloomington: Indiana University Press, 1987.

McLaurin, Allen. *Virginia Woolf: The Echoes Enslaved.* Cambridge: Cambridge University Press, 1973.

McNees, Eleanor, ed. *Virginia Woolf: Critical Assessments.* 4 vols. New York: Routledge, 1994.

Minow-Pinkney, Makiko. *Virginia Woolf and the Problem of the Subject: Feminine Writing in the Major Novels.* New Brunswick, NJ: Rutgers University Press, 1987.

Phillips, Kathy J. *Virginia Woolf Against Empire.* Knoxville: University of Tennessee Press, 1994.

Roe, Sue, and Susan Sellers, eds. *The Cambridge Companion to Virginia Woolf.* Cambridge: Cambridge University Press, 2000.

Ruotolo, Lucio. *The Interrupted Moment: A View of Virginia Woolf's Novels.* Stanford, CA: Stanford University Press, 1986.

Silver, Brenda R. *Virginia Woolf Icon.* Chicago: University of Chicago Press, 1999.

Zwerdling, Alex. *Virginia Woolf and the Real World.* Berkeley: University of California Press, 1986.

Suggestions for Further Reading:
Mrs. Dalloway

(in addition to the works cited in the introduction)

Barrett, Eileen. "Unmasking Lesbian Passion: The Inverted World of *Mrs. Dalloway*." In *Virginia Woolf: Lesbian Readings*. Edited by Eileen Barrett and Patricia Cramer, 146–64. New York: New York University Press, 1997.

Bishop, Edward. "Writing, Speech, and Silence in *Mrs. Dalloway*." *English Studies in Canada* 12.4 (December 1986): 397–423.

Bloom, Harold, ed. *Clarissa Dalloway*. Major Literary Characters Series. New York: Chelsea House, 1990.

Bradshaw, David. "'Vanished, Like Leaves': The Military, Elegy and Italy in *Mrs. Dalloway*." *Woolf Studies Annual* 8 (2002): 107–25.

Cunningham, Michael. *The Hours*. New York: Farrar, Straus and Giroux, 1998.

Edwards, Lee R. "War and Roses: The Politics of *Mrs. Dalloway*." In *The Authority of Experience: Essays in Feminist Criticism*. Edited by Arlyn Diamond and Lee R. Edwards, 161–77. Amherst: University of Massachusetts Press, 1977.

Froula, Christine. "Mrs. Dalloway's Postwar Elegy: Women, War, and the Art of Mourning." *Modernism/Modernity* 9.1 (2002): 125–63.

Henke, Suzette. "*Mrs. Dalloway*: The Communion of Saints." In *New Feminist Essays on Virginia Woolf*. Edited by Jane Marcus, 125–47. Lincoln: University of Nebraska Press, 1981.

Hoffmann, Charles G. "From Short Story to Novel: The Manuscript Revisions of Virginia Woolf's *Mrs. Dalloway*." *Modern Fiction Studies* 14.2 (Summer 1968): 171–86.

Jamison, Kay R. *Touched with Fire: Manic Depressive Illness and the Artistic Temperament*. New York: Free Press, 1993.

Lippincott, Robin. *Mr. Dalloway: A Novella*. Louisville, KY: Sarabande Books, 1999.

Low, Lisa. "'Thou Canst Not Touch the Freedom of My Mind': Fascism and Disruptive Female Consciousness in *Mrs. Dalloway*." In *Virginia Woolf and Fascism*. Edited by Merry M. Pawlowski, 92–104. Houndmills, UK: Palgrave, 2001.

Miller, J. Hillis. *Fiction and Repetition: Seven English Novels*. Cambridge, MA: Harvard University Press, 1982.

Prose, Francine, ed. *The Mrs. Dalloway Reader*. By Virginia Woolf et al. Orlando: Harcourt, 2003.

Richter, Harvena. "The *Ulysses* Connection: Clarissa Dalloway's Bloomsday." *Studies in the Novel* 21.3 (Fall 1989): 305–19.

Scott, Bonnie Kime. *Refiguring Modernism*. 2 vols. Bloomington: Indiana University Press, 1995.

Squier, Susan. *Virginia Woolf and London*. Chapel Hill: University of North Carolina Press, 1985.

Tate, Trudi. "*Mrs Dalloway* and the Armenian Question." *Textual Practice* 8.3 (Winter 1994): 467–86.

Thomas, Sue. "Virginia Woolf's Septimus Smith and Contemporary Perceptions of Shell Shock." *English Language Notes* 25.2 (December 1987): 49–57.

Wicke, Jennifer. "Mrs. Dalloway Goes to Market: Woolf, Keynes, and Modern Markets." *Novel: A Forum with Fiction* 28.1 (Fall 1994): 5–23.

Woolf, Virginia. *Mrs Dalloway*. Edited by Morris Beja. Oxford: Shakespeare Head/Blackwell, 1996.

———. *Mrs. Dalloway's Party: A Short Story Sequence by Virginia*

Woolf. Edited by Stella McNichol. New York: Harcourt Brace Jovanovich, 1973.

————. "Modern Novels." In *The Essays of Virginia Woolf*. Edited by Andrew McNeillie. Vol. 3, 30–37. San Diego: Harcourt Brace Jovanovich, 1986.

Wright, G. Patton. Appendix I: List of Textual Variants in *Mrs. Dalloway* by Virginia Woolf. Edited by G. Patton Wright. The Definitive Collected Edition. London: Hogarth Press, 1990.

Films

The Hours. Produced by Scott Rudin and Robert Fox. Directed by Stephen Daldry. Screenplay by David Hare. Paramount Pictures and Miramax Films, 2002.

Virginia Woolf's Mrs. Dalloway. Produced by Lisa Katselas Paré and Stephen Bayly. Directed by Marleen Gorris. Screenplay by Eileen Atkins. First Look Pictures, 1999.

Virginia Woolf Annotated Editions

Top Woolf scholars provide valuable introductions, notes, suggestions for further reading, and critical analysis in this paperback series. Students reading these books will have the resources at hand to help them understand the text as well as the reasons and methods behind Woolf's writing.

Between the Acts
Annotated and with an introduction by Melba Cuddy-Keane
978-0-15-603473-9 • 0-15-603473-5

Jacob's Room
Annotated and with an introduction by Vara Neverow
978-0-15-603479-1 • 0-15-603479-4

Mrs. Dalloway
Annotated and with an introduction by Bonnie Kime Scott
978-0-15-603035-9 • 0-15-603035-7

Orlando: A Biography
Annotated and with an introduction by Maria DiBattista
978-0-15-603151-6 • 0-15-603151-5

A Room of One's Own
Annotated and with an introduction by Susan Gubar
978-0-15-603041-0 • 0-15-603041-1

Three Guineas
Annotated and with an introduction by Jane Marcus
978-0-15-603163-9 • 0-15-603163-9

To the Lighthouse
Annotated and with an introduction by Mark Hussey
978-0-15-603047-2 • 0-15-603047-0

The Waves
Annotated and with an introduction by Molly Hite
978-0-15-603157-8 • 0-15-603157-4

The Years
Annotated and with an introduction by Eleanor McNees
978-0-15-603485-2 • 0-15-603485-9

Each volume includes a preface by Mark Hussey, professor of English and women's and gender studies at Pace University, and editor of *Woolf Studies Annual*.

Harcourt | HARVEST BOOKS
www.HarcourtBooks.com